A BIRD IN WINTER

Louise Doughty's ten novels include *Platform Seven*, recently filmed for ITV; *Black Water*, a *New York Times* Notable Book of the Year; the bestseller *Apple Tree Yard*, which was adapted for BBC One; and *Whatever You Love*, nominated for the Costa Novel Award and the Women's Prize for fiction. She has been nominated for many other prizes including the *Sunday Times* Short Story Prize and the CWA Silver Dagger, along with creating and writing the hit BBC drama *Crossfire*. Her work has been translated into thirty languages. She lives in London.

LOUISE DOUGHTY

A
BIRD
IN
WINTER

faber

First published in 2023
by Faber & Faber Limited
The Bindery, 51 Hatton Garden
London EC1N 8HN

This export edition first published in 2023

Typeset by Typo•glyphix, Burton-on-Trent, DE14 3HE
Printed and bound in the UK by CPI Group (UK) Ltd, Croydon, CR0 4YY

The right of Louise Doughty to be identified as author of this work
has been asserted in accordance with Section 77 of the Copyright,
Designs and Patents Act 1988

*This is a work of fiction. All of the characters, organisations,
and events portrayed in this novel are either products of the
author's imagination or are used fictitiously.*

A CIP record for this book
is available from the British Library

ISBN 978–0–571–32218–3

MIX
Paper | Supporting
responsible forestry
FSC® C171272

Printed and bound in the UK on FSC® certified paper in line with our continuing
commitment to ethical business practices, sustainability and the environment.
For further information see faber.co.uk/environmental-policy

2 4 6 8 10 9 7 5 3 1

To Ruby
(aka Jill Dawson)
for everything

Snow is a strange white word;
No ice or frost
Have asked of bud or bird
For Winter's cost.

Isaac Rosenberg,
'On Receiving News of the War'

PART 1

*And dawn, I think, is the hour when the pariah goes out
. . . it is the hour of the persecuted, the damned, for no
man was ever born who could not feel some shade of hope
if he were in open country with the sun about to rise.*

Geoffrey Household, *Rogue Male*

1

The truth is in the picture. Alaska. When I can see the whole picture, when I have decoded all the detail, I will know what really happened: I will know what made me run. All I have to do is keep looking at the picture and sooner or later, I will work it out.

Here is the picture.

Alaska has floor-to-ceiling windows and is on the corner of the building and is always cold. That's why we call it Alaska. The glass is one way, of course – from the street below, if you looked up, you would see nothing but a row of navy-blue panels. In the centre of Alaska is a large oval table with a glass top and chrome legs. Around the table are a dozen chairs, also chrome, with white leatherette upholstery. Apart from the table and the chairs, the room has no other furniture. The walls are palest grey, empty of decoration.

I am sitting at the oval table, in a middle seat, my back to the door. Kieron, our boss, is standing by the floor-to-ceiling window and facing out, surveying the city. Our side of the building looks away from New Street and the Bullring so he's gazing across the Town Hall car park, the A38 and the business district of which our outfit is a small and discreet part. The sky that lowers over Birmingham is hidden by cloud so white and thick it looks like solid matter, impenetrable.

I look at Kieron. He has his back to me but is standing at a slight angle – I can see his face in semi-profile and I wait for some sign, a muscle twitching in his cheek, perhaps, to give away what he is thinking or feeling, but he remains expressionless. He is holding his cup of coffee and lifts it from its saucer to take a sip, but his torso stays so still I have the notion that his arm is operating independently, as if he is a tin soldier with jointed limbs – emotionless, robotic. Killers come in all shapes and sizes, after all: sometimes they wear uniforms; sometimes they wear soft-white shirts.

Carmella is sitting opposite me, her back to Kieron, looking down at the papers in front of her with an intense expression. Ranged round the end of the table, James, Samuel and Kit are in a cluster like starlings on a fence. They are no more than boys, after all; I don't think one of them is over thirty-five. They like to be proximate to each other when there is trouble: safety in numbers.

We all have coffees in front of us and there is a plate of pastries in the middle of the table, mostly untouched, although a few moments ago, Carmella picked up one of them, a croissant, and tore the end from it, posting it into her mouth and putting the rest of it back on the plate, leaving a small scattering of pastry flakes on the table as she did. She and I have always made an effort to disagree with each other in meetings; it's a pact we have had since the day we walked into Alaska together and she angled her head towards me and whispered without humour, 'Make sure we don't always agree with each other, or the boys will say we're dominating them.' When Kieron is in full flood, I know it would be a tactical error to meet Carmella's gaze.

At this point, though, I could really do with meeting her gaze. I want to know what she thinks about what we have just been told – but all she does is stare down at her papers when we all know the papers have just become irrelevant. The three boys sit at the end of the table, looking winded. Nobody knows what to say.

As I sit there, digesting Kieron's announcement, he walks back to the table and puts his coffee cup and saucer down on the glass tabletop. He turns and reaches out, resting his left hand lightly on Carmella's shoulder, and at that point – she couldn't help herself, I realise later – she raises her gaze to mine, keeping her expression so effortfully blank that what she is thinking could not be clearer. I feel myself rise, and as I am rising what I am thinking, calculating, is: *It's no more than thirty paces to the lifts.*

———

My father was an insomniac. If I woke in the night, I would hear him moving around the house – we lived in a crumbly old place. You could scarcely take a step without a floorboard creaking. One night, I remember slipping from my bed and padding out onto the landing. I knew my father was somewhere in the house, moving around, and I had the desire to comfort him.

I was around five, I think – my little brothers were babies and slept in cribs in my parents' room. I paused outside the door of the master bedroom, which was ajar, and peered in. My mother was asleep on her back, snoring softly. The boys' cribs were next to each other beneath the window. I could see the shape of them, small lumps like slugs, unmoving. The curtains in my parents' room were thin and moonlight illumined the room. They had a blue candle-wick bedspread that was rumpled and awry. My mother was half uncovered, one solid leg exposed and her nightie rucked up at the hip. If I had been a bolder child, I might have padded over to her side of the bed and covered her, but I withdrew from the doorway and walked down the landing to find my father. I was so small, so light, that the floorboards didn't creak for me.

I found my father at the far end of the landing, silhouetted in a window that looked out over the untidy sprawl of our back garden. He was smoking and staring out at the scrubby lawn, the hedge, the fields beyond. Our house was the last one in our road before the open countryside – turn of the century, huge sash windows that rattled in their frames in winter. A stray high explosive had taken out the rest of the street in 1940 and it had been rebuilt with modern brick semis and bungalows. Only our house remained as a relic of the pre-war world, detached in more ways than one.

I remember thinking, *He is lonely.*

He turned as I approached. 'Bird,' he said. He had called me Bird for as long as I could remember. 'What are you doing up?' He asked it idly as if he neither wanted nor expected an answer, looking back out across the garden then lifting his chin and tilting his head back to exhale a fine column of smoke towards the ceiling.

I stood by him in my long cotton nightie and leaned my head against his hip. He put his left hand on top of my head and stroked my hair. His downward motion was firm, as if I was a cat. We stood there for a while, my father and I, communing in silence.

'What are you looking at?' I said eventually.

He inclined his head towards me and whispered, 'The moon . . .'

I stared out of the window at the sky. 'Where is it?' I asked. From where I was standing, I couldn't see any moon.

'Oh, it's always there, Bird,' he replied. 'Even when you can't see it, it's always there.' His cigarette had burned down and he looked at the glowing tip between his fingers. 'The moon follows you wherever you go. Sometimes it's fat and round, sometimes it's just a thin curve and sometimes you can't see it at all because of the cloud cover, but it's still there.' He made the moon sound like a searchlight that you could never escape.

My five-year-old self did not yet understand that my parents had independent thoughts and lives, that they existed beyond the perimeter of my own world. Even so, I understood enough to realise that my father was afraid of something out there in the dark – or, perhaps, afraid of its illumination.

Apparently, before the age of two we don't understand that when our mother or father leaves the room they continue to exist in another place. As far as the infant is concerned, it is as if the person they depend upon to stay alive has just dissolved into thin air. No wonder toddlers scream all the time. It isn't bad behaviour – it's existential despair.

I was around eight when I came to understand that my father was a liar.

'I'm going to France, Bird,' he declared one day with a flourish, 'shall I bring you back some cheese?'

'I would like a doll in national costume, please,' I replied in the solemn, respectful tone that I had learned worked best with my father. I had a book at the time, a large illustrated book like a children's encyclopaedia, called *National Costumes of the World*. I spent hours lying on my stomach on my bed leafing through it, imagining that I was Mila from Switzerland in a white apron with a red cross on the front or Kakalina from Hawaii with a garland of flowers (Kakalina had a better outfit but Mila had a dog). I craved a physical collection. I had already planned how I would arrange it on the shelf above my bed. So far, all I had was a Dutch girl in tiny clogs, with stiff blonde plaits made of straw.

My father laughed as if I was joking. 'A string of onions round the neck and a stripy shirt and beret?'

Well, if that's what they wear . . .

He was gone for over three weeks. When he returned, I waited for a doll to be produced. I didn't expect it when he first walked in through the door – my brothers and mother were there and of course he couldn't bring presents for all of us, but I was his favourite, after all . . .

It was three or four days after his return that I first had a chance to encounter him alone, one Sunday morning. My mother had taken my pious little brothers to church – my father and I were both atheists; we had discussed it. I waited until the coast was clear, then went to find him in the front room, the room that would have once been called a parlour. He had given up smoking a year or so previously but this part of the house still held a base note of cigarette ash, and in my memory the light from the bay window has a misty quality.

He was sitting in his favourite armchair, reading the newspaper. This was back in the days when papers were so huge that men in armchairs could hold them up and disappear – and so I stood in front of my father and spoke to the paper. The headline that day read *ALDERMASTON MARCH TO REACH LONDON*, above a photo of men in coats and hats at the front of a crowd holding placards and banners.

'Dad,' I began, spoken as one syllable, then repeated as two. 'Da-ad . . .'

'Ye-ees . . .' he murmured from behind the paper.

'How was France?' I was beginning gently, by taking an interest in his trip.

He lowered the paper. The Aldermaston March, whatever that was, collapsed in on itself as it descended to his lap. 'France?' he asked.

'Yes,' I said.

For a brief but unmistakeable moment, his face went blank. 'Oh, France, yes *France*, yes, thanks, France was grand.' He raised the paper and spoke from behind it. 'Your mum will be back soon, Bird, there's a good girl.'

I left the room with my expression knitted. *My father is a liar. He hasn't been to France at all.* It was the first time I remembered him underestimating me but far from the last.

'Your father is in hospital.' My mother called me on a Tuesday afternoon, which was unusual – we generally spoke on a Sunday. I was thirty-five years old. My father would die before I was thirty-six. *Your father is in hospital.* Later, I was to find my mother's phrase a little odd, as if the man in hospital was primarily mine. Perhaps she was acknowledging that losing a husband was one thing but losing a father quite another. 'I've called your brothers. Louis thinks he can make it over tomorrow.'

My father had had a stroke, she went on to say, that morning, a small one, they thought. He had been bending over by the bin and as he stood up, he staggered and put his hand out to the kitchen counter to balance himself. 'My eyesight's gone all blurry,' he had said.

She helped him into a kitchen chair and they both might have dismissed the incident as him straightening too quickly, apart from the fact that she noticed his left foot was dragging as she helped him sit down.

The CT scan later confirmed the stroke was mild – but that was the way it often went: the small stroke is a warning, a shot across the bows. The colossal one gets you later, as it would my father.

She told me the hospital he was in – it was one I didn't know, but when I looked it up, I saw it was on the right side of Coventry for me to drive there from London and arrive by mid-evening.

Then she said something that confused me. 'He's in ward C3. It's the psychiatric ward.'

It was only on the drive to the hospital that I thought back over the last year and realised how much my father had deteriorated and how my mother had been hiding it from me. I had noticed, in my busy, distracted way, that he was often absent or inattentive when I visited – asleep in the armchair sometimes, 'resting upstairs' at others. But now I recalled this strange blankness in his gaze when he looked at me on arrival, how he would stare for several minutes until something I did – a familiar hand gesture or turn of phrase – would unlock his memory and he would smile and declare, 'Bird! How are you?'

This has been coming for a while, I thought as I pulled into the hospital car park, even though I wasn't too sure what this was, as yet. I was not yet alarmed enough to think of the implications. In the front of my thoughts, as I crossed the car park in the dark, the black tarmac slick with rain, was annoyance that my mother had not told me a while ago about my father's condition.

I hadn't visited them for three months and was unprepared for the changes in him – the haphazard stubble, the concave cheeks, the wary look in his large dark eyes. When I got to his room, I had to stand by the door, taking a moment, while my mother rose from her chair beside his bed saying, 'Sit with him for a bit while I just visit the bathroom.' Her face was drawn and I felt a rush of guilt – they had clearly been having a much worse time than they had let on, while I had been so busy with work, saving the universe.

My father was staring ahead, motionless. Apart from the fact that his eyes were open, he might have been asleep. 'Go and have a coffee, a sandwich,' I said to her, while still looking at him. 'You can update me when you get back.' She nodded, stepped towards me and embraced me briefly, the flats of both hands pressing my back, gratitude as well as affection in her grasp.

'I won't be long,' she said softly as she closed the door behind her.

I sat by my father's bedside and took his hand and he turned his head, stared at me with a liquid gaze devoid of recognition, turned away again. It upset me, the way he had stared at me, so I looked at his hand, the green bulges of veins beneath the skin, the long dark hairs on each finger. I noticed that his fingernails were neatly clipped and wondered that he had the presence of mind to do that recently when the ability to shave properly had left him. I thought about his personal vanity and because I could not mourn him yet – it seemed too soon, unseemly – I mourned the loss of his vanity instead, and of all it represented.

'Thing is . . .' His voice was surprisingly strong and clear. 'Thing is . . .' he repeated.

I looked at him but he wasn't looking at me, he was looking straight ahead. He had gone silent again, as if he had already said what the thing was. Then he spoke again.

'If D467 doesn't make contact within twelve hours we need to notify all personnel.' He paused again. 'Bratislava.'

11

My mother would only be a short while, I knew. Cellular phones, as we called them back then, were still unusual – strange to think it now, but if you got one out in public, people would ask you why you had it; as I left the room, I glanced up and down the corridor before I took mine out of my handbag. It was ten o'clock at night and no one was around. They had put Dad in the side room most distant from the general ward. I looked up and down, at the receding lines of walls and doors. There was a faint buzzing sound from the yellowish lights in the ceiling above me. Apart from that, there was nothing, no one, just the grey and cream-coloured shapes of an empty hospital corridor.

I hesitated. I knew I should call the duty line, but my first instinct was to contact Richard Semple, my father's former protégé. I felt for my father's vulnerability. I wanted someone who knew and cared about him to deal with this. But I followed procedure, dialled, gave the code followed by my identifying details, and got a duty officer. 'I need to talk to someone about my father, Robert Berriman,' I said. 'He's retired and he's just been admitted to the Newland Infirmary, it's a few miles south-west of Coventry. He's had a stroke but I think he's also early stage dementia and he's talking.'

The duty officer asked for more details then said, 'Hold for a minute.' While she entered them into Mainframe, there were some clicks from her keyboard, then a pause, a few more clicks.

While I waited, I continued glancing up and down the corridor. I hoped it wouldn't take long – I didn't want my mother to return and see I was standing outside the room.

After a short while the duty officer came back on the line and said, 'Thanks for calling it in, we're aware.'

After I had hung up, I stood for a moment in the grey and yellow corridor, watching the empty stretch of it, listening to the faint buzz of the lights and a small ticking sound. A tiny moth was trapped somewhere inside one of them.

When I had my mandatory psychological assessment for the Service, the psychiatrist was an elderly white man with a beard. 'If you were to show me a typical family photograph from your childhood,' he said, 'describe it to me, who is in it, where are you all sitting relevant to each other?'

The picture that came into my head was of our evenings watching television. We had a large black and white set in a mahogany cupboard in the corner of the room. In this picture, my mother was cuddling the twins on the sofa while they threw rivalrous glares at each other; my father was in his armchair, his gaze intent. Every now and then, he was annoyed by the faulty diction of a presenter or newsreader and would correct them out loud. I was cross-legged on the carpet, ostensibly watching the television but also watching my father and the tight little unit that was my mother and brothers. Clear-eyed, I thought of myself later in life, divining everything.

Timothy and Louis were around three in that picture. Tim was plump and self-satisfied, a solid square of a child – already it was apparent he would be good at PE and feared in the playground. Later in life, he went into insurance and made a ton of money in some obscure aspect of it that I never understood, something to do with commercial shipping. He moved to San Diego and married an American who always called me *honey* with the distracted air of someone who couldn't quite remember my name. Louis was the weakling, thinner and paler than Tim, close and affectionate with our mother and very, very quiet. For much of his childhood, there

13

were concerns that he was, in the parlance of the time, 'a bit slow', but nothing was ever confirmed. One day, he would relocate to Madrid to take up a professorship in linguistics. Apparently, he's quite notable in his field.

Both of the twins were obsessed with our mother at that age and clung to her, competing for her attention. When we watched television in the evenings – usually the documentaries my father insisted upon – they would snuggle either side of her in their pyjamas, tucked into the fleshy valleys made by her torso and ample arms, Louis sucking his thumb and Tim twisting the hair behind his right ear round a finger. She would pull them in tight and say happily, 'It's lucky I have two arms.'

'We were a very loving family,' I replied, 'it was a secure childhood, happy. Very normal.'

Dr Beard paused for a moment, then said quietly, 'That's not what I asked.'

I once asked my mother whether she had minded her husband never talking about his day at work, his disappearances, the silences that fell in our house. I was in my early thirties and had been in the job myself for just over a year – I couldn't understand how anyone, male or female, combined it with a normal family life. I was curious.

It was a Saturday in March. The weather was unexpectedly warm. I had arrived the evening before and would stay till Sunday morning. I still thought of it as 'going home for the weekend'. Dad had retired the year before, aged sixty, although he had been taken off active duty ten years before, of course. He was lucky to have hung on another decade in an administrative role but even so, it had happened too early. He was restless, still fit and strong, still going away for days at a time for reasons that were unclear – sometimes I wondered if he was having a late-in-life affair, although I look back now and think he simply couldn't drop the habit. Mysteriousness is addictive, after all – it puts us at the centre of the story.

Mum said he went out for a long walk several times a week, up to the shops or the War Memorial Park, supposedly to stay fit, but I suspect he just couldn't bear to be at home all day. I look back now and feel sad. You never stop being what you are, in our line of work. The prospect of stopping must have felt like a kind of death to him, and all the disappearing and exercising in the world no more than postponement – and, of course, as it would turn out, he was right. He could glimpse the clouds on the horizon. He was frightened of them.

He had gone out for a walk around town, despite my mother's protestations, taking some tea in a flask and a piece of fruitcake wrapped in greaseproof paper – we weren't to wait for him, we were to go ahead and have lunch. I was secretly pleased. I liked talking to my father and I liked talking to my mother, but my relationship with each of them was different: we talked about different topics, used different phrases even. When we were all together, we resorted to small talk, the lingua franca of any family.

His departure reminded me that whenever Dad left the house, I had always taken it for granted that the explanation he gave may not be true.

I broached the subject casually, while my mother served us a Sunday roast on a Saturday because I had to leave after breakfast the next day. We had been talking about the fact that Dad had gone out, so it was natural enough for me to slip in, 'Did you mind, ever, him going places, I mean? The job.'

15

My mother was of that generation of women trained to not-mind all sorts of things – but there's a difference between an outward show of not minding and really not minding. We've forgotten so much, already, what it was like for women of her age: you gave up work upon marriage, you didn't have your own passport or bank account, no name on the mortgage. How similar women were expected to be – salt 'n' pepper curls, A-line skirts, headscarves – and how according to men, *women* were like this or *women* were like that, all one homogenous lump who thought and felt the same, all day long.

Plenty of her women friends had it worse than her, in that era. I could remember suburban Coventry in the fifties and sixties very well. Joy Kendall who lived opposite couldn't leave the house on a Saturday without her husband standing in the bay window with his forearm lifted, watching his wrist the whole while. If she returned a minute later than her estimate upon departure, he would come to the doorstep as she walked up the road and you could hear him yelling at her from across the street. Mrs Carlton from number fifty-two had a husband who was sleeping with the local librarian. My mother merely had to be discreet and uncomplaining – as far as I knew, that is.

So when I asked her, 'Did you ever mind?' and she gave one of her dreamy smiles, I was expecting her to reply, 'No, not really . . .'

Instead, she said, as she ladled potatoes onto my plate, 'Well, there was only one time that I minded.'

I waited.

After she'd served me, she lifted a trio of potatoes from the dish and held them above her own plate for a moment before inclining the spoon to let them slither down – she always loved new potatoes in the spring, with butter, and chives from the garden, chopped finely with the kitchen scissors. She was in her mid-fifties then but her curls always stayed salt 'n' pepper; her hair never went entirely white. She would die in her bed of an aortic aneurysm, at the age of seventy-nine.

She lifted her napkin and pressed it to her lips, even though she hadn't eaten anything yet. She looked down at her plate. 'It was our first morning as a married couple. We were having breakfast at the hotel, and he poured me some hot chocolate and said there was one thing I had to promise.' She raised her cutlery, then put it down again. 'I thought he was about to say, you know, you must always be faithful or, I don't know. I could tell it was serious, maybe it was, maybe, if I become disabled you must put a pillow over my face – he had a horror of being incapacitated or trapped in any way, you probably remember . . .'

This anecdote was already as long as almost anything my mother had ever told me about her life. I stilled my breath.

'Instead, he said to me, as soon as we are settled in the house, you must pack a bag, not a suitcase, a shopping bag, the kind of thing you might use if you were just going out for the day with a friend. It must have a change of clothes and some money I will give you, in an envelope. If I am away, or even just at work for the day, and I phone you, and I say to you, can we have steak and kidney pie for supper, we haven't had one for ages and I've a real hankering for one, if I ever say that, then you say yes but I'll have to get to the shops then, and you must go and get the bag and leave the house immediately. Immediately, I mean, you put your shoes and coat on, and you're gone . . .'

She pushed a potato around the plate with her fork, then lifted her knife and cut it in half but still didn't eat. 'Well of course the

17

first thing I said was, where will I go? He said, when you've packed the bag, show it to me, and we'll agree where the envelope with the money will be hidden. There might be a second envelope next to it, which will have instructions. If there isn't, you walk to the railway station, along the main road, not down the cut-through, and you sit in the waiting room and wait for instructions. You make sure there are other people around. If there's no one else in the waiting room, go and sit on a bench outside.'

I wanted to ask questions, but I knew that if I seemed too keen for detail it could frighten her off. When my mother talked about herself in any way, she became like a small deer. It was important not to startle her. I picked up my own fork and toyed with a piece of lamb on my plate – she had given me the crispy pieces from the edge that she knew I liked.

'Of course,' she continued, 'all sorts of things fell into place then. I think I had always known, but I minded that he hadn't told me before. He was telling me now I was his wife, but that meant he hadn't trusted me enough to tell me until we were married, as if I might run off or something, as if he didn't believe I loved him enough to stay with him regardless.'

She looked down at her plate, lifted her cutlery and began to cut her lamb up into small pieces. 'So I said to him, why are you only telling me this now, on our first morning of married life? And he said,' she gave a small smile at the memory, 'he said, well I didn't think it would be on to lean down and whisper it in your ear at the altar.'

We were both eating now, having managed the tricky business of commencing the meal without halting the conversation.

'What about when we were born?' I asked.

18

'Oh, he said to me, when you were about three or four months old, you do remember our conversation, don't you? He didn't need to say anything else. We both knew which conversation he meant. It was easy when you were babies. I just packed a nappy bag, there'd have been no questions with me carrying one of those. It was harder when you were older, of course, knowing what to put in, because I never knew how long it would be for, and of course when there were three of you there wasn't room for much.'

'Did you ever discuss it again?'

'There was no need,' she said, frowning as if a piece of meat that she had put in her mouth was chewy. She swallowed hard. 'About once a year I looked at the bag and changed the contents a bit, a small book, or some colouring pens to keep you occupied, underwear, that sort of thing. I was only guessing.' She paused and looked at me with something like amusement. 'It never actually happened. To tell the truth, I don't think there was much chance it would – it was more so that your father had peace of mind.'

I thought of how my father had insisted on a gravel drive in front of our house, so you could always hear the postman's approach in the morning. I thought of how he went around the house at least twice each night before bedtime, locking all the doors, unplugging all the electrical devices, then checking all the doors were locked again. I thought of the great washes of silence within which our lives as a family had been conducted, the great, wide, slowly flowing river of it, how we had all just let that river of silence carry us along.

'The gravy's gone cold already,' my mother said, putting a hand out and laying it along the side of the gravy boat. My mother's gravy boat – white porcelain with a gilt rim – what a pleasing design it had, the great wide tongue to pour the gravy over, like the stone ledge of a waterfall made smooth by time. 'Shall I give it a minute in the microwave?'

And so I suppose it was always in my blood, running I mean – perhaps not running itself so much as the preparedness to run – the capacity to go through each day always being ready. If you grow up with that, you come to think of it as just something inside you that you live with, like mild asthma, or an allergy to seafood. It doesn't dominate your life, you just feel a low-level awareness of it all the time, an instinctive vigilance that you hardly ever think about.

And then, one day, something happens, and while part of you is still in whatever situation you are in that day – in a meeting, perhaps, with five of your colleagues, in an office called Alaska with a glass-topped table and the flakes of a half-eaten pastry scattered around – the other part of you is getting hot inside, your breath rough in your throat, and you are already thinking, *When I get to the lifts, if one of them opens as soon as I press the button, that will be the quickest way to the ground floor, but if both lifts are caught on another floor then, to save precious seconds, I should take the stairs.*

2

It's less than thirty paces from Alaska to the lifts – I am walking swiftly but calmly and I estimate: twenty-three. The corridor outside our offices is empty. Thank God, I think, for one of my thoughts as I stared at Kieron in the meeting was, *They might be outside already.* They will be on their way to the building, though. As I hit the button to go down, I imagine a small group of ordinary-looking men in suits outside the lifts on the ground floor, hitting the button to go up. The thing about the Department of Standards, or DOS, is that it's staffed by the most mild-looking people you will ever meet – it's as though they train them on how to appear innocuous. If you passed one in the street you might guess them to be a middle manager in a high-street building society, or a geography teacher, perhaps.

The lift doors open immediately – it's mid-afternoon and the lift is empty. As it sinks, I feel the power of descent, as though gravity is pulling me down. My ears pop, or feel as if they pop; the roots of my hair tingle. I breathe through my nose and tell myself this is all psychosomatic. The lift stops three times on the way down, each time collecting a single person: a woman with a pink streak in her hair and large rimless glasses, a tall, blond-haired man, a young man with a beaky nose. I clock each of their identifying features in turn without looking at them. Already, I am hyper-alert and – weirdly – I have time to feel impressed with myself.

Back in Alaska, up there on the seventeenth floor, there will have been a small silence after my unexpected departure from the room,

21

an exchange of looks, and as the lift descends, I try to picture what is happening. The meeting will continue for a short while – it will take them a few minutes to work out I'm not coming back. James likes to ask informed questions phrased in a way that suggests he knows the answer but is still eager to learn. It's probable he is buying me vital seconds.

We reach the ground floor. The lift doors slide open with a *ssshhhh* . . . and I can see straightaway that there's no one waiting in Reception. The barriers to exit into the lobby are those hard plastic triangles, canine shaped, that protrude from wide metal posts on either side. You need your pass to get in, but on the way out they are automatic – the barriers spring apart as you approach, then snap shut behind you. As I sweep through them, I raise my hand to the man behind the desk. It's Denis today, plump and reassuring in his smart uniform. He raises his in return. As we bid each other farewell, it is as if the gestures are in slow motion, as if our hands are rising and falling in encapsulation of all my working years, my ascension up the ranks to becoming Kieron's deputy, my rapid descent into – what? I don't yet know. In that simple act of raising my hand, I am saying goodbye to more than two decades in my profession along with a great deal else besides.

And then immediately, with no conscious memory of pushing through the revolving doors, I am outside and standing on the wide, shallow steps that lead down to the piazza, breathing in as I go. I have the sensation that I have just dived into a river on a hot day. It's shocking but refreshing, and as long as I keep swimming, I'll be fine.

It's an eight-minute walk from my office to the shop. I've walked it many times and know how to negotiate the backstreets passing as few CCTV cameras as possible. I am on automatic pilot. If I think about what I am doing at all, it is only to congratulate myself on the thoroughness of my preparation.

An elderly man stands behind the counter – I'm guessing he's the uncle; he's been there with Adil a couple of times when I've been in but this is the first time I've seen him minding the shop on his own.

'Hi,' I say, 'I'm Sue, it's my stuff in the back.' I gesture towards the storeroom as I speak.

He looks at me with a steady, clear-eyed gaze. I gesture again and he gives a short sharp nod, then turns.

I follow him to the back. The door to the storeroom stands open but it's too tightly packed with shelves to allow us both in, so the uncle steps back to allow me inside, while remaining in the doorway watching me and glancing back over his shoulder in case another customer should come into the shop.

I step forward and pick up the holdall, which is tucked down at the bottom of a stack of shelving containing a neat row of boxes of Cup a Soup: cream of mushroom, chicken noodle, tomato and basil.

'Thanks,' I say to him as I leave.

The concrete unloveliness of New Street looms – joint worst station in the country, tying with Liverpool Lime Street and East Croydon, so they say, and soon to be knocked down and rebuilt, bit by bit. Inside, I head to the ticket office – it's quiet, there are four desks with staff behind them and only three customers. I walk casually to the empty desk and ask the slow-moving, softly spoken man behind it for a single to London. I pay in cash. I don't need to glance up to the corner to the left and above me to see the CCTV camera trained on me because I've done my homework and I know exactly where all the cameras in this ticket office are.

Back out on the concourse, I stand beneath the wide information board and crane my neck like all the other worshipful passengers. A Euston service is due to leave in seven minutes. It's already boarding. Perfect.

On Platform Five, I enter the train by the door immediately after First Class and walk down through the carriages until I find a double seat facing backwards, tucked close to the luggage rack. It is the work of a moment to take my two phones and slide them into the narrow gap between the cushion and the wall. Then I rise from the seat and go straight into the toilet in the vestibule.

Inside, I twist the handle on the lock and it slides home with a satisfying *thunk*. I dump the holdall on top of the toilet, yank at the broken zip and pull out a lightweight raincoat, some trainers, leggings and a beanie hat. I pull my skirt down over my hips and pull the leggings on top of my tights, folding and stuffing the skirt back into the holdall along with my block-heel court shoes and neat tailored jacket. I'll have no need of office wear for a good while now, but I'll hang on to them just in case. I slip the raincoat on top of my shirt and zip it up, stuff my hair into the beanie. There are some clear glasses in the pocket of the raincoat. In less than a minute, I'm unrecognisable unless you manage to get a close-up of my face. Outside the loo, I turn towards the front of the train and walk down towards the engine. It's a relatively quiet service, only one in four seats occupied. Within a couple of minutes I have exited back onto the platform towards the front of the train.

The next train to Glasgow leaves in twelve minutes. I'm calm as I head towards it. Two police officers are standing by the ticket barrier chatting to a guard. From the corner of my vision, I can see their demeanour is relaxed – one has his elbow lifted, resting on a barrier. The other has removed his hat.

Even so, once I am settled on the Glasgow train – again in a double seat close to the luggage rack and toilet, the position in which I am least likely to be joined – I look at my watch and wonder at the acre of time that is the remaining eleven minutes before departure.

Eventually, the doors to the train clunk shut with appropriate weight and solemnity. By contrast, the whistle is high and satisfyingly shrill. The train begins to move, but slowly, like an old man with creaky bones. The platforms at New Street Station are all underground and as the train creeps forward, the view out of the window on my right is of a high black wall smeared with green moss, a prison wall, the light above it distant, and then we enter a pitch-dark tunnel and the train is still so slow, the wheels screeching and crunching. It is not until we exit at the far end of the tunnel that the train picks up speed. *At last, at last,* I think, with the turning of the wheels. Kieron may have made the phone call about me already, but my preparations have been thorough. *Flavia, I'm coming.* The buried thought deep inside us – we do everything for two reasons after all: the reason, and the real reason.

Suddenly there is a sky of palest blue and thick green trees and the grey metal fencing that runs alongside the tracks as the wheels turn faster and faster and we are out in open countryside before we know it, speeding along past the warehouses beneath the low scudding clouds and nobody but me knows what I am doing or where I'm going: what a secret, soaring thought. I'm hurtling away from my life. I've done it. I've gone.

3

It all goes swimmingly until we get to Carlisle. I am no more than eight miles from the Scottish border when it begins to go wrong.

We have not long pulled out of Oxenholme. I have been staring out of the window at the Lake District wishing that instead of being stuck on a train, I was on foot in a wilderness – wouldn't fleeing that way be much more exciting? Be careful what you wish for, as they say.

We have come to a stop some way out of town, far enough out for fields to stretch either side of the train. The sky is still pale blue but if I look ahead on the left-hand side I can see clouds, bunched and darkening, massing together like an infantry unit preparing for attack. I shuffle to the aisle seat so I can look down the train and see a ticket inspector in the carriage ahead. He is beaming at passengers while he asks for *All tickets and railcards, please* and bumping against the side of the seats as though the train is still in motion, laughing at his own joke. I have a valid ticket, bought six weeks ago, but he's the type who pauses to chat to customers, which makes me nervous. I rise, pick up the holdall, and start walking down the train to the rear carriage. As I do, the train begins to move and for the briefest of moments I have the illusion that although we are picking up speed, I am stationary.

In the rear carriage, I spot a set of seats around a table at the far end that look empty. It is only as I sit down, a little heavily, that I see there is a woman in her thirties with an infant on her lap

26

sitting in the seat diagonally opposite mine, facing backwards. Next to her is a child around six, leaning against her mother's shoulder and sucking her thumb.

Startled by my sudden arrival, the woman glares at me and I see that on one cheek there is a bruise, only partially disguised by powdery foundation. It is in a shallow crescent shape beneath one eye and already a purple-greenish colour, with a glow of yellow that blurs the edges, as light can sometimes blur the edge of the moon. I bet that hurt before it discoloured, I think. Now the swelling has gone down the pain will have diminished, perhaps so much that she feels a flush of surprise when she looks in the mirror. Or, perhaps, she might be so accustomed to bruises she never really forgets they are there. If you are beaten a lot, then your safety depends on you never forgetting.

Our eyes meet and in the same instant I observe what is all too obvious in her – the bruise, her hidden position on the train, the quiet, glazed look of the child – she sees something in me, and I almost want to lean forward and say quietly, *It isn't what you think. My situation is different. That fellow feeling you've just spotted, it's not the same.*

She gives me a cool look, then turns her face to the window. I don't know whether I am more embarrassed by my seeing her or her seeing me, but I rise from my seat again, pick up my holdall and head into the vestibule at the very rear of the train, an empty space where nobody will come. I have an overwhelming desire to act.

I take my burner phone from my coat pocket. I turn it on and dial as the train picks up speed again and soon we are thundering towards Carlisle.

It answers after four rings. 'Stuart,' I say, 'Sophie Lester. We spoke in May.'

There is a short pause. 'Ah yes, Sophie, yes of course, of course!'

I am just in time, he says. End of September is my last opportunity. After that, the weather will be too bad to sail.

It's late August – the end of September leaves me with four weeks to go and in an ideal world, I'd be out of the country within days.

'You don't have anything before then?'

'Sorry, next one is full and I can only do so many, only so many people that crazy!' He bursts into one of those *hahahaha* laughs.

I make a calculation – I've always known I would have to go to ground for a few days at the very least and I have the wherewithal. This isn't catastrophic, just a hold-up. I consider offering to bribe Stuart to toss one of the earlier participants off his manifest, but it might make him suspicious and that I cannot afford. 'Sure, just as long as you're definitely going then.'

'Oh yeah, I have to, still paying off the loan! Hahahaha!'

After a few unavoidable pleasantries, I bid Stuart farewell, hang up and consider my plans. Four weeks. I will have to divert my route, take my time over each stop – a zigzag course would be good, that's okay. I've studied my Ordnance Survey maps of Scotland so often over the last few weeks that I've practically memorised the whole country. It will actually play in my favour: it will add a note of randomness to what I do next.

I should message Vikram, I think, using the code we agreed in advance.

It is at this point, as I'm standing in the rear vestibule of the train as it approaches Carlisle, about to text my solicitor, that something really bad happens – so bad that I have to go through a series of thoughts in order to calibrate just how bad it is.

The phone in my hand vibrates.

The only phone call I have ever made on this phone is to Stuart the yacht guy, just now, and I withheld my number. Nobody has this number. It is an *unknown* caller.

I lift the phone to my ear.

'Heather . . .' His voice is low, almost a murmur. 'Phones on the London train, bit obvious. Doubt that's where you're headed.'

I say nothing. I wonder where he is, whether he's back in his corner office, or whether he's still standing in Alaska, having dismissed everyone else, looking out over Birmingham.

'It's okay . . .' he says. Is there a slightly breathy quality to his tone? I am trying to work out if he sounds frightened. 'They already know you're not going to London, so this is what . . .'

I hang up the phone and turn it off. I stand where I am for a moment or two, biting the inside of my cheek and confronting the possibility that I have not been nearly as clever as I thought.

He didn't say *we*. He said *they*. This is – potentially – very bad news.

The train pulls into Carlisle. I get off, shouldering the holdall. I don't glance into the train but as I pass the woman with the two children, I have the feeling she is looking at me.

Carlisle Station is unexpectedly pretty – a vaulted glass roof, ironwork, stone. This calms me a little as I head for the exit, walking ordinarily, so as not to attract attention of any sort. As I reach the exit barriers, two men in slacks, one wearing a herringbone coat, the other a mac, come walking swiftly towards me, their faces set. I keep my expression neutral as I show my ticket to the guard while watching the men out of the corner of my eye. There is another guard at the far end of the barriers, next to an open gate, and they flash warrant cards at him, discreetly, without pausing their stride. I can't risk looking back so I don't know if they are heading towards the train I have just left or whether they are here about something else. I need to stop somewhere and regroup, but I want to be further away from the station.

I stride off in what looks like the direction of town, passing a church and two solid round towers the shape of the castle pieces we used to have in an old wooden chess set. I don't stop as I go by but glimpse a plaque that says something about a citadel and think, you've built your citadel, it's going to be okay. So Kieron was already tracking your phones – you suspected as much. The burner phone is too old for GPS but him having the number is a deeply alarming development.

I head down a road called English Street, which strikes me as mocking when, if I'd stayed on the train, I could be nearly at the Scottish border. Perhaps I've been precipitate – or perhaps the train is still sitting in Carlisle Station while those plainclothes officers walk up and down the carriages looking for me.

I am walking through a pedestrian precinct and see that at the end of it there is a Victorian-looking building with wide steps leading up to a Tourist Information Centre and beneath it, a café. I wonder if I can risk going in to pick up a local map and decide that I can't – but I can sit in the café, which is wide and open plan, with seats inside and out, and have a clear view right down the precinct.

He didn't say we, he said they.

We call it *sweeping the room*.

One of the visiting speakers on our surveillance training course was seventy-eight years old – such a long string bean of a man, pale and bony, white-haired, manner as cool as a glass of water – he came to talk to us in jeans. Jeans on a septuagenarian, we loved it. His tone of voice had a mid-Atlantic inflection. Although he was elderly, kindly, there was something sexually alert about him, a slight crackle in the room, like a radio signal from a planet in a distant galaxy.

He was there that morning to give a PowerPoint presentation about various cases he had been involved with. We had quite a few of these sessions, historical examples of successful missions and, sometimes, the unsuccessful ones, everything that could and had gone wrong. In those talks, we got to learn from the missions the public never hears about – the terrorist attacks that were foiled and how, the demonstrations where invaluable intel was garnered, and why.

And sometimes, we got to learn about the things that had been missed, the real reason six or fourteen or thirty-two people had lost their lives when nobody should have died. The men and women who gave those talks had something haunted about them, sometimes apologetically so, sometimes tinged with defiance. Ancient Mariners, all of them.

The man in front of us that day had retired as Chief of Field Operations with special responsibility for liaison between the friendly powers – the CAZAB nations. He had been out in the field on active service, then had direct management of operatives on active service. He had travelled all over the world: he had secretly run the world. We were putty in his hands.

When it came to the question-and-answer session, we moved swiftly to the thing we all really wanted to know: what is it like to be you? Here was a man who had progressed through decades of doing what we were training to do. He had lived the life and come out the other end. A pale, bony portent – he was what we would become if it all went according to plan.

One of my fellow trainees, Ahmed, he was called, supernaturally smart and destined to rise quickly through the ranks, raised his hand and said, 'But don't you miss active service? Isn't civilian life a bit boring?'

It was what we were all thinking, of course. This man in front of us might be a veteran but he was at the end of the journey, a husk. We were hot, fleshy pupae, just bursting to emerge from the cocoon of training.

Our visiting lecturer raised his white eyebrows. 'Boring? Civilian life?' He was sitting perched with one buttock on the edge of the desk at the front of our class. He lifted his hands and let them drop into his lap. 'Son, nothing could be more fascinating. Every room you walk into, every restaurant or café, every street you stroll down. You never lose it, you know. Sweeping the room. It's a habit you'll never shake. And after a while, well, you think to yourself, it finally occurs to you, I'm not looking for the bad guys any more, it's not my job any more. I'm not looking for the threat. And then you realise, you can use that skill just to read people out of pure interest, and you think how amazing people are. That old lady, that schoolboy – you glance at them and read their whole lives and you think my God, what a gift God gave us, human beings I mean, to be so . . . *various*. I don't know if you know that poem . . .'

At the mention of God, the atheists in the room, most of us at a guess, gave an inward roll of the eyes. I thought, smugly, they've all missed the reference to Louis MacNeice – but not me, because my mother was an English teacher. The schoolgirl swot in me was

32

already planning how I would get one over on competitive Ahmed at break time by nursing a coffee in a plastic cup and saying to him, 'You don't know that poem? "Snow". It's amazing.' Maybe I would reel off a couple of lines. *I peel and portion a tangerine . . .*

'The thing is . . .' our visiting lecturer said, and something in his tone of voice made us sit up. His languid demeanour was gone. All at once, he was speaking with passion and seriousness. 'The thing is, everyone will tell you about the negative side of it, the habits of mind you develop, how the whole of your life, you will always live with caution and paranoia, how sometimes it will kill you, the loneliness, because you can't really talk to the people you love best, but what people don't say is, it's a gift. Every day, the rest of your lives, it's like you have a kind of X-ray vision into people's souls, you see people in a way civilians just aren't trained to do, and it's marvellous. It's a gift.'

Behind me was a solid woman called Charlotte. Together, she and I were the oldest in the class – most people there had been recruited in their twenties. I had come via the WRAC and a spell in the City; she had moved sideways from being a police detective and as a result thought of herself as a bit ahead of the game. I heard her mutter under her breath '*Well he's really drunk the Kool-Aid . . .*' and I wanted to turn round and say 'Shut the fuck up.'

Sweeping the room. Anyone, without any sort of training, can look around as they enter a place, of course; the trick is to do it without anyone realising you are doing it.

Inside the café, there are eight people. Three women sit round the table closest to the door, wearing T-shirts and cut-off trousers and sturdy shoes – a regular walking-and-coffee group, at a guess

– stirring their drinks with spoons and talking quietly to each other. None of them look round as I enter. An elderly man with a hearing aid is sitting on his own at a neighbouring table reading a free newspaper, the cold dregs of a cup of tea beside him and a certain wet-lipped vagueness in his look.

Two twenty-something mums with toddlers in strollers are in the middle of the café. One lucky mum has managed to get her toddler to sleep and is pushing the stroller to and fro with one hand. The other is picking up chips from her plate and absently passing them down to her very-awake child, a boy, who stuffs the chips into his mouth in one go and lets out a small squawk for more as each chip is swallowed. In the far corner is a middle-aged man, quietly rocking in a wheelchair, with his carer, a young woman. They both have plates of pasta in front of them.

As I push through the door, a ninth person – for the purposes of this quick analysis, the toddlers didn't count as people, by which I mean they were unlikely to leap from their strollers brandishing warrant cards and handcuffs – follows in behind me. I go over to the fridge to give him time to get ahead of me, but he follows me there too, selects a can of Tango and goes straight to the till. I linger a bit, picking up a bottle of water and putting it back down again, glancing over at the boy as I do.

He looks to be around sixteen – I get a good look at him as he pays then goes and sits on the far side with his back to the wall, facing out into the café. I think how I always used to choose a can of fizzy drink if I had to sit anywhere for a while because it's less likely that a waiter clearing tables will take it from you.

The boy is staring straight ahead and looking sullen. He is looking as if he should be meeting a group of friends in the park but has had a massive falling out with one of them who has threatened him with a beating if he shows up, so he's not going, and now he's in worse trouble because he'll look like a coward. He looks as if he's thinking of going shoplifting and getting himself caught just so that he can post on Facebook that he was nicked, and then he'll have an excuse.

But then being baby-faced is a great advantage for a field operative. A teenager always has an excuse for having his hood up, if needs be, or smoking on a street corner, and they are so ubiquitous most people give them no more than a glance – and if they do notice them, they are a bit afraid of them and a bit ashamed of being afraid.

The café is very quiet, full of people who have nowhere else to be and no music is playing so everyone is talking quietly. I approach the counter – it's self-service – and say softly, 'Cappuccino, please . . .'

The young woman behind the counter replies mildly, 'Large or small?'

'Small.'

'To have here or takeaway?'

Just give me the fucking coffee. 'Here.'

I pay, take the coffee from the woman, turn and go and sit at a table facing the boy with his back to the wall – not directly opposite, a couple of tables away, but so that he and I still have a clear view of each other. The woman has put two sachets of sugar on the saucer and I lift them one by one and flap them to separate the granules inside, even though all I'm going to do is drop them into my pocket. My holdall is beneath the table and I draw it in between my feet.

I picture Alaska. I picture Kieron standing at the floor-to-ceiling window, his back to me but at a slight angle, his taut stance: he has a neat body but well-honed, a thick ridge of muscle across the back of his shoulders, rising to his neck, visible beneath his expensive shirt – he has good taste in shirts, I'll give him that. There was something about the way that he put his coffee cup back down on the table – I picture him and watch the cup's soundless descent as if it's a magician's sleight, where your attention is caught by the performance of one hand while something is secreted in the palm of the other.

He didn't say we, he said they. If he meant us, the Service, the DOS, he would surely have said 'we'. The implications of this make my breathing shallow, even though it's what I have suspected for a while.

I have a choice. I can turn on the burner phone and make a call – Richard would have officers here within the hour – while I sit safely in full view in a public place. They would bring me in. I would take my chances with the investigation. I'll be risking arrest, prosecution in a secret trial, jail time . . .

Then I think about what Carmella told me just before the meeting, about Collins.

I haven't even crossed the Scottish border yet. I can't give up that easily. I just have to disappear even more conclusively than I thought. I want to call Vikram but I can't risk that now, not if the burner phone is compromised.

The coffee is lukewarm, weak. The milk feels viscous in my mouth. I rise from my chair and pick up the holdall. I glance at the boy – he raises his head at the scrape of my chair and looks at me before dropping his gaze again. Of course he isn't one of us; if he was, there is no way he would have stared at me as I left. No one knows where I am as yet – I'm still one step ahead of all of them and need to stay that way. I'll go to the nearest public toilet. I have scissors; I have other clothes, dirtier clothes. I wish that I had savoured the cappuccino rather more; it's going to be the last one I'll have for a while.

4

I find the uninviting brick cube of a public toilet just beyond the Civic Centre at the far end of the shopping precinct. Inside, it smells of bleach and piss and everything is metal: the doors to the cubicle, the seatless toilet – there is a tiny metal sink set into the wall with a metal nozzle that dispenses water, soap and air in that order except there is no water.

I lock myself in a cubicle and pull my next set of clothing out of the holdall: pale-grey tracksuit bottoms – the colour selected because it will show up dirt – a thin hoodie with frayed sleeves and a brown bomber jacket made of some cheap felt material, very worn, that I bought in a charity shop. The raincoat, glasses and small Timex watch that I've been wearing so far go into the holdall. I take scissors to my hair. It was in a shortish bob before and I don't need to take that much off, just make it more ragged, tuck it behind my ears.

As I leave the toilet I think about how I must walk now, how I must sit and stand. Being an outcast is mostly body language. It will come naturally, soon enough. One night sleeping rough, one rainstorm, the collective effect of a few scathing looks from passers-by – before long I will be returning the hostility with my gaze. I can feel the process beginning already as I walk down the pavement towards a distant motorway and the clouds I saw from the train drift over Carlisle. Rain begins to needle on my head, as if the weather knows what I am about and has decided to make my disguise just that little bit more authentic.

*

It's probably thanks to the rain that I get a lift within twenty minutes – that and the fact that I am a small person huddled in a too-big jacket. From a distance, I look fragile: a student on her uppers, perhaps. By the time the driver who pulls over for me gets a good look at my dirty clothes and middle-aged face, I am sliding, damp as a dog, onto his leather passenger seat with a 'Thanks, mate, where you headed?'

He glances at me for a moment before he says in a strange, flat monotone, 'Maybe I'm going all the way.' He guns the engine as he pulls off the hard shoulder.

I face forwards and don't speak as he drives; nor does he. I don't feel good about this one, but maybe he's just a grumpy bastard. I keep my eyes on the road ahead, and only realise we've crossed the Scottish border when I see a sign for Gretna Green. Since devolution, it has to be a proven matter of national security for the Service to ask for help from the Scottish police, which doesn't mean they won't, of course, but it makes it slower and more bureaucratic.

As we pass the sign, the driver glances my way and, with a grin in his voice but that same flat intonation, says, 'Maybe we should stop off and get married, what you reckon?'

He's a big man, barrel-chested. His pale-blue businessman's shirt is short-sleeved and showing fleshy, freckled biceps; the buttonholes are pulled into ovals around the small white buttons. Through the gaps in the fabric, I glimpse long hairs in soft, pale flesh. All my life, men have underestimated me because I'm small.

I keep my gaze ahead and don't answer, hoping that if I stay silent, he will take the hint. I really want to get as far as I can on this ride before I have to tell him to pull over and let me out. And anyway, the more I speak, the more clues I will give him about myself.

39

After ten minutes more of silence, he reaches forward and pushes a button on his dashboard. The car fills with music, a boy band of some sort, singing in harmony.

We drive for around an hour, not speaking, the music just a touch too loud and very slightly distorted. We are past Lockerbie but still on the A74 when, without saying anything further, he hits the indicator and pulls left, first into the slow lane and then onto a slip road that curves around to reveal a secluded lay-by – later I will think, he knew the area well. He pulls in at a diagonal, brakes, yanks on the handbrake. There is no preamble, no attempt to pretend he just wants a bit of a chat. Before I have time to say anything, he has clamped his left hand onto my upper thigh, his fingertips and thumb digging in either side of my leg. I wait for him to say something or lean in, but he doesn't. Outside the car, it is raining hard and the drone of traffic from the motorway is drowned by the percussion of raindrops on the roof. The sky above is blurry. I look at his hand on my thigh – I could reach over with my left hand, grab the little finger and lift it back so sharply it would crack the joint open before he even knew what was happening, forestalling his cry of pain by jamming my right elbow into his throat. But he's just the shitty sort who would go to the police, whining that he only picked me up because he was worried about the safety of a woman hitchhiking on her own and look how she repaid him, all because he wouldn't hand over his wallet. They would ask for my description.

The moment stretches. The radio is still playing, a thumping dance tune now.

The motorway traffic, the beat of the music, the rain on the roof – the grip on my thigh does not loosen and I do not move.

Then, emboldened by my stillness, he turns and looms towards me – my hands go up to his chest, fingers splayed wide and muscles tensing, and at the same time I hear the loud purr of an engine and another car pulls into the lay-by right in front of us, a Range Rover with rooftop storage, the bobbing heads of three children in the back. Before the engine has stopped, a woman has leapt out from the passenger seat and opened the back door on her side, lifting her arms to extract a child.

I pull on the door handle – central locking is on.

'Let me out,' I say.

He still has his hand on my thigh but has turned to look ahead. The woman is standing by the grass verge, bent over and comforting the child by rubbing its back – it looks as though the kid is vomiting. There is a loud dull *thunk* from the driver's side and the father appears round the back of the car.

The man removes his hand from my thigh, although he has been gripping so hard the pressure remains insinuating. In a few hours, I will have bruises.

'Fuck off then, you old cunt,' he says, pronouncing the monosyllables in a bored voice, as if he doesn't care enough to summon any real venom. He flicks off the central locking.

I scoop up my holdall and spring from the car and without glancing back, turn and run to the rear end of the lay-by, then head down a steep slope of brambles and nettles to a gully that runs parallel to the road for a few metres then widens and empties into an open field.

I have put three fields behind me before I see another main road in the distance. I'm heading north, by the light, and it's mid-evening

41

now. It won't get dark for a while yet but the grey clouds above are imitating dusk. It's raining hard and the second-hand bomber jacket is like one of those soft holey sponges you use to mop the kitchen counter. I begin to shiver, and I recognise the depth of my shuddering as a kind of delayed shock – not so much shock, perhaps, but the drain of adrenaline that occurs after a situation. Strange, I think. I didn't believe myself to be afraid, but my body is acting as if I was.

There is a row of trees at the edge of the field and as the rain hardens I head for it, stumbling on the ridges of dark, fallow earth. When I reach shelter, I put my holdall down and squat on top of it, huddling down with my arms crossed over my chest, shuddering, even though it isn't cold. I'm fit, but I'm out of practice. After a moment or two, my thoughts become logical and I stand up, extract my showerproof raincoat from my holdall and put it on top of the bomber jacket. It's polyester and the plastic-bag effect will mean my body will warm up the damp jacket.

I'm hungry – it always annoys me in films when people never seem to get hungry. I think of the plate of pastries on the table in Alaska and am grateful I ate one of them in the kitchen before the meeting began, but that didn't count as lunch. Alaska, how far away that seems already. I can scarcely believe I was sitting round a glass-topped table in a business suit only a few hours ago. I could eat the sugar sachets in my pocket, that's what I saved them for, but I should keep them until I'm really short of calories. I don't have a water bottle either. I need to find a shop before too long but, more than that, I need to think about where I will shelter when night falls – I won't get into another stranger's car today. I don't trust myself not to hurt them next time.

The rain has lessened but the tree above me is minimal protection. It's the kind of rain that has no need of motion; its mere existence is damp enough – a fine drizzle that is scarcely visible yet has soaked my clothing, my flesh. It feels as though it has permeated to the bone. I think of my hiking rucksack back in my flat in Birmingham, with its secret pocket in the base that unzips to reveal a bright-pink foldable rain cover with an elasticated trim that stretches over the whole thing. I think of my thick grey walking socks and waterproof trousers. I think of all the protective items that my salary and my status as a paid-up and functioning member of society have allowed me to purchase in the past. I feel much more exhausted than the hour warrants, which is not a good feeling. I need somewhere to sleep.

I see the underpass as I cross the neighbouring field: it forms a low bridge over a wide ditch. Above it, a slip road leads to a dual carriageway, the one I spotted in the distance from across the fields. It is a low curve, a shallow crescent similar in shape to the faded bruise on the woman's cheek. As I near it, I see that it is dark and damp-looking and because of the fading light, it is only when I am almost at the entrance I notice a figure on the ground, huddled against the wall. From the stance, the inward turn of the shoulders, I am guessing the figure is slight, but it's wearing a huge puffa jacket, a man's-size jacket coloured scruffy black that has become so soaked with rain it is shiny and soggy, the sleeves hanging heavily down. I stare at the figure, its face invisible beneath the huge hood, and wonder how cold it must be, squatting there weighed down by the wet puffa jacket's clammy embrace. It must be like having the physical embodiment of moisture draped over you, soaking you, owning you. Then I wonder what the person inside might have drunk or smoked to be insensible to that level of physical discomfort. Or perhaps there is a peak of misery so total that you don't need to drink or smoke anything, that misery itself renders you numb to misery. I am about to turn away and find somewhere else to shelter when, face still invisible, the figure speaks. It is a woman's voice, age un-betrayed by cracking or inflection, with a soft Scottish accent.

'You can stay if you like,' the voice says. 'I won't hurt you.' Then there is a kind of snorty half laugh, a throaty intake of breath. One soggy arm rises, indicating a place a few feet away against the wall of the underpass. 'He's gone. Don't know where he's gone but he's definitely gone.'

'Thanks,' I say.

I go over to the place, deep in the interior of the underpass, where I find a fleece blanket, once baby blue but now covered in dirt, in a muddled pile comprising some newspaper, a battered, broken suit-case and a heap of twigs. If the figure in the puffa jacket is planning on lighting a fire down here, I won't stick around. It might draw attention and I don't fancy dying of smoke inhalation either.

'Here,' says the woman's voice – I'm guessing she's elderly – and she reaches out a foot to indicate a thin plastic bag on the ground between us. 'In there.'

I lean forward and look in the bag. There's a carton of milk, whole milk, and a half-used roll of loo roll.

'Have it,' she says. 'I got given four of them by an Indian lady because they were past their sell-by. She gives me all sorts – she's really nice. S'okay but won't keep the night.'

I pick up the carton – it's unopened – and wonder if the figure in the puffa has really had three pints already today or the truth is

44

she just doesn't like milk and was trying to make me feel okay about drinking it. I open it and give a cautionary sniff. It smells alright. When I drink from it, its temperature is not much different from the lukewarm cappuccino I had in Carlisle, although there is the merest hint of a cheesy tinge – by the morning, it will be on the turn. My stomach gives a lurch of revolt, but it's better than nothing and the thing is, puffa lady is nearer the entrance than me and I can stay hidden here; she will act as an early warning system if anyone approaches.

'What you call yourself, then?' the woman asks. It's an unexpected question and I'm tired so I answer without caution.

'Bird,' I reply, and know straightaway that was a foolish thing to say. If this woman is questioned at any time, it will give me away – the Service knows every detail of my childhood and my file will be linked to my father's. I've been Heather the whole of my professional life, but Bird will be in my records somewhere.

The woman reaches up and pushes her hood back – and I see that she is barely a woman, more a girl. She can't be more than sixteen, eighteen at most, with the pallid skin of someone who has been malnourished for an extended period and filthy brown hair and a stark gaze. Her gaze is as old as her voice.

'I'm Dina,' she says. 'Where you from then? Don't look like you've been doing this all that long. You got anything to smoke?'

I shake my head. 'No, not all that long, couple of weeks.'

Dina stares at me, then pulls her hood back up over her head. When she speaks, her voice is dull. 'You'll get used to it.'

The light at the entrance to the underpass fades minute by minute. Dina and I sit opposite each other, me further inside than her but

45

both wet, both cold. Outside, the rain continues to fall. Beneath the underpass, drops are shaken from the ceiling by the thunder and rumble of traffic overhead, but that too fades as darkness falls and gradually I start to drift in and out of consciousness. At one point, I raise my head with a start – I was nodding as I fell asleep – and look to my left to see that Dina has slid at a diagonal against a soggy pile of flattened cardboard boxes and is breathing deeply beneath her damp, clammy hood. The hood is slightly askew and the side of her pale face is just visible in the gloom. With her eyes closed, she looks about twelve.

I lie down with my head on my holdall and pull the filthy baby-blue blanket over me. It stinks, and I think the smell will stop me sleeping, and then I am asleep.

5

It is dark when I wake. Dina is motionless. I lie there for a while, not even attempting to move, thinking about things I don't want to think about.

Outside the underpass, down the grassy slope, grey light begins, so gradually it is barely perceptible. Slowly, the traffic above my head picks up. I watch dawn break and still I do not move.

There is a sudden blare of a horn from a driver right above our heads and Dina starts awake, looks round, then lowers her head again. Eventually, I raise myself on one elbow.

At the top of the grassy slope, I stop to look around. At least it isn't raining at the moment. In the middle distance, there is the dull roar of traffic on the dual carriageway – and to my right there is a service station: petrol pumps, a car and lorry park, a supermarket.

Before I continue my descent, I reach into my pocket and turn the burner phone on. For a moment, nothing happens, then, just as I am about to slip it back into my pocket, it gives a single shudder. I look at the text, black letters on a grey background.

Call me. We can sort this.

He was always going to go for reasonable to start with, I think. The threats will follow, as sure as night follows day; and there are two further messages beneath, sent late last night – he goes for a mix of flattery and threat.

Don't be stupid. You're not a stupid woman so don't be stupid.

The final one is more blatant – unwise of him, I think. It was sent gone midnight. I wonder if he had been drinking.

Don't make me do something I don't want to do.

Reading his messages, I divine a note of hysteria beneath them.

I turn the phone off and head down the slope, hobbling a little, my legs still stiff. I think about the night manoeuvres I went on in my youth – how much more quickly a young body recovers. I'm too old for this.

Considering how early it is, the car park in front of the supermarket is busy; the early risers with long journeys ahead of them are already en route. Two caravans are parked in the lorry park, both hitched to family estates. A quartet of lorry drivers are chatting next to one of their vehicles, stretching, drinking from thermos flasks. I wonder how many of them slept in their cabs the previous night; that prospect seems luxurious as a hotel room to me now.

I lean against the fence and pull the phone from my pocket but don't turn it on, just lower my head over it as if I am texting, scouting out the car park and the entrance to the supermarket. I've brought my holdall with me, so I have cash, but if I go inside in this state, I will draw attention. I don't want the supermarket manager calling the police as a pre-emptive measure. After a while, I wander over to the entrance.

I put my holdall behind me and sit down cross-legged on the floor of the concrete porch outside the supermarket's sliding doors, hood pulled up, my arms around my knees and my beanie hat on the ground in front of me, flattened to form a bowl as if I am hoping for loose change. To my right, the doors swish open and closed, open and closed. People come in and out of the supermarket and no one gives me a second glance.

At one point, a security guard, a short white man with unconvincing epaulettes on his black uniform jumper, comes to the entrance and regards me, but when he sees that I'm not bothering anyone, he turns away. I'm in the full beam of the CCTV here, of course, but whoever invented hoods was the friend of people like me, the hiders and skulkers, the spies and criminals, the just plain desperate.

From where I am sitting, I can watch the cars pull in – the one-way system of the car park means that every car has to drive past me before turning in search of a space. Within ten minutes, I've seen exactly what I'm looking for, a small Kia with a woman driving and a toddler in a car seat in the back, next to him two suitcases with a plastic crate of toys on top. Strapped to the roof rack is a travel cot. A single mother going on a long drive: perfect.

She parks in the row of parent-and-child bays nearest to me, three cars along, opens the back door and hefts out the toddler, a plump boy still in his pyjamas, who she carries on her hip to where a discarded trolley rests not more than four metres from where I sit cross-legged on the floor. The child looks sleepy and grizzly. I'm guessing she won't be long.

Ten or fifteen minutes later, she emerges, the toddler sitting in the front of the trolley, which contains a large packet of nappies and another of loo roll and three plastic bags on the top in which I glimpse an eclectic mix of groceries – a jar of pasta sauce, a family-size pack of Liquorice Allsorts, a bottle of red wine. Go mum.

I rise and follow her as she walks back to her car, my hand delving in my pocket, keeping my distance and looking down while moving

49

as swiftly and silently as I can – she's too preoccupied to glance behind her.

I've timed it just right. She has the nappies, loo roll and three bags to unload – five items, that's two turnings from the trolley to the open boot. She slams it shut and for a minute I think she might be fastidious enough to lock the car but thankfully, no. The bay to return the trolleys is right behind where I was sitting, a few metres away; the car will be in full sight and the keys are in her pocket. She wheels the toddler in the trolley back to the bay. I will have several seconds while she lifts him out, hefts him onto her hip again and pushes the trolley one-handed into its allotted space, fiddling for the pound coin she will get for returning it because even when you've got your trolley for nothing, you still really want the pound you get for giving it back.

I reach the car and open the boot, the phone in my left hand. I see what I need straightaway, a folded newspaper on which she has placed the toddler's wellies and her own walking shoes, beneath it the felt of the boot's floor lining, frayed and detached at the edge where it meets the chassis. I slip the phone under the edge of the felt and grab the wine from one of the shopping bags and a paper bag from the bakery section.

'Hey! No!'

She has spotted me. I turn to see her halfway between the super-market entrance and her car, angry but too afraid to approach me. The security guard has come to the door, but it's started raining again and the chances of that fella chasing me are zero.

I raise the bakery bag apologetically, turn and scoot off.

The security guard will raise his hands and let them drop so that the palms slap his thighs, then turn back into the supermarket shaking his head. What can you do? The woman will give him a look of contempt – perhaps raise her own hand in a *what are you even for* gesture – but that will be the end of it. She'll return to the car, toddler still on her hip, check that nothing is missing apart from the baked goods and the wine. She'll check the bags in the back seat as well even though she saw that I was only at the boot. She will swear softly beneath her breath as she slams the boot closed. As she straps the toddler in, she will brush his fringe back from his forehead and feel a sudden rush of gratitude that no harm has come to her or her child and all she's lost is a bit of shopping and really, couldn't it have been a lot worse? Don't you hear about stabbings during such minor robberies these days?

As she reverses out of her parking space, she will give a small wince of guilt, perhaps, remembering the pound she recovered for returning a trolley that wasn't hers, thinking how the figure in the dirty coat with the hood pulled up was probably just hungry and really, wouldn't she have handed over some food or some loose change if asked, after all, and what kind of experience leads a person to be begging outside a supermarket, so desperate that when no one drops any coins in front of them, they'll steal food from the boot of a car?

By the time she thinks of me again, the mobile phone that is any-one's last chance of contacting me and my last chance of blowing it by answering will be – with any luck – a hundred miles away.

I was hoping for doughnuts or a pasty but the paper bag I have stolen contains four plain bread rolls, two white, two brown. I eat one of the brown ones as I head back up the slope. I feel free and clever and light without the phone. If I have a qualm about getting rid of it, it is that I can't keep Vikram informed – but we've planned for that eventuality. I have learned the lessons of the previous day and I'm ready to move on. I am still one step ahead of them all, I think.

I look back now and I think I was like a youngster playing hide and seek in a garden, a child who ducks behind a slender tree trunk and convinces herself that as long as she turns to face the trunk and keeps both hands over her eyes then because she can't see anyone, that means she can't be found.

Beneath the underpass, amidst the cardboard boxes and the damp and dirt, Dina is lying where I left her, face hidden. I stand next to her for a moment, wondering if she'll stir, but she's the kind of unconscious that looks like a coma – she doesn't move or twitch. She could be dead. I lean in but can't catch the sound of any breathing above the steady thrum of traffic on the slip road and the drip-drip of water from somewhere nearby. I put the bottle of wine between her and the wall, angling it slightly so that it's propped up, and put the bag of bread rolls next to it. Bread and wine. It isn't much but at least it isn't milk.

Before I descend the slope again, I look back at the low underpass and see that if anyone passed by at that moment, they would make the same mistake that I made when I approached the evening before. They wouldn't realise there was a person there. All they would see was a heap of rubbish against a wall.

6

As I walk towards the dual carriageway, I think of Dina. I didn't even check whether she was still alive . . . the bleakness of dying all alone like that, somewhere like there. There's a solid weight in my chest that at first I can't identify – is it grief for her, the life that had brought her there? To my sorrow, I realise it is not grief, or at least not for Dina, it's guilt, the weight I am feeling. *Go on, off you go, off on your own business, just like you always do. This isn't the first young woman you've let down, after all. Won't be the last either.*

She loved bears. It became our thing, me bringing her a new bear each time I visited. It reminded me of my desire to collect dolls in national dress. She had dozens of them. Once, as a joke, I brought her a unicorn with a fluffy white pelt and a horn in rainbow colours. I mistook our deal – a new bear each time I visited – as a kind of secret language on the same level as an in-joke between adults. She took one look at it and burst into tears. I didn't make the same mistake again.

One evening, I remember, I was putting her to bed. She was around four or five, I'm guessing; her mother was downstairs cooking dinner. I loved doing the bedtime routine when I visited, pouring whatever small maternal instinct I possessed into this small time with her, this dark-eyed girl who reminded me of myself that age, so much so that occasionally I forgot she wasn't me.

I had read her a story – I don't think it was the all-time favourite, *We're Going on a Bear Hunt*, but it almost certainly featured a bear in some guise or other. Bears in children's books were incredibly versatile – they were schoolteachers and explorers and nurses; they drove trains – you got the feeling that human supremacy on earth was a sort of cosmic joke, that the bears could be doing everything, given the chance, and probably make a better job of it. Also, in children's books, they tended not to eat people. I wondered how my darling girl would feel when she found out about their dietary preferences in real life – it would be worse than the moment she realised Santa didn't exist.

I had finished the book and put it to one side and was sitting by her bed while she became sleepy, talking to herself in a kind of musical chant, something about sandwiches and a butterfly and a boy at nursery who was mean. I was half sitting, half lying on the edge, resting the side of my head against the headboard, stroking her soft, fine hair as her eyelids fluttered. I was already turning my mind towards the goblet of full-bodied red wine that would be waiting for me downstairs on the kitchen table, breathing.

'Feather . . .' she murmured. She had been unable to pronounce my name as a toddler and *Feather* had stuck.

'Yes?'

'Look . . . this is secret . . .' She flailed with a small hand to the shelf of soft toys to the right of the bed and grasped the paw of a synthetic-looking white bear in an upright sitting position. I remembered it. I had brought it the previous Christmas, wrapped up in white paper decorated with bears in Santa hats. I was proud of the paper, although she had ripped it off without comment.

The bear was a special light-up bear. When you pressed a button on its tummy, it glowed in different colours from within.

'*This is secret . . .*' Her voice was a whisper. '*Mummy doesn't know . . .*'

54

I noticed that *Mummy*. She often used her mother's first name, as a lot of only children of single parents do. I had only observed her saying *Mummy* when she was crying or upset.

Her eyes were open now. The thought of the secret had woken her up. She held the bear up with both hands and pressed the button – the bear lit up blue, shining through the white translucent fur.

'That's good,' she said softly, more to herself than to me.

She pressed again. Green.

'That means the grass is growing,' she said knowingly. Her lower lip trembled. 'No don't . . .' Her voice became a whisper again. *'Please don't, bear . . .'*

She pressed again. Yellow. A smile spread on her face, although she still looked at the bear, not me. 'Yay! Sunshine!'

She began to breathe heavily, in the same way she might if she were preparing to do a really big jump. She pressed the button and the bear lit up red, and all in one movement, she threw it across the room and turned into her pillow with a cry of anger and fear.

I rubbed her back while she whimpered and shook her head, face down in the pillow. 'It's okay,' I said, a little uselessly. I was good at games and stories, less good at tantrums or distress. 'It's okay . . .'

'It's *not* okay . . .' she insisted, turning her face to look at me, eyes wide. 'Red means that Mummy is going to *die!*'

I stroked her head and smiled and said, 'No, darling, your mummy isn't going to die.'

She threw herself onto her back then and said brightly, as if I was a bit stupid, 'Yes, she is. And you. Everyone dies. When we're old.' She lifted her fingers and wiggled them, then added, with relish, 'And then we turn into a *skell*ington . . .'

*

55

Later, over lasagne, I told Flavia. She rolled her eyes. 'That fucking light-up bear. No end of dramas but she won't get rid of it. You would think someone in toy development would have said a red light wasn't a good idea. Designed by a man, obviously.'

'Sorry,' I said.

She shook her head. 'It's not the kind of thing you'd think of, if you don't have your own child, I mean.' It wasn't the first time Flavia had casually dismissed my opinion on the basis of my childlessness – and at that point, I had a strange train of thought: if Flavia *did* die, I could adopt Adelina. How bizarre, and how stupid, when I had never wanted my own child, let alone to raise someone else's. I knew the idiocy of it, but . . . the silkiness of her hair, the way she would lisp *Feather*, her perfect hard little teeth; these things tugged at me, gave me a yearning sensation that felt like an equal mix of pain and pleasure, illogical in its impurity.

On the train going home the next day, I laughed at myself, remembering that thought. I was off to Geneva that week, for a liaison symposium. I was still very junior at that point, but I had been chosen over others in my cohort to do a presentation on information exchange and if it went well, there was the chance of a secondment. Thatcher had been re-elected, the IRA were active on the Continent and cross-European co-operation was all the rage – they were even digging a tunnel under the English Channel. The secondment would mean being in Geneva for six months. I really wanted it.

Flavia and I never talked about my work. She had been interviewed as part of my vetting when I was recruited, of course. At the time, I made an airy reference to my job being civil service, access to classified documents – like most people in my line of work, I generally found the trick was to make it sound really boring.

It wasn't difficult to fend off questions from Flavia about my life because she didn't really ask that many. Most of the time I didn't mind – although occasionally I minded a lot. I knew she thought my frequent absences from her and her daughter's lives were down to me being a bit useless, and as excuses go, that was pretty plausible. And the truth was, visiting once in a while – that was perfect. I wasn't a parent and didn't want to be. I was the bringer of bears, arriving to shouts of excitement and two little arms in the air. I got the good bits. What moment of madness had made me think I might want to do it all the time?

The last ride I hitch is from two women who run a hat shop who are going all the way into the city centre to make a delivery. I get out at George Square, thank them and go to Queen Street Station toilet, where the change machine for people who need twenty-pence pieces to get into the Ladies isn't working, but this is Glasgow and a smiley, chatty group of women gathers, nodding and greeting me even though I'm a down-and-out. We wait patiently for someone to exit the Ladies who, on seeing us, holds the barrier open so we can all enter. In the cubicle I pee, and wait until it sounds quiet outside before I emerge from the cubicle and wash my face and hands in a sink. I'm keeping this disguise but I need to look respectable enough to go into a baker's or grocery store and buy myself some breakfast. One croissant, one pint of warm milk and one stolen bread roll in the last twenty-four hours doesn't cut it.

A few minutes later, I am sitting on a bench in George Square, bacon and egg butty in one hand and large bottle of water in the other. My disguise is still so complete that no one gives me a glance, and the butty is so good that, for a moment, I have the illusion of being free from fear or anxiety, as if I am what I look like and no more.

It lasts no longer than it takes me to finish the butty. The precariousness of my situation descends upon me. I look at my hands. Egg yolk has dribbled down the palm of one hand, sticky, already hardening. It's not just that Kieron had the number of the burner phone – it's that he was still able to make the call and send those texts later in the day. That means he is not in custody, and I won't be safe until he is, and maybe not even then. If I can't leave the country for another four weeks, then I need to get off the streets. It's time to go to ground.

I am in one of those mixed streets that you get in every inner city in the UK, a few modern, gleaming business buildings, alternating with nineteenth-century lumps of stone – dirty stone. We're only a year on from one of the biggest financial crashes in modern history, after all. The grime is still on the walls here as everywhere else.

As I pass a tall narrow Victorian building, the wooden door at the bottom of it opens and a family emerges, luggage in tow: a husband with a large wheeled suitcase, wife with a smaller case and a boy aged around eight wearing a brightly coloured backpack. They don't speak as they pull the door closed behind them but their clean-cut looks suggest American or Canadian to me. They stand on the doorstep of the building as I pass. The husband is checking his phone.

I go a few metres further, cross the street, double back a few paces and squat down on the doorstep of a building opposite, pulling up my hood, to watch the family. I now have the leisure and opportunity to watch as many people as I like, after all. It's one of the few compensations, television for the homeless. The husband and wife exchange a few sentences – I can't hear what they are saying because of the passing traffic, but from their gestures and expressions I am guessing they are having a light argument about which way to go. The boy is silent, as if this happens a lot and he has learned patience over the years. The wife sighs and looks at the ground, blowing air through her cheeks, then the small family set off. There is a clock tower on a building at the end of the street that tells me it is 10.25 a.m. I am guessing check-out time is 11 a.m. There are no windows on the ground floor of the building but of the three floors above, the first two have closed grey blinds – only on the top floor are the blinds open. When the family are out of sight, I cross the road and settle down in the doorway the family have emerged from.

Next to the building where I am sitting there is a small café. After ten minutes, a young staff member, a slight girl, Italian- or Spanish-looking, comes out and, with a shy smile, hands me a coffee and a flapjack in a paper bag with a see-through plastic front. I'm not a fan of flapjacks – if I want porridge I'll eat porridge, thanks very much – but I gesture thanks by lifting the coffee cup in salute.

I've been there over an hour. I'm sitting in the full sun. My water bottle is empty and I need to pee: being thirsty and having a full bladder at the same time is such a double-ended discomfort. It feels unfair.

Eventually, a cleaner appears. She's a short, solid woman, thick hair in a cut that could have been chopped with an axe. She wears diamante earrings. She isn't carrying any cleaning equipment – that must be inside the building – but she is already pulling on a pair of creamy-coloured disposable gloves.

She has almost reached the doorway when she sees me. She stops and glares: I'm in her way. No kindly café girl, this one – I can see it in her face. Her life has been hard too, and she isn't begging on street corners. She works for every penny.

I rise from the step and back away, raising the coffee cup again, this time in a kind of clumsy, apologetic salute that says, *Don't mind me, missus, sorry to be in your way, I'll just finish my coffee then I'll be off.*

She makes a small huffing sound as she mounts the single step and her finger flicks over the keypad. I watch the shape it makes: a pushchair. As soon as the door has slammed shut behind her, I lean in and take a look at the keypad to confirm: one nine eight five. 1985 – the year I was recruited. All I have to do is think of Richard, with his slicked-back hair and paternal smile. There was a movement of her hand to a corner of the keypad after she had put in the code, but she was so practised and quick I didn't catch whether it was bottom left or bottom right. It's either Richard Star or Richard Hash. The keypad is still making a tiny fizzing sound.

I pick up the holdall, cross the street again and resume my original position in the doorway of the building opposite. I watch the windows. The ones on the first and second floor of the building keep their blinds down – the cleaner must be in the third-floor flat, and although it is too high up for me to be able to see in, I spot the shadow of movement inside once or twice over the next hour. By now, I am busting for a pee and dizzy with dehydration. If she doesn't emerge soon, I will have to go and find a discreet alleyway, but then I might miss her exit.

It's one o'clock when the cleaner leaves the building. Great, check-in for any future guests is likely to be four o'clock, three o'clock at the earliest, which gives me a bit of time. She's carrying a black plastic dustbin liner, tied at the top, which she dumps beside the public bin in front of the café before setting off with her stout stride, on to her next job.

I give it another fifteen minutes in case she's forgotten anything and comes back, wait until the young woman in the café is busy serving someone at the counter, then I cross the street swiftly, glancing left and right as I approach the doorway and key in the code. One nine eight five *hash*. The door buzzes and I'm in.

It slams behind me with a sonorous clang. I like a heavy door. The street noises vanish. The hallway is narrow, cool and carpeted, everything cream-coloured and filled with a kind of dusty hush. I stand for a moment to orientate myself. To my right, on the wall, are three lockboxes marked A, B and C, with combination locks. I can see just by looking at them how sturdy they are: even with a metal implement it wouldn't be easy to jemmy them open. Best to see if the door of the flat itself is less sturdy – these days it's often easier to break a door than a lock. The air in the stairwell remains dusty as I head upstairs. The wallpaper on the walls looks freshly painted over but coming away at the joins. The whole building has a newly refurbished but under-used feel, which suits me just fine.

There's an old Yale lock on the door to the flat, the sort you can slip open with a debit card. I have long since discarded my old wallet, but I have a debit card in the new identity I can't risk using yet, so I slip the lock with it then push at the door. It gives but doesn't open. I look down to the point of resistance and see another lock at waist height – a mortise – that will definitely need an implement. I go back down to the entrance level where there was a large cupboard set into the wall. I open one of the double doors and there amongst the buckets and mops and shelves stacked with clean linen and towels is a stepladder and a toolbox. In the top compartment of the toolbox I find a chisel, a heavy, sharp one like my father used to have in his shed in the garden, with a well-worn wooden handle. I feel the weight of it in my grasp – it feels good. I'll hang on to it afterwards; who knows when it might come in handy?

The top-floor flat is light and airy – open plan, and much bigger than it looks from the front of the building. I stay away from the kitchen windows, which face the main street. At the back, the windows look out over a small courtyard walled by neighbouring buildings with drainpipes and frosted glass. There's a small bedroom with a single bed next to the sitting room and when I go back into the hallway, I realise it's a maisonette. Upstairs I find another floor with a large bedroom and extra bathroom built into the eaves.

I go back down to the kitchen, staying close to the counter, and open the fridge. It's disappointingly empty – but there's a coffee machine and a glass bowl of pods and, in the cupboards, salt, pepper, a bag of pasta, olive oil and a few other basic food items including an unopened box of muesli and a jar of honey.

In the sitting room, I find what I really need – the information folder about the flat including the name of the letting company and a phone number. I can't remember when I last saw a phone box on a street corner – I might have to return to Queen Street Station – but a quick call to the agency and I'll soon be able to find out whether the flat is empty, and how long for. I can't rent anywhere without a credit card, but now I have access I can squat in it indefinitely as long as I know that nobody else is about to show up.

It's only as I'm about to leave the flat again that I spot them – the sandals, placed neatly next to a sofa that is upholstered in fake-looking brown leather. The sandals are almost the same colour, hence easy to miss. I stare at them with the same hostile look I might give a spider I have just discovered in the bath. They look too expensive to belong to the cleaner – they must belong to the woman who checked out with her family just now. I do a quick calculation: she won't realise they are missing until she gets an opportunity to unpack her case. With any luck, they were on their way to Glasgow Airport to get on a plane. Either way, they will know they can't return to the flat because they have left the keys in the drop box downstairs, so they will have to ring the rental company. I must be careful, not get complacent – but then I would have to be careful anyway.

I make myself a coffee and sit on the brown sofa for a bit, leafing through the instructions in the folder – how to work the dishwasher, recommended local restaurants – then I leave the flat, making sure there are no signs of my habitation in case anyone comes by while I'm out. I take my holdall even though it's a pain lugging it around the streets. If anyone shows up while I'm gone, all they will find is a mysteriously broken door.

My call to the rental company, asking about flats in that area but saying I'm unsure about my dates, establishes that the one I am squatting in has no booking till mid-September. As I walk back to it, I contemplate the prospect of staying there until then – the longer I can hide out this way, staying off the streets as much as I can, the greater the chance of the trail going cold. All the same, I will only be able to relax in the evenings when there's no chance someone from the agency could drop by.

That first evening, I cook myself a huge bowl of the dried pasta and drizzle it with the olive oil and grate a small bit of the cheese I bought in a corner store. I've also got a bag of salad. I sit on the tasteless brown sofa with my feet up and it feels good for a while – this pasta, this flat, this solution.

My mood alters as darkness falls. I can't put a light on, of course, so as dusk gathers inside the flat as well as outside, I rinse the plate and return it to its place and wonder what they are all doing . . . why isn't Kieron under investigation yet, or arrest? The Service will be looking for me, there's no doubt about that, but could anyone else be, already? I'm longing to speak to Carmella and find out what happened after I left the meeting, but it wouldn't be safe to call her even if I had a phone. The uncertainty is getting me down; it is hard, not knowing how afraid I should be.

Fear is a waste of time, I say to myself sternly as I extract a spare duvet and blanket from a hallway cupboard and make myself a bed on the plastic-leather sofa. As long as I prop the sitting-room door open, I can see out into the hallway and have a clear view of the door.

Just as I am drifting off, the security light in the stairwell flicks on. I am up and off the sofa in a crouching position almost before my brain has time to acknowledge the movement of my body. I wait in that position, heart thumping, doing the action-required assessment in my head – the whereabouts of my holdall (against the wall), the time it will take me to grab it and head up the stairs to the upper level (four seconds, maybe), the magnitude of the sucking noise the skylight in the smallest room will make when I open it (loud enough to be heard downstairs in the flat? Almost certainly). I remember that a small dressing table stands directly beneath the skylight: it won't be difficult to haul myself out.

I stay in that position, though, I do not run, even though my heart is pounding in my chest. After two minutes, the light goes off again. All is silent, dark. The light must be hyper-sensitive – that happens a lot with security lights. I lie back down but it takes far longer than it should to still my thumping heart. I am hot, sweaty and the flat is full of shadows, the street outside far too quiet.

I go back to sleep eventually but have a restless night – the light going on wakes me at least twice more and even when it doesn't, I start awake several times.

In the morning, I'm woken early by sunlight on the plain white walls. I sit up and look around and realise that although the first impression the apartment gives is one of being smart, a more accurate adjective is bleak. The open-plan sitting room and kitchen feel wide and echoey, and there are no pictures on the wall or coloured cushions on the sofa. I'm guessing it's new to the rental market and hasn't had that many customers as yet – it's not a great street, hence the low uptake at this time of year. I wonder if American dad was a cheapskate, his wife furious that he booked this place when they could have had something in a nicer part of town, or a hotel – or perhaps it was the other way around.

After that first disturbed night I make a better plan: I decide to sleep on the single bed in the downstairs bedroom, but before I go to bed, I go upstairs to the large bedroom, and open the skylight just a notch. I find a black dustbin liner in a kitchen drawer, then put my holdall in it, folding it over but not tying the handles. I go back upstairs, stand on the dressing table, lift the skylight and put the bin liner on the ledge outside, then pull the skylight so it's almost closed but without pressing down the handle to fasten it.

Then I do a practice run, timing myself on my watch. I can get up the stairs and out of the skylight in three seconds. Back downstairs, I pull the heavy glass-topped coffee table in front of the door to the flat and on top of the table I construct a winter tree made up of a clothes rack and ironing board taken from a cupboard in a hall, and then decorate it with wire coat hangers from the wardrobe in the big bedroom. I will be sleeping close enough to the door to be woken by the hangers if anyone tries to come through it, however slowly and carefully. The glass-topped table won't stop them for more than a few seconds if they decide to rush the door but I will hear them loud and clear. I sleep fully dressed.

On the fourth day, I go out to buy a few food items. I'm using what I can in the flat; I still want to husband my cash as much as possible. I call the letting agency and apologise, telling them that my work dates keep changing, that's why I haven't confirmed, but is that top-floor flat still free? Then I return to the building with a thin plastic bag containing some fresh bread and hummus and tomatoes and let myself in with the keypad quickly, efficiently – I always check the friendly waitress is busy or absent before I approach the door. I have the strangest feeling as the door clangs shut behind me and I trot up the cream-carpeted stairs, almost as if I live here now. Later I will think, I was getting careless.

I use my debit card to slip open the Yale lock.

Inside the hallway, I close the door behind me gently, advance a few paces, then stop and stand still. Something is wrong.

I am in the doorway leading through to the open-plan sitting room and kitchen. I stay very still. My senses prickle.

I look around. I can't see anything that has been moved. The information folder is where I left it, on the sofa at a diagonal. The footstool is in the same position it was when I last sat there and rested my feet on it. None of my belongings are left carelessly about because I have been stowing everything I haven't had on my person in the holdall, which is still hidden on the roof. I look around the bare open-plan room. What is wrong with this picture?

The sandals are gone.

In the same instant, I hear the heavy clang of the street door downstairs.

Seconds later, I am lying on my stomach on the tiled roof, my holdall in the bin liner on my right and the skylight I have just pulled myself out of on the left. I have left it very slightly ajar, so I can hear what is going on in the flat.

The sounds are indistinct at first – footsteps, one pair of heeled shoes, one set of workman's boots. Then voices, a light female voice, a gruff male one, both with Scottish accents. I am guessing that someone from the office has been sent round to pick up the sandals and has discovered that the mortise lock on the flat door was broken – I couldn't jemmy it without scratching the paint on the door frame. She has returned with a workman. I was lucky she came by to get the sandals while I was out – unlucky she returned with a workman when I was back.

Then I hear the boots clump up the stairs to the top bedroom. I withdraw my head and flatten myself down against the roof, but I can't risk further movement in case a tile on the roof is loose. There is a momentary pause while he walks around checking the top floor, then a dull thud as he closes the skylight and presses the handle into the lock position. Great, I think, that skylight will only open from inside. I'm stuck on a roof. Thank God I took the precaution of hiding my holdall up here.

I stay on the roof for what must be nearly an hour – I want to make sure they have gone before I move because I have no idea how much noise my movement will make inside the flat. Once I get myself down to street level, I will have to leave Glasgow immediately in case they report the break-in, in case someone, somewhere, is joining up the dots.

I risk craning my neck and peering down through the skylight – from that angle I can see the table beneath it and the bottom half of the bed, the bedroom door, which is open, and a bisected section of the top landing of the flat. Traffic noise floats up here from the city and I have to turn my head to listen. All seems quiet and still. I wait a bit more, then I begin to edge my way, testing each tile before I rest a hand or knee or foot upon it, towards the far side of the roof. I can see one of those maintenance ladders with a cage over it, hoops of iron so that if you slip off the ladder, you stand a chance of staying in the cage rather than falling backwards and plummeting down to the street or back yard below. Here is something I never confessed to my superiors when I was a field operative – vertigo. But I'm strong and good at climbing as long as I don't look down. If there is a maintenance ladder, there must be a way down through this or a neighbouring building, somehow, and I have the chisel in my holdall, which I am holding across my chest by means of slipping the handles up each arm. I wasn't going to sling it across my shoulders in case the weight toppled me backwards. I risk a quick glimpse round to make sure I can't be seen on the roof from any other nearby buildings, catching a wild and dizzying panorama of white sky and grey cloud as I do. I close my eyes. I can do this. Given the choice between what I have to do now and dealing with another arsehole like that one in the car, I'd take the arsehole in the car any day.

Down on the ground, legs a bit shuddery, I head straight to Queen Street Station. I have a twenty-pence piece on me this time and as soon as I have bought a ticket from the machine and checked the train times, I go to the Ladies. I have to become a different person again.

This time, I emerge from the Ladies toilet as a middle-aged woman on a solo walking holiday. All the clothes I wore to be homeless are now flattened into the holdall and I am wearing the leggings again and a fitted grey T-shirt from M&S with a lemon-coloured – and, crucially, clean – sweatshirt knotted round my waist. On one of my scouting trips while I was in the flat, I discovered a sports outlet sale, seven minutes' walk from the station, and I hurry there now. I have thirty-four minutes before my train.

The sale is in some kind of church hall on a side road set back from the main thoroughfare. I get an end-of-season rucksack for thirty-five pounds and some sale-price walking boots, good-quality ones, for sixty. At the counter, as I pay a long-haired man in cash, I pick up a pack of hiking socks, three for a pound, and some sunglasses for two quid. In an alleyway behind the church hall, tucked out of sight behind a skip, I take off my trainers and stuff them into a side pocket of the rucksack, then transfer the items in the holdall to the rucksack, arranging each pocket so I will remember where everything is. There is no time to linger over my transformation, but it feels so good to stand and shoulder the rucksack: the weight feels so much better now it is properly distributed. My last act is to toss the battered, broken holdall into the skip – I'm finished with that persona now. Job done, I brush the dirt from the palms of both hands with a brisk criss-cross motion before I turn away.

It's more than five hours on the train to Mallaig, but we pop out of Glasgow and are through the suburbs in no time. Beyond Helensburgh, the train runs along Gare Loch, then across land for a bit and alongside Loch Long – which is indeed very long – and the wooded hillsides that rise above the lakes are blurred by the drift of a light summer mist. My heart soars in the way it only soars in Scotland, remembering my first visit all those years ago. I'm going to take my time to get there – I've already decided on a roundabout route.

The small times seem like hinges sometimes. That village was the place I could have said *I love you, let's work something out*, the place at which my life might have turned on its axis, all those years ago, rather than continuing along the line that led me here. It was the place I learned that Adelina was going to exist.

The train passes along a row of trees close to the track and sunlight flashes through the trees, brilliant and startling, making my eyes flicker like they do when you look at one of those old-fashioned little books where flipping the pages puts a cartoon in motion. With one small gesture, you bring a character to life.

7

It's pouring with rain by the time I get to Mallaig and windy enough to make an umbrella useless even if I had one. The port is only five minutes' walk from the railway station and I have half an hour before the ferry is due. Beyond the tiny terminal, little more than a kiosk, there's a solid white-haired man in a hi-vis jacket overseeing the row of cars waiting to board a large ship that is docked at the end of the ramp. Its vast triangular bow is lifted into the air as if the front quarter of the ship has broken off from the rest of it, as if it is a whale or some other beast of the ocean, upper jaw agape, about to swallow cars.

'That for Armadale?' I ask the man.

He chuckles and says, 'No, lassie, you're going on something much smaller than that.'

He tells me where to wait, in a bleak, open-sided structure like a bus shelter, and I watch the cars board the large ferry, although around a dozen vehicles wait behind in the queue for the small one, a little chugger, white and rusting, that is revealed to be waiting in the bay as soon as the large one has departed.

I'm the only foot passenger. The solid white-haired man comes to check my ticket and I ask, 'Where's the best place to sit on that ferry?'

In a matter-of-fact manner, he replies, 'Inside a car.'

It will rain for most of the time I am on Skye and when it won't, low cloud will cover the island, a kind of drenching mist that seeps into your hair and clothes with such soft intensity it might as well be raining. I am destined to spend this part of my flight ambling around Portree alongside the disconsolate tourists, and when I'm not ambling I will lie low in my B&B on the edge of town. It's against my every instinct, this zigzag route to the top of the country. Every bone of me wants to be in constant motion – but I can't risk arriving at my destination too early, which means I am forced to take my time. At least I made the call to Stuart before I got rid of the burner phone.

It isn't easy to find somewhere to stay – I spend the first night in a grassy hollow. Eventually, I hit on the idea of going to the least prepossessing part of town, a stretch of new builds on a main road, where I find a modern suburban home with no view and a sign saying VACANCIES in the window.

The elderly man with thick glasses who answers the door looks me up and down with suspicion. I explain that I have just come over on the ferry but hadn't done my research and had no idea how hard it was to find somewhere to stay without pre-booking and I've lost my credit card wallet to boot but luckily I have cash and I can pay upfront if he likes. He stands back and opens the door to admit me into a white-painted hallway with an immaculate grey carpet. A door on my right is open to a primrose-yellow breakfast room. Next to the door there is a little stand with a guest book and pen and a figurine of a Royal Scots piper. The landlord lowers his chin and stares pointedly through his thick glasses at my boots. Then he swivels his gaze to a sign on the wall to my left that reads: 'Leave your outdoor shoes in the hallway box. Slippers are provided for your comfort in the rooms.'

I bend to unlace the boots.

He shows me a small single room on the ground floor, to the left of the front door and only available, I'm guessing, because it's so tiny. Propped up on the bed is a little cardboard sign that says 'Smoking will incur a £100 cleaning fee.' The room is at the front of the house and the sound of the passing traffic is a dull and constant roar.

'This looks perfect,' I say.

I pay him upfront for five nights and he leaves me alone in the room. I slide the straps of my rucksack from my shoulders, take off my waterproof and hang it on the hook on the back of the door, then go over to the tiny kettle on a plastic tray in the corner. Next to it is another note: 'Absolutely no takeaways or cooking in the bedrooms.' When I go out later that day I see he has turned the sign in the window around to read NO VACANCIES.

On the third morning, something odd happens. I go to my room after breakfast, intending to go on a hike in a bit if the rain clears, lie down on the bed and realise that is precisely where I am going to stay. I don't want to leave the room.

I lie on top of the bed for a long time, quite still, on my back with my hands behind my head, a soft grey blanket pulled up to my neck, staring at the white ceiling and listening to the traffic swooshing by, the patter of rain on the windowsill, the trickling sound from a nearby drain. I feel adrift, like a hot-air balloon that has slipped its moorings while empty.

For a few hours, there in my small white box, I give in, give up – and deliver myself to every moment of weakness I have ever felt. It is the strangest feeling. I know that if I looked out of the window at any time during those hours and saw two police officers or Service

73

personnel passing along the path, on their way to ring the bell of the strict landlord's front door, if I heard the sing-song ding-dong of that doorbell, I would not even move. I would lie where I was, on the cool white linen with the warm grey blanket over me and continue to stare at the ceiling, waiting for them to barge in the door because I no longer care about where I am going or what I am going to do or even who I am. It is a morning of pure surrender.

Around noon, there is a light tap on the door and a young woman's voice with a local accent calls out, 'Cleaning!'

'No thank you,' I call back, and roll over on my side, pulling the soft grey blanket up over my shoulder and closing my eyes.

On my last full day, I come back from a walk into town to check the buses and let myself into the room to find a handwritten note placed at a neat diagonal on the corner of my bed nearest to the door. *Your room is booked from tomorrow, please vacate your room by 11 a.m.*

Breakfast is served until 9.30 a.m., so even though I wake early, I pack up my things and wait until 9.25 a.m. in order to avoid the other guests. When I get to the primrose-yellow breakfast room there is a place setting for one in my usual spot, the gloomiest corner. My unsmiling landlord comes to take my order wearing his navy-striped apron, holding his tiny notepad and tiny pencil. I ask for the full Scottish, black pudding and everything. I might be sleeping rough again tonight, after all.

The breakfast room is quiet – most people have gone and there's just an elderly couple in the far corner talking quietly to themselves. The landlord brings my breakfast and a pot of coffee but doesn't refer to the fact that I'm checking out that day.

When I come out of my little white room at 11 a.m., rucksack on my back, I half expect him to be standing in the hallway to make sure I leave on time, but he isn't there and when I stick my nose into the breakfast room I see it is cleared and empty. As I open the front door I look at the figurine of the Royal Scots piper on the stand and give it a little salute of farewell, one soldier to another.

I step out onto the narrow pathway that runs along the main road – there's a bus to the Kyle of Lochalsh around noon so I have plenty of time. It's raining again.

Goodbye, Skye. I know it's beautiful, but it's been strange and misty, my time here. I'm ready to move on to my next stop, even though – or perhaps because – the thought of it waiting for me has been like long, wavy grass and a deep, cold river and thick, oozy mud and a big, dark forest and a swirling, whirling snowstorm. Can't go round it – how does it go? Can't go under it.

Oh no.

8

The railway station at the Kyle of Lochalsh is a pleasing oddity – a tiny place right next to a small ferry port – the Inner Seas right there, Skye straight ahead, the mainland to one side and, to the other, the Inner Sound and the route to the Outer Hebrides. Gulls wheel and shriek overhead in a light-blue sky that, even in summer, holds a touch of ice. It makes me sigh with pleasure – there are so many different ways to escape. The two-carriage train is on the platform already, empty and waiting with its doors open. This station is the end of the line – any further and you'd be in the sea. I get a takeaway coffee from a kiosk and sip it watching the fishing vessels, the small industrial boats. Yellow cranes are ranged on the quayside, next to bundles waiting to be lifted on board. I feel calm.

There are fewer than a dozen people in my carriage when it leaves – I suppose the train will scoop up more from the villages and small towns as it crosses the mountains and valleys of the Highlands. I'll be rejoining it later, but for now I'm getting off at the second village: Duirinish, then Plockton.

Two other people dismount from the train with me – one sets off down the hill to the village on foot while the other gets into a car. I sit down on a bench to wait until they have gone, drinking from my water bottle. The line is still single track at this point and the station only has one platform – opposite me is woodland. Behind me, the occasional vehicle passes along the road. In the silence in between there is birdsong, a light wind soughing in the trees.

I have already decided to take a roundabout route to the cottage – this stop isn't just strategic; after all, it's a pilgrimage – and part of me is hoping that if the little house of my memory is empty or derelict now, after all these years, I can camp out there for a couple of weeks. Wallowing in memory, you might call it, but it will also have a practical function. My route from here to where I need to be in three weeks will take no more than three, four days maximum if I go there directly. I need to spend time somewhere and here is as good a place as any on a practical level – or as bad as any, I suppose, if we're talking about how it might make me feel.

Go easy on yourself, I think, as, instead of turning right out of the station down into the village, I cross the road and leave the path to head up the ridge.

It is pleasing to be walking up a steep slope with a rucksack, leaning forward into the gradient so that the load on my back is still above my centre of gravity. To have boots on my feet again, equipment, and to be in open countryside . . . The sky above me is blue, with drifting clouds that are snowy white on top, the colour grading gradually towards the bottom through palest grey to dark, darker, darkest. There is a richness to the browns and greens beneath me: the bracken is both fresh and bone dry, lurid green and the colour of a brown envelope. I enter the woods that run along the ridge with a sense I am more hunter than hunted, and I step carefully, look around through the gaps in the trees. I must be no more than a mile from the village but I could be in the middle of nowhere.

It takes longer than I remember to get to the cottage – but last time, we walked down through the village and along the path. There's no mistaking the direction I need to go in, though, I remember it

77

exactly – it must be the furthest habitation on the edge of the village, at the end of a dirt track and huddled beneath a row of trees. I'm approaching from the side as I come through the forest. I remember the first time I saw it, how the low bothy-style shape of it made it seem as though it was crouched down beneath the shelter of the pines, enclosed and safe. I could see immediately why she chose it.

I descend the ridge once I'm past the other houses and then come down through the trees. If my memory is correct, I'll emerge close to the cottage somewhere around here and I should be able to view it from the side. The pines are so thick it is only when I have traversed almost to the edge of the treeline that I can look across a short patch of fallow field to where the tiny white house crouches – and at the same time I see, to my disappointment, that there is a car parked in front of it. I'm more than disappointed – I'm gutted. I realise how much my fantasy of it being a derelict hideaway has fed me with hope. What a fool.

The boot of the car is up and there is a suitcase next to the door of the cottage, which stands open, although there is no one in sight. I stay hidden behind a tree and watch for a while. After a few minutes, a couple in their sixties emerge from the door. The wife pulls the suitcase over the lip of the step and then turns to help her husband, who has begun unloading bags of groceries from the boot.

I watch them from the safety of my hiding place, as hostile as a cat. They look comfortably off to me. The woman is wearing a drapey fine-wool cardigan over skinny jeans and the kind of lace-up boots that could be walking boots but look equally chic on a village high street as you head towards the café to get an oat-milk flat white. I imagine her pursing her lips over her reusable coffee cup while she wanders around little craft shops and galleries, thinking about how much she likes coloured glass. The man is tall and has thinning grey hair – ex-banker, I'm guessing. He looks like the kind of man who pauses after he has made a banal statement and then stares at you, waiting for an admiring smile before he proceeds.

So that's all the cottage is now, a holiday let, an excellent base from which to explore the beautiful surroundings of the West Coast of Scotland. Later, when they have unpacked their shopping, maybe had a cup of tea, they will head out for an exploratory walk before the light begins to fade and the midges come out. When they come back, they might even light a fire – it's Scotland after all and even in the summer it can be pretty nippy in the evenings. Perhaps one of them, the man I'm guessing, will make a nice risotto. Asparagus. Lemon.

I watch them from the shelter of a tree, hidden from view. I think of how, from this position, it would be easy to pick them off – the man first as he bends into the boot, then the woman, one in the chest as she comes back out of the house to see why her husband has slumped against the back of the car. I think about how it might feel to have the weight of a weapon in my hands – the much-maligned SA80, perhaps. The vast majority of people go about their ordinary business, day in, day out, and never stop to think who might be watching them.

I was crazy to come here after all this time. What made me think that the past would be waiting for me, just because I needed it as I fled from the present? Wasn't that the kind of solipsism that made me so bad at relationships before?

The past is dead. I hate everybody. I hate myself most of all.

I wait until the couple are inside and have closed the door behind them before I cross the fallow field and emerge onto the path. It isn't a public footpath, there's no stile, and as I climb the fence, I catch my leggings on a curl of barbed wire and tear a small hole in them. It doesn't improve my mood.

Walking back into the village along the track takes a lot longer than I remember.

The bay: what did she call it? That detail has long since gone. It forms a broad, shallow arc with a road that runs along it and white houses ranged along the road, looking out over the inlet – a small hotel, a pub, a tiny art gallery. It's low tide and the inlet is a wide stretch of moss and pools and shingle. As I walk along the path I see the car park at the far end where we sat on a low stone wall and ate ice cream. I walk to it now and sit in the same place on the same wall, opposite the tiny island that you can cross to on foot when the tide is low, with gorse bushes that were in their full flush of yellow when I came before. There's a bench on the island, facing where I am sitting. You can sit and look at the island, then you can wade out to the island and sit on the bench and look back at the village. Criss-cross that small strait of water as many times as you like; whichever bench you are on, the prettiest view will always be from the other bench.

A small white boat chugs round the island and heads for the pier at the end of the car park – it looks like the seal-spotting boat, the one she made me go on, but the man who took us out was elderly back then; he must be long dead now. I watch the boat pull up and disgorge four passengers, a family with two teenage children. They walk past me on their way back to their car, chattering in English accents about the seals they saw and their whiskers, their eyes.

Behind where I sit, the ice cream shop on the corner is still there. She had vanilla and I had mint choc chip, that much I do remember, and even the flavours of ice cream we chose seem significant to me now, emblematic of our contrasting personalities. It comes to something when you're trying to imbue a single-scoop cone with significance. Go on then, have your wallow, I say to myself. A little weak sun comes out. I preferred Plockton at the end of winter – was it March or April, when I came before? Early spring: yellow gorse, slate roofs, charcoal clouds . . . There was snow on the distant mountains across the bay, back then. It made more sense. In the summer, it's just a visitors' destination, bleached of significance. How is it possible for a place to be both full and empty at the same time? When it is full of memories.

After half an hour or so, I swing my legs back over the low wall, to head up the steep hill to the station. I thought I might spend a fortnight here but it's turned out to be no more than a couple of hours. Perhaps that's as it should be. One more stop to make before I get back on the train and head to Inverness.

I can't remember exactly where it is – but I know I will be able to see the stone arch from the path. I don't even know who built it – if I had a phone on me I could google it, of course, but I don't, so I can't. There's a little wooden sign pointing to the arch from the path. 'Open Air Church'. I don't remember that being there before. I turn off the path and head up the small steep slope.

The arch is wide and leads into a broad gully with a floor of rough grass and high walls of stone lined with a slope of scrubby bracken and gorse. There is no roof, of course, that's the point. I think of her standing in the middle of the grass, both arms lifted wide, and turning in a slow circle, her dreamy face lifted to the sky. *Isn't it amazing?* I feel suddenly angry. All that sentiment – it annoyed me even then. What good did her beliefs do her, how did they protect her from what happened that day, when all she was doing was walking down the street on her way to the shops?

I don't want to waste any more time here: I did enough of that looking at the cottage, gazing out over the bay. I turn right and go straight to the place she pointed out, the place she made me promise to look if anything ever happened to her.

The scrubby earth slopes upwards steeply here and the bracken is even more overgrown than it was before. I have to slip my ruck-sack from my shoulders and lean it against the arch before I drop on my knees in the earth and begin to dig with my hands, cursing her roundly for the fool's errand I am on because of a long-ago oath and only because I came here hoping to hide. Otherwise, I swear to God, I really, *really* would not be bothering. I'm not the sentimental sort.

I curse her for my dirty hands, the soil beneath my fingernails. I curse her for making me promise I would do this and I curse myself for sticking to the promise. I'm about to give up when my fingernails scrape against wood and a splinter lodges at the very tip of an index finger.

I sit back on my heels, suck the finger, then after a suitably solemn pause, I extract the box.

I don't know where she got it from – it's smaller than a shoebox and very plain. I'm surprised it hasn't degraded over the years, but it's covered in some kind of varnish that has faded and peeled here and there. As a precaution, the contents inside are wrapped in a plain white plastic bag. I lift it out and peer inside, then pull the

82

contents out, one by one: a small velvet bag with a pretty bit of string enclosing the top – inside it is a silver link bracelet. I hold it up. There's also a see-through plastic wallet, A5 size, which contains several paper packets of photographs; some school exercise books; a tiny sewing kit; a jewellery box with an old-fashioned, broken watch . . . and a small white envelope.

I take the envelope and hold it, looking at it warily, as if it might disintegrate in my hands. One word on the front: *Heather*.

To buy myself time, I put everything except the letter back into the plastic bag, which I fold over and slide down into the main compartment of my rucksack. I have to leave the box here, so I re-bury it. It won't fit in the rucksack and even if it would, I'm damned if I'm lugging it across the North Sea. Then, seated at the bottom of the steep slope, I put my rucksack back on but prop the end of it a little higher than my backside on a rough stone immediately behind me, so I'm still wearing it and can rise straightaway in case anyone else comes along. Only then do I open the letter.

Dear Heather,
How strange to think that if you are reading this, I will be gone. I struggle with the idea that the world will carry on when I have disappeared from it. You know that I believe in another world – but I share your problem with believing they can both exist at the same time.

Anyway, I will try to imagine you holding this and me not existing any more and I will hope that doesn't happen for a very long time and that most of my fears now are unnecessary. God willing, it will be in many years to come.

I hope whatever you are doing with your life right now, you are happy. I worry about you. You like running away – most of all running away from the things that make you happy. What's that about, as you would say? Fear of losing them, I suppose, mia cara amica. Well, that's a longer conversation than I have time for at the moment – you'll be arriving soon and I want to finish this before you do so that I can tell you about it while you are here.

So here it is. I love you very dearly, Heather (I never could get used to calling you Bird). I may not be here any more, but I give you everything here. The silver chain bracelet in the small velvet bag is an exact replica of the one you gave me – can you believe it, I found it in a shop on my way here. That pleased me so much, it felt fated, it was what gave me the idea. In here are also some childhood things, some photographs, my school exercise books. They aren't of any importance or value except to someone who loved me and at the moment that's pretty much looking like you, you're it!

Apart from the thing that is coming, that is, and who knows when that thing might care for tokens one way or another – so you must be the custodian of them in the meantime, and pass them on when I am dead.

So, on that subject, most of all, I gift you this: responsibility. It is the greatest gift that I can give you, Heather, my dear friend. It might look like a burden but I promise it isn't. It's frightening, and exciting, and many other things – but it isn't a burden. If you ever read this, it is a privilege I will no longer have, and so I am giving it to you. Responsibility – it is not something to run away from. Instead, you should seek it out, or shoulder it gladly, if it comes to you. It's what makes our lives worth living, my friend, I do believe that most sincerely. I don't need to explain any more because by now, by the time you are reading this, you will already know.

Please please love her as much as I love you.

There is so much more I could say but I'm writing in haste because the 11.17 will be here soon and it's going to take me a while to walk through the village and up the hill. I hope you haven't brought too much luggage – as soon as you see me you'll realise I can't help. At least it's downhill on the way back. I can't wait to see your face when you see An t-Ob for the first time – yes I've even picked up a little Gaelic, well, place names and numbers, that's it.

84

I've thought of the perfect hiding place for this letter, already pre-pared, and I'm going to tuck it safe away on the way to the station. The sun has come out to greet you, dear Heather, and I'm so excited that I'm going to see you soon.

It's such a beautiful spring day. On days like this, the village and the bay are so lovely. You can't believe it will ever be winter again.

I love you, ti amo, tha gaol agam ort,

Always,

Flavia xxxxxx

I sit there in the rough grass for a long time, holding the letter in my hand and staring at it. After a while I notice that the paper is fluttering in my grasp. I am crying, and once I have begun to cry, I cannot stop. I am sitting in a hollow in the middle of nowhere outside a remote village on the West Coast of Scotland and I am whimpering and snivelling like a small animal in a trap. I press my other hand against my face as tears stream down. My mouth is open but my howl is silent.

Flavia. And Mum. Everyone I care for is gone. I've had to run away from all the people I work with, everything I own, and no one in the world knows where I am. Even the people hunting me can't find me. I gulp as I stifle my sobs, fingers splayed over the harsh rectangle of grief that is my mouth. Salty tears run down my cheeks. I'm so lonely I am nauseous with it.

It doesn't last; when you are in your darkest moment, your most heart-freezingly miserable, you are already at the bottom and will soon be heading back up. It is human nature, human will, if you like. We can't die of grief, however much we may think we can or want to: deep inside, too much, we need to live.

85

My sobs subside. In a few minutes, I will push myself off the slope, fold the letter and stuff it into a pocket, then, stiffly, like an old person, climb back down to the path and turn right to head up to the station, continue my flight.

Was it there, in Plockton, when I was at my lowest, that it happened? Was it in Glasgow, perhaps, when I spent those four days in a flat I had broken into, imagining myself to be in no hurry at that point? Maybe it was even earlier – perhaps he was on the train and disembarked with me at Carlisle, but no, I hitched that lift, it can't have been then. Or later: Inverness? I will never know. All I know is that somewhere on my journey to the furthest reaches of the British Isles, at some point, I was found and followed by a man who had been sent to kill me and I didn't even notice the point at which he picked up my trail.

I didn't even notice – I can't stop thinking about this. Where was I, at that point, and what was I doing? Of all the things I have learned or been told about or worked out for myself, that's the one thing I will never know. I agonise over it, sometimes, and find myself remembering how I sat there in the secret hollow outside Plockton and cried with loneliness. It's fanciful – but I can't help feeling as though that moment of weakness let him find me, as if that small orgy of self-pity cracked open something that let him in.

In idle moments, I trace that journey in my head, following the pictures of my memories as precisely as you might trace a route on a map with a fingertip, trying to work it out. There, and there, no, maybe there? Surely, if I think hard enough, look hard enough, I will be able to see the man they sent, somewhere in my peripheral vision, a figure behind me but getting nearer and nearer as I look back over my shoulder. He is growing, morphing: a shadow, a shape, visible then invisible in the way that a nocturnal creature is revealed then shrouded by the slipping and sliding of clouds across the moon.

PART 2

The way to accelerate the multiplication of money was to be close to power . . . to spot the places where power was suddenly exposed, like a seam of ore torn open by some tectonic shift.

Tom Burgis, *Kleptopia*

9

Preparation is everything, that's what we learned in the army, although I wasn't an army officer as such, I was an Acting Captain in the Women's Royal Army Corps. They didn't let us girls join in with the boys back then. We didn't go to Sandhurst, we didn't bear arms and our training timetable at the WRAC centre in Camberley included – I shit you not – flower arranging. But my experience in the WRAC was all about Flavia too – and what happened to Flavia was why I left after less than six years, and if I hadn't set fire to my commission I would never have ended up in the Service. Swings and roundabouts, as they say.

I left the Women's Royal Army Corps towards the end of 1981 – although to say I left is something of a sophistry. The GOC of SE District made it clear I could resign immediately on the grounds of compassionate discharge or I could wait for a court martial that would in all likelihood end with discharge in disgrace, but I guess that's what happens when you swing for a senior officer, even if he deserves to be swung for.

Looking back, it's the raised hopes that I object to. We were encouraged to take ourselves so seriously. When I went up before the Regular Commission Board at the age of twenty-two – three days at Westbury – I was awarded my commission with one caveat: I had excelled at the physical challenges and individual tasks, they told me, but my weakest point was my co-operation with the rest of my syndicate. It was something I needed to work on if I was to be true officer material one day. I needed to be more of a team player – God, how I hated that phrase. 'A cadet whose only desire is to win the Sash of Honour will not be liked or respected by her peers,' a kindly Major told me, inclining her head and giving me a twinkly little smile that made me want to slap her. *Liked?* Respected, yes, but *liked*? I nodded, of course, expressed myself eager to take the feedback on board – in truth, if being first over the obstacle course had required me to push one of my fellow applicants face down in a cowpat, I would have done it in a heartbeat.

Marching to the 'Pride of Lions' or 'Early One Morning', room inspections every morning – first you, then your kit – learning military lore and map reading, visiting the Units and the London Stock Exchange and the Old Bailey so we understood how the society we would supposedly defend with our lives actually worked. I loved it all to start with, but when I looked back after my disillusionment, all I could think was why were we taught all these things when we would be allowed to do so little? Supervising the stewardesses, overseeing the clerks, training other women whose job upon commission would be to train other women too.

Over at Sandhurst, the passing-out parade was attended by the Queen. We got our parents. But at least mine seemed to enjoy it. They looked the smartest I had ever seen: my father in a navy suit with a double-breasted jacket and shiny buttons, hair oiled, shoes polished to a perfect shine. I had never seen him stand so tall and proud, his lips pressed together in a tight beam of satisfaction. Mum was dressed as if for a wedding, in pale yellow, with heels that made her walk very carefully, holding tightly to my father's arm. She smiled bravely through the whole thing, even though it was freezing and she disliked both dressing up and being cold. We had been told in advance that as it was such a brisk day, we could wear two pairs of the regulation tights – Boots' Brown Haze – but the whole Company had to agree to wear either one pair or two pairs so that our legs would be the same colour beneath our skirts.

While we waited in line, I watched my father greet our training staff and saw how they inclined their heads in a brief, sharp nod – recognising something in him, a man with training, and I thought, *thank God*. I've no plans to give him a wedding or grandchildren or an Olympic medal – but at least I am giving him this.

After passing out I was stationed in Richmond, North Yorkshire, where I supervised the stewardesses, the maids who took cups of tea to officers in the mornings. Later, I would be involved in such tasks vital to national security as doing spot checks on the women's barracks in the middle of the night, to see if any of them were in bed with each other.

Green knickers. Regulation issue green knickers. I remember those. But I hadn't joined the army for the brown tights or the green knickers or the spot checks on young lesbians – I didn't give two hoots what the NCOs got up to as long as nobody was using their rank to take advantage of someone else. Looking back, the writing was on the wall, although later some of my former colleagues who stuck it out longer than I did told me of interesting postings to Rheindahlen, and one of them narrowly survived the 1987 bombing by the IRA. If I'd held on I might have got to Cyprus with the Slimeys, perhaps, not that they allowed many women into Military Intelligence, but it would have been an awfully long wait, and I would have had to do a lot of simpering at male officers a great deal less able than myself.

And before any of that could happen, came Flavia.

When I first saw Flavia, she was sitting on the floor, knees raised, hair a-tumble, boot on fist.

There was a long corridor with a polished wooden floor that ran between our rooms at Camberley like a deep, dark canal, and the very first week of training it became our habit to sit there of an evening and talk while we bulled our boots. I arrived a little late that evening and was about to walk further down the corridor, where two of the new friends I had made, Frances and Claire, were working rags around the seams in time with each other and talking. We were all still at the stage of feeling our way around each other, working out who we liked and didn't like – within a week our friendship groups would be set in stone for the rest of training, but at that point things were still fluid.

Communal bulling was already a ritual – we had all intuited, without ever being told, that it was about a great deal more than making sure the toes of our boots were shiny: it was about making sure they were all the same level of shiny. The connection between polishing your boots and hauling a fellow soldier out of a foxhole while mortars exploded above your heads may seem tenuous to a civilian, but we understood it instinctively. Everyone dressed for it in tracksuit bottoms – which the privately educated girls called *tracky bums* – and vests, but Flavia was the only one of the group who had loosened her hair. It fell in a full black waterfall down her shoulders, and that was the first thing I noticed about her.

She looked up as I approached with my boots in one hand and

shoe-cleaning kit in the other. She was dark-haired and dark-eyed like me, but without my sallow skin or pinched features. Her complexion was the creamiest white, her cheeks plump. Before too long, I would come to feel as if I was her shadow, the version of her that might have existed if all light had been sucked out of her. She looked up at me with an expression I would also come to know, as if a small huff of amusement – a not-entirely kindly sound – was about to burst out of her.

Instead of joining the girls I had already befriended, I stopped, rested my back against the wall opposite Flavia and slid down it until my arse bumped against the shiny floor. Bulling might have been a communal ritual – a moment of bonding in the knowledge that come the morning we would all face the same inspection – but I only had eyes for her.

I opened my kit and took out my two brushes, knitted together by their stiff hairs, and a small selection of rags. I couldn't see my tin of polish – I must have left it in the corridor the previous evening, or perhaps someone else had picked it up. It wasn't like me to mislay something and it was going to be embarrassing to ask if I could borrow someone else's. As I raised my head, Flavia – I did not yet know her name – slid hers across the floor like an ice hockey puck. I felt a rush of gratitude, not so much for the polish as the rescue from humiliation. I picked it up, twisted the metal clasp and flipped the lid. I saw that it was brand new, the surface of the polish pleasingly unbroken. I looked at her and she jutted her chin upwards, saying, 'Keep it, I've got this one.' I noted that she had slid over her new polish, rather than the one she was already using, which was empty enough for the shiny bottom of the tin to be visible at the centre.

I raised my eyebrows. 'Thanks,' I said, a sardonic note in my voice. My priority at this point was avoiding the indignity of seeming too grateful.

Our gazes met in a smile that already felt collusive. I suppose if I was superstitious I might say that the history of our relationship was written then, in that first look. Either way, it was far from the last time that Flavia would know what I needed before I knew myself.

We swapped stories that first evening, talking in the corridor long after the others had risen from their positions and gone off to iron their uniforms or dust the shelves above their beds in order to arrange their toiletries precisely before inspection. It became our habit to talk a lot in the evenings to come.

Flavia had been born in Italy and spent her early years in Lombardy as the only child of a widowed mother – her father had died of a heart attack when she was two years old. Her mother had been an only child so there were very few aunts or uncles or cousins on the scene. In Italy, she said, it was very strange to have so few relatives, and as she was growing up, she realised that she had lost not only her father but the brothers and sisters she might have had. (When I told her I had two brothers but wasn't close to either of them, she looked at me like I was mad.)

She idolised her dead father – there were photos of him in silver frames all over the house. He had been tall and handsome; her mother was small, and shy, and cried a lot. When Flavia was eight, her mother met and married an Englishman who had come to teach English at a local college where they lived in Cremona. He had family back in the UK and Flavia and her mother didn't have much family anywhere, so two years later, the family moved back to

England and Flavia spent the rest of her childhood in Basingstoke. Fair to say, it was something of a shock.

Her stepfather was very good to her, loved her, raised her as his own, and the marriage was happy, but Flavia's mother hated living in England, hated the cold, the grey skies – mourned the life in Italy that she had never really had. She and her new husband didn't have children themselves, so Flavia never got the siblings she longed for. 'I wanted a sister more than anything in the world. I was always trying to make best friends with other only children at school and persuading them to prick their fingers so we could swear blood pacts.' She laughed when she told me this. 'It never worked out.' We were both oddballs at school for different reasons; we talked a lot about that.

When she was fifteen, she started asking more about her father, and her stepfather – not her mother – sat her down and told her that her biological father hadn't died of a heart attack, he'd been an abusive alcoholic with cirrhosis of the liver and she and her mother were better off without him. It was the catalyst for Flavia to suddenly engage with all the teenage stuff: discovering vodka, smoking behind the science lab at school, but she scraped her way into a redbrick university through clearing and must have pulled her socks up at some point or she would never have got through Westbury. I suppose she ended up in the army for the same reason as a lot of people: whatever all her friends were doing didn't work for her. She was looking for something else.

Because Flavia and I both had thick, defiant hair, we would do each other's buns in the morning. All hair had to be off the collar, of course, and around three-quarters of the women had short cuts, which saved them vital minutes in the mornings. On a typical day, the door of my room would burst open and in would come Flavia, still in tracksuit bottoms and her vest, nostrils flaring. 'Oh my God, *rapidamente*, come *on*, you idiot!'

'Good morning to you too . . .' I would pull the grey blankets over my head and she would rip them off, plonking herself down on the edge of the bed.

'Come on, come on, come on!'

As I raised myself up on my knees, she swung to the side and turned her head so I could kneel behind her, holding a hairbrush that I'd grabbed from the shelf behind me: a few firm brushes, a twist, and I was flipping the fine brown net over and over, my mouth full of pins.

The first time I did this, as I pushed the last pin in, pressed it to check it was firm, I noticed the elegant row of dark hairs, like very fine fur, on the back of her neck, shining against her pale skin, and it occurred to me that if I was a man, I would lift a hand and stroke the back of her neck with my forefinger.

'Now you, quick!' She jumped up and pushed me down, hand on one shoulder.

'Oh God, Flavia, I've only just woken up, let me *pee* . . .'

One of our Majors was a Glaswegian, and so Flavia replied, in the worst Glaswegian accent I have ever heard, 'There'll be *nae* time for *peein'* when the *bullets* are *flyin'*!' And then we were so helpless with laughter she could hardly fix my bun, and in the end I had to push her out of my room so I could get dressed in time with both of us still doubled up, inarticulate with mirth at our lateness, her impulsiveness, the absurdity of our chosen careers.

The other women all thought we were lovers, but we never were – not in the way they meant, at least.

I could say so much more about those days: there was a kind of innocence, a purity to our ambition, our patriotism, our belief that we were, in our own small way, making a contribution, keeping democracy safe. We never realised, in the seventies and eighties, the magnitude of what we were up against. We were young, we were good at what we did, and we thought that was enough.

After I was posted to Richmond and while she did her tour of Germany, Flavia and I stayed in constant touch – when she came back to the UK, we saw each other on leave weekends, holidayed together a couple of times. She came to stay in Coventry with me when I went home.

I met her mother and stepfather just once, at a rather awkward lunch we had with them in a Sunday carvery, local to them where they still lived in Basingstoke. Her stepfather was pleasant and dull – his year teaching in Italy was clearly the most exciting thing that had ever happened to him; he still talked about it. Everything about him was sandy: sandy hair, sandy skin, sandy moustache – I'm surprised he wasn't called Sandy. Flavia's mother stared at me while I talked in a way that made me feel uncomfortable, as if she had a feeling I was a bad influence on her daughter and was trying to work out precisely how.

Then, gloriously, we were both posted to HQ SE District for a spell.

My first thought on arriving in Aldershot in 1981 was that it was a town that had yet to leave the seventies – mind you, I had to go back there in 2001 and it felt as though it still hadn't. On that later visit, a full two decades after I had been stationed there as a young officer, I walked from the station to meet my contact – my equivalent liaison officer with Military Intelligence – and thought that perhaps there are some places that take on the air of a particular decade. The UK was in a short and shallow recession at that point and would soon recover, but the town seemed to have an air of brave hardship about it. Perhaps that's true of any army town. As I waited in a café in the pedestrian precinct, I saw the same off-duty soldiers I used to see when I was stationed there myself as a young woman – tight T-shirts, no coats, walking around as if their hackles were permanently raised. I also saw something I had never noticed twenty years before: the stringy-looking older men with haunted gazes sitting on benches with beer cans in their hands. I wondered if they were a new feature or if they had been there twenty years before but, with the callowness of youth, I hadn't noticed them. I saw how the young, muscled types walked past the older men without a glance – they could not see, or would not acknowledge, a portent.

When I first arrived there in 1981, I knew I was becoming dis-illusioned with the army but I hadn't fully acknowledged to myself just how much. I was on my Grade 3 Staff appointment by then, a Staff Captain in Int and Sy, as we called it. Flavia was an Officer Instructor in the Army School of Catering. There were still over a hundred pubs in the town back then, mostly to cater for the NCOs – the townies knew the squaddie pubs and had the good sense to steer clear of them.

I saw a soldier thrown through a plate-glass window once – off duty, of course. A group of us, me and Flavia and three others, were

100

standing outside the fried chicken shop on High Street, eating chips after a night in the Weaver's Arms. A group of privates in jeans and cut-off T-shirts were sitting at a window table. It was winter but they wouldn't have dreamed of wearing coats when they had biceps to display. Occasionally you would see one who had deigned to drape a thin scarf round his neck but only with the ends hanging loose – if he wrapped it round his neck, his fellow soldiers might call him a *poofter*. They all had platters of deep-fried drumsticks coated in some brown crumbly mix and I happened to glance through the window at them at the same time as another soldier, passing by on his own, took a sharp turn, walked calmly into the chicken shop, picked up one of the seated men and – before his companions could react – threw him bodily through the plate-glass window, out into the street.

There were three or four other groups standing around and most of them let out a loud cheer before heading over to see if the soldier on the ground was okay. Meanwhile, inside the chicken shop, a massive punch-up started that seemed to involve the assailant, the victim's friends and everyone who had been waiting in the queue for their chicken.

I turned to ask Flavia whether we should break it up – it was much easier to do that as a woman officer than a man – and saw she was now standing a few feet away talking to a tall officer who I recognised vaguely. She was laughing, no, *simpering*, looking down at the ground, then back up at him where he towered above her, and as I watched, he reached out a hand and took hold of a bunch of the hair on the back of her head in his fist. I could see her face in profile and she was smiling as he tipped her face up to him – and in that moment I realised that it wasn't a passing man who was chatting her up, but someone she had known for a while who had spotted her in our group and come over. They were just outside a pool of lamplight, scarcely visible in the dark, and everybody else's attention was on the fight. As he lowered his own face down to her, she closed her eyes.

I never found out what offence the soldier who was thrown through the window had caused to the one who did the throwing, but I was told that the following weekend, he went back to the chicken shop to apologise to the owner and give him a wad of cash for his troubles. As he left the shop, he saw his assailant from the previous weekend heading towards it, also planning to give the owner a wad of cash with apologies. So the first soldier, the one who had been thrown out of the restaurant, picked up the second soldier and threw him *into* the restaurant through the newly replaced window. After that, the owner gave up replacing the glass and left the window boarded up. I don't think it affected his custom.

He was a Lieutenant Colonel, the tall officer, a Commanding Officer in Provost Company, married, of course, and it was strictly against the rules, so strictly that it happened all the time. Flavia hadn't confided in me because she knew I would disapprove, she said. Her downfall came unexpectedly, one Tuesday evening. I was on my way to Senior Lieutenant Bianchi's room to ask her about her next leave dates and as I approached down the corridor, I saw four other women gathered round her open doorway and heard weeping from Flavia's room.

I pushed the others out of the way as I approached.

Flavia was sitting on her bed, leaning forward with her hands over her face, and howling – actually howling, like a small child.

On the floor of her room, at her feet, was an open case with a few objects thrown into it: a bag of toiletries, a small and seemingly random selection of clothes. There was a broken china mug on the other side of her room.

'What's going on?' I asked.

'All I did was ask if she was okay,' said the woman next to me, a tough little terrier of a woman called Minnie, a PT Instructor in 10 Company. 'You try.'

I stood in the doorway and looked at Flavia, at where she was sitting on the edge of the bed, helpless in her distress.

'Fuck off,' I said to the other women, then went into Flavia's room and closed the door behind me.

Flavia had 'lost her name' – that's what they actually called it when you were in disgrace, although most of the time they didn't even know your name. She was gone that very evening and when I begged her to talk to me about it, explain what had been going on with Michael and what had happened, she wept and told me not to get involved. She'd be in touch, she said – and with that, she was gone.

The following weekend, I tried ringing her mother and her step-father. Sandy, whatever his name was, answered the phone and told me Flavia was taking a break and it was best I didn't call again – she didn't want to speak to anyone from the army for a while. *Anyone?* I thought. How was I suddenly anyone? When I begged him to pass on a message he paused and said, 'I'll tell her you've called,' then hung up the phone.

The next night, there was a mess dinner that I knew the Lieutenant Colonel would be attending. I stayed on the base while the others went into town and towards the end of the evening, I crossed the wide-open spaces in the dark and waited outside the Regimental Dining Hall – I told myself I wanted to give him a piece of my mind but now I think there was more to it than that. I was about to behave in a way that would produce the result that I had, without knowing, wanted for some time.

It was 10 p.m. and moonless, pitch dark. I watched him step out of a yellow-lit doorway with a group of other officers. They all paused on the doorstep for a smoke. He was silhouetted against the light, and I could see how he flicked ash from the end of his cigarette with an elegant matinee-idol tap of his forefinger. Tall and rangy, he had a loose way of standing, as though he was comfortable in his own skin. After ten minutes or so, he dropped the stub and ground it into the step with a smart to-and-fro motion of his heel, then bid his fellow officers farewell with a lift of his hand. They were still smoking and somebody else would probably end up picking up his stub as it was considered bad form for officers of their rank to leave them on the ground. He turned to walk behind the hall and down through the alleyway formed by two close rows of barracks; he was the only one of his group heading back to married quarters.

I followed him until the unpaved strip of path turned down between the backs of two barracks where there were no windows. The grass was still wet after recent rainfall and my approach was silent, but halfway down, he sensed my presence and stopped, looking back. He was in dinner dress – I was in civvies. There was a moment of query in his features, then a slow smile. In the faint moonlight he looked handsome, closely shaven, neatly browed – I had a sudden and vivid image of how he might clip his nasal hair in the mornings. I could almost hear the tiny click of the clippers.

I knew I couldn't mince my words – there wasn't time. He would probably turn and stride off as soon as I spoke, or someone else might come along. I only had seconds.

'You're a total fucking shit,' I said quickly but calmly. 'You know you are. You may think there's no consequences and maybe there aren't, but every single woman on this base knows what you're like and . . .'

'Heather,' he said pleasantly, facing me squarely. 'I haven't had the pleasure yet.' He stepped towards me, his expression still relaxed. I knew his approaching me was intended to be threatening but I wasn't having any of it. I stood my ground.

'You're no fucking officer,' I said, my voice hissing and low, 'you're a disgrace to your uniform. You're just some adulterous toerag like any other toerag out there, you're just . . .'

His legs were much longer than mine and a single step brought him up close. He reached out one hand and grabbed the back of my head, lacing his fingers in my hair and pulling my head back sharply, tipping me off balance in a gesture that was the dark version of what he had done with Flavia just outside the lamplight, an instinctive mockery of it, and to this day I cannot see that gesture performed romantically on film or TV without knowing that, in its essence, it is nothing of the sort. My scalp contracted; my throat was exposed and pulsing. My eyes pricked with tears and I had time to wonder, momentarily, if he was mad enough to actually hurt me – but he was far too much of a careerist for that. The backwards contortion and stretching of my neck had narrowed my windpipe. I made a single low gulping sound.

He bent his head towards me. 'Not my fault you didn't get anywhere, but when it came to me, *Heather*, I assure you . . .' He released the back of my head. I staggered but stayed upright.

He regarded me for a moment. I wondered if he was drunk, the kind of drunk that seems very sober. 'She makes a sweet sound when she fucks,' he said, and turned away, sauntering off with a raised salute of one hand. *Goodnight to you.*

You can get over hatred of somebody, I suppose, but you never get over hatred that is blended with fear: that one, it's like indelible ink. I was determined to prove I wasn't afraid.

I ran after him. At the end of the barrack walls, the path opened up into a small square before the next row of barracks. Four NCOs were standing in a huddle near one of the doors and I saw them, of course, but by then I was too furious to care. By the time I caught up with him, he was well into the square where there were tall lamps in the corners that lit the scene. I may have shouted, I'm not sure, but he turned back with a louche *This is getting tiresome now* expression on his face just in time for my small hard fist to catch the underside of his left jaw.

I wish I could say it made a satisfying sound of some sort as it connected, but it didn't. It did, however, hurt me enough to know it had also hurt him – and it was worth it all, including the end of my army career, to see the look of disbelief that came over his groomed features in the same instant that the squaddies by the nearby block let out a whoop of glee.

10

After I left the army, I moved to London and registered with a temp agency. Work was easy to get: a lot of companies liked to employ ex-military as we generally showed up on time with our shirts ironed and our shoes polished. I had joined the WRAC full of patriotic fervour, the passion my father had instilled in me, that one of the highest callings I could aspire to was to serve the Queen and defend democracy. Now I joined the rush-hour commute on double-decker buses and had earnest discussions with my office colleagues about whether the prawn sandwiches from M&S were basically mayonnaise with pink bits.

After four months, I finally heard from Flavia. I was angry with her by then – the friend I had defended, just disappearing like that. This was before mobile phones, before email or social media – if you didn't know where your friend had gone and the only phone number you had was for her parents, then that was the only way you could get in touch. If they didn't pass the messages on or she didn't reply, that was it. During that time, I imagined that if she ever got in touch again I would be distant with her, aloof. She would be devastated by my coolness and apologise over and over again.

As it was, my phone rang one evening when I was at home alone in my flat watching television, and I was so surprised when I picked up the receiver and she said, 'Heather, Heather it's me,' that I didn't even ask her how she had got my new number (turned out she had rung my parents for it, of course).

'Oh my God!' I said, my voice high-pitched with delight. 'How the hell are you? *Where* are you?'

She was laughing down the phone. 'Thank God – I thought you'd be furious with me.'

And like the helpless idiot that I always was when I was with Flavia I replied, 'No, no, of course not, I was just worried . . . I didn't . . .'

'I'll tell you everything, I promise, when you come and stay.'

'Stay where? I don't know where you are.'

'Plockton,' she said. 'I'm living in Plockton, well for the time being, probably not for that long. That's why you have to come.'

'Where is Plockton?'

'Look it up, I want to know how *you* are.'

I told her about my new job, my flat, how there was an elderly couple in the flat downstairs with no fewer than six tiny, yappy dogs. I tried to ask her about herself, her mysterious disappearance, what had happened with Michael, but she kept saying she'd explain everything when I went to visit.

We both went to get our diaries so we could sort out a date. I returned clutching my Filofax and slim gold biro. The phone receiver was lying on its side on the countertop in my tiny galley kitchen and before I picked it up again, I stopped and looked at it. Flavia was on the other end of the line. In a second, I would pick up the receiver and we would arrange a time for me to go and visit her, and I paused right there in my own small kitchen, staring down at the phone, diary in hand, to appreciate that moment.

I slid the receiver between my shoulder and my ear while I used both hands to hold the Filofax and the pen. 'Go on,' I said, 'when do you want me to come?'

'As soon as possible.'

I called her back the following evening after I had checked with my agency that I could take the Friday off to make it a proper weekend. I had promised Flavia I would look up Plockton and how to get there.

'Eleven hours?' I said as she answered the phone. 'How can anywhere in this country be eleven hours on the train? You're not even right at the top.'

'That's if you leave first thing,' she said. 'But the other thing you could do is get the sleeper to Inverness from Euston the night before. I'd do it that way if I were you, come over from there in the morning. You're doing a bit of a dog leg but the ride over to the West Coast is so beautiful, it's good for your soul.'

'Okay, sure,' I replied, although being the cynic I was, I wasn't sure about the *good for your soul* bit. A view was a view, after all. 'I'll have to see if there's a sleeper on the Thursday night.'

This second call was more awkward. During the first, we had heard the giddiness in each other's voices, responded to and mimicked each other's delight. Making an arrangement had sobered us. There was a lot to discuss when we met, after all.

Good for your soul. It reminded me of the element of Flavia's personality I had never got along with – her spirituality, her insistence that there were higher purposes or things in the ether or whatever. She had been done over by the army. In my view, that wasn't something to be turned into *everything happens for a reason*. It was something that should make you want to break somebody's jaw.

I lost my cynicism around 6 a.m. on a Friday morning in the early spring of 1982, when I lifted the grey blind on my sleeper compartment and, having left London Euston dark and rainy the night before, saw snow-covered mountains reflecting the early-morning light. Whatever shred of my internal sceptic was left dissolved around four hours later after I had changed trains in Inverness and headed west, crossing the country from coast to coast, the landscape so wide and empty . . . Lochluichart, Achanalt, Achnasheen . . . water, mountains, sky, mist – broad valleys with small lakes and scrubby copses of fir – I wondered that the army had never sent us there to train. And I wondered at my own ignorance. For an outdoorsy sort of person, why had I spent my life in boring, built-up England? Why hadn't I been here before? I still didn't know what was going on with my friend, but I understood there might be more than one reason why Flavia had left England, and why she had gone so far.

She was waiting on the platform as I got off the train and the first thing I noticed was that she was visibly pregnant. I felt my face go slack as I walked towards her.

She held out her arms in an expansive gesture, glanced down at the rise of her belly, then back up at me. 'Surprise!'

We linked arms as we walked down the hill towards the village – Flavia was chattering. 'We're going to go through the village but you're probably hungry so we won't stop now. I've got some home-made soup on the stove. My place is the other side of the village – I can't wait to show you, but we'll take a look at the bay and a few other places as we're going past, you can do that, can't you? You're not bursting for the loo or anything?' I had the feeling she was talking so much because she didn't want me to ask any questions just yet.

The road down into town was steep but halfway down she stopped and said, 'Here, as we're passing, I want to show you something.' She pointed to where a small steep slope led upwards, out of sight of the path.

In the middle of the Open Air Church, Flavia turned in a circle, the full three-sixty degrees, her arms partially lifted and face tipped to the spring sunshine, a seraphic smile on her face. 'Don't you think it's magical?' she said. 'Christians worshipping in the open air, in secret maybe, when they had to. It must have felt so special, to have the sky witness the strength of your belief.'

I looked around, to please her. 'It feels more pagan to me.' Open-air worship made me think of people dressed in animal skins sacrificing a goat on a stone, drinking the blood from a goblet, perhaps. By firelight. I had a sudden image of the unfortunate goat, tied down to the stone, on its back with its eyeballs rolling in terror and teeth bared. Is it possible to tie a goat down on its back?

She turned to me and her look was soft and serious. 'Will you remember this place, do you think?'

I knew she wanted me to feel affected, but really, as far as I was concerned, it was just a grassy hollow. 'Yes, of course,' I replied, to please her.

'Good,' she said, 'I want you to remember it for years to come.' She came up to me, took my arm again and said, 'Come on, my rational friend, not everything is explicable right away, but we will skip the rest of the guided tour for now. That soup is waiting for us.'

'Good, I'm starving.'

*

We passed through the village – Flavia gesturing expansively to the pretty little bay – and then turned down a track with small fields either side. At the far end was a low, small, whitewashed house. To our left was a tightly knitted area of forest – dry-looking pines packed so close, the darkness of the wood's interior came right up to the edge of the field as if it might spill over and flow towards us.

When I remember this now, I strain to take myself back there and look more sharply, as if I might see my future self many years hence, partially concealed beside a tree trunk, watching the cottage and fantasising about having a sniper's rifle lifted, peering down the sights.

There was no front garden to the cottage, only a patch of gravel where many years later I would see, to my disappointment, a parked car with its boot open, suitcases. Flavia told me she had a small hatchback but it was at the garage. She opened the wide wooden door and we stepped into a hallway with a staircase straight ahead, tiny sitting room to the right and, to the left, a kitchen with a stone-flagged floor.

'Leave your bag there,' Flavia said, pointing to the bottom of the stairs. 'I'll show you upstairs later – there's only one bedroom so we're sharing. Let's get the soup on, I eat like a horse these days.'

To the side of the staircase were two large suitcases, upright with their handles raised. 'Do you have other guests?' I asked drily.

She smiled. 'No fear, just you. That's all my stuff in there.'

I raised an eyebrow.

'I don't own anything here, it's all rented. I keep most of my personal stuff all ready to ship out quickly if I have to.' I thought of my heavily pregnant friend lugging her two large cases out of the wooden door, tipping them into her hatchback, driving away in a hurry with her hands clutching the wheel, and I felt sick to my stomach. Why is that always in the back of our minds: *what's my exit route, where's the door?*

She slipped off her mac, turned and hung it on a peg to the side of the door. She lifted her hair clear of her collar and I saw she was wearing a small silver bracelet that I had bought her for her last birthday. She caught me noticing it and beamed. 'Ah good,' she said mysteriously as I followed her into the kitchen.

The kitchen had roof beams with hooks and an old-fashioned range that looked as though it had been there since ranges had been invented, but it wasn't giving out any heat – there was a gas hob to the side of it. The walls were painted with some kind of crumbling distemper – the whole thing had a 1930s feel to me. It felt like the kind of place that would have a woodshed out back where you would store up food and fuel against the coming winter.

I sat down at the table while Flavia went about opening cupboards and closing them, disappearing into a small room she called the pantry and coming out again. Objects appeared in front of me: a tub of hummus; several different small cheeses in waxy wrappers arranged neatly on a wooden chopping board; a china plate with gilt edging and a dark crack running from its centre. My friend's shirt was taut across her belly, and yet I sat there without helping her. If it was winter, I thought, I would be shivering, unable to warm up – and yet it was spring. Flavia had opened the back door to a small garden, the air outside gleaming. The knowledge of how her life, and so our friendship, was now changed, was sinking in. I thought of how she had kept the huge news of her pregnancy from me for months and months.

Flavia placed a small blue milk jug on the table and I picked it up and angled it, looking at it as if I'd never seen a milk jug before.

'This is nice,' I said, 'where did you get it?'

Flavia stopped and turned. 'Are you annoyed at me?'

I put the jug down. 'I'm just pleased to see you,' I said.

'You are.' Annoyed, she meant.

She turned on a gas ring beneath the saucepan of soup on the hob. It took her a couple of goes to strike the match and when she held it near, the flame leapt into blue with a *whumphing* sound.

'It's just . . .' I said. 'You just disappeared.'

She lowered the heat on the soup, 'I know,' she said. 'I owe you an explanation.'

'You don't owe me anything.'

'Yes, I do.'

She leaned back against the kitchen counter and regarded me seriously, softly. 'When I told Michael I was pregnant, he told me to have an abortion. He knew I was Catholic when he slept with me but that's not the point. When I said no, he held me against the wall with his hand around my throat . . .'

My eyebrows rose and my chin went down. I stared at her.

'I didn't tell you because I knew how upset you'd be. You still had a career in the army. I didn't want to ruin things for you.' She smiled. 'And then you left anyway.' She raised her hands, let them drop. 'I found out what happened, by the way. I was angry with you. I had been trying to keep you out of it.'

'You just disappeared,' I repeated, feeling how shameful my solipsism was but unable to dampen it. 'I didn't know where you were, if you were okay . . .'

'I know,' she said. 'But I didn't want to tell you the full story, it wouldn't have been fair on you, and I didn't want you to have to lie if you were asked where I was, if Michael came looking for me.

And I needed time to think. I was scared, things got bad. I said some things I shouldn't have about his wife and family, threatened to expose him, stupid really, got him off the hook, morally I mean. He turned pretty nasty. He's a very strange man.'

I thought of the image of Michael tapping the ash off the end of his cigarette in the dark after dinner with his fellow officers, casually, as if life was pleasing to him.

'Are you safe now?' I felt the capacity for murder rising in me. I knew myself to be capable of it. The world is divided into two sorts of people, after all: those who are capable of understanding and negotiation, even towards evil, and those who are constitutionally primed to hunt down someone who has hurt or damaged somebody they love and do something bad to them in return. I fall into the latter category.

She turned and continued her lunch preparations, giving the soup a stir, flipping the lid on an old-fashioned metal bread bin, selecting bread rolls to put on a plate. 'I think so,' she replied. 'No one knows where I am. I'm just renting here till the end of next month, that's why I wanted you to come now, to see it. I've fallen in love with this place – I'd stay if I could.'

'Don't you have, I don't know, appointments and stuff?' I said, gesturing towards her taut belly.

She gave a small smile at my ignorance. 'That's mostly in the early stages. After the anomaly scan they tell you to just go off somewhere and grow. I knew if I didn't get away from Basingstoke I'd go insane. My mother kept telling me her parents would have put her out on the street if she'd given them a bastard.'

So she was at home when I called.

'I've got plans, I need to move to a city to give birth to this one.' She placed her hand on her stomach. 'I'd love to stay here, but it's too remote when I'm on my own. I'm thinking Manchester – I've got a cousin there.'

I thought about how relaxed Michael had been when he had grabbed my hair and pulled me backwards, just enough to unbalance me, nothing that would leave a mark.

'Is he dangerous? Have you filed a police report?'

Flavia shook her head. 'Saying what? It wasn't like that.' She stopped what she was doing for a moment and sat down in a chair, cradling her bump. 'It's hard to explain, but there's something in him that's determined to win. I just know that if he ever shows up in this one's life, it will be bad. I know if he saw the baby, he'd try and interfere, demand his rights, just to spite me. He used to call me crazy, a crazy Italian. You should hear what I said back, mind.' She smiled at me then, and any lingering resentment I might have felt about her disappearance melted away. 'I've been very thorough, made preparations, I promise, for now and in the future, and you're very much involved, but maybe I needed time away from you to realise how much I wanted you to be part of my new life, and actually it would have been impossible if you were still in the army, but now . . .' She gave a happy shrug, leaned forward and rose from her chair.

I blew air out of my mouth.

'I know,' she said, serving soup and bringing the bowls over to the table, 'it's a lot to take in. Let's eat.'

I lifted a spoon of soup to my lips – some thick tomato and vegetable mix – and, of course, because Flavia made it, it was delicious. It filled me with a deep warmth from the inside, blossoming out from inside my body. I felt myself open. I was here with my friend, and it was not that she had lost interest in being my friend

116

or moved on – she had her reasons, and they were good reasons, and now she wanted me in her life.

We talked about the army a bit – she told me about how much she had wanted some geographical distance from it all. She had visited this coast on holiday with her mother and stepfather when she was a child and loved it. She had gone to the local library in Basingstoke and gone through the Scottish telephone directories until she found the local hotel here. At first, she had asked about renting a room on a weekly basis, she was after a stay of eight to ten weeks. They had said that wasn't possible but told her about the cottage, available for a short-term let. 'I came up with my cases having not even seen a photo!' As soon as she saw it, she knew she had come to exactly the place that she needed – to walk and rest and plan. We talked about her mother and her stepfather – her mother had been devastated that her daughter was going to be an unmarried mother. It had caused a lot of tension, but Flavia was pretty sure she would come round once the baby was born.

After a while she started asking about me, what I had been doing since I left. I talked about my parents in return – she'd met them several times and found them charming, thought my father was 'quite good-looking', which I had thought hilarious and disgusting at the same time.

I told her I was doing temporary work here and there in London, job-hunting and thinking about working in personnel – she asked if I had a boyfriend. I dodged the question.

'Heather,' she said casually at one point, as she split open a soft white bread roll with her fingers, 'are you gay? Because if you are and haven't told me, I'll be quite offended.'

I hesitated, wondering what to say. I hadn't had a boyfriend in the army, but that wasn't because I didn't want to sleep with men, it was because I was concentrating on the job. I had had several boyfriends when I was at university. And there was a man I was seeing in my current temp job. I was doing a maternity cover with an oil company in Holborn. He was a surveyor. We hadn't slept together yet, just had some overheated lunches clutching hands beneath a pub table, but it was pretty much a done deal.

'I fuck men.' It was a bald statement, shiny and bald. I said it like that to shock her, but I shocked myself, the way I just came out with it. It made me realise something, sitting there eating Flavia's soup: I loved Flavia, but I fancied men. At the risk of sounding obvious, I liked the maleness of them. I liked a broad, hard chest, a chunky wrist or ankle, body hair and odour. I liked the way they were different from me, felt different, tasted different, smelt different. In my third year at uni I got caught sniffing one of them too obviously, breathing in his maleness. He was a geography student called Barry. It was quite hard to explain.

Flavia was unperturbed, raising an eyebrow at me, but whether that was at the crudeness of the statement or because she was sceptical, I couldn't say.

I scraped the last of my soup from the bowl.

'Oh, salad!' she said, lifting her hands. 'I was going to make a salad!'

I knew that if I didn't prevent her, she would rise and wash her hands, even though she had washed them as soon as we got in, and make a salad with the purple lettuce sitting on the drainer, its roots still muddy where she would have pulled it from the garden that morning.

'Sit down,' I said as she began to rise. 'We've got plenty here.'

118

'Okay, I'll do the salad with supper,' she said. 'Anyway, you still haven't told me if you're gay.'

'Honestly, I don't know what I am.' I paused, reflecting on the fact that when I said 'honestly' it was, in fact, honest. I gave a small, high laugh, so she knew I was not about to indulge in self-pity. 'Alone, that's what I am.'

She was sitting perpendicular to me. She gave a small smile, turning in her chair and leaning forward as much as her belly allowed. She took my long-fingered hand in her plump, soft one and placed it on the taut rise of her stomach.

She looked at me, held my gaze with a small smile. We both waited. Above the sink, a bluebottle buzzed against the window-pane. On the wall behind her, an old-fashioned wooden clock was ticking arrhythmically.

And then, on cue, the child inside stirred – it was like a rumble of rock beneath the crust of the earth. A small earthquake is coming, I thought.

'You're not alone, silly,' said Flavia softly, still looking at me. 'You've got us.'

A little point of bone nudged the palm of my hand, a tiny elbow or knee or foot, pressing through the layer of flesh and skin between us to greet me with a prod.

That was the first time I met Adelina.

11

It's odd how I feel now, when I think back to the weekend Flavia and I spent together in that cottage. It was not much more than forty-eight hours, and yet it stretches in my memory with the quality of a long summer, the winter before receded, the winter to come in a distant and scarcely imaginable future. We were with each other every second of those hours. It was a one-bed cottage with a wide double bed upstairs in a low-ceilinged bedroom, so we shared the bed and in the night I woke several times when she stirred to go to the toilet. 'Sorry . . .' she murmured sleepily as she clambered back onto the firm mattress, '. . . occupational hazard.' At one point, I woke for no reason and lay there in the warmth and the dark, just listening to her breathing beside me.

In the morning I was sluggish and sleepy and she brought me coffee in bed and opened the low window for fresh air. We sat up in bed together with our drinks and giggled like schoolgirls – although she was only drinking water. 'I can't touch coffee now, imagine!' she said. And that seemed funny too: an Italian who couldn't drink coffee.

'I love this bare room,' she said at one point with a sigh. 'It was an old lady who died here, in this bed in fact, some aunt of the woman at the hotel. They'll probably sell it, but you know, her home, her furniture and things, I feel her spirit here.'

I found the thought pretty creepy myself, but decided not to mention that. 'Mmm . . .' I said.

'I'm just treasuring the moments, to be honest. It'll all be different when the baby comes. I love how temporary this is, how all I have to do is *be*.'

Later that afternoon, she persuaded me to go for a trip around the bay on a rickety little boat owned by a local man and see the seals hanging out on the small rocky islands. Groups of them lay, fat and mottled, lifting their heads to gaze at us. I asked how close we could get to them and the elderly man driving the boat said that if I sang a song out loud, the seals would come and swim round the boat, but I suspected it was just for the amusement factor of persuading me to sing. Luckily for the man, and Flavia – and the seals – I've been tone-deaf my entire life and had the good sense to refuse.

As I helped Flavia off the boat and onto the wobbly pontoon, I noticed that she was still wearing the silver bracelet – a delicate thing, a chain of links with a thin clasp, the kind of thing I would lose or break in an instant. She caught my gaze and her lips pursed, the corners of her mouth lifting in the same seraphic smile she gave when she turned in a circle, arms lifted, in the Open Air Church. 'I wear it all the time,' she said.

As we walked down the pontoon, back towards solid land, I wondered if the unsteadiness of it was making me queasy, for what else could explain my irritation? Is this what being pregnant does to you? I thought. Make you all dreamy and content? If so, you can keep it.

But Flavia always had that quality, a kind of calmness, as if there was something solid and grounded inside her that she could return to, whatever life threw at her. Even when she had her occasional flashes of anger, she never seemed to lose control entirely. There was something in her that was unshakeable. Sometimes you want to shake unshakeable people, just to see what happens.

As ever, she picked up on my mood, took my arm and beamed, pulling me close. 'Come on,' she said, 'I'm going to buy you an ice cream – it's amazing here, almost as good as home.'

She had vanilla. I had mint choc chip. We got them in cones and sat on a bench looking out at the bay, the island with the bench, yellow gorse aflame, the distant, snow-topped mountains. I understood the pull of the place: it was a perfect place to come and hide.

'It's hard to explain,' she said. 'It's not straightforward. Winning is everything to him – if he finds me, and sees my child, he will want to interfere, and it won't be good. I'm not frightened of him in the way you think, but I have to plan. I'm going to be a single mother, just like my mother, history repeating and all that. And so I have to think ahead, be responsible.'

History repeating? I hate the idea that we are controlled by our histories: what a cop-out.

She had finished her ice cream quickly. She scrubbed at her sticky fingers with the small, plasticky napkin they had given us but all it did was dissolve into shreds. 'I need to wash my hands. He was one of those men, you know the sort, those men who say they love you but they're so vehement, it feels like they're saying the opposite.'

I knew the sort, every woman knows the sort, but I didn't sleep with that sort of man. I had more sense.

I felt tired all of a sudden. I was growing a headache. I didn't want to talk about Michael any more, or men of any type; I wanted to go back to the cottage and have dinner then watch television with Flavia's feet in my lap and then go to bed.

The rest of the weekend was lovely. Flavia was happy to be with me and once I relaxed I was happy too, and during the course of that weekend, I felt a new accommodation was growing between us: she talked about her plans – if she settled in Manchester, how often would I be able to come up and see her and the baby? I began to see that us both leaving the army would lead to something good. I would get a job I liked instead of temping, Flavia would have a baby, and I would be like a godmother or very special auntie. It would be like having a family of my own without the day-to-day commitment – maybe, it would be great.

On the Sunday, she walked me back up to the station – slowly; it was a steep hill for her now. She stopped by the Open Air Church and pointed up towards it, saying, 'You'll remember it, won't you?'

I successfully quelled the flush of irritation I might have felt at her labouring a point I didn't even comprehend.

We reached the station twenty minutes before my train and sat on a bench – there were only two other passengers at the far end of the platform, and we talked idly for a while about our parents, the army.

'Do you think there's going to be a war?' Flavia asked. She meant the Falklands.

'Probably,' I said, and marvelled at our detachment. We were just civilians now. The people who were arriving for the Inverness train would look at us and see two ordinary women in their late twenties, one pregnant, seated on a bench.

She put her hand on my knee and smiled at me. 'I know what you're thinking,' she said. 'You're feeling annoyed you're going to miss it. You aren't going to stick it out, working in an office – I mean, it's just not you.'

'Well, what else will I do?' I said, a whiny note in my voice. 'I wouldn't go back into the army even if they'd have me – arrange fucking flowers in the mess room while the boys sail off to the South Atlantic? Anyway, I've pretended to my parents that I really like civvies.'

'I can't believe your father was convinced by that!'

'Oh God,' I said, laughing. 'Every time he tries to give me career advice, I have to change the subject. I can't bear it, you know what he's like.'

'You'll find something,' she said airily.

Alright for you, I thought, you have your purpose in life all sorted now.

As the train appeared in the distance, we rose. I picked up my weekend bag.

Flavia said, 'Here,' and pressed a small note into my hand. 'Read it on the train.' I looked at her and she said, 'I've hidden a box of precious things, nothing worthwhile, I know you'll think it's silly.' The train was drawing to a halt and the other passengers were moving towards the doors, but she took my hand to detain me a moment longer. 'Maybe one day if you're unhappy, you'll come back here. I came here so unhappy, and it mended me.'

We clutched each other awkwardly – I was scared of pressing against her too hard. 'What the hell are you on about?' I said, a smile in my voice.

She stepped back from me and smiled in return. 'I know I can rely on you,' she said, resting her hand on her belly. 'Call me when you get home,' she said. She was so beautiful, so calm. I forgave her everything. 'I'll let you know when I've decided about the move down to Manchester. You need to come and see me again before I go pop.'

I got a window seat on her side but she waved once then turned away as soon as the train began to move, just as I knew she would. She was sentimental: watching a disappearing train would make her feel sad.

As we picked up motion, I opened the note she had given me and found instructions and a little drawing of the Open Air Church with a cross marking the place where she had hidden the small box of precious things. I was to go and collect it if anything ever happened to her. And I was to promise, faithfully, that if I was ever lost or unhappy in the future, I would think of coming to Plockton just as she had, of being healed by it.

As we sped through the landscape, I watched the view, the beautiful view, with the note on the table in front of me, only folding it and putting it in my pocket as we neared Inverness. What a silly gesture, I thought, shaking my head. Well, that was Flavia. I was looking forward to getting back to London. One ball of ice cream was enough. I didn't really have a sweet tooth.

I had slept well on the train coming up and wondered if I would again on the sleeper back down that night – I hoped so. I was going straight to the office when I got into Euston the next morning and having lunch with the surveyor. *You aren't going to stick it out, working in an office.* She had a point about that, although it took nearly three years, in the end, for her to be proved right.

Flavia moved to Manchester six weeks after my visit to Plockton, and had a beautiful baby girl, Adelina, and for the first few months,

I visited as often as I could, every second or third weekend – she had a spell of post-natal depression and needed help.

I remember those early months so clearly – Flavia was in a dark place. I did the night shift when I stayed, feeding baby Adelina from a bottle, testing the heat of the milk on the inside of my wrist as I remembered my mother doing when she fed my little brothers, then holding her against my shoulder, a tea towel draped beneath her sleepy head for the reflux. The thing you don't realise about small babies until you hold one is how dense they are, how hot and heavy, like a tiny nuclear device – so small, and yet they explode the world.

Flavia's depression improved sharply after six months and eventually she felt up to travelling down to London on the train, Adelina in one of those bucket seats you clipped to a frame. I had to pick them up at Euston, though, and drive them back to my place through hideous traffic.

Cooking was never my strong point, but I had gone to some trouble and made coq au vin – it wasn't that easy to find proper pancetta back then, or even shallots. It was bubbling gently in a low oven when we got back to my place and as we stepped in the door – Flavia holding Adelina, me lifting the pushchair and her case – she inhaled and said, 'Oh my God, what is that amazing smell?'

She gave Adelina a bottle, winded her, and then folded a blanket and laid it on the kitchen floor to put the baby down while I served up for us – green beans, crusty bread.

As she sat at my rickety little kitchen table, she looked at the coq au vin and beamed. 'Heather, this is fantastic – I've given up cooking for myself completely, proper grown-up food instead of mashed-up baby leftovers, thank you . . .' I felt a small glow.

'I bought a new casserole dish for it,' I said. 'I realised I didn't really have one, no point for just me, it was nice to have a . . .'

'Bibbedy bibbedy bibbedy . . .' said Flavia, looking down at Adelina, who was lying on her back on the floor, waving her fists and beaming up at her mother.

'I've joined this boot-camp class on Saturday mornings,' I said, 'it's an absolute killer but the women in it are brilliant.'

'Well, any kind of exercise is out for me for a while,' Flavia replied. 'Oh *pudding*, are you Mummy's *clever* little one?'

Adelina was kicking, bending her knees in a little froggy motion then straightening her legs again, her small body full of energy, bursting to do all the things it wasn't able to do yet. Flavia had yet to comment on the coq au vin beyond saying that it was better than baby food – no, better than leftover baby food.

At that point, Adelina stopped kicking and braced her arms. A dense, concentrated look came over her face, which went an interesting shade of puce.

'Uh-oh,' said Flavia. 'Great timing, Pumpkin.'

She bent down and picked Adelina up, hoisting her onto her shoulder as she rose, then turned and picked up the nappy bag from where she had left it against the wall.

'I've just served up,' I said.

'Trust me,' Flavia replied, rolling her eyes, 'it's in all our interests that I do this straightaway.'

She went through the double doors that separated my small kitchen from the sitting room with the bay window and closed them behind her.

She was gone a long time. I could hear noises from the sitting room, a mixture of burbles and baby talk (reasonable enough, I suppose – she was talking to a baby). Every now and then, the words would dwindle into murmurs and become small animal sounds. At one point, Flavia sounded as though she was blowing bubbles on Adelina's chest – at another, as though she had picked up one of her little feet and was making farting noises against the soft pad of Adelina's sole.

I sat back in my chair and raised my glass of red wine to her empty chair. The coq au vin cooled on our plates.

Eventually, Flavia returned. The baby was now dressed in a green all-in-one thing with poppers.

'Thank God I had a spare sleepysuit,' Flavia said. 'That was a really volcanic explosion.'

'You can spare me the details,' I said.

Flavia put Adelina back down on the floor, reached into the nappy bag and pulled out a see-through plastic ring with little coloured balls inside, handed it to her baby. She took the sanitary bag with the dirty nappy in it over to my kitchen bin. Then she went to the sink and washed her hands, very thoroughly, drying them on a tea towel.

She sat back down and looked down at her plate, where her coq au vin was congealing, the sauce becoming grey and inert.

She indicated my plate with a jut of her chin. 'You didn't need to wait, you could have carried on without me.'

We both picked up our knives and forks and continued our meal in silence, the only sound the clink and squeak of the cutlery on our plates and the occasional happy gurgle from the baby on the floor.

When Adelina was two and a half, she went to a nursery and Flavia began a freelance job writing advertising copy and started dating again. Michael never did come after her, as she had feared. Sometimes, the things we dread do not happen. It's important to remember that.

I have to be honest: for me, it got a lot more interesting when Adelina could talk.

Feather, she would call me, when she was old enough, running towards me with a chunky little wobble, fists clenched and damp, a sparkle in her eyes.

After a year of temping, I retrained and spent two years in the personnel department – as they were called back then – of a large accountancy firm based in the City. For the first three months, there was the adrenaline of learning a new role. After that, I was bored out of my brains. It was around this time that I began sleeping with older men.

Older men were generally impressed by my army training. It wasn't what they expected of someone slight and sallow like me, who wore court shoes and pencil skirts and pale polyester blouses. It's tempting to conclude I was lazy, at that age, but it was more than that. I had been trained to follow orders, not initiate – sensitive young men my own age, the nice ones who waited for me to demonstrate interest, seemed like too much of an effort. Confident, good-looking ones like Michael revolted me. Older men often had an endearing world-weary but kindly quality – at the same time they knew what they wanted. Being ten or fifteen years younger than them was as good as being beautiful – and so they wanted me.

I liked the look on their faces when we got into a bedroom and I slipped off my heels, reaching up both hands to remove my hair clip and giving my head a light shake so that my thick black hair fell down on my shoulders. I would glance at them with a shy smile: cheap trick, never failed. They would walk towards me, all convinced they were being masterful. After I left the army – and thanks in part to my encounter with Michael – I had signed up for Krav Maga classes and did them every Tuesday and Thursday evening, along with boot camp at the weekends. The older men I chose were sweet, the way they thought they were in charge, and I was naturally too tactful to mention I could probably break their arm.

It was silly behaviour, in retrospect. Who knows why I did it. I think I was looking for something that older men had that I wanted, I just never quite worked out what that thing was.

I met Richard Semple at a dinner party. He was around ten years my senior, the kind of man you'd call a silver fox nowadays, although I'm not sure the term existed then: slender, a little too smart for my liking, slicked-back hair, handkerchief neatly folded in his breast pocket. I preferred them bulky and rumpled. The next evening, he called me at home, having got my phone number from the hosts, and asked me if I would like to have lunch at his club – he had already established that it was not far from where I was working at the time. I assumed he wanted to sleep with me, like all the other middle-aged men, the Davids and the Rogers and the Thomases. Back then, men didn't ask women out for any other reason, after all.

The ones who wanted to lunch you at their clubs were very much of a type, but I wasn't averse to it. They had exceptionally good manners and were happy to keep the conversation going without me doing too much work.

As soon as we were seated at a corner table, before the waiter had even brought the menus over, Richard asked if it was alright if he ordered for both of us – we only had an hour, after all. I said of course. We had a gin and tonic while we waited, then a game terrine, followed by a glass of dry white with a main course of cheese soufflé – a speciality of the club, served hot and fluffy with a butter lettuce salad on the side. So far it had been small talk – he asked me a lot of questions, which part of my geography degree had I enjoyed the most, did I like living in London . . . He parried any questions I asked him in return – married men often did that, though.

When it came to my experience in the army I was, of course, a little cagey about why I had left, but frank about the frustrations I had experienced there, how little use it had made of me and the other women.

Richard looked at me over the table, just a casual glance, nothing heavy or meaningful, and said, 'Well, considering your family connections, it's surprising you haven't had a tap on the shoulder, isn't it?'

I looked back at him. I had said nothing about my father. This man had done his homework – or rather, someone else had done the homework and passed it on to him.

He regarded me – a proper look this time. He put down his fork. 'Until now, that is.'

'You know my father?' I asked.

He tilted his head a little, from one side to another, in a light, dismissive gesture that suggested that although that may have been a factor in the matter we were discussing, it was not something he wished to dwell on. This conversation would include the information he wanted it to include, and no more.

It explained something: when we had met the week before, I thought he had an air of authority, like a barrister or a surgeon, and had been a little surprised when he said he was a 'middle-ranking' civil servant – the two hadn't quite matched.

Nonetheless, I persisted. 'Have you spoken to my father about me? Because you should know I've always been resistant to discussing my career with him – he's tried.'

He pressed his lips together and raised one eyebrow a very small amount, much in the way that a teacher might with a precocious and slightly annoying pupil. 'I'm not going to answer that question for the time being, and if you ask him, you'll get the same response.'

I opted for silence.

After a while, in the tone of a man making a concession, he said, 'What I will say is that your father would probably agree with me that a woman of your abilities is wasted in a personnel department.'

I was guilty of coyness back then, I'm sorry to say, and as well primed as any woman of my generation on how to accept a compliment, even a patronising one – especially a patronising one. I looked at Richard with an expression that suggested I was pleased, flattered, and thinking about it, when there was not one ounce of doubt in my mind.

I was thirty years old. Flavia and Adelina were the only two people I was really engaged with on any meaningful level – I visited when I could, but I wasn't involved in their daily lives. My job bored me. Men of my own age bored me. Even I bored me. By then I had saved up enough to buy a small flat in Upminster, of all places, and filled it with coloured clutter that didn't suit me (it was 1985; red teapots and chequered tea towels from Habitat were all the rage). I went running in the park and did a lot of physical fitness classes. I had a small circle of friends. I visited my parents back in Coventry at the weekends, not nearly often enough. I slept with older men for recreation. I'd recently joined a dance class.

The cheese soufflé was cooling on my plate. Excitement had robbed me of appetite. 'What happens next?' I said.

12

I was fifteen or sixteen when I came across my father in the garden, hands and knees on the grass, elbows bent and back ramrod straight at a strange, tense diagonal, bottom in the air, his nose almost touching the grass – as if he had lost some small but precious object and was trying to locate it by sniffing. It was winter. The grass was stiff with frost. His body was shaking but it seemed to be more than the cold; it was an elemental kind of shudder, as if our lawn, crusted by winter, was a tremulous surface. He was hyperventilating.

I didn't know what to do. I looked back at the house as though my mother might appear, but I knew she was out at the shops. The boys were at football practice and she would be picking them up afterwards. My father and I were alone.

We only had one neighbour, elderly Mr Watson, and he never ventured into his garden in winter. To my right, and at the back, were the wide fields, fallow, mud in great lumps, open countryside, a stretch of trees with blackened branches. I looked up at the hard white sky and it too seemed unrelenting. I understood that the safety of our family had always been tenuous, that we were on the very edge of town and the very edge of something else as well, as if we might drop off at any moment and be lost in the landscape, a place of white sky and rocks of mud where the cold would not even acknowledge us as human.

There was something wrong with Dad. I always knew that, although for many years all I got by way of explanation was oblique references from my mother to 'what happened during the war'.

What came first, the chicken or the egg? Ask any surgeon or para-medic, any police officer or firefighter or war photographer – or spy. Do those jobs warp your personality so you can perform them well, or did you choose them because they suited you in the first place?

After training, during our probationary year, we all had temporary secondments with our sister organisation – it was thought important at that time that we understood each other's work at ground level, and because these secondments involved a bit of travel and a bit of intrigue, they were everybody's favourite part of the induction process. One evening, I found myself in a small town in Switzerland by the shores of Lake Geneva. I had been tasked with going to a nearby café the following morning to watch a man have his breakfast. All I had been told about the man was that he ate breakfast in that café every day. I was to observe him, and anyone else that he spoke to – I hadn't even been told why that particular date was significant or who or what I was looking out for. I had a photograph of him, that was all.

I had arrived in the small town by train the previous afternoon and checked into the hotel that had been booked for me. The evening was mine, so I went for a walk by the lake and looked at the yachts and the huge houses with their front lawns and green-painted shutters. Bankers, counts, heiresses of some sort – I tried to guess who lived in these giant houses on the quayside. In London or New York, someone that wealthy would hide behind the fences that their money had built, but this was Switzerland. The rich lived in a world of the rich and their front gardens were openly visible from the quayside path.

It was out of season and there weren't many people around. I bought a crêpe and ate it while sitting on a bench looking at the lake. I would have rather had a proper meal, but it was the sort of place where a woman dining on her own in a restaurant might get noticed, whereas a woman sitting on a bench looking a bit lonely was unremarkable. It was grey and quiet. A soft rain that smelt of grass fell lightly upon the rich people and their huge houses. Snow-topped mountains loomed on the French side of the lake and I tried to work out which one might be Mont Blanc.

I walked back to my hotel, which overlooked a paved pedestrian street of fashion shops, all closed for the evening and no doubt selling clothes I could never afford: I was on civil service rates now, after all. I had taken something of a pay cut to join the Service. I had already scouted the café where I needed to be at 8 a.m. the following morning. At the reception desk, a young woman was sitting with her head resting on one hand, looking bored. She didn't even glance at me as I passed, holding my room key by its large wooden fob.

My room was a long rectangle, plain and white, with gleaming oak floorboards. There were tall windows at the end that you could open wide, a low wrought-iron railing to stop you falling out. I opened the windows and lay on the bed, my head propped up with pillows, and stared out at the sky, waiting for the evening to pass. I felt what I can only describe as a deep kind of peace.

Chicken or egg? I thought of my father. I thought of what I might have inherited from him without even knowing it. I didn't talk to him about the job – I would do that later, I thought, when I was more established. I wanted to make my own mark first. All the same, I couldn't help wondering, was it always inevitable I would end up doing this?

All I knew was that I felt a deep calm, there in that Swiss hotel room in the small town by a lake. I was exactly where I should be, doing the job I wanted to be doing. I felt entire, complete.

In truth, the early part of my career was the bit I wasn't very good at. There were officers who loved running agents, who became deeply attached to them on a personal level. To lose one of your agents, for whatever reason, was considered personally devastating as well as a bad mark on a professional level. I never enjoyed it, myself. The needs of our agents made me uncomfortable: they were too human, too vulnerable, too fearful. If they weren't paranoid before they worked for us, they were pretty soon, after all, and when they became paranoid, they panicked. They forgot the safety signal, or they got it the wrong way round – coat buttoned for everything is safe, open and loose for abort – and that was even worse than forgetting altogether. If they weren't wearing a coat at all, at least you knew they were struggling. Panicking people are unpredictable.

When you were running agents, there weren't any barriers between the personal and the professional – you could be rung up in the middle of the night by a Lebanese PhD student you had placed inside an anti-war organisation at Portsmouth Polytechnic to see if it was being run out of Moscow, and he would be crying down the phone because he thought someone had looked at him funny in the canteen or he missed his mother in Beirut. Being a spy is one thing. Looking after other spies who never really wanted to be spies is quite another.

Some of them just needed the money, of course, but many of them needed ideological persuasion, or wanted to be drawn on my ideology. I always found it best to explain – truthfully – it wasn't that I was particularly *pro* our government; on the contrary, I didn't actually like our government all that much. It was just that I was fiercely *against* governments who wanted to imprison their own citizens, torture them in basements or execute them without trial. I didn't care what that government called itself or what form of politics they preferred to pursue. I just thought Mister or Missus General Public had a right to walk down the street without the risk of arbitrary arrest. This wasn't a line: it was true at the time and still is – but I know now it was never as simple as I pretended, and that to claim it was, was an evasion. Who was I trying to kid – them, or myself?

The row with Flavia came about five years after I had entered the Service, and although it was nothing to do with my work, I still wonder whether it would have happened otherwise: or is blaming my job just another evasion? Like most catastrophic, friendship-ending rows, the catalyst wasn't important – there's a difference between a cause and a trigger, after all – but it involved me helping out with Adelina's eighth or ninth birthday party. Flavia had plenty of mum-friends from Adelina's school, but they were all married and the occasions when other families had two parents to do these things were the occasions she found most difficult. She liked me being around to help with the parties not just because I was surprisingly good at organising games of musical bumps or sleeping lions – the kids all looked at me and saw a headteacher, I think – but so that there would be someone there to collapse on the sofa with afterwards, to talk to about how that kid Simon was a liability or the moment that we both thought little Genevieve was going to vomit.

It wasn't as if I didn't have a good reason – it was work. And it wasn't my fault that I couldn't explain to Flavia the nature of my work, couldn't justify why sometimes I had to change my plans at short notice or go quiet on her for a stretch of weeks – okay, over the last two or three years perhaps it had been months, sometimes, not always.

I visited the weekend before the party, just for the Saturday night, and told her then, as we prepared a meal together after I had arrived, 'By the way, I don't think I can come up for the party next weekend.' She looked at me, then turned away and carried on chopping tomatoes.

She was off with me for the rest of my stay. When I suggested on the Sunday morning that we take Adelina to the soft-play centre – a place I loathed – she said, 'She's got homework, they've started giving it every weekend now. I told you.'

I refrained from replying, it isn't going to take all day, is it? Instead, I said, the epitome of mildness, 'Well in that case why don't I go down the shop and get the Sunday papers?'

We ate pasta with Adelina at 6 p.m. – kiddie pasta – and Flavia said, as I carried the bowls through to the kitchen at the end of the meal, 'Do you mind rinsing them before you put them in the dishwasher?'

After supper, we sat in the sitting room – Adelina was allowed to watch some kids' telly as long as she had brushed her teeth and got her pyjamas on first – and Flavia and I leafed through the papers, her reading the arts and fashion sections, me reading the news, the only sound between us the rustle as we turned the pages.

Adelina was lying on her stomach on the carpet, watching some old-fashioned feature film – a country home and a group of children

139

who had discovered dinosaur bones in the woods, or possibly a dinosaur, men with blunderbusses, women in aprons with frills who said things like 'lawks a'mercy!' She was a little bored by it, thumping her feet on the carpet behind her, chin propped on her hands. The sound was up rather louder than I would have allowed. Without turning her head to me she said, 'Heather . . .' She could pronounce my name properly now. 'Heather, are you a widow-lady?'

Flavia did not help me out. She just looked at me, one eyebrow raised very slightly, coldly amused.

'No,' I said to Adelina, turning the page to a news report of the IRA shooting in Lichfield. Domestic terrorism was more on our agenda than ever.

'What *are* you then?'

Flavia closed her magazine and dropped it onto the sofa next to her. 'Come on you,' she said to Adelina, 'story time.' She picked up the remote and flicked off the film and Adelina jumped to her feet without complaint. She was such a pretty child – thick dark hair, pale skin, the image of her mother – although something of a tomboy, thank God, not into all that pink plastic rubbish that got foisted on girls that age.

'I'll do it,' I said, rising briskly from my seat. 'Come on, Pumpkin, what's it going to be?'

Before Adelina could answer, Flavia said, 'I'll do it. You sit down and read the papers. Put your feet up.'

I always did the bedtime story before I went back to London.

Adelina turned to me – I opened my arms to her, and she ran over and threw her arms round my waist. I bent my head to hers and kissed her hair. 'See you soon, Baby Bear,' I whispered to her.

'Come on you, upstairs,' said Flavia a little too brightly.

They left the room hand in hand, Flavia beaming down at her daughter. Adelina did not look back.

By the time Flavia came back downstairs, I had made myself a coffee and was sitting on the back patio. It was June and the evening was still warm.

'Do you want one?' I asked as she joined me. 'I'll get going soon.' It wouldn't hurt her to remember it was a big chunk out of my weekend, coming up here, I thought. I had a meeting at the Home Office at 9 a.m. sharp the next morning. It was already on my mind.

She sat down on the garden chair opposite me without speaking. We sat in silence for a few minutes.

I put my coffee cup down on the garden table. 'I do have my own life,' I said. 'I'm sorry, I know you want me here next weekend, but I can't always be a presence just whenever it suits you to have an extra pair of hands.'

Flavia's last relationship had been with an electrician, the divorced dad of one of the kids at school. It had lasted for a year or so and she'd gone pretty quiet on me for the duration. When it ended, as all her relationships seemed to, with some degree of acrimony, she was back on the phone to me every weekend in a trice. I couldn't remember the last time she had asked me anything about my life. Okay, so I might not have been able to answer truthfully, but I would still have liked to be asked.

'I know you prefer to be an absence than a presence,' she said then. 'Because when you're an absence you're in control, aren't you? You're the one who gets to decide when you come and go. And you have all the satisfaction of knowing you're being thought about but none of the bother of commitment, or being considerate to somebody else's feelings because that's actually quite—'

'Fuck, where has all this come from?' I knew she was annoyed with me but I had no idea there was all that resentment in there. I looked at her and saw that she was white-faced with anger, her mouth in a small, tense moue.

'. . . *quite* hard work, isn't it? Like, you have to actually *do* something, behave with consideration, or something . . .'

Silently, over the weekend, she had reached this place of anger. There was nothing I could do except try to lower the temperature. If I responded in kind then it would become a full-blown shouting match, maybe with swearing or door slamming, entirely lacking in any kind of logic or progress in understanding, and that wasn't my style. *I've got a bloody four-hour drive ahead of me,* I thought.

I kept my voice measured, reasonable. 'You seem to think it's deliberate, manipulative. I'm not, whatever it is I'm doing, I . . .' I dried at that point because, accidentally, I had just conceded that I was indeed doing something.

The concession took the wind out of her sails. She looked momentarily deflated. She mumbled, 'Well, Adelina's upset and it isn't actually a comfort, hurting people accidentally. *Oh, I didn't mean it that way,* it still hurts . . .'

It seemed as though the heat had gone out of the situation. Then, all at once, having been the pacifier so far, I felt something rising in me – so quickly I hardly knew where it came from, something sudden that, on analysis, had clearly been building for a while. I heard myself say, 'Don't throw Adelina at me – she's a child, she'll be fine. *You're* upset. Maybe you've just been looking for an excuse to be upset because in any situation being the victim is the place where

142

you feel most comfortable, which is why single motherhood suits you down to a tee, because God forbid you actually took control of your life and stopped dating losers for five minutes.'

She stared at me then, and the calm expression on her face should have been a warning, but like a complete and utter idiot, I ploughed on. In fact, far from cooling down, I warmed up a notch. I was on a roll, and it was downhill all the way from there. 'Everyone has bad things happen, everyone has bad relationships, everyone feels alone most of the time. You deal with it, you turn things round, instead of playing the fucking victim all the time. What kind of example are you setting Adelina? You really want her to turn out like you?'

Her voice was level, icy. 'Well, funnily enough, there are some situations you can't control when you have a child to care for. Your child has to come first. If you were a mother yourself, you would understand that.'

I was not having that. 'I'm not a mother because I've chosen not to be. I've made, you know, actual choices, and I take responsibility for those choices. Maybe you should try it some time.'

When she spoke, her voice was light. 'How was I supposed to choose when I got accidentally pregnant? He came inside me without even asking me. He said he just assumed I was on the pill and when I told him he held me against a wall with his hand round my throat. In what part of that situation was I supposed to take control?'

'You could have done as he asked,' I said, mimicking her light tone, 'and had an abortion. Then you could have carried on having affairs with any number of married men.'

We each stopped and drew breath, as if we were high-wire artists who had set off from opposite ends of a rope strung above a perilous canyon and had paused, facing each other, hoping that

143

the other would turn around and go back, knowing that if either of us wobbled the rope, we would both fall.

She looked down at the garden table, a small rusty thing made of iron, unsteady on its feet. I looked at her, willing her to look up, and if she had, maybe I wouldn't have leaned forward a little and said the stupid thing I said next. 'We can all play the victim card – is that what you're going to teach Adelina? Fuss you made over one grazed knee yesterday, you'll turn her into a right crybaby, but maybe that's what you want because blaming fate or God or whatever is *so* much easier than being a grown-up and taking responsibility, so when *she* gets up the duff by a married man, I suppose you'll be pleased.'

She looked at me then, and spoke in a tone of voice that was clear as a bell on a silent Sunday morning, musical but full of meaning – a tone of voice that made it obvious she was speaking quite literally, and that she really meant it. 'Fuck off.'

And I did.

For the whole of the drive home, I rehearsed all the things I wished I'd said – the better, more articulate ways I could have put my point of view across. I got home still angry, and I stayed angry. All those nasty little digs at my single status, totally uncalled for. I didn't really know what had happened; all I knew was that it had been coming for a long time.

Anger is exhausting, though, and within a few weeks I was no longer angry, I was sad – and I was sorry then, alright, but sad-sorry, not really sorry, so I still didn't call to apologise, even though by then I had a feeling I had probably overstepped the mark in some of the things I had said. Flavia didn't call either.

Then came the time when it all felt too late, because in addition to the original apology, I'd have to apologise for not apologising before. So even though the balance had shifted, and I felt that the original argument was, probably, mostly my fault, the long silence was both our faults, and it didn't feel fair if I was the one who had to apologise. And all that not apologising, all that silence, became like a fast-flowing river that got colder and colder and eventually hardened into ice. The silence polarised us: she was Arctic, I was Antarctic, or the other way around – it didn't really matter. There was an entire turning world between us.

My father had his stroke that autumn, and somehow that made me angry with Flavia too, that she did not know my father had had a stroke, that she had no idea what I was dealing with. Even so, I still assumed we would make up, somehow, in some indefinable future. First of all, I thought, well, before Christmas, because if I wasn't working, I usually spent Christmas Day with my parents then drove up to Flavia and Adelina for the dull period between Christmas and New Year. As it turned out, I ended up working that Christmas, and the day after Boxing Day, I drove to Coventry to be with Mum and Dad.

'Aren't you going up to Manchester?' my mother asked, when I explained to her that I could stay for a full week.

'No,' I replied, 'it's more important to be with you and Dad.'

'Oh,' Mum said. 'Oh, that's lovely, but I'm sorry we've messed up your plans.'

And then, of course, I felt a bit bad.

But with work and everything, before I knew it, it was nearly Adelina's next birthday and I was worrying about whether to send a present or not – would Flavia just send it right back, after my long silence? – and before I had resolved that issue in my head, my father died and my life became about that for a while.

My father died at the age of sixty-eight, and the questions I had postponed asking him, about his career, his life, would now go unanswered forever. Life became something different, and that something different didn't have Flavia or Adelina in it, and for a while that felt okay.

After a few more years in the Service, I realised that I wasn't an agent-runner or a field operative or any of the things that made most people want to join – the only thing I had really liked about my fieldwork experience was the bit that other people disliked: the loneliness. I was a strategist. I preferred computers to people – they generally did what you expected them to do (except when they didn't, of course). Even when I was travelling for work, I was at my happiest when on an aeroplane with a folder full of figures on my lap, working out the best way to suggest liaison strategies with one of our partner services, constructing an argument based on facts, assessing other people's fieldwork. The bit that interested me was not a popular area of work – it wasn't glamorous. Liaison with foreign services, or with our sister service, or Special Branch, or other partners in the UK, all the record keeping, the paper-work: it's the bit that people never think about, the bureaucracy that supports the action. And because I was good in an unpopular area, I rose through the ranks quite quickly, with a reputation for thoroughness. Before I knew it, I was no longer an ambitious thirty-something with a daddy complex – as I moved into and through my forties, as fifty loomed, I morphed, quite effortlessly, into the efficient workaholic that everybody wanted when they wanted a job done well.

Flavia never contacted me – and I wish I could say I missed her, but the truth was that in those years I didn't, really. I missed Adelina, if I thought about her – so I tried not to think about her. My reputation as someone married to the job did me no harm when it came to men – there were lots of men. I worked in a male-dominated field and the married men I consorted with were grateful for my discretion and lack of demands; for my part, I liked that they made no demands in return. We understood one another. The thing about having always fancied middle-aged men is that once you're middle-aged yourself, it's no longer weird.

Only once in a while did I feel sorry for myself, on the rare occasions that I got drunk on my own and stayed up late playing midnight jazz on the ghetto blaster in my kitchen and dancing, slowly, carefully, singing along in a tuneless murmur, enjoying the acidity of an ice-cold white wine, still swaying as I tipped the glass.

13

Richard was my mentor for a while after he recruited me, although he went on to have a meteoric rise up through the ranks and within a couple of years we lost touch. He came to my father's funeral, though, and at the wake – tea and beer and sandwiches in a local hotel – he and I fell to talking about Dad, about how he had taken Richard under his wing, how as a young officer, Richard had always been grateful to him.

As things thinned out, Mum and I went out onto the steps of the hotel to see people off, while Tim and Louis were inside, settling up. When Richard departed, he embraced us both warmly and murmured to my mother, 'Anything you need, Jenny, anything at all . . .' We watched him as he got into his Jaguar, reversed out of his parking space and set off down the hotel's drive, moving our hands in gestures that suggested we were cleaning a window together very slowly.

'Did you get to talk to him?' I asked. 'We had a nice chat.'

'Richard Semple,' my mother said, then gave the smallest of pauses. 'Be a bit careful with him.'

'Why?' I asked.

She looked down, pressing her lips together, a frown on her small features. She was a person who had the greatest of difficulty with an unkind remark. They never formed easily in her mouth. She folded her arms. 'I would describe him as a man who always has his eye on the main chance. Your father liked him, but he was wary of him.'

Dad was wary of a lot of people, I thought as we went back inside.

As it was, it would be over two decades before Richard and I found ourselves in the same department, the Joint Administrative Department that oversaw all areas of the Service and our partner organisations. We were both well past active duty by then and he was an elder statesman: urbane, relaxed, patrician in a way that was a little more earned. Physically, he barely seemed to have aged. The swept-back hair was white, but he still wore a handkerchief in his breast pocket, and it was only when I got to know him again that I realised it wasn't that he was young-looking now, so much as that he had been old-looking back then.

He must have been nearing retirement by the time he became my boss – I was in my fifties. Technically, he was my boss's boss, with overall responsibility for four internal departments, but he wore his authority lightly – I never once heard him raise his voice – and would be more disappointed than angry when you screwed up. He reminded me of my father, in some ways, the good ways.

It was late in 2006 that he called me into his office to ask me to consider moving to Birmingham and joining a new unit that he was setting up. He knew my mother was still alive and still lived in the West Midlands and he asked after her quite often – later, I was to realise there was a lot else he knew.

Friday afternoon had arrived at the end of a long week: I was feeling tired and jaded. Richard made me coffee – normally, he didn't offer. He told me about the unit, part of a drive to establish regional bases for the Service. There had been a skeleton staff there for six months, he said, doing feasibility studies and so on – Liaison

2.6 they were calling it. It was to give oversight between our different departments and outside agencies.

'Why haven't I heard of this before?' I asked him, scanning the departmental brief as I sat the other side of his desk, the un-drunk coffee in front of me.

Richard was leaning back in his chair, all slender fingers and knowing smile. He leaned forward as I looked up. 'Sheila doesn't want to spare you, but I've explained to her why I think you'd be ideal. Officially, you'll move sideways as deputy, but in fact you'll go up a grade, I'll see to that. Parity with Sheila, technically, could stand you in good stead if you want to go for departmental head in a year or two.'

I raised an eyebrow at the non sequitur and pressed my point. 'An entire offshoot of Liaison is being set up and there's been no . . . ?' I dried to a halt, looking at him.

He pressed his lips together in a thin smile, then placed the fingertips of one hand on another sheet of paper in front of him on his desk.

'What you're holding in your hand is the official brief. What the new unit in Birmingham actually is, is this.'

He swivelled the piece of paper around and pushed it towards me.

I picked up the second piece of paper. L2.6 was nothing to do with liaison – well, only tangentially. That would be our excuse for contacting people. Its actual job was as an offshoot of internal investigations, with special responsibility for assembling evidence and drawing up preliminary suggestions for the official lines of enquiry. Richard was creating an offshoot of one department that was actually an offshoot of another. L2.6 was being created to help him catch dirty spies.

150

'Does Sheila know about this?' I asked, scanning the sheet. Being told something my immediate boss didn't know was a plus, for me, as I'm sure Richard was well aware. I liked Sheila, but she had no intention of moving sideways or retiring. Unlike active spies, who were shuffled off at fifty, in Administration we were allowed to hang on till a grand old age. She was creating a bit of a logjam at the top of the department.

'No,' Richard said, 'Sheila does not know. No one in Liaison does. As far as they are concerned, you'll just be out there doing feasibility studies for new ways of working, answerable directly to me. That's why you'll go up a grade on the sly – it's got to look more like a demotion than the other way round. The DOS will continue in London as we are.' He raised his hands. 'You know how difficult our job gets once we're officially involved . . .'

'All those rules and procedures . . .' If he picked up on my ironic tone, he chose to walk past it.

'Pre-investigation, if you like. One of my Level Five officers, man called Blythe, is setting up an office in a tower block in Birmingham. It's so unglamorous people will assume you've been sent there as a punishment, sorry about that. At the moment it looks like it's barely working, only three staff so far, half empty, tumbleweed blowing down the corridors . . .'

'When in fact it's a fully functioning Death Star?'

'Correct.'

As usual when I was in front of Richard, I felt a strong need to hide my excitement, to hide any emotion in fact. 'I'll need all the current case studies as soon as possible.'

'Of course.'

*

I spent the next month preparing for the transfer. In the office, I affected an air of weary resignation about my sideways move. 'Birmingham . . .' I said, if one of my colleagues asked. 'I told them I wanted a change, but Birmingham . . .'

One of my Level Twos, Talia, cornered me in the Ladies toilet one day to say how she thought it was really unfair I was being sent there. 'You know why they've done it? It's because Sheila has three teenagers and they know she wouldn't want to uproot the whole family. It's discrimination.' Talia was thirty-eight and a childless workaholic herself – she looked at me and saw her future.

I was used to people's assumptions that I felt put upon. 'Well, I'll be close to my mother,' I said. 'She isn't getting any younger.'

'God,' said Talia, peering at her own reflection while she washed her hands ferociously, over and over. 'We always end up with the caring duties one way or another, don't we? There's no escaping it.'

Richard's plan was clever. Liaison was a huge part of the Service and it was understood we had our fingers in all sorts of pies, including contact with our partner agencies abroad. Before the Second World War, the secret services of various countries didn't really talk to each other – for obvious reasons, the clue is in the title – but thanks to the Soviets we all realised a little more co-operation was called for. The Americans, the Canadians, the Australians, the New Zealanders and us – the CAZAB circle, it was called, or Five Eyes – all got together. CAZAB was a big secret for years, until spies started writing books, and then the Services finally realised that information exchange was everything. As it was globally, so it became inside the UK – Liaison may sound innocuous, bureaucratic, but actually we're the tent pegs that hold everything up. Five, Six, the Met, Home Office, Foreign

Office – you could call it the UK equivalent of CAZAB except they were all in competition as well as co-operating with each other – everyone vying for their own slice of that public-funding pie. Liaison was responsible for managing all that, oiling the wheels.

Internal investigation was another matter. Spying on spies is hard: they know how to cover their tracks. Once they get wind of the fact they are being investigated, you've had it. The official line within the Service was that Liaison Department was full of nothing more than paper-pushers, there to make sure that co-operation between Five, Six, the MPS Special Branch and their county equivalents ran more smoothly than it had in the past. This new unit, as an offshoot of Liaison, was, therefore, the perfect way to gather evidence on spies before the Department of Standards launched an official investigation.

The housing market in London was buoyant that year, the rate of increase at a thirteen-year high, according to the papers. I sold my flat for more than twice what I had bought it for and while the paperwork went through, I started browsing online estate agents and finding out just what I could get for my money in a nice suburb or town on the Coventry side of Birmingham. Would I go for the four-bedroom Victorian terrace with a garden front and back? Or the modern detached property with its own driveway on the out-skirts of a village? I had never planned on returning to the West Midlands, but here I was in middle age, successful but in a bit of a career cul-de-sac, with a whole new move ahead of me. People who have families get to have different phases of their lives imposed upon them – those of us who don't have to create them.

*

Occasionally, I thought of Adelina and calculated how old she was, where she might be. It was well over a decade since her mother and I had last been in touch. Would she have gone to university, graduated? She might even have children of her own. I imagined the dark-eyed girl I had known transformed into a young woman. I imagined the conversations she and I might have had in her mid-teens, when she would have gone through a phase of hating her mum like all teenage girls do because we resent our own premonitions. I would think about how I could have been a kind of honest broker, looking at things from both points of view, how in years to come they would both express gratitude to me for how helpful I had been during that difficult time, the hours I had spent on the phone talking to one or other of them. I would think of the place I could have had in their small family unit, a kind of elder, an honour.

One of the case files I reviewed in preparation for my new role in internal investigations involved a young woman, some years older than Adelina and nothing like her in many ways, but a clever young woman such as I assumed Adelina to be. She also had an unusual name, Aurora, but then there were quite a few odd things about Officer Aurora Morgan. Aurora was a gifted young woman, parents both mathematicians based in Oxford, double first in maths herself (she'd lived at home throughout the whole of university, she played the flute to Grade 8 and bred hamsters as a hobby), not particularly intuitive or realistic – the sort of person who convinced herself that she was cleverer than the system. She also had a gambling habit that she had managed to hide during her assessment – it's getting pretty hard to hide that kind of thing these days. Since the advent of internet banking, it's easy to investigate an officer's financial affairs, as I know to my cost.

Gambling habits are a big red flag for obvious reasons – any pressing need for money makes you vulnerable to being turned, and a compulsive habit is never a good thing whether it leaves you open to blackmail or not. Somehow, she had come to the attention of the Chinese. The information she was passing over was very low grade, some out-of-date protocols regarding her department's communications analysis. It was so low grade she would have been able to convince herself there was no real harm done, that she was getting a lot of money for not very much; she might have even thought she was taking her Chinese handler for a bit of a ride. But that's the way it works. To start with, they ask you for something that has little or no intrinsic value – its main purpose is to ensure you are compromised.

We had caught her early. Her handler was biding his time until she rose up the ranks and had access to something more important. She wasn't a very good liar, Aurora. I had already read the transcript of her interview so watched the video carefully in order to analyse her behaviour. The moment she was presented with the evidence against her, her face became entirely expressionless, but even so, it was like a pane of glass through which you could watch her thoughts turning. She had small, pale features, a narrow nose, a pinched mouth. She was a skinny, twiggy little thing – I read in her slight body something I thought her interlocutors had probably missed, the history of an undisclosed eating disorder, starting in her early teens and only partially conquered. None of the men who had interviewed her had noted it, but I saw it in the tense strings of her arms, her undeveloped chest, the bony shoulders. I had been an adolescent girl myself, after all.

In the video, she was leaning forward in her chair, listening to the investigating officer, hair back in a neat ponytail, expression blank but intent. The IO handed over a clip file with a sheaf of paper on it – the records of all her contacts with her Chinese handler. A single glance told her what it was.

I imagined her looking down at the sheaves of paper with the same efficiency she applied to a bet when she gambled, the same swift ability to calculate. And what she would have been calculating was this: arrest and prosecution in a secret trial, jail time inevitable, or an offer to triple. All this while she hardly moved a muscle – but I could see it happening behind her eyes. She'd already doubled, now she was going to triple. How hard could it be? I could see her thinking. Self-delusion afflicts the very clever as much as the rest of us – you could argue it afflicts them even more.

I had been asked to write up my reviews and I noted in my conclusion that, in my opinion, letting her triple was unwise. I suggested they root out her childhood medical records – I bet there was something there she had managed to hide in later life, some obsessive psychological issues of some sort. I thought if the Chinese suspected she was tripling, they would get her to quad-ruple and she would go on and on, always chasing the next bet, playing worse and worse odds, until she didn't know herself who she worked for herself any more. There are certain personalities that can't row back, they can only go on and on, and the worse it gets, the further they go.

She was atypical, that one. Mostly it's men who turn, and mostly for the most obvious of reasons: sex or money – ego or vanity or greed. Humans are frail.

*

Thinking back to that now is painful: how confident I was, when I reviewed the case of young Aurora, that she was so different from me, that I would never have got myself in the sort of mess she was in. Hadn't I had a successful career, after all? Wasn't I incorruptible? I was, but as I was soon to learn, being incorruptible didn't mean you would never make a mistake. In my case, the mistake also involved money, but it wasn't gambling and it wasn't illegal, not to start with.

There was a house in Coleshill I really wanted, the full country-life fantasy – it was empty occupancy and if I didn't move fast I would lose it. My London estate agent assured me my flat sale was progressing well, but my buyers were in a chain and they were having some issues securing the mortgage extension they needed to buy my place at the asking price so we needed to give them a bit more time. My move to Birmingham was imminent, so I took out a bridging loan – it was either that or lose my dream house. It was the kind of thing it was obligatory to declare at work, of course, but there was no hurry. I'd just had a re-vet because I was moving post and it was only a six-month loan. The sale of my place in London would go through well before the next vetting round.

A week after Richard had confirmed my transfer but before I made the move, I went down to Birmingham to visit the new office. I walked over from New Street Station to the business district, where there seemed to be a flourishing of construction sites throwing up buildings in strange shapes: some of them with a silver fascia, some with a curved roof or a gleaming glass front, all punctuated by dereliction and surrounded by swooping dual carriageways. I hadn't been to Birmingham for years and it was even more confusing than

I remembered – if an alien was dropped in the city centre, I thought, he would feed back to his superiors that he had been inadequately briefed.

The unimaginatively named New Tower was the only completed building in a wide semicircle of office blocks around a plain concrete piazza. Revolving doors spun me into a large atrium of white marble with a huge reception desk running the entire length of the back wall. A lone security guard sat behind the desk. He didn't look up as I entered. To one side was a horseshoe of squashy orange sofas but nobody sitting on them – hardly anyone around at all, in fact. I liked this: the sense that what I was joining was something new, to be created.

I gave my name and received my visitor's pass, then took a turn around the echoey atrium, wondering what went on here apart from us. To one side of Reception there was a board with half a dozen nameplates and over twenty slots waiting to be filled. We were calling ourselves Stoke Colman Import & Export Ltd, and at the sight of that deceit, up there on the wall, I felt a small surge of pleasure. It never gets old: the little venal glee that people in my line of work get from being something other than what we pretend to be.

One of the lifts to the right swished open and a tall, solid woman in a buttoned yellow cardigan came out. As she approached me, her hand was already outstretched. 'Heather, welcome, I'm Carmella.'

I took her hand in mine; it was warm – she was bespectacled and professional and I thought straightaway, *Ally*.

Carmella gestured through the barriers, slapping down her own pass to allow me in. She saw me looking around as we walked towards the lifts and explained, 'Only around a third of the offices are let at the moment, we got a deal for being an early occupier. I don't think there is anyone above us or below us yet. They're still fitting out some of the lower floors.'

On the seventeenth floor, there were white double doors, windowless, directly opposite the lifts. Carmella pressed her pass against the ID register, a small box to the right of the doors, then pushed one open and gestured me in.

Inside were carpeted corridors, glass cubes of offices, brand-new desks – a couple of them occupied at the far end to the right – but Carmella gestured to the left.

'I'll show you round, then I'll take you in to meet Mr Blythe.'

I risked a direct question. 'What's he like?'

She allowed herself the twist of a smile. 'You'll see.'

She showed me the small galley kitchen and the Ladies toilet, told me I would have a choice of two offices, seeing as so few of them worked there at present. As we headed down the corridor she stopped at an open door and gestured in. 'This is the meeting room.' I stepped inside and looked around: floor-to-ceiling windows, a huge glass oval of a table.

'It's cold in here,' I said.

'Welcome to Alaska.'

14

I moved back to the West Midlands in January 2007, at the height of my career: an important new role, the trust of one of the most senior figures in the Service, and a pay rise that came with enhanced pension prospects. My mother was delighted about my return to the region, and I found that living closer to her removed a whole layer of guilt about how often I visited her even though I didn't do it any more often. My mere proximity felt generous.

Within a year of my father dying, Mum had sold the family home, a decision that surprised me at the time: I had assumed the old house would always be there, the nest that allowed me to fly. It was one of the few things I was sentimental about – but my mother wasn't, clearly. One Saturday morning, a few months after Dad had died, I rang her and she said, 'I can't talk now, darling, the men are coming any minute.'

The men, as it turned out, were not the mysterious foreign assassins my father had always feared: they were a local clearance company. My mother told me later that she took them from room to room and pointed at objects. 'That can go, yes, all of that. And that cupboard. There's nothing in it, well there's lots in it but it's just junk, it can all go.' She didn't even look through the cupboards to check whether there was anything important muddled up with the old Christmas cards and packs of light bulbs and half-used wrapping paper. 'If I put something important in there and forgot it then it wasn't that important, was it?'

Maybe my mother had always been like this, I thought at the time, practical, firm, doing what had to be done – maybe I just never noticed because my father sucked up all the oxygen in our household. He was so complex, so open to interpretation: my mother hid in plain sight.

She moved into a modern bungalow in a village called Baginton on the outskirts of Coventry. It didn't have a great deal to recommend it, as far as I could see. It was just one of those anonymous suburbs that are all over the Midlands, East and West, plain brick houses with uniform gardens in new developments that never seemed to have any kind of centre, just one sprawl blending into a neighbouring sprawl. She had sold the old house for a tidy sum and even after moving costs and giving some to my brothers to put by for her grandchildren, my niece and nephews, she had the money to buy a two-bedroom bungalow outright and some savings to supplement her state and widow's pensions. The second bedroom had a single bed for me in case I ever stayed the night. I never did.

She asked me if I wanted a sum of cash to compensate me for what she was giving the grandchildren since I didn't have any children of my own. I said no – this was when I was still living in London with only myself to think about and although I wasn't exactly well off, the financial difficulties I would get into later would have been unimaginable to me back then. Instead, she made it clear to us all that in lieu, I would inherit the bungalow. My brothers were happy with that arrangement; it also gave me sole responsibility for concluding her affairs when she passed away, as well as looking after her in the meantime.

Not that she needed much looking after, to be fair. She made friends very quickly, although how she did it when there was nowhere to meet them and nothing to do is something I never worked out. They were mostly widowed women like herself – she was, after all, from that generation that married men five or ten years older whose life expectancy was ten years shorter. She often had news of them to tell me: 'Joan's only son got married behind her back, just imagine, to a woman fifteen years older who's been married twice already.' Or 'Neesha is trying to lose weight, but I said to her, at our time of life, Neesha, I think we've earned our cake.' Alone and in her seventies, she appeared to become a kind of friend magnet. I wondered if other women, sensing her kindness and openness, waylaid her in the street.

She came to see my house in Coleshill three days after I moved in. The huge front sitting room was still full of packing cases – that was going to be my holding room for the time being. It had a beautiful, original bay that had subsidence and was falling off the front of the house; I was already getting quotes from builders to get it fixed. I hadn't worked the heating out yet, so the whole place was freezing, as if it was holding the cold. It had been unoccupied for two years before I moved in. It was going to be a project.

Mum stood in the hallway, looking at the curved banister that led up to the first landing. The house was so icy we both kept our coats on.

'Guess what,' I said as I hung my car keys on the little iron hook by the door, 'there's a conservatory, come and see.' The conservatory, adjacent to the kitchen, looked out over open fields. There was a lone donkey that lived in the field neighbouring mine. I had already nicknamed him Fred. It had occurred to me that the land I now owned was big enough to build a granny annex if Mum ever

162

reached the point where she could no longer live independently. After so many years of living in London, landowning was a novelty. I was enjoying my negotiations with space, with emptiness: I was full of imaginative and unfeasible ideas about how I was going to use it.

I turned to see Mum's face creased with concern as she looked around. 'It's amazing, I mean, well done you, but aren't you going to rattle around a bit?'

We walked through to the light, airy kitchen, and I said, 'I haven't worked out the oven yet, I think it might be broken.'

'Let me have a look,' said Mum, ignoring the arm I had stretched out towards the conservatory and stalking briskly across to the oven, where she bent to examine the controls.

I watched her. I was fifty-one years old and a senior officer in the Joint Administrative department of the British Intelligence Services and my mother was intent on showing me how to turn on my own oven.

I had never been much of a one for credit cards, but what I discovered about debt is that the larger it gets, the more you seem to spend. It's all about proportion. If you have nothing, then losing fifty quid is pretty rough: if you are fifty thousand in debt, losing fifty quid is neither here nor there.

When I moved into the house, the repayments on my bridging loan were sixteen hundred a month, so buying some white goods and a sofa on credit and adding eighty to that seemed more or less immaterial. Taking out a loan to pay a builder seemed like a good investment too – it would only make the house more valuable when it was fixed up, after all – it wasn't like spending money on a holiday. When the sale of the flat went through, it would all be sorted, everything would be paid off.

Every now and then, I pressed my estate agent back in London for an update and he said it was all going swimmingly. The current buyers had gone a bit quiet on us, their solicitor wasn't very good, but if they ended up dropping out, it would actually play in our favour. The way house prices were going up and up, the longer it took to sell the flat, the more I would make eventually, more than enough to cover a few months of extra shelling out on the bridging loan. In actual fact, we should be *hoping* my buyers would pull out – then we could put the flat back on the market for another, ooh, at least another twenty-five grand, he thought. In anticipation of this happy outcome, I kept spending on doing up the house.

I hired a local builder to fix the bay and a few other things that needed doing: the downstairs shower room needed ripping out, some rewiring – those old houses – but it was going to be beautiful when it was done. At the weekends, I took to cruising car-boot sales, on the hunt for authentic furniture. I even bought a vintage – for which read *broken* – toaster, because I was sure I could get it fixed and I thought it would look so right on the kitchen counter. There was a lot of kitchen counter to fill, after all. I decided that a porcelain cup with a thin crack running from rim to base was quite charming because it was decorated with flowers and came with a matching saucer.

Did I ever think of Flavia during this time, as I made a home for myself? Did I ever consider why I was investing so much in all these objects – or ever wonder, as I admired the pretty, broken things that

I bought, whether it might have reined me in a bit if I had someone to turn to and say, *Look at this, what do you think?*

The London estate agent called in April. My buyers had indeed pulled out, he said, but he wasn't worried. Their mortgage lender's valuation survey had come back sixty thousand pounds lower than the flat was worth – which was just ridiculous, the estate agent said. Were they trying to tell him how to do his job? He wasn't worried, he said again. My place was great, he had a string of buyers on his waiting list who would jump at it. I could get lodgers in if I was anxious, but he wouldn't advise it – keep the place clean and tidy and it would sell in a trice. Empty occupancy was a great plus – maybe he'd put it back on the market just a little lower than the original price; that way you tempted the buyers in, and you could well end up with a bidding war. Before he rang off, he told me for a third time that he wasn't worried.

In the meantime, there was the job.

I had met my new boss on that first visit, when Carmella showed me around. At the end of the guided tour, she had taken me to the far end of the corridor, where a discreet door opened up, deceptively, to the largest of the individual offices on the whole floor.

Mr Blythe sat behind an expanse of desk. He was talking on his phone as we knocked and entered. He raised the flat of his hand in greeting to Carmella who gestured me to an armchair the other side of the desk, set at an angle. Only as I sat down in it did I realise it was just that little bit softer and lower than it needed to be if you wanted to have an equal conversation with the person sitting on the swivel chair opposite you.

165

'Got to go, got to go,' he said into the phone. 'Someone *vee* important just walked in the door.' He slammed the phone down and jumped to his feet, rounding the desk with his hand extended. 'Kieron.'

'Heather.'

'Heather, Heather, wonderful to meet you, you come highly recommended. I gather we're very lucky to have stolen you from London.'

I'm as vulnerable to flattery as the next person, of course – although it felt awkward, from my low-seated position, raising my hand to his. He grasped it and looked at me: ginger-haired but greying at the temples, square-ish face, around seven or eight years younger than me at a guess, average height, firm frame, a broad gold band gleaming on his wedding finger. Not my type, physically, but our gazes met and in retrospect I am convinced I knew two things about him from that first locked gaze: one, we were going to have sex, sooner or later, and two, it would be a terrible mistake.

We set about our work with alacrity, me and Kieron and Carmella – between us we investigated the names that were flagged up to us by London, all unofficially, of course. I was in charge of writing the personal histories. We called them the ologies. In criminal law, when the police are investigating a murder, they draw up a complete history of the victim: family history, education, work appraisals. It's called a victimology. 'How's the ology going?' one of my workmates might ask about a particular case. My problem was that, unlike the police, I had to be subtle: I could only find out the facts about a person that I could garner without alerting them to the fact that they were being looked into. My favourite part of the job was inventing personas with which to make enquiries. Sometimes I would be Miriam, a student, writing a PhD and needing some information for my research. Sometimes I was Sally, a data information analyst. My favourite was probably Rowena Gallant, a private investigator. I used her when I needed to really nose around, and I only got caught out once, by a solicitor who specialised in whistle-blowing and security matters, Vikram Khatri. He must have advised some of our people because he paused when I introduced myself over the phone, then said, 'So, Rowena, would you have been a private investigator for five years, or six?'

Carmella oversaw online investigations, with the help of a Level Two, James – he would rapidly acquire two colleagues; tracing anyone's online behaviour was often a time-consuming business. Kieron ran the financial enquiries. We were a tight-knit team, compiling dossiers on our former colleagues in a way that would have earned us a deal of enmity, had it ever come to light. We developed something of a siege mentality, holding weekly meetings on our targets and giving them nicknames. We even started having sweepstakes on whether or not we would discover anything suspect about any given individual.

For a while, it would all work very well: we had some notable successes, such as our unmasking of an officer called Collins who worked under Richard at the DOS and had extremely suspect contacts in Kazakhstan. The financial crash, when it came, was an opportunity for money launderers the world over. The new breed of billionaires in the former Soviet Union didn't just buy yachts or homes in Mayfair: they bought politicians and bankers and the staff of any institution that might look into their activities. You get money by being adjacent to power, after all – and it works the other way round as well. Our investigations suggested Collins had been taking bribes from a minister in Nazarbayev's government. We could not discover what he had been offering in return – presumably something the minister could sell on to Russia or elsewhere – but it was thanks to our information that the DOS was able to haul him in and try and work that one out before he could cover his tracks.

We would never be thanked publicly, within the Service, I mean, so when the news of Collins's detention by the Service came in, Kieron gathered us all in Alaska and broke out a bottle of Prosecco. The six of us toasted ourselves and then he declared that he was taking us all for dinner – a new Italian had opened up in the piazza.

It was a Thursday and the place was already busy with office workers when we got there – we got the last empty table. The music was very loud. Carmella and I ordered another bottle of Prosecco. The boys all had pints. When the waiter came to take our food order, Kieron rocked back in his chair holding the menu up and slapped it with the back of his hand. 'We'll have one of each flavour except the margherita and six plates!' he shouted. 'On me!' he hollered as the waiter turned away. There was a note of hysteria to his happiness, and I wondered if he was feeling relieved as well as triumphant. Our failure to discover what Collins was offering in return for the bribes had bothered me.

Kieron and the boys were yelling to each other across their pints.

Carmella leaned in to me and murmured, her mouth close to my ear, 'You think he's so happy because it's one of Richard's? Doesn't look good for the DOS, does it?'

The same thought had occurred to me. The DOS had been employing a corrupt officer right under its nose – Kieron had been tracking the man's finances for two years, apparently. It didn't make Richard look good.

I wondered where the unfortunate Collins was right at that moment. It had been a dawn arrest. Collins would be sitting somewhere in a suburb of London, probably, in what we euphemistically called a safe house. In effect, he was being held prisoner while we gave him a very ugly choice: prosecution in a secret trial followed by a long and isolated prison sentence, or witness protection if he co-operated. The witness protection might be tempting if he had been selling secrets on an ideological basis, but if he had been selling them to the highest bidder – in other words, to gangsters – then there would be a price on his head for the rest of his life. Those people tended not to mess around. The DOS would be taking a carrot-and-stick approach. They would be offering to take care of him on the one hand while on the other pointing out that even if he didn't talk to them, the gangsters would assume he had, particularly if someone hinted to them that he had . . . Either way, he would never feel safe again – so he could feel not safe on his own in prison, away from his family, with the constant threat that the Service might trade him, in which case he would probably end up with a bullet to the back of his head within six months of stepping off a plane somewhere in Central Asia. Or he could feel not safe within the protection of the Service, relocated with a new identity, a slim chance at a new life for the whole family. He had a wife and four children.

'Well,' I murmured back to Carmella, 'Collins being dirty is great for Kieron all round.'

'Don't knock it,' she said, 'it's the first time in office history that he's bought us dinner.'

'*What?*' said Kieron, leaning across the table to catch our conversation. 'What you two gossiping about?'

Beneath the table, Carmella nudged my knee with hers and I spluttered into my glass of fizz.

The camaraderie of a small unit was new to me, and I liked it. It was cosy, there in the restaurant with my little group of colleagues and seven different flavours of pizza on the way. A couple at a nearby table were glancing over at our drunken-shouty gang, and I saw how we looked through their eyes – a noisy, self-confident huddle, leaning in, tight with each other, celebrating something.

There was only one blot on the landscape, and it had nothing to do with work.

15

My dream country home was turning into a disaster – a decision made too fast and with too little prior research, a basic error of which I was ashamed.

It took nearly eighteen months for the London estate agent to sell my flat for the realistic price at which it should always have been offered. By then, I was in an unspeakable amount of debt. I could not apply for an extended mortgage on the country home without declaring the other debts and informing work – who would want to know why I had breached protocol by not declaring the bridging loan. I was lucky it had not already shown up on my annual re-vet. Well, that's what I thought at the time. Later, I was to realise luck had nothing to do with it.

Fed up with spending all the hours I wasn't at work negotiating with builders or worrying about the possibility of rising damp, I decided to sell up, at which point I discovered I had paid well over the odds for a beautiful but crumbling house that was little more than a massive cash sponge with subsidence. By the time I finally got rid of both properties, I was left still servicing over a hundred and eighty thousand pounds of debt.

The vintage furniture I had bought proved impossible to resell – 'brown furniture', it's called, worthless. Some of it went on Freecycle, which at least meant someone had use of it. Most of it went to the dump. The builder's escalating bills had all gone on necessary but invisible renovations that hadn't made the house any easier to sell.

*

One Sunday morning, around six weeks before I would leave my so-called 'dream house' for good, I walked to the bottom of my patch of land, where a low mist hung over the wide nettle patch I had never got round to clearing, to say good morning to Fred the donkey with a carrot, and found the neighbouring field was empty. I stood for a moment by the rickety fence and looked out across the fields, the roofs of distant houses, the white sky. I wondered if Fred had died. How did that happen, exactly, with donkeys? Did they just lie down on their sides in the damp grass and die?

The neighbour's house was a modern two-storey home on the far side of Fred's field. I had befriended their donkey but had never seen the neighbour themselves. It came to me that the village was empty, soulless, that I had bought into something I didn't even understand. I wondered if the things we do are little more than reactions to something we had previously failed to do. If so, it suggests a monumental failure of imagination.

From somewhere far off, a dog gave out a single rusty bark, then the morning was silent again. How had this happened? I was the kind of person who was good at things, competent. I didn't make these sorts of mistakes.

I turned back to the house.

It was around three months later that I found myself in a hotel room after a conference in Cheltenham with Kieron Blythe, my boss, eight years my junior and with the kind of dense, honed body that average-looking men sometimes have, a body they have worked on hard to compensate for a lack of looks or height. I preferred them older than me, tall and loose, a little rumpled round the edges. Like I say, he wasn't my type.

I had moved into a rental flat in central Birmingham. It came fully furnished and I'd been unable to sell most of my furniture: I'd had to pay someone to take it away. My total debts were now a little short of two hundred and thirty thousand counting the remainder of the bridging loan, my credit cards and my debts to the builders. I had just had a default notice. I was going to have to declare it at work and, at the same time, explain why I had not declared it before. A Section 8 disciplinary investigation would be launched and I didn't know what would happen, but the very least of it would be removal from my current position in the Birmingham unit, a return to London, a city I could no longer afford to live in, in a lowly administrative role – and that was the good outcome.

When I thought about losing my job, a wave of nausea would wash over me. It would paralyse me, in the same way that a person facing a tidal wave might decide there was no point in running; it was best to go limp and let the water crash over them. I was nothing without my career and I knew it.

So I was there, with my boss, in a hotel room in Cheltenham. We were both drunk, but I was drunker.

I was sitting in a chair while he leaned forward from where he was perched on the edge of the bed – it was a small room – and ran one finger down the inside of my elbow. His fingernail caught in my skin.

I had been talking about selling my house, not the full story, of course. I had murmured something about being fed up with the commute, how much easier it was now I had moved to a rental in the centre of town.

He let me burble on for a bit, watching me intently. When I dried to a halt he said, 'It's okay . . . I can help out, you know, strictly between you and me.'

I looked at him.

'Your vetting comes direct to me,' he said, 'and whether or not it goes any further is my call. Look, I've been through the circumstances. It has no bearing on your work, none at all.'

I said nothing. I wondered how long he had known, and why he hadn't said anything to me before.

He sat back a little and raised both hands, 'Look, sorry . . .' He slurred *sorry* a little, and I wondered – but only later – if the slurring was genuine. 'Inappropriate time to raise it, but you know, you started talking about it and just looked so worried.'

Later this conversation would become drenched with significance, of course, but like the idiot that I was, my reaction at the time was surprise, then – I am ashamed to admit – gratitude. My boss was covering my arse. Had been for a while, it would seem.

There was a mirror on the other side of the room. As he leaned back in towards me, I caught a glimpse of our reflection in it, me seated in the chair, him angling forward, just before I closed my eyes.

We didn't look at each other, during. It wasn't that kind of sex. At one point, I opened my eyes to see that he was reared above me, head tipped back, eyes closed, dreamy expression on his face. He gave a small wince. The reflexive physical response I was experiencing died. I clenched myself and increased the small lift of my hips in order to conclude the business faster.

Afterwards, I knew there would have to be a polite interval before I could extricate myself. We lay on the bed together, facing each other, and I regarded him thoughtfully, while he gave me a grimace that said he knew I was regarding him and he was enjoying it.

174

Kieron Blythe, Head of Liaison 2.6 – okay, it was a department within a department, but he was head of it, a big fish in a little pond, reporting directly to Richard, and his position meant he had multiple indoctrinations, including access to Net Intelligence 8, as we called the then web-monitoring service. If you're going to keep an eye on the people who keep an eye on other people, you need all their tools at your disposal, after all. I wonder what he wants next, I thought, career-wise, particularly now he's kneecapped Collins. Does he fantasise about Richard's job, eventually, Director General one day? The relationship between the two men seemed an odd one to me – they shared a taste in expensive shirts, and Richard had clearly brought Kieron on, groomed him for big things, but he must know that Kieron would be nursing patricidal tendencies.

Kieron smirked at me. 'Go on . . .' he said.

'I'm just wondering why you wanted to do that.'

He shrugged. 'Because I could.'

My eyes widened as if I was hurt and he smiled reassuringly. 'Hey, only joking, kiddo . . .'

Kieron Blythe would have to be handled with care from now on. I had made myself vulnerable to him, which would play in my favour – but he must not suspect, at any point, that I was mocking him.

I sat up and lowered my feet to the floor, taking it slowly and carefully. So, he was the kind of boss who liked to have something on everyone. I'd met that type before. The Service was full of people who wanted to win. *No real harm done,* I thought. He was married, after all, a wife who lived in London with one young son; he went back there at the weekends. Didn't I have something on him now, too?

He had used what he knew about me to bed me: so what, as long as he thought he was in charge, he would be manageable – and actually, it could end up saving my career. It would buy me time while I thought about what to do, how to dig myself out of the financial hole I was in. There was no relish in being so transactional, but as I sat there on the edge of his bed, turned away from him, I couldn't help thinking that if a fifteen-minute shag was the price I had to pay for Kieron Blythe not reporting the state of my financial affairs back up to Richard, I was getting the protection cheap.

I leaned forward and picked up my bra from the carpet. It was white, lace, and it came to me that I had worn that underwear set to the conference on the off-chance – I just hadn't imagined it might be Kieron. I hadn't come here aiming for him, which meant he must have come here aiming for me.

My back was to him where I sat on the edge of the bed. As I triangled my arms to fasten my bra, he said, 'I actually thought you were a lesbian.'

Oh God. So he fancied the challenge. It was a good job he couldn't see my face. 'You mean, I have short hair and don't waste time flirting.' I kept my tone light. 'You aren't the first man to think that.'

'No, it's not that,' he said and, unexpectedly, I felt him stroke my spine with one finger, beginning at the top, the back of my neck, and tracing my vertebrae all the way down, skimming over my bra, right down to my tailbone. It was a far more intimate gesture than the sex we had just had. I tried not to shudder.

'Your army days,' he said. 'I met someone who knew you at a family party last year. According to him you had a massive lesbian crush on his girlfriend, the one who died, and you punched him in the head. It was quite the story.'

I sat where I was, breathing. I arranged the expression on my face, turned to him.

He smiled. 'I know, coincidence, eh? My cousin Ruth had a wedding anniversary and I got talking to this bloke, ex-army, just got chatting, I was making conversation, saying how I worked in import and export and someone in my office was also ex-military . . .' He shook his head in amusement. 'Pretty intriguing, you must admit.'

'Which girlfriend? Who died?'

'Some mad Italian.' He misread my face and sat up in bed, giving a small inhalation. 'I didn't tell him anything about you, I didn't breach protocol! Just said I knew someone called Heather who had been in the army years ago and his face lit up. Tall guy.'

I have performed many physical feats in my time but probably the greatest was the one I performed that night, the one where I rose and finished dressing while making light conversation with Kieron before getting myself back to my own room.

I went straight to the bathroom and vomited the wine I had drunk into the toilet – I used my finger down the back of my throat – before I opened my laptop and googled Flavia Bianchi.

Flavia had died four years ago. 'Bus Crash Tragedy': the *Manchester Evening Argus*. The driver had had a heart attack at the wheel and ploughed into a queue at a bus stop outside a shopping centre. It was one of those incidents that is briefly big news, then disappears the next day. Three people died: Randeep Chowdry, a pensioner, a three-year-old called Finn Goldney, who was strapped into his pushchair next to his father, who survived, and Flavia Bianchi, mother of two. The only detail it gave about her was the tragic twist so beloved of accidental-death reporting: a witness said that Mrs Bianchi was actually walking past the queue at the time. As the bus approached, the child in the stroller dropped a soft toy. Flavia had paused, picked the toy up from the pavement and then squatted down to return it to three-year-old Finn. Flavia and the youngster were killed at the scene – the elderly man died later in hospital.

I wondered if she had her back to the bus, if the first thing she felt was a push, and then it was all over quickly, or if she saw it coming towards her and knew what was about to happen and had time for a moment of fear, of horror. *Died at the scene* might mean 'died instantly' – or it might mean 'lay crushed and broken and in terrible pain while they waited for the ambulance'.

I thought of how scathing I was when I read her note on the train from Plockton to Inverness, about her fears of dying one day, her obsession with it – the daft idea of burying a box with a note for me, her sentimental conviction that she should leave something behind for me. *I know you will think this is silly*, the note had read, *but when I was a lonely child in Italy I always thought, whatever I do, it won't be normal. And then I joined the army. And I always thought, I don't think I will have a normal family, husband and children and so on – and I had Adelina. And I feel that my death won't be normal either. It's a Trinity of sorts. I know what you will think of this!* Well, she was right, wasn't she? She was right and I was wrong.

I closed the laptop lid and went to lie down on the bed, where I curled into a foetal position. *Mother of two.* So she had married, or had another child by one of those awful lovers. At least Adelina would have someone. I wondered how she was told.

178

Thinking about Adelina felt as if someone was sliding a fine but long needle between my ribs. Four years. All that time, I had been walking around, concentrating on my work, living my life, having my own pathetic little adventures, and all that time Flavia had been cold in the earth or ashes, and I hadn't even known that she was dead. I covered my face with my hands. I stayed there a long time.

16

The city-centre flat I had moved into was the diametric opposite to the dream house: an antiseptic new build no more than ten minutes from the office and resembling an office in some ways — white walls, echoey, a small stainless-steel galley kitchen. It came with minimal furniture and built-in cupboards and white goods. I brought nothing with me but my clothes and personal effects in the full knowledge that, for the time being at least, I was going to live a purely functional life. At times it felt as though I had moved into Alaska. It was exactly what I needed.

I developed an obsession with tiny things — I bought a small toiletry bag and resolved that all my toiletries should henceforth fit into it, including a foldable travel toothbrush. I started wearing sports underwear — I threw out the white lacy bra and all the other underwear like it, the thongs, the translucent slips I had bought for myself back in the days when I wanted to impress a one-night stand or have a drink and masturbate to myself in the mirror on a Friday night when there was nothing on the telly. Instead, I bought plain black knickers, the seamless sort, made of fabric so fine it was like wearing a slippery layer of extra skin and, crucially, they would pack down so neatly that ten of them laid flat took up no more space in a bag than an envelope.

I didn't buy any plants or hang any pictures or mirrors on the walls — anything decorative disappeared from my life. It was all about utility. I bought a small glass teapot and a glass cup and started drinking jasmine tea with no milk, admiring the translucence of my beverage at the same time as I admired the transparency of the receptacles I used to serve it to myself. I browsed fancy design websites in an effort to persuade myself this was a style choice but in my heart of hearts, I knew something else was going on, something I didn't yet understand.

My house was gone. Flavia was dead. It was as if I was losing all my previous selves like a lizard sloughing off skins. I had even shed my own competence.

At times, I wondered if I was becoming ill.

After the Cheltenham conference, Kieron and I carried on as normal at work, and I assumed, with relief, that he was just one of those men who lost interest as soon as he had slept with you. Then came the evening when we were both leaving the building at the same time and he said, as we emerged from the revolving doors onto the concrete piazza, 'Fancy a drink?'

I really, really did not want me and Kieron to become a thing, but I knew I had to be careful how I turned him down. 'Oh God, I'd love one,' I said, making myself sound as regretful as possible, 'but I've promised to go over to a friend's house.'

He took the rebuff cheerily enough. 'Another time.'

Then, as he trotted down the shallow concrete steps ahead of me, he stopped, turned back and said, 'Or maybe I could bring a bottle of wine over to your place some time?'

'Sure,' I said with a bright little smile, and he trotted off into the night.

I couldn't help admiring his honesty. He wasn't pretending any kind of romance – he didn't want a full-blown affair, just the occasional shag.

There's a way to get rid of such men. You take them to the pub and you tip back the Sauvignon as if Sauvignon-rationing is about to be announced, and you put your hand on their thigh, halfway between the knee and their groin area, then you lean in and get a little tearful and ask if they have any real feelings for you because you just want to know where you stand. They can't get out of the door fast enough. I hoped it wouldn't come to that with Kieron.

But then, as I walked home through the dark streets of inner-city Birmingham, I thought about the crowing tone in his voice when he told me about meeting Michael at his cousin's wedding anniversary, and how his reaction to that weird coincidence had so obviously been *Great, I've got something else on her now.* I thought about Flavia, and how it still hurt that she was dead, and how I found out that she was dead through Kieron Blythe, of all people. Flavia's name in his mouth – even though he didn't know and hadn't used her name – filled me with a kind of impotent hatred for him, for all men, in fact. Kieron and I could pretend to carry on as normal at work but it was not normal, we both knew that, not because we had slept together, but because of what he knew about me, the hold it gave him over me, and because whatever happened between me and him, I would not forgive him for the way Flavia's death was nothing but a bit of juicy gossip, some quirky fact he had picked up about me from the horrible Michael at his cousin Ruth's party.

It was not long after that things started to get weird.

I was gradually clawing back my financial affairs, although I was still in a great deal of debt. After a little research online on a computer in Birmingham Library, I had discovered a strategy for managing unmanageable repayments. The trick is to stay one step ahead of legal proceedings by demonstrating what's known as a 'willingness to pay'. I had got into the habit of defaulting on a monthly payment, then ringing to apologise and paying part of it – even a minimal amount makes it much less likely that they will issue a court summons. A judge looks a lot less favourably on a company that takes you to the cleaners if you can demonstrate you are doing your best, however small your best might be. My main strategy was to minimise the possibility of anyone instigating proceedings against me – because even Kieron would be obliged to refer that one upwards.

It was in February, some time around the middle of the month, that I rang the loan company, euphemistically called Thoroughgood Asset Management. I was pretending that I wanted to confirm they had received the two-thousand-pound payment I had made on the twelfth while in fact laying the ground for the March payment being a little delayed – then when it was, I could point out that I had warned them.

'Yes,' said the young woman on the end of the line, 'we got that safely, thanks, and the thirteen thousand five hundred came in the next day.'

It was a gloomy day, that day. By three in the afternoon, the light was already failing through the glass walls of the office – it had been a long winter and it was far from over yet. Carmella had left for the day, something about her childminder being off sick, and the three boys were busy at their terminals. I walked down to Kieron's office and went in without knocking.

He looked up as I came in.

I pressed my lips together, then walked over to the chair on the other side of his desk, sat on it and said, 'What's going on?'

'Ah,' he said, sitting back in his seat, 'I didn't think you'd be noti-fied. I was going to tell you about it asap. Listen, I *have* been trying to get you down the pub for a while now – it's not really office talk.'

I lifted my hands. '*Thirteen fucking grand?*'

'Look, I'm going to have to trust you here . . .' He left a pause, looking at me a little pleadingly, before continuing. 'It's like this, okay. I inherited from an uncle, lung cancer, six months ago. It's just come through, but I can't tell my wife. None of your business why I can't tell her, but I can't, we're having some issues, okay, and finances are relevant. It's a loan, not a gift. I was going to explain that before you found out about it. No hurry, none at all, in fact – you can pay me back when you've finished paying off the loan, no biggie.'

'You want me to help hide your assets in the event of a divorce?' I could not prevent a note of incredulity entering my voice.

'Well, that's a rather brutal way of putting it.'

'You knew that if you put it in my bank account I'd give it right back, so you put it into my loan, which would make that impossible.'

'Okay, it was underhand. I'm sorry, I should have discussed it with you first. I know it's a big favour, but look, I've been watch-ing your back for some time here, so I'm just asking something in return. Trust me, I have my reasons.'

So that was why he had been protecting me – in order to call in the favour at a later date. No such thing as a free drink. I was embarrassed by my assumption that it had been about sex.

As I rose from the chair, he said, 'Let's get that drink some time. We've been so busy here, it's ages since we've had a proper catch-up. I feel bad now, I know it was a liberty. Seriously, I'd really like that.' He got up and walked round to my side of the desk. He took hold of the sleeve of my blouse – it was a blouson-style thing, grey with white buttons and full sleeves in a slippery synthetic fabric. He rubbed the silky material with his thumb and forefinger. 'I like this,' he said.

I treated him to my most level and sceptical gaze.

He pulled a face. 'I could do with a shoulder to cry on, to be honest, things are pretty rough at home.'

I did not answer as I left the room.

I walked back along the carpeted corridor to my desk.

If Carmella had been in the office, I might have gone to her and said, 'Look, I need to talk to you about something, it's a bit of a long story.' But she wasn't.

If I had been based in London, I might have rung Richard's PA and said, 'Can you find me half an hour with the boss as soon as possible?'

Inaction doesn't feel like a decision, just postponement while you make the right decision: but not making a decision is often the worst decision of all.

I avoided being alone with Kieron for a while – what kind of favour was he going to ask next, particularly if he carried through on his offer to bring a bottle of wine round to my flat? Luckily, work was busy for both of us, but around a fortnight later, I was in the tiny, windowless kitchen, stirring a cup of tea and peering into it trying to guess whether the milk I had just added to it was still fresh, when in he breezed, whistling to himself, and headed for the fridge.

He opened the door, paused, and turned to me, about to say something. To head him off at the pass I said, quickly and casually, 'What's the latest on Sidcup Man? Is there any other milk in there?'

Sidcup Man was an officer of sixteen years' service – lived in Sidcup, Kent, which for some reason we found funny – who was suspected of a relationship with an immigration firm in London that was, in its own turn, suspected of organising entry into the UK for someone we were pretty sure was KGB RB, the Belarusian secret service. The investigation was still in its early stages – there were suspicious movements in his finances, that was all. The DOS was asking for regular updates but as far as I knew had not launched anything official.

Kieron was at the fridge. 'There's almond milk.'

'Ugh,' I said, 'not in tea.' It was time I brought in some of my favourite jasmine blend from home.

'DOS have told us to drop him, they've wrapped him up.'

'Oh, I didn't know they'd even got going on him.'

The dropping of cases wasn't, in itself, all that unusual – we were an internal investigations unit; our job was to follow leads that went nowhere, happened all the time. People are human, and even people who had nothing to hide often behaved as if they did – as I knew all too well. In fact, it was no exaggeration to say that since I had been working for Liaison 2.6, it aroused my suspicions if someone had nothing about them that aroused suspicion. It *was* unusual, however, that the DOS had come to that conclusion before we had even finished our preliminary report.

Kieron left the kitchen. I poured my tea down the sink and boiled the kettle again for an instant coffee. I had an uncomfortable, indefinable feeling. I did a body check on myself – arched my shoulder blades back towards each other – and thought maybe I'm just tired. I couldn't remember the last time I had an unbroken night's sleep. I had got into the habit of a glass of

186

wine or two with dinner in front of the television. I had let my personal fitness slip.

I put the carton of almond milk back in the fridge and closed the door, leaning and resting my forehead on it. The metal was pleasingly cool and the effect anodyne. *You're tired, you're not sleeping well*, I thought. *You need to take more exercise.* Maybe that was what was wrong with me.

When I was at university, I would go hiking at the weekends with a rucksack that had three bricks in the bottom while my fellow students were getting legless in the SU bar and copping off with one another. That's how keen I was to join the WRAC (and no, funny you should ask, I didn't have that many friends). Competence, physical competence, was everything. A soldier had to be ready to march at any time. Why I bothered to keep myself combat-ready when we wouldn't even be given live firearms training is beyond me now – but it stayed with me, the desire to be ready for something that may never come.

The Saturday after my kitchen conversation with Kieron, I drove south-west out of Birmingham. I loved the Waseley Hills, the Clent Hills – the Malverns were my favourite – but I didn't want to go that far that day. I liked to go early in the morning, so I could have a good hike and be away from the area before the weekend families arrived. There was nothing better than arriving in a car park, setting off in my boots with a water bottle and a protein bar and, just before I headed into a field or up a hill, looking back to see that my car was the only vehicle there.

I went to a village on the Worcester and Birmingham Canal – I was out of shape and so planning an easy walk, three to four hours

187

maybe, on a circular route that would bring me back to the village. Maybe I would treat myself to a half of dry cider and a ploughman's in the pub after, if I was back in the village early enough to miss the lunchtime rush.

I was the same weight I had been in my twenties, a little more wiry perhaps – my hair had a few strands of white and my skin puckered more easily – but I had the small, tough body of a much younger woman. When I'm elderly, I sometimes thought, I'll be one of those leathery old ladies with chicken flesh and stringy arms who is surprisingly strong and good at DIY, even though I'm not all that good at DIY at the moment. Well, that was the plan.

It was at the end of my walk, as I headed down the high street, that I stopped in front of a second-hand bookshop. It wasn't so much the shop that drew my attention as something in front of the shop, the kind of display unit that second-hand bookshops often have to entice customers, a wide drawer on legs that means books can be displayed spine upwards for people to trail their fingers across when looking for classic novels or old Penguin editions or whatever takes their fancy – the bibliophiles' equivalent of the vinyl record shops you still see down backstreets in cities. The books they leave out front aren't valuable or they'd get lifted – it's battered paperbacks, mostly, some in rows with the spines so degraded and curled all you can see is the folds and stitches beneath.

I daresay a disintegrating paperback of *Far from the Madding Crowd* might call to someone but it didn't make my fingers twitch. What caught my eye was a row of burnt-orange objects with cream-coloured spines. I stopped and picked one up: a vintage Ordnance Survey map for Dumfries and Gretna. I looked at the spines, a random selection of Scottish locations: Dalbeattie, Kirkcudbright, Stranraer . . . I felt a sweet kind of sadness wash over me, an airy, floaty feeling as if I was drifting skyward like a hot-air balloon and a rope around my ankle was loosening.

I spent a few minutes selecting the maps that I wanted and added a couple that I didn't. Looking back I wonder if I was already aware, subconsciously that is, that I mustn't create a pattern, that arbitrary selection was my friend.

The windows of the shop were filthy – through them I could glimpse a book-lined cave, low-ceilinged, the colour of strong tea. A man with stubble wearing a round hat and fingerless gloves sat on a chair behind the counter, and in the children's section at the front of the shop, a young girl sat on a low stool, leafing through a picture book.

As I pushed into the shop, the maps in my hand, a bell above the door gave a small tinkle and the man with the stubble looked up from where he was rolling a cigarette on top of a fat biography of Churchill. He lifted the cigarette and slicked it horizontally across his tongue as I approached, looking at me with the air of a man who was calculating how much I might be up for paying for what was in my hand.

I held out the Ordnance Survey maps – eight of them in all, faded, tatty round the edges.

'Going on a long walk?' he remarked laconically as he put the cigarette down on top of the biography and reached beneath the counter for a large paper bag. He put the paper bag beside his till, took the maps from me and fanned them to see how many there were.

'Dad,' said the child on the stool. I glanced round. She was head down, intent on her picture book. 'Can we do this one day?'

'No,' the man replied, 'I've told you.'

He looked at me, licked his lips again. 'Twelve pounds.'

The old maps should have been no more than a quid each but I wasn't about to haggle. I handed over a twenty-pound note. As he gave me the change I said, 'I'm a local artist. I cut them up, make collages.'

His look told me all I needed to know about what he thought of local artists.

As I left the shop, I saw that the child was reading *We're Going on a Bear Hunt*, a large edition splayed open, covering her knees.

I pulled at the door handle with unwarranted force and the door stuck in its frame for a microsecond before springing open. The bell tinkled loudly and as I exited into the village street, I paused to catch my breath and told myself, it's okay, it's just pain, that's all, that bad feeling that you're feeling right now, that's all it is – pain, made more piquant by regret perhaps, but mostly pain.

When I got back to my car, I sat in the driver's seat for a moment with the door open – a fug had built up inside. I bent and unlaced my walking boots, then reached over to place them in the footwell on the passenger side, where I had left my old trainers.

On the passenger seat were my water bottle and the paper bag containing the maps.

I took a slug of water and put the water bottle back down. I picked up the paper bag and slid the maps out, fanning them across the passenger seat, looking at them. Why did I buy these? Then I thought about Collins and Sidcup Man, and how it was interesting that we had had two very different cases with a similar pattern recently – evidence of the receipt of money but no real evidence of what they were doing for the money.

I sat back in the driver's seat of the car.

It was the Monday after that that Carmella tapped on my door. As well as her own caseload, she managed the Tech Training Programme – the colloquial term we used for the process of making sure we all stayed up to speed on new internet research programmes – it was as essential for what we did as it was for a firearms officer to do regular weapons training.

She half opened the door and leaned in as I looked up. 'Combating remote malware installation,' she said, 'London next week, place has just come up, you're going.'

'Am I?' I said absently. I hadn't been to London in ages. A few days away from my problems in Birmingham was attractive, I had to admit.

'Yup,' she said, 'I'll email you the programme.' She closed the door.

It was more the boys' department than mine, but hey.

And so it came to pass that the following Monday lunchtime, I was crossing the foyer of the Connaught Building in Bloomsbury.

I was walking briskly across the chevron-patterned tiled floor of the reception hall, looking down and admiring it, when a voice called out, 'Heather!'

I stopped and turned. Richard was looking particularly dapper that day, in an immaculate suit, his thin white hair combed back over his head. His smile was warm. I hadn't seen him in person since our recent success – it had surprised me a little that he hadn't come to Birmingham to debrief and update us all, but then considering

191

all the other cases he had to deal with, maybe our preliminary investigations were not as important as we liked to think.

He leaned into me, grasping one of my elbows with a bony hand, his grip just one notch too tight. 'We must have a proper catch-up soon,' he said in a tone of voice that suggested if I wasn't in my fifties he might have added *my dear*. 'It's been an age.'

I felt a moment of weakness then, a desire to take all my worries to a male authority figure, like a maid with a wicker basket full of apples. *Here, have one. Have as many as you like.*

'Well done on Collins,' he said, with what seemed to be genuine warmth. 'Way to go our end, of course, but we're all very pleased. Seems to be going swimmingly in Birmingham, guess we won't be tempting you back to London any time soon?'

The chasm between how Richard thought everything was going for me and how everything was really going was so large I could have tumbled into it.

I smiled back and said, 'Thanks, yes, that was a good one, wasn't it? Thanks to Kieron, though, got to say, he's like a dog with a bone.'

'How are you finding Mr Blythe? Good at the job, but an arrogant little bastard, isn't he?'

I was surprised by Richard's disloyalty – although I enjoyed it, of course. I rolled my eyes. 'He doesn't like to be wrong, does he?'

'Certainly doesn't . . .' Richard leaned forward, took my elbow again and pressed his dry cheek against mine by way of farewell. As he turned to go, he said, 'Well, tell him I hate to admit it, but he was quite right about dropping Ian Barrett – either he's clean or a really good cleaner-upper. We can't justify a full investigation.'

He turned smartly on one heel. 'Don't be a stranger, now,' he said over his shoulder as he strode towards the exit.

I crossed the foyer and mounted the wide staircase, my hand running lightly along the curve of the pleasingly worn wooden banister; the seminar room hosting the afternoon's session was just at the top of the stairs. The conscious part of my brain was thinking I should ask for clarification on something about the morning session that I hadn't fully understood, but the unconscious part was chasing another thought, following the thread through the minotaur's cave of my subconscious.

Ian Barrett was Sidcup Man.

So, after leaving an interval of a couple of weeks, on a Tuesday when the sky outside was an odd greyish-pinkish colour that suggested there was pollution in the air drifting over central Birmingham from an industrial unit somewhere, I stood in Kieron's office, in front of his desk, and said casually, 'There's something I don't understand about Sidcup Man. If we'd got a positive trace on the school fees' payment then why did the DOS drop it?' Having your children's private school fees paid by a dodgy connection was a common way for people to avoid a bribe going through their own bank account. But that wasn't the point of my question.

'I agree,' he said, lifting his hands. 'According to them it turned legit, family friend, so a little odd, but the connection checked out. They'll keep an eye, obviously.' He looked at me as if he agreed with my concern, shrugged, added, 'I know.'

I left Kieron's office and walked back down the corridor to mine. I sat at my desk and looked at the odd-coloured sky and wondered what to do now that what I had suspected since my canal walk was true. I thought of myself buying maps of Scotland that I didn't want or need – and how at the time I hadn't understood why my hand had reached for them – but how my subconscious was one step ahead of me and making preparations. Kieron Blythe was corrupt. His modus operandi was planting evidence – convincing evidence – that suggested other people were doing what he was doing himself, and however he was pulling it off, he had developed an effective enough system that it was withstanding further scrutiny by the DOS. He had condemned Collins, somehow. He had exonerated Ian Barrett. There were probably lots of genuine cases in the mix, but he was also using Liaison 2.6 as his personal fiefdom, to control the directions that the DOS looked in, and when they looked away.

Collins. Barrett. And probably, eventually – me.

17

'What's wrong?'

I had come to my mother's house on a Sunday. We were in her front garden – it was spring and her shrubs were in bloom, great green things that squatted in a bulbous row along her tarmac drive, looking to me like something from an episode of *Doctor Who* that pretends to be inanimate but moves towards you when your back is turned. My mother was clearing dead twigs from beneath the shrubs using two flaps torn from a cardboard box. I was pretending to help.

I stood by her, holding open a garden refuse bag, and looked at the curve of her back as she bent over the twigs. She had spoken while her face was lowered.

I had never confided in my mother, either when things were going well or going badly, yet she always had a radar for when something was up: she knew very little of my life, but she sensed a great deal.

She straightened up – her hands in her garden gloves holding the pieces of cardboard, the pieces of cardboard sandwiching twigs and leaves – and repeated the question. 'I can tell, you know. What's wrong?'

Funny, no matter how old you get, there are times when you are with your mother and you want to allow your lower lip to tremble and your eyes to brim because even though you know your mother doesn't have a magic wand any more, part of you never stops being the small child who thought she did.

Another chunk had been paid off my loan, two days ago, from a different account than had paid the last chunk, and I hadn't challenged Kieron about it this time because I needed him to think I was collusive while I decided on my next move – but the longer I left it, the more guilty I would look when it all came out.

'I'm okay,' I said, 'I'm just really tired, work is full on.'

She gave me a steady, clear-eyed and sceptical gaze.

'Do you remember Flavia?' I said.

My mother dropped more twigs into the bag and used her forearm to push her fringe back from her forehead. 'Yes, of course, you two were so close until you got that promotion. I was sorry you lost touch. She sent me Christmas cards every year though, for a few years at least.'

'Did she?' I hadn't known that.

'Yes, then I think she must have moved, I don't know, went quiet.'

'She died,' I said. 'I found out a while ago, I've been meaning to say.'

My mother's face softened with distress. 'Oh, that's sad. She can't have been all that old.'

'A traffic accident, in Manchester.'

Gently, rain began to fall. We both turned towards the house.

'Did you write to the daughter?' my mother asked. 'What was she called?'

I shook my head, even though I was behind her and she couldn't see. 'No, I thought about it, but I don't know what I'd say. We hadn't been in touch for years, after all.'

'You should write to her,' my mother said then.

I've got a few other things on my mind right now, I thought.

We went into the kitchen and while Mum washed her hands at the sink, I leaned against the countertop and waited for her to ask more about how I was.

196

'Pass me that teapot down,' she said as she dried her hands on a tea towel.

A few minutes later, as I carried the tea tray through into the lounge, I got to the point of my visit, asking casually, 'Do you remember that old phone I gave you, years ago, the Nokia?'

I had given my mother an early-generation pay-as-you-go, a small grey brick – but within a few months she had taken out a contract that came with another phone.

'Yes,' she said, putting down the tray, 'it's in the sideboard, do you want it?'

The following week, on the Wednesday, I worked until nine o'clock in the evening with the door to my office closed. I had a good excuse: I was taking a couple of days off for a trip to Margate, where I had been before for mini-breaks, sometimes with my mother, sometimes without. It was where she had grown up – but on this occasion, I was going alone.

One by one, I heard the others leave. The lights came on across Birmingham, a constellation in the gathering dusk, then it was dark outside and the windows became black mirrors that I was careful to avoid gazing into, unwilling to be arrested by my own reflection.

I heard the cleaner arrive and begin to hoover, empty the bins. I waited until he tapped on my door, opened it, and said, 'Oh, I'm sorry, miss.'

'It's alright,' I said, smiling at him, rising from my chair. 'Come in, it needs a clean. I'll go into one of the others.'

'I can do the big room first.'

'No, it's fine, come in, I'm nearly done anyway.'

I threw some papers into my briefcase and picked up my coat from the back of my door.

In Kieron's office, I left the door ajar, dropped my coat over the soft chair and laid my papers out on Kieron's desk. Then I took a cloth handkerchief out of my pocket to put over my fingertips.

I started on the desk drawers – they were all locked and, as was procedure, he would have the key on him. I tried a combination of my key and an extended paperclip without success.

I brought his keyboard to life and entered the half-dozen pass-words that came to mind, one-fingeredly – his date of birth, his son's date of birth. He had mentioned both his wife's and son's birthdays in recent months. Then I tried his wedding anniversary and parents' dates of birth: it's amazing what you can find out about someone from both public and Service records, and that was my speciality, after all. Nothing produced results. Outside, in the corridor, I heard that the cleaner had finished my office and was going into Alaska. I listened to the near-but-distant drone of his vacuum cleaner for a minute. *Fuck*. How was I going to find out any more without leaving traces of what I was up to? If I was going to report my suspicions about Kieron to our masters back in London, I needed more than what I had, and I needed a good explanation as to why I hadn't gone to them before. I had let him hide the state of my financial affairs and pay money into my loan, which made me look complicit. Accusing him without further evidence was going to look as though I was only doing it to exculpate myself.

In the meantime, I had started making plans. But what would I do about Mum?

I rested my elbows on Kieron's desk, steepled my fingers and pressed the fingertips together and thought of the way I had sat in that chair in the hotel room back in Cheltenham, and how I had just let it happen.

The light from the corridor altered. I looked up. Carmella was standing in the doorway with her coat on.

'What are you doing in the boss's office?' she asked, crossing her arms and leaning against the door frame.

'Oh,' I said vaguely, blowing my nose on the hanky then stuffing it into my pocket. 'I thought you'd gone home.'

'I wouldn't get too comfy,' she said sardonically. 'He isn't going anywhere any time soon.'

'No,' I said, 'I'm just staying out of the cleaner's way for a bit.' I rose from the chair. 'Anyway, I prefer my office, the light is better.' I picked up my coat, shrugged it on. 'If you're heading out, I'll come with you.'

We walked down the corridor together, exited the double doors.

In order to make his reports back to the DOS watertight, wouldn't Kieron need an ally in investigations? I thought of how closely Carmella and Kieron worked together, how she had been in the office from the moment Richard had set up the new unit. Didn't she have any suspicions of her own? If not, why not? Maybe he had something on her too.

'Fancy a quick drink?' I said as we walked towards the lift. 'I'm off tomorrow.' Quite apart from my suspicions, I felt a sudden and overwhelming desire for Carmella's company. Right at that moment, I wanted, very badly, to spend an hour with someone I genuinely liked, someone who would make me feel my life was less cold. I knew this was contradictory.

'Nah, I'd love to, but I'll be in right trouble if I don't get home.'

Of course. She had a husband and two children. She had a house, a garden, a life.

We approached the lifts together. I said, 'Going to take the stairs, need the exercise.'

She raised an eyebrow in farewell – I caught it just before I turned and blundered with pointless vigour through the door to the stairwell.

Holidays are an odd business when you are single. By and large I've found that self-catering is best avoided: you are liable to find yourself sitting in a rented flat or house looking round the room and realising the only thing you are taking a holiday from is the paint colour of your own walls. I've always resisted going on holiday with friends, though – too much like having a favourite scarf that you wrap round your neck a bit tightly only to realise it's irritating you even though you still like the colour.

But my trip to Margate wasn't a holiday – it was a weekend away to make some sort of decision, although in retrospect, it came to seem more like a rehearsal.

Margate is a long way from the West Midlands, but we used to go there to visit my mother's family when we were all small and, in any case, the distance was part of the attraction. I needed to do some sitting on trains and staring out of the window.

The flat was on the third floor of a tall, narrow building with curved corners, a bit art deco I suppose. There was a slightly dank bedroom at the back and a tiny kitchen, but the sitting room was on the corner of the building and had three bay windows with elegantly swooping glass, overlooking the sea. This was its selling point when I saw it online. I was planning on doing a lot of staring at the sea.

On the first morning, I went for a long walk along the shingle shoreline. My feet scrunched on the gravel, sinking into it with a satisfying stony rumble. It was late spring but a stiff wind slapped my overlong fringe across my face – I thought, *I've let it get unkempt, I'll book a cut when I get back.* Neat hair and exercise made me feel strong and capable. The sea heaved gently; seagulls wheeled overhead. The perpetual nature of a seaside walk, the steady availability of it, made me feel calm, more in control. I needed this, I thought, to remind myself of what was possible.

After the walk, I came back to the flat and made a salad in the tiny kitchen, then slumped on the sofa, feet up, and ate the salad while I stared out to sea. The wind had died down, but the water was layered and rippling with so many different colours: it was an empty sea, this sea, in blues and greys and browns depending on the light. There was a dull-red freight ship on the horizon: I watched it while I ate but it didn't move. I stared at it so much, it ceased to seem real: it began to seem like a portent – what of, I didn't know. I thought of Flavia and I thought of my mother and of all the people that everyone has, the people that hold them and pin them in one place. I thought of how un-freighted I was in comparison with most people.

The North Sea. There was nothing between me and Scandinavia. I thought about that fact as I sat there, staring at the motionless ship.

On my last full afternoon, the Saturday, I neglected to close the curtains as dusk fell. I dozed a little, my half-drunk tea cooling on a side table, and when I woke, I saw a dark figure on the far side of the esplanade, standing motionless by the painted iron railings. The figure was in silhouette and distant enough in the faded light for me to be unable to see whether it was looking out to sea or facing the flat and staring up at me.

I sat motionless, waiting for the figure to move, but it did not. There were no lights on in the flat yet, so I knew I couldn't be visible, but all the same, I waited until it was fully dark outside, the figure swallowed by night, to rise and close the curtains. Only then did I switch on the lights.

As I walked over to the kitchen counter to make myself something to eat, I thought, *This is what you will face, twenty-four hours a day.*

I was due to check out at noon, but the next morning I woke early enough to walk into town and get myself a cooked breakfast.

The light was full and clear, the sea new-looking, calm. I crossed the road and turned left where the esplanade sloped down and levelled past a scrubby cliff and the site where they were building a new contemporary art gallery, part of the refurbishment that the Kent coast has been undergoing for some years – the road has been renamed Turner Way.

In the morning light, there were no dark figures, motionless and watching, just a few townspeople walking their dogs, a handful of tourists like me. I paused and looked out to sea, resting my elbows on the railings and watching the tide – high tide but on the turn, I thought. The dull-red freight ship on the horizon still hadn't moved. It had been there since I arrived on Thursday.

Kieron was corrupt in some way or another, I was pretty sure about that, but I also had no reason to think he was going to report my financial difficulties – how could he when he was up to his neck

202

in something himself? If I kept quiet about whatever he was up to, he would keep quiet about me. That was the point, wasn't it?

But what he was up to might be really bad – whereas I had just been an idiot. How could I let him continue if my suspicions were correct? It would be the most appalling dereliction of duty. My silence had already been collusive.

But talking of duty . . . I had my mother to think of. The bottom line was this: I had no firm evidence of what Kieron was up to either way, and while Kieron had no idea I suspected him of anything, I had the option of just dropping the whole thing, didn't I?

Turn away.

On the journey home, I was almost happy – it was a train ride of three and a half hours with two changes, but I had decided to carry on doing nothing. That's how easy it was.

I changed trains in London and had time to buy a coffee at Euston. I found a window seat and settled to drink my coffee while the train pulled out. As it did, I watched the backs of flats with their metal balconies overlooking the tracks, the building sites, the scrubby, weed-filled patches of land, all the in-between spaces that I had been so close to falling into. But I hadn't fallen into them and I wasn't going to. I was on a train with a window seat facing forward and nobody next to me so I could put both elbows on the armrests. Just before Watford Junction I saw, across the fields, a pall of black smoke rising from a fire somewhere and felt grateful that whatever it was, it wasn't my problem.

I had to change trains at Rugby. I stood on the platform waiting, still holding the empty coffee cup, and glanced around. All the people standing near to me with their children or their suitcases were just ordinary people standing on a railway platform with coffee or tea in cups or bottles of water or sandwiches and I thought, I'm one of them, an ordinary person. All these months of worrying that I was doing nothing, when all I had to do was decide to do nothing, and then I would feel okay.

Dusk was falling by the time I got home. The flat was only eighteen minutes' walk from New Street. I'd travelled light, as I always did, and stopped off at M&S to pick up some chicken and a bag of greens for my supper. I felt fine as I wandered home, cutting through Chinatown, past the Hippodrome.

My flat was in a brand-new development, with a pedestrianised centre and a series of paths, the blocks comprising layer after layer of dwellings identical to mine occupied by couples or single professionals. The residents I had seen were all much younger than me – they were starter flats for people who had yet to accumulate much furniture, or objects to put in or on the furniture. The walkway to mine was lined by the yellow-brick apartment blocks on either side, with balconies and windows in grey aluminium – my flat was at the far end, just before it opened up into another street.

I turned the corner, then pivoted swiftly into a nearby shop. If you had been observing me, you might have concluded that as I was ambling along, in no particular hurry to be home, I had suddenly remembered a grocery item I really needed.

Once in the shop, I went to the refrigerated cabinet at the back and stood in front of it, looking at the different tubs of margarine as if I liked some obscure brand and was hoping to find it there. After a few seconds, I selected a packet of mature cheddar that I didn't want or need, then turned back to the shop's entrance. By the door, there was a tall rotating stand, sparsely occupied by a few greetings cards in cellophane wrappers. Using this as cover, I was able to look through the glass door of the shop and down the walkway towards my flat. Around half the people in the block had drawn their curtains already and light shone from behind them – the cold grey flicker of television sets.

From my vantage point, I could see my flat – the curtains were open, as I had left them when I departed three days ago, and all appeared to be in darkness.

But I knew what I had seen as I turned the corner into the walkway. My flat was on the upper ground floor and, at the front, had a square-shaped bay that jutted out. I had seen a brief glow, small and mobile, moving around inside my sitting room. I had seen the glow for a fraction of a second before it disappeared, as if a firefly had been snapped inside a box. Fireflies are yellow, though – aren't they, yellow? This was white.

They didn't pull down the blinds because that would have given away that somebody was inside the flat and they couldn't put the overhead light on for obvious reasons.

I calculated the number of seconds it had been from when I turned the corner: I had walked into the shop, one second, gone straight to the back and stood in front of the cold cabinet for maybe three or four seconds to let myself process what I had seen, selected the cheese and walked back to the greetings card stand – another second. I had been standing in this position for two to three seconds – call it eight seconds in total. They would be gone. Either somebody was tailing me or waiting in a car nearby – I didn't have time to observe if there was anyone sitting in a parked car before I went into the shop because I had been looking at my flat and that little fleeting glow from inside. Whoever was inside would have been notified of my imminent arrival, snapped off the torch and left, probably by the back sash window – there's a catch on that window but no extra lock. I'd never needed one because I was on a raised ground floor and there was a basement flat beneath me with a walled courtyard. A couple called Ali and Karim lived there – they invited me once in a while to drink mint tea and eat baklava.

The walkway was empty now. At the far end of it, two cars were parked on the street, not far from my flat, but nobody was inside them. If the lookout had been parked at either this end or the other, they would have driven away while I was reaching for the cheese.

The greetings card rack was on a stand. I turned it slowly, round and round and round . . . it made a soft squeaking noise. I watched the street. Out of the corner of my eye, blurrily, a blue teddy bear wearing a cowboy hat slowly entered and departed my peripheral vision.

The young woman behind the counter was texting and hadn't looked at me.

I watched my flat, still turning the stand. By the time I have paid for my unwanted packet of cheese and walked to my front door, they will be long gone, I thought, melted into the night.

As I left the shop, I took my keys from my pocket and held them in one fist, the sharpest key, the Yale lock of the communal door, protruding between two fingers. A neighbour, a very skinny young man whose name I didn't know, came out of his flat on the other side of the walkway and raised the folded newspaper in his grasp in acknowledgement as we passed each other – I nodded in return.

I looked into the bay window as I mounted the steps at the front but all looked normal inside.

As soon as I entered the flat, I knew I was not mistaken. There was a different quality to the air, a degree or so colder than it should have been – a window was open somewhere. I walked over to the kitchenette at the back and, sure enough, the sash that overlooked Karim and Ali's basement courtyard was raised. Even though the back of the block had always been secure, I was certain I had not left it like that when I departed for my weekend away. I'm not the kind of person that forgets to close a window before leaving the house.

The next thing I checked was the entrance hall cupboard – inside was a scruffy holdall left over from my move, where I was keeping the Nokia and some cash I had been saving, squirrelling away a bit more each week. I looked down at the holdall, squished into the bottom of the cupboard next to the ironing board. Had the handles always been flopped over in that direction? I couldn't remember. I pulled it out, checked the phone, checked the cash – everything was as I had left it, as far as I could tell.

Something else was wrong. I put the lights on and checked under the bed, the wardrobe, every cupboard – even the ones that were far too small for anyone to hide in. Everything looked undisturbed, including my computer and the papers on my desk.

I went into the bathroom and saw immediately: the toilet seat was up. I leaned forward at an angle, tentatively, as if looking over a precipice. The bowl of the toilet was full of yellow piss. Floating in the yellow piss was a cigarette butt. This wasn't a search: it was a warning. I stared down at the cigarette butt, reached out a hand and pushed the flush handle – I watched the water while it churned.

The piss would be gone when the water settled but the cigarette butt would still be floating there. I would be forced to pick it up with my fingers and put it into the bin because that was why it was there, to force me to do that.

Sometimes I think of the seven seconds or so I stood there looking down into the churning water and I think what a pity it is we can't bend time, project forward to make the necessary connections, join up the dots. If we could, I might have been able to see myself in four months' time, standing waist deep in the freezing black water of a Scottish loch on a moonlit night, looking down into the pale face staring back up at me as it floated in the water, and wondering if it was the face of the man who had pissed into my toilet, torn the butt off a cigarette he had no intention of smoking because the smell might alert neighbours there was someone inside my flat and dropped it, lightly, efficiently: all for me to find when I returned from Margate having changed my mind.

18

Later that evening, I called my mother. 'Oh good,' she said, as she answered her phone. 'Nice to know you're back home safely. How was it? The weather wasn't great here.'

I felt a twinge of guilt – I could have taken my mother to Margate with me, after all. She had a good social life but she rarely went away. She loved the seaside.

'Oh, it rained there too but it was still nice,' I said vaguely. 'Mum, I've just been thinking about something I've been meaning to say,' I said. 'I'm really sorry but I can't find that set of keys you gave me, they must have got lost in the move. I thought they would turn up here, that's why I didn't mention it, but they haven't.'

'Don't worry about that.' My mother laughed. 'Nobody is going to want to burgle this place – my telly must be ten years old.'

'I know, but I'd feel happier if we changed the locks, maybe get you some window locks and an alarm while we're at it. I'll pay, it's no problem.'

'I think that would be a bit daft, to be honest.'

'Better safe than sorry.'

'You sound like your father!'

On Monday, I went into the office at 8 a.m. When the others arrived, I had already cleared a load of emails and was sitting with my office door open and my feet up on my desk, eating a cheese and ham baguette I had bought on the way in.

'Good weekend?'

I looked round. Kieron was standing in the doorway. He didn't normally come to ask me how my weekend was.

I did not lower my feet from my desk or swivel my chair. 'Great,' I said, glancing at him while I extracted a long thin piece of cheese and held it above my mouth. 'Fantastic light, that coast. You ever been to Margate?'

He hesitated. 'No, no I don't really know Kent at all.'

I took my feet off my desk, lowered my legs, swivelled, tossed the remainder of the baguette into the bin by my desk. 'That was actually pretty disgusting.' If he was hoping to find me tense or frightened in any way, he would be disappointed. I don't know what my display of bravado was for, exactly, other than I was hoping to discomfort him.

'You should have got it toasted,' he said as he turned away.

Perhaps he didn't know about the warning. Maybe all he had done was say to someone, somewhere, *My deputy is onto something but I'm handling it*. If so, he was not in control of what might happen next. I had some masticated baguette stuck in one tooth – my tongue probed at it. It could not be a coincidence that the break-in at my flat came just after Carmella had seen me in Kieron's office. Perhaps she had made some casual remark, on the Thursday or Friday. 'Heather was keeping your seat warm the other night, you know.' Perhaps she went to him and told him because she knew he would want to know.

After that, I became more careful. I changed the locks on my flat and arranged for a locksmith to come to my mother's house as soon as possible – cue much eye-rolling from her, and remarks about what an incorrigible worrier I was. I installed more encryption on my laptop at home. I varied the walking route I took to and from the office. In the weeks after the break-in, I saw no evidence that I was being watched or followed. Another tranche of money went into my debt and Kieron and I did not speak of it, but continued to be entirely professional with each other: my demeanour round the office was cheerful and relaxed at all times. I was hoping that if I acted like I had got the message, there would be no further threats. It was not a reassuring thought.

One Monday morning meeting as we were all ranged around the table, sorting through our papers before swapping notes on a target of our investigations, Kieron said casually, 'By the way, everyone, you might be interested to hear, it would seem Collins has disappeared.'

We all looked at him.

'What do you mean?' I said. 'He's disappeared, or been disappeared by someone else? I thought he was in custody.'

Kieron kept looking down at his papers, laying them out neatly, side by side, straightening the edges. 'Don't know yet,' he said. 'Just heard on the grapevine that he's gone. Maybe he was co-operating and they relaxed enough to lose track of him, who knows? Maybe they didn't protect him quite as well as they promised.' He picked up a biro from where it lay on the table beside his papers, clicked it on, clicked it off, clicked it on, clicked it off . . . still, he did not look up, but murmured as if he was thinking out loud, 'Which would be pretty awful for poor old Collins, really . . .'

I glanced at Carmella. She did not return my look.

That night, when I got home, I performed my routine check of the flat – the tiny, invisible thread I pasted over the front door each morning and over my cupboards, my laptop. Nothing untoward.

I put a moussaka in the microwave and stood watching it go round and round, listening to the hum of the machine. When the pinging sound came, I did not move for a moment, just stood, stupidly, looking at it.

After my dinner, I went to the cupboard in the hall and extracted the holdall, then took it into the bedroom, where the curtains were already closed, and put it on the bed while I hauled out the plastic bags of clothes I had been collecting, emptying them out onto the bed, then kneeling down to practise my folding technique, working out just how much would fit.

The call came two weeks later, while I was at work, and when I put down the phone I rose steadily from my chair and walked a few paces down the corridor before calling out, clearly and loudly, 'Carmella . . .'

Carmella came out of her office, took one look at my face, and walked swiftly towards me.

Behind her, I could see Kit emerging from the Monitors Room, looking to see what was going on, but I shook my head at him. I only wanted Carmella.

My mother was dead.

I had not phoned her for several days, neither had Tim or Louis. Her body was discovered because the postman noticed that a water bill he had delivered two days previously had not been picked up from the mat and the curtains to the bungalow were still closed at midday. The paramedics broke in and found her in bed. She was lying curled in the foetal position, I was told. There were no signs of forced entry to the bungalow, nothing amiss.

She hadn't seen a doctor in the previous fourteen days and wasn't being treated for any condition, so a post-mortem was done as a matter of course. The results came through within a week and I studied them closely, of course, and phoned the Coroner's office, but there was no doubt. She had an undiagnosed aortic aneurysm. It would have been developing for years. The rupture, her subsequent death, would have been very quick. Better that than a cerebral aneurysm, the doctor told me quite chummily – my own manner had been so brisk and practical that he talked to me like a fellow professional – you get a blinding headache with one of those. Really, with someone as generally healthy as my mother, there was no reason why it should have been picked up any earlier, he added; I shouldn't blame myself, it was just one of those things. Better that than cancer, better than Alzheimer's, the doctor said – a shock for the surviving relatives, but really, for the elderly person themselves, a blessing. He actually used that word.

It hurt me that she died alone, that she had lain undiscovered because neither my brothers nor I had called. But I was glad she was in bed and not on the floor. It was the death my quiet, kind mother deserved.

For a while it was all I could think about, the fact that she was gone, the gone-ness of her, the empty space in the world where she used to be.

I could have taken her to Margate with me. She would have loved that.

At the funeral there was a fine turnout of the friends she had made in her widowhood. (Would I have that many at my funeral? I couldn't help thinking it.) They sat in a row, pale and wan, maybe wondering if they were next up for a swift and unexpected demise. I looked at them and thought about the stories my mother had told me, wondered which of them was which. It was the only way to get through the small speech I made.

I quoted Louis MacNeice, the final stanza of 'London Rain'. I didn't even know if it was one of Mum's favourites, but it felt right. '*My wishes now come homeward, their gallopings in vain . . .*' At the last minute I swerved away from the line about lust and jumped straight to, '*Falling asleep I listen to the falling London rain.*' It was more about me than Mum, of course.

My brother Louis, his namesake, the most beloved of all of us by our mother, I had always felt, came over from Madrid and did the formal eulogy. He and I had a nice, if stilted dinner after – our lives were so disparate, it was all small talk. Tim couldn't get there from the States but arranged for the whole thing to be videoed so he could watch it later. I tried not to resent him, but it was an effort. It wasn't that he hadn't made the journey, that I understood all too well: it was his pretence of involvement.

My mother was a good person and her love was a good love to have, an unobtrusive love. None of us had returned it well enough.

Louis returned to Madrid the morning after the funeral – it was left to me, as her sole executor, to wrap up our mother's affairs. It was not a difficult process: she had left her papers in order – and her possessions too. Any sentimental items from our childhood had already been shipped out to Tim or Louis – the photo albums from our schooldays, some medals belonging to our father.

When I went round to the bungalow the weekend after her funeral, I felt a sweet sadness as I unlocked the extra locks I had had installed on her door – a waste of money, of concern, as it turned out, and yet it comforted me that I had done that for her.

Inside, the house already had the strange stillness of a place uninhabited. It no longer smelt of her.

It didn't take long for me to sort her clothes, her shoes – everything had been left neat and clean and it was simply a matter of me putting things in plastic bags and piling them by the front door in order to do a hit 'n' run on the local charity shop on my way home. I smiled to myself as I opened a drawer of balled-up tights, the neat divide between black tights on one side of the drawer, brown and neutral-coloured ones on the other. I remembered how chaotic and cluttered the old house had been, with five of us in it, the boys screaming around all the time, my father's books, my mother's sewing machine and teaching papers, the big kitchen and the unsteady chairs around the wooden table – when he was eight, Tim cracked his head open on the flagstones after rocking backwards once too often during supper. Years later, you could still see the darkened trace of the blood that had soaked into the mortar between the tiles. Tim used to bring visiting friends of his into the kitchen to show them.

I thought about how neat and tidy my mother became once she downsized, that side of her personality asserting itself with startling rapidity once she was a widow and her children grown. From my – admittedly limited – observations of family life, it appeared you were destined to accumulate a mountain of objects that would peak as the children reached young adulthood. That pinnacle achieved, you were then destined to spend the next two decades shedding the objects you had spent the previous two decades collecting. Unless, like my mother, you downsized drastically and did it in one fell swoop.

In terms of hoarding, my mother had made one exception: her favourite reading matter after poetry, *Gardener's World*. Each month it had arrived in a translucent sheath of biodegradable plastic – and each month she had placed the new edition on top of the pile of old editions next to the sofa, until they had grown into a stalagmite that reached the top of the sofa's armrest. I picked up slithering armfuls of them and transferred them to the hallway, ready for the recycling bin. At the bottom of the stalagmite, anchoring it to the carpet, was a large hardback atlas, a coffee-table atlas of the sort you might order from a Sunday supplement, in a cardboard casing with a shiny picture of a globe on the front.

I picked up the atlas and stood for a moment, holding it and feeling the weight of the world – it was an old edition, I remembered it from my childhood, and my interest in the world came back to me, my curiosity about my father's disappearances, the dolls in national dress. I took it to the dining table and slid it out of its casing – it had a plain navy-blue cover, rough to the touch, with embossed gold lettering: *The Modern World Atlas*. I lifted the cover and flicked through it: the world was such a huge thing. There were so many places in it.

I took a pile of *Gardener's World* out to the recycling bin and as I crossed a patch of damp grass my feet went from under me and the magazines flew from my arms. I landed on my back, so hard that for a moment I could not breathe. My shoulders rose briefly as I gulped in air and breath returned and I realised that, although winded, I had landed as squarely as any gymnast. I may have cried then, for my mother, cried because she was gone and because I was alone.

Afterwards, I lay still, relaxing into the pleasant hiatus that comes in the moments after you have been weeping with grief. The act of being motionless was so intensely pleasurable that I stayed there, allowing my limbs to relax.

The sky above was clear, the air mild and I remembered how, as a child, it felt amazing, magical sometimes, to lie on my back on the grass and gaze up at the great arc of the sky: the small sparkles of white air that twinkled like fairy dust, the cloud strata, the infinite space of it all.

I lay there and breathed.

My mother was gone.

The last thread had unravelled.

I stared at the great curve of the sky.

19

I chose a shop down a small side street in the misshapen hinterland behind New Street Station. It was one of those half-newsagent, half-café places – some groceries and toiletries at the back and two small round tables at the front where you could sit after getting a coffee from the plum-coloured button machine next to the counter.

It was a grey, empty Saturday. As I pushed my way in, dragging a large wheeled suitcase behind me, the young man behind the counter looked up from the textbook he was studying, yellow highlighter in hand. I glanced around. The shop was empty. There was a CCTV camera behind the counter, but I knew I wouldn't find a shop like this without one, so it was a risk I'd have to take.

I parked the suitcase by one of the small round tables at the front of the shop and bought a coffee from the machine, along with a sticky-looking sand-coloured muffin in a plastic wrapper. The young man served me with a nod, a shy smile, then returned to his textbook. I sat at the table and drank the machine-made coffee and forced down a sugary bolus of the muffin, sighing and looking at my watch, long enough for the smiley young man to glance over a couple of times, maybe wonder who I was waiting for. After around twenty minutes and an extra-long sigh, I rose from my seat and walked over to the counter, where I pulled a long face and said to the smiley young man, 'Look, this sounds funny but . . .'

I explained my problem. I had just arrived from London. I was moving to Birmingham at the end of the month. I was supposed to be meeting a friend who was going to take my wheelie case of stuff to her house and look after it for me, but she had childcare issues and couldn't get here for another couple of hours. I wanted to do some shopping but I didn't want to lug my case around. Could I leave it with him, just until lunchtime? I slid a two-pound coin across the counter.

Sure, said the smiley young man, no problem – he could put it in the storeroom; he wouldn't be able to do it if his uncle was around but it was him who was the boss for most of the summer. His uncle was opening another business in Wolverhampton. He tried to refuse the coin, pushing it back at me across the counter, 'No, no, lady, you bought a coffee.'

'I'll buy another one when I get back,' I said cheerily, pushing the coin back his way before I turned to go. 'Seriously, you are really helping me out.'

I went to the station and read *The Times* on a bench for a couple of hours, then returned and collected the case two hours later as promised, buying another cup of coffee and thanking the young man profusely.

Two weeks later, I returned. The young man recognised me, asked me if I'd moved to Birmingham yet, and I said yes, thanks, I'm between the cities, moved half of my stuff, trying to get it sorted. I asked him how his studies were going. He told me he was beginning to think that chemical engineering had been a mistake. He was between his first year and second year and was wondering about physics. He asked about my new flat and I told him I'd got the decorators in and they were driving me crazy. 'I'm still living out of suitcases and the place is full of plaster dust.'

I dropped in a couple of times more, claiming it was on my way to work, and it was on my fourth visit that I asked – look, I've got some boxes I've got to collect from my old place but there's no room in the new place while the builders are still in. It's just junk I really should throw out but I can't sort it until the decorators have gone. I'll give you a tenner a week in cash if you let me leave it with you. Even a small storage unit is going to cost me loads more than that and they want contracts and a three-month minimum and it would really help me out – it's just a couple of boxes.

The nice young man who wasn't sure he wanted to be a chemical engineer, Adil was his name, was more than happy to help.

I brought the boxes round in a cab a week later and Adil helped me carry them from the cab boot and back seat into the storeroom, where they stacked neatly against the far wall. 'Look,' I said, 'if you want to look inside go ahead, just so you know there's no heroin in there.' We both laughed. I was a polite middle-aged lady, small and ordinary-looking: I couldn't be more innocuous. If he did look inside, he would see that the one labelled 'Kitchen Bits' was indeed full of kitchen bits, the few objects I had taken from my mother's kitchen before I got the clearance people to finish up, the favourite things that I had watched her use often: a set of mugs, the gravy boat and, for good measure, the egg slicer she used to cut hard-boiled eggs into neat, uniform slivers that she laid across iceberg lettuce before pouring salad cream on top. There were three boxes in total, medium-sized, none of them sealed, each of them labelled and containing exactly the sort of household junk as described in neat marker-pen capitals on the side. In addition, there was one of those zip-up plastic bags people use to go to the laundry containing bed linen, and the battered grey holdall.

The holdall was the only item I had any plans to retrieve from the shop – the rest of the stuff was just to lend weight to the story.

220

Inside the holdall now was an old, tatty jumper, visible beneath the half-broken zip, and underneath the jumper some spare tops and trousers, underwear, a couple of hoodies. In a side pocket of the holdall was a half-empty carton of tampons, some old scissors, a sliver of soap in a translucent plastic container. Stitched into the lining of the side pocket, beneath the tampons, were the items of fake ID I had acquired in the name of Sophie Lester, the burner phone and the cash.

Vikram was my best bet when it came to legal advice. I had spoken to him several times during the course of my work; usually he represented the kind of people I was trying to pin down and told me he couldn't help. But once, he contacted a colleague of his in London for us and helped the Service open negotiations with someone the colleague was in touch with. I still pretended I was a private detective when I called him, and he still pretended – a little drily at times – that that was what he thought I was. Vikram wasn't daft.

I called him from the car on a Sunday afternoon, when I knew he visited his allotment not far from the village where he lived, which was between Coventry and Solihull.

'Vikram, Rowena here, sorry to bother you on a Sunday . . .' I happened to be passing by, I said, so I was going to drop by the allotment to say hello. It was a personal matter, I was hoping he could find me a solicitor who could do probate for me on my mother's estate as fast as possible.

Vikram gave a small pause on the other end of the line – there was nothing in our previous professional contact that warranted me calling him on a Sunday afternoon, but if you had been listening in on the call you would have gathered from my tone of voice that we were old chums.

'Sure,' he said. 'I've got some iced tea in my mini-fridge – I run it off the car.' His tone mirrored mine: old chums. Like I say, Vikram wasn't daft.

The bit about needing to do the tax form quickly was true. I had put the bungalow on the market, instructing the estate agent to keep the price low, and had had an offer on it immediately, subject to probate. My purchasers were a downsizing, retired couple, cash buyers, who could move immediately. I had already opened an offshore account in which to hide the proceeds when they came through.

My mother's death was saving me in more ways than one, and it was only the peril of my situation that prevented the guilt of that from overwhelming me. It had upset her when I sold the dream house. I had never confided in her the real reason, just said that I had 'taken on a bit much'. The disaster that was my personal finances was far from the only thing about my life I hid from her, after all.

It was a still day – funny, how that detail has stuck. No cloud covered the sky, the sun was unseasonably hot, and there wasn't so much as a whisper of a breeze: it felt as if the weather was holding its breath while it waited to see what I would do next. Vikram and I had talked about his allotment in the past because my parents had had one. He lived in a village called Chadwick End. It was good for commuting, he had said, without mentioning where he commuted to, which made it sound as though commuting was a pastime like clay-pigeon shooting or golf. The allotments were half a mile from where he lived – I parked two streets away all the same and walked there. On a warm day, there would be plenty of people around, so I put on a sun hat that I had in the car.

Vikram had described his plot – the last one on the right, next to the wooden fence, but he had not described how he had turned his shed into a mini home from home. As I approached it, I could see that it was the largest on the allotment, with windows either side of the door that had little net curtains, and in front, next to two deckchairs, a small collection of garden ornaments: a stone angel covered in moss, a wire chicken, a couple of gnomes. I had the feeling the collection was ironic.

Vikram was standing in front of the shed looking out for me. And as soon as we had shaken hands, he said, 'Rowena. Shall we sit inside? Sun is a bit on the hot side, isn't it?'

I nodded, smiling. Vikram was a small man, dark-skinned and curly-haired, with a ready grin – I had a feeling he had spent his life wrong-footing people by being relaxed and friendly, disguising just how sharp he really was. I liked that about him.

'Yes please.'

He went outside and brought in one of the deckchairs.

'I'll get the other,' I said.

'Good,' he said. 'Put it there. I'll get the iced tea.' He disappeared round the back of the shed.

I looked around: shelves with tubs of gardening tools, multiple hooks from which hung spades and forks. At the rear were bags of compost. The shed smelt warm.

He came back in and handed me a plastic bottle of iced tea. We each sat down in a deckchair and he looked at me and said, 'Well?'

'My mother's bungalow was worth more than I thought,' I said, 'but it's still well under the inheritance tax limit. I know we still have to do the form, though . . .'

While I was speaking, I got my phone out of my pocket and held it up for him to look at while I turned it off. I nodded at him.

He got his own phone out of his pocket and did the same. Then he looked at me. 'I confess I'm intrigued,' he said. 'Are you here to tell me you've become gamekeeper turned poacher?'

'In a manner of speaking.'

It occurred to me, while I explained my predicament, to wonder if Vikram would think me some kind of crazed fantasist: I didn't look like one or talk like one, but I might have just been the sophisticated version.

After I had finished speaking, we discussed my legal options. Then he said, 'I have to be honest, Heather, if it is right that this man is as adept as you say, at planting evidence against people, I mean, then you are in trouble. The only people I know of who have defended their positions in the way you will need to are the whistle-blowers who fled abroad.'

'I know,' I said. 'That wasn't an option while my mother was alive, but now . . .'

'Can I turn my phone back on?' he asked. 'I've got a suggestion.'

I nodded.

We waited a moment while his phone came back to life. His finger passed over it, then he lifted it up to show me: family photographs. The first was of three teenage girls with the most beautiful and varied looks – one with jet-black hair and pale features, another with a waterfall of honey-coloured locks but a complexion similar to Vikram's. He could not stop himself beaming with pride. 'My wife

224

is Norwegian,' he said. 'We're the full rainbow.' In that moment, he looked like a man who felt that all was right with the world, that there was no problem he could not solve.

'They are beautiful,' I said with a smile.

'The middle one is a bit of a terror,' he said happily.

He showed me a picture of all five of them together – then another of all five of them on a visit to Norway surrounded by more than a dozen very white blonds. 'My wife's extended family,' he said. 'They live in the north. I think she's related to most of the town, there are hundreds of them.' He pointed at a bulky-looking man at the end of the row. 'He's the black sheep. He's the only one of them who left town, and he just went a few miles up the road.' He talked a bit more about family life in Norway, shaking his head and saying, 'Imagine, she grew up in the fjords, and she ends up in a cul-de-sac in Chadwick End, and know what? She loves it! She says the English countryside is beautiful . . .' He shook his head with the air of a man who could not believe his luck. Then he clapped both hands on his knees, levering himself upwards out of his chair. 'Sangeeta's definitely the best for probate,' he said, 'she'll sort you out in a jiffy. I'll walk you back to your car, did you park by the entrance? Hope you parked in the visitors' bit – the owners get very sniffy if you don't.' He dropped his phone onto his deckchair as we left the hut.

At my car, he rested his hand on the roof while I searched through my pockets for my keys. 'I hope you're wrong, Heather,' he said.

'So do I,' I replied.

'And what if you're not wrong? What then?'

We looked at each other and something passed between us. It

was seeing my own concern mirrored in another person's face. It made everything real.

'I'll be in touch,' I said.

'Do,' he replied. 'Be safe.'

He stood there while I got into my car, lifted my hand, reversed. As I pulled away, he was still watching me with his sweet, relaxed smile, hands in pockets.

Aksel. The black sheep would turn out to be called Aksel.

20

The pastries: the pastries were unusual, and perhaps if I hadn't been hungry I might have noticed this – it was mid-afternoon, a week after my visit to Vikram. I had been working through lunch and hadn't eaten since breakfast, just drunk a lot of coffee.

Kieron never brought in pastries to a meeting.

The signs taped to the wall in our small office kitchen were universal to office kitchens all over the world – I was to be reminded of them later when I stayed in the B&B on Skye. 'If you are the last to leave in the evening, please turn out the light' or, 'Fridge emptied every Friday' and, the battle cry of office managers everywhere, 'Wash your own cups and mugs!!!'

'Pastries,' I said as I came into the kitchen where Carmella was filling the kettle. A thin bag sat on the countertop next to a large plate, the grease from its contents bleeding through, darkening the paper.

'Croissants,' Carmella corrected me tonelessly. 'Kieron brought them in for the meeting.'

If I had been more attentive, less hungry, I might have picked up something in her voice, but instead I was remembering that, a while back, I had seen some of those little plastic cartons of jam, the kind of thing you steal from a hotel breakfast buffet, in one of the cupboards.

'Bloody hell, what's got into him?' I said as I opened and closed cupboard doors, and when I remember doing that now I feel as though a great swan was batting its wings in my face and I didn't even notice. 'Must be some announcement coming.'

While Carmella boiled the kettle to fill the cafetiere, I opened the bag and slid the croissants onto the plate with the same reflex of helpfulness that we were both guilty of around the office, despite our seniority. Then, having failed to locate any jam, I leaned against the counter and ate one of them, holding it in one hand and tearing off pieces with another, popping them into my mouth and watching Carmella make the coffee. She seemed quiet. She wasn't looking at me.

She poured the contents of the kettle into the cafetiere, and I watched the swirl of boiling water fall onto the black grit of coffee grounds and the steam lifting out of the glass and wondered what was going on. In a tone of voice that sounded rather lame even to me, I said, 'No lunch.'

She smiled with her lips pressed together. Then she glanced behind me and said in a low, quick voice, 'Have you heard the rumour?'

'No, what?' I asked.

She stepped towards me and her voice took on a sudden husky urgency. 'Collins. I asked a contact in the DOS what the story was, off the record. Officially, nobody knows what has happened to him.'

I looked back at her.

'Heather, listen – unofficially, they think he's dead. Rumour is he wouldn't co-operate, total denials, so the DOS let him go and passed the details of his whereabouts on.'

'On to who?'

Her face looked wretched, full of things she was not allowed to say.

Kieron bustled into the room, clapped his hands together, saw me with a half-eaten croissant in my hand and gave me a happy look.

I lifted it apologetically. 'No lunch,' I said again.

Normally, this would draw a sarcastic remark from Keiron, but instead he said, 'You've plated them, marvellous!'

He took the plate and in a small, dense movement, turned and lifted his hand to gesture us into Alaska with a briskness that said, quite unmistakeably, *Well let's get on with it then.*

Carmella turned back to the counter, added the cafetiere to the tray with the white cups and saucers and picked it up, carried it through. Kieron followed her.

'*Plated,*' I said out loud to the empty room. 'Is that even a verb?'

I pulled a face, swallowed the last of the croissant and bent to brush the flakes of pastry from my skirt.

It was carefully choreographed, I realise that now. He spent the first hour of a three-hour meeting on the results of the Statistical Threat Analysis survey for the West Midlands region and then announced, when we were all losing concentration, that there was something else we had to discuss.

'Right,' he said, lifting the sheaf of papers in front of him and tapping the bottom edges of them once on the table before putting them to one side. 'You'll have to forgive me for springing this on you all.'

We all looked at him. He rested both forearms on the table, knitted his fingers, leaned forwards slightly with a solemn air – but he didn't look at any of us in particular.

His tone was apologetic, but there was no indication of the full seriousness of what he was about to say – I thought he was about to tell us that an urgent investigation had come in and we would have all leave cancelled for the next six weeks, which sometimes happened.

'I'm sorry to say this . . .' His voice slowed. We all looked at him. 'I hope you all understand this is out of my control.'

He had our attention now – but still, I did not guess.

Opposite me, Carmella was looking down at the table.

'The DOS has slapped a Section HD4 notice on us, all of us, effective immediately, effective as of now.'

Our department was being frozen. We were being frozen. We were all to be placed under investigation.

I had been present when this had happened in other offices, when investigating officers walked in as the announcement was being made and everybody had to take their hands from their keyboards immediately and rise from their chair, touching nothing on their desks, while the goons went from person to person, holding evidence bags, noting everything they put in them, divesting each individual of all communication devices, even watches. I wondered if, while we were all sitting in Alaska around the glass-topped table, they were already waiting in the corridor outside. That would explain why Kieron had spent an hour on the Statistical Threat Analysis survey – to give them time to assemble.

I wondered if Kieron was scanning us discreetly for our reactions. I could tell that my face was registering the same blanket shock as everybody else but I, of course, was the one who had least cause to be shocked.

Kieron got to his feet and walked the two paces to the floor-to-ceiling window, taking his coffee on his saucer with him. He gazed out at the vast grey stretch of Birmingham, lifting the cup to his

lips in a leisurely manner that suggested to me he was performing
for our benefit, in order to give us time to absorb what he had just
told us. I used that time to listen hard to the acoustics outside the
room. As far as I could detect, there was no one in our offices or the
corridors. Not yet. It would be difficult for them to enter our offices
without being heard by any of us inside the room. They could be
waiting outside the windowless double doors that led to the lift
area, of course, or they could be downstairs. Or Kieron could be
exaggerating the whole thing for his own purposes, as yet unknown.
He could be bluffing, to see how we would all react. *No, to see how
I would react.*

Kieron turned and placed the coffee cup in its saucer back on the
table, then pivoted smoothly, reached out his left hand and placed
it lightly on Carmella's shoulder, tightening the fingers in a gentle
squeeze.

I stared at Carmella.

Carmella looked back at me and although it was only momentary, the message in her gaze, the fear, could not have been
more obvious.

Go. Go now while you still can.

PART 3

Anyone with more than one excuse is almost certainly a liar.

John le Carré, letter to Stanley Mitchell,
6 January 2001, *A Private Spy: The Letters of John le Carré*

21

The truth is in the picture. But the picture is never quite the same picture whenever I look at it. Sometimes, what I see – with a certain failure of logic – is myself, rising from my chair by pressing lightly on the table with the fingertips of both hands. Did I mutter 'Excuse me a minute'? Or 'Just going to the loo'? Or did I say nothing at all as I turned to the door? They must have all looked at me, but I don't see their faces: I see mine.

At other times, what I see is the coffee cup in Kieron's hand, descending as he lowered it. In the images I have of that meeting, he lowers it again and again.

Staring at a memory should be like staring at a painting – if you wanted to peer at what is going on in the bottom left-hand corner, you could just look, but the pictures in our heads don't work like that.

It's two and a half hours from Plockton to Inverness. Around halfway through the journey, I leave my coat on my seat and the rucksack in the rack above me and go to find the toilet at the back of the little two-carriage train: the other people in my carriage look like locals and there's an unsmiling elderly lady sitting diagonally opposite me. Nobody is going to nick anything.

Was he on the train? Did I go past him as I made my unsteady way to the loo? The train was half empty until we got much closer to Inverness. Surely I clocked each passenger out of habit – I don't remember doing it but it's instinctive and I don't recall not doing it either – yet in my memory there is no young man with pale skin and dark hair, slumped in his seat, maybe with a hood up. I was thinking about Flavia, and about Alaska, but surely I did not neglect to notice who else was on the train? He may not have been there at all, of course.

I return to my seat, to staring out of the window. As we pull into Achanalt, it comes to me: it was the way Kieron put his hand on Carmella's shoulder, that was what was odd.

Kieron is right-handed, and was holding his saucer and cup in his right hand. Carmella was sitting on his right. The normal thing would have been to put the coffee cup down on the table, then pat her shoulder with his right hand as he sat down – but the way he pivoted suggests to me, now I think about it, that his instinct was to put his hand on her as quickly as possible. She and I are staring at each other across the table. He wants to get to her, to give her shoulder that light squeeze – was it for reassurance? *You've done the right thing.* Was it a threat?

When Carmella looked at me – perhaps I over-interpreted the *run* I saw in her eyes, but what was unmistakeable was pain. I liked her, she liked me, and she knew something I didn't. Kieron's announcement was no surprise to her, I'm sure of that now. He told her beforehand that our department was about to be put under investigation, and that I was the chief suspect. She could not warn me of that – but she could hiss to me in the kitchen: the rumour about Collins.

When I arrive at Inverness, it is to find bright sunshine overhead and the streets shiny after recent rainfall, as if the whole city has been washed thoroughly just before I got there. It's a short walk to the bus station, which is unlikely to appear in any tourist guide to the must-see places in Scotland, but it's good to be here – this is the last leg of my journey to the furthermost point of the British mainland.

I buy a one-way ticket to Thurso – it's going to take four hours and it will be dark by the time I get there. I will have to find somewhere to stay by turning up on the off-chance, or sleep rough like I did the first night on Skye, but the thought that the next day I will get a ferry that will finally take me away from the British mainland is making me careless with excitement. Dawn should break some time between six and seven at this time of year. If I have to kip in a field outside Thurso tonight, it's not the end of the world.

A queue of five of us has built up by the time the driver opens his doors – he lets us onto the bus even though there is another twenty minutes till departure, then he gets on himself and leaves the door open. A fellow driver comes to chat with him while the bus waits: they are talking about bus spotters. I didn't know there are bus spotters like train spotters, but apparently so. Our driver is complaining that one took his picture the other day. 'Had it up on UK Bus Spot in minutes.' I am reminded, not for the first time on my flight, that there will come a time, soon perhaps, when everyone and everything is surveilled.

Would I really not have noticed him on the bus? Could I have been that careless? I had a good view of everyone who got on and off during the journey. Nobody rang alarm bells.

I have a picnic with me, the finest Inverness Bus Station has to offer: a ham and cheese sandwich, a can of orange Fanta and a packet of crisps. I crack open the Fanta and crisps before we depart but decide to save the sandwich in case I need it for an emergency breakfast in the morning – perhaps I can get a proper meal in Thurso, if the bus arrives on time. I feel like meat, and a glass of red wine. My mood is almost celebratory.

Just before we depart, a young woman gets on the bus and offers a ticket. The driver asks for her student discount card. She reddens and hands over something from her pocket. The driver looks at it, thinks for a minute, then says, 'Have you got another one of these at home?'

The young woman gives a mute nod. 'You've brought the wrong one with you,' he says, 'the out-of-date one. Never mind, remember next time.' Our driver is a man who not only lets a young woman on his bus when he shouldn't, he invents a narrative to spare her humiliation. I feel in safe hands as he turns the huge steering wheel and the big yellow bus bumps and grumbles its way out of the station, heading north.

We are out of the city and tanking along a straight road that slopes gently downwards, forestry either side, mountains in the distance. Soon we are crossing a huge loch on a long, low-lying bridge, water either side. I glance around and see that the woman across the aisle from me is reading a paperback, and I think how in every part of the world that is outstandingly beautiful, the tourists come and gawp without regard to the people who live in it, who have lives to be lived – and hasn't my flight made me quite the philosopher? I don't remember having time for profound thoughts when I had a full-time job that meant I neglected my friends, my mother. Not much time for staring out of windows then.

We pull into Dornoch and park up for ten minutes so that various amongst us, myself included, can use the loo – that Fanta has gone right through me. Later, I doze for a bit and wake at Lybster, where I see the sea directly ahead through the windscreen as the bus pulls round the little square houses – it feels as though we are dropping some people at their door.

As we leave Lybster, dusk begins to gather and I feel a growing discomfort, a restlessness. Perhaps it is the fading light, but from this point on, the journey time seems to extend, our destination more distant with each passing mile, and before long, it takes on a hallucinatory quality. We are winding round the coast of the very top end of the British mainland now: expanses of water, glimmering in the gloom, appear first on one side of the bus and then the other. I am hungry and disorientated. Why are bus journeys so much more exhausting than train journeys? I wonder. Something to do with fear of death, I guess.

The dusk goes on forever. The houses are mostly grey and low, built to crouch down from the wind. There aren't even any sheep in the fields. We do several more stops in Wick to let people off in the growing gloom and a couple more people get on. Everyone seems to know each other.

Eventually, we arrive at Thurso. Darkness has fallen. The few remaining passengers descend with me and the yellow bus pulls away. My fellows melt into the night. I feel as if I have come to the ends of the earth.

I am alone in a town of solid stone buildings and I should probably begin a trek around to find a guest house, but I'm hungry and more tired than I should be considering I have just spent four hours sitting down. The plastic sandwich squashed into my rucksack holds

239

no appeal. Behind me, back down the street, I can see a warm glow from a small restaurant, the only thing open in a strip of shops. My feet take me there.

The small restaurant is completely empty. I wonder if they are about to close, but a very young waitress comes forward with a smile as I enter and gestures me towards a round table just inside the door. She hands me a menu while she talks through the specials of the day. I can't believe I have got all the way here when I was on Skye only this morning and I would like to brag about it, but instead, I order gratefully. A large glass of Malbec arrives on my table with pleasing rapidity. The bowl of the glass is broad in my palm, the wine dense and flavoursome. It warms me from the pit of my stomach.

I am tucking into a plate of beef, braised for three days, according to the waitress, and it's falling apart in my mouth in a very satisfying manner, when two handsome middle-aged men come into the restaurant and, seeing another late diner, greet me as warmly as if we are friends, before sitting down two tables away and starting to talk about power stations. I eavesdrop as I eat, and from their conversation guess that they are work colleagues, one somewhat senior to the other, doing a tour of local electricity-generating sites. They glance over at me from time to time. They have an air of availability – perhaps they've been travelling for a while and are bored of each other's company. One of them in particular is sending me open looks and I know that if I walked by their table on my way to the toilet, he would say something to engage me in conversation, maybe invite me to join them for a drink. It wouldn't mean anything in particular, it would be just light entertainment, but I feel a fleeting pang of regret that it isn't possible. The beef and the Malbec have lulled me. I am thinking as if I am normal.

Outside the window, it is now very dark. I ask the waitress for the bill, and when she brings it over I ask about guest houses, keeping my voice low. I don't want the men to hear where I am being directed: a certain amount of caution has re-established itself. The waitress is local, of course, and it's a small enough town. She makes two suggestions and I memorise her directions. There's one that sounds a bit out of town, but she describes how to get to it along a road that runs parallel to the sea. It's a big old house, she says, run by an elderly couple, and they always have room.

Outside the restaurant, I shoulder my rucksack, and as I cross the road, I glance back at the small glow of it. Perhaps the thought I had then was a kind of premonition. *Should I go back and talk to those two fellas, after all?* The restaurant was warm; inside it, I was safe.

The heavy meal has made me sluggish – I hope I can find the guest house quickly. I imagine myself in a wide, cosy bed – I will be asleep within minutes. I walk in the direction the waitress described, along the dark streets of Thurso. No one else is around. The occasional car passes, but I'm the only person on foot; it's often the case in small towns where everybody needs a car to get anywhere. To my right is the distant rumble of the sea, audible as a bass note beneath the high alto of the wind.

It is cold now. The moon is a pale smudge behind the cloud. The waitress described a narrow side street to the left at the point where a wall ends – five minutes' walk up that, she said, just past the postbox, is the guest house. I turn at what I think is the right place and suddenly am bathed in the icy white glow of a security light – I'm halfway up someone's drive. From inside the house, directly ahead of me, there comes ferocious barking. I do a brisk U-turn, hoping that the householder isn't the type to release the dog to investigate. I get back to the main road with my heart thumping a little faster and increase my pace, so much so that as the houses become sparse I begin to think that, in the darkness, I must have missed the side street altogether.

I stop where I am.

The night is dark; the wind blows; the street is empty. Should I go back to find the guest house, or press on and find a sheltered spot to sleep rough, out of town? I can head to the ferry terminal at first light, after all. I'm longing for a bed, but some instinct is making me feel unwilling to turn and head back into town. Have I let the barking dog spook me?

Something is wrong.

On my right, a stone wall stands between me and the sea, which is lost in the darkness, invisible. I can hear the waves crashing onto a pebble beach, a whooshing sound followed by a low rumble as the retreating breakers drag pebbles and stones back into the water. On the left, the buildings have thinned to almost nothing – there are a few low, square houses set back from the road. Ahead of me, the road is swallowed by the night. I turn and look behind me. All is darkness, shadows. Around a hundred yards back, there is a black vertical stripe of a lamp post with a small, contained pool of light at its foot. The wind blows and the waves crash and I know I have no alternative but to keep walking and see if there is a place ahead, where the town gives way to fields, because if I stay far enough ahead it will be so dark out

242

there, I will be able to hide. There's no doubt about it. I feel it in my bones. I am being followed.

I am no more than a mile out of town but there's no light pollution out here; the night is pitch black. The wind is still blowing. I turn away from the sea to strike out across the fields. The sound of the waves fades away as I head into the open countryside and I can hear the breath in my throat. Above me, clouds scud across the night sky and every now and then the darkness is briefly illumined by a glint of moonlight, enough to see the landscape ahead: then the glimmer fades as another cloud drifts across the moon.

I run, stumbling on the uneven ground, the tufts of grass. As long as I put enough distance between me and him, I will be able to hide. He'll never find me in this pitch-black night. Looking behind me will slacken my pace – I will do it only when I have found somewhere to shelter. Now I am away from the sea and all is quiet, all I can hear above my breathing is the scruffing noise of my rucksack on my back as I run, the thin tinny jangle of some loose change in my pocket – in the silent, starless night, these small noises seem deafening. I have set up a steady pace, though. I'm fit, and I know I can keep it up a long time.

The clouds shift across the moon again and in the brief glow I see, less than half a mile away, a small loch shaped like an oval platter lying flat in the fields, with a rim of trees on the far side and a row of rocks to the left of the shoreline. It's the only cover for miles: apart from that, the fields stretch unbroken. I need to reach the rocks. As I head for them, I risk a glance behind – do I see him then, a moving shape in the distance, back towards the path, something darker against the dark?

For a moment, I doubt myself; perhaps I am fleeing from shadows. Maybe, when I find somewhere to hide and the thumping of my heart slows, I will laugh at my mistake – and as I nestle down to sleep, somewhere, I will shake my head and reflect that I've let the loneliness and anxiety get to me. Maybe. But I can't risk stopping to be sure.

The soles of my boots slam against pebbles – I slip and stumble. I have come to the end of the field and reached a shingle slope that leads down to the loch: if I head towards the rocks at speed my boots will make a crashing sound against the stones – but the alternative is to go back and then strike out left or right across an open field, and if there *is* anyone behind me, they will catch me then. I'm fit and strong but I'm a small woman with a heavy rucksack – the hard reality of that is sending adrenaline coursing through me. I have no choice but to run across the shingle; it feels as though the crunch of my boots on the stones rings out across the countryside. I can only hope it's an aural illusion born of fear.

When I reach the rocks, I crouch down behind the largest and slip my rucksack from my shoulders. I peer round the rock, across the shingle, up the rise and to the open field beyond. All I can see is blackness, but I can't stay here. It's too obvious a place to hide and only a couple of rocks are large enough to crouch behind. If he spotted me heading this way, I'll be easy to find. I scrabble with the openings of the rucksack's side pockets, feeling a smooth wooden handle, grasping for the things I cannot afford to leave behind. My wad of cash, false passport and debit card are all in the same Ziploc bag, which I shove into the left-hand pocket of my waterproof and zip securely, calculating the loss of what I am about to abandon, recalibrating. I might be able to come back for it – but for now, all that matters is speed.

After a moment or two, my pockets now full, I stay low and leave the shelter of the rock to head towards the shore – a row of bushes lines the approach to the trees. If I can make it to that, I should be impossible to spot as I head towards the cover of the wooded area.

I am no more than two metres away from the bushes when a cloud slides away from the moon and silver light illuminates the stretch of shingle I am trying to cross. I turn.

He is standing around fifty metres away, at the top of the rise. His silhouette suggests he is wearing a close-fitting coat of some sort. The hood is up, and tightened, making a smooth oval outline of his head. He must have a beanie hat on underneath it because the silhouette of his head seems disproportionately large. He stands with his legs slightly apart, braced. He is holding something in his right hand.

The moonlight is full now. It makes the shingle slope between us glow wet-black as it rises and levels in shallow steps.

Behind me is the loch. The water is soundless and the wind has dropped. All I can hear is my own breath.

I am facing him as he stands on the ridge looking down and although I can't see his expression, I know he is looking at me. The sky behind him is dark but his silhouette is darker still, a hard shape against a velvet blur. My father was always afraid of the moon.

This is how it happens, I think, by the side of a small loch in the middle of nowhere in Scotland, on the furthermost reaches of the main island of the British Isles. Five decades of life, two of them in a profession I inhabited too well, all my mistakes and selfish behaviour, months of indecision followed by two weeks of flight – and it has all culminated in this place, this moment. I think of all the diversions and hesitations that have led me here: the four days

I spent echoing around an empty flat in Glasgow, the pilgrimage to Plockton, the bus journey, even the meal I ate earlier when I sat in a restaurant for over an hour at a table next to a glass door . . . In my thoughts, the trail that has led here; my whole life, in fact, is condensed into this one distinct realisation: everything I have ever done, every choice I ever made, was leading up to this moment. I was so close to escaping. I have come to the end. I have been found.

The wind picks up. I hear it on the surface of the loch; the water behind me gives a small shush and sigh. My chest heaves and falls, filling my lungs with air. I was afraid, as I crouched down behind the rocks, but now, looking at him, I have reached a place beyond fear, a place where practice and resolution join and I think with cold clarity. Here, right in this moment, I experience neither fear nor panic but an intense sense of my own alive-ness.

He stands above me, a stark cut-out of a figure, motionless. He is waiting to see what I will do.

I cannot go left or right – if I run along the shoreline he will cut me off at a diagonal. I have only one choice. I turn and stride into the loch, splashing loudly as I stretch my legs against the drag of the cold water. I hear the crunch of the shingle as he runs down the slope towards me. My only hope is to get as far out as possible and pray he is a weaker swimmer than me – I reach inside my pocket.

The stones beneath my feet give way to soft mud. I struggle against it, slipping and sliding. The edge of the loch is so shallow that the water is only up to my waist when I hear him right behind me, splashing through it. I stretch out and try to kick off against the mud so I can swim, but my feet gain no purchase and I hear a swoosh, a grunt, as I feel him catch hold of a handful of my coat on my left shoulder, yanking me backwards and pulling my head down beneath the water. I close my mouth just in time and the water rushes over me, fills my ears, shocks me to the core, but I force my eyes open to look up and see his face looming above, just above the surface, a white face, blank and intent, dark eyes staring. He has bent his head down close to watch me as I drown. Our faces are inches apart and yet he is above, breathing air, and I am underneath and the surface of the water is the border between life and death. Our eyes meet as he brings his other hand to push me further down. I have no more than seconds before he wins by sheer strength and I summon everything I have ever felt hatred for, all the men like Kieron, Michael – even Richard and my father, even the ones who thought they were okay – and Flavia's fate, that split-second thing that shouldn't have happened, my hatred for that; every ounce of training and determination and strength I have ever possessed goes into my right arm as I push up against the mud with my feet, propel my arm above the surface of the water and drive the chisel directly into his left eye.

His arms lift and fling wide on either side as he releases me. He makes a terrible sound as he goes backwards, an inarticulate cry of horror, shock and pain. I am upright and on him immediately, and as I push him down, as he was pushing me just a moment ago, I feel no hesitation, no panic, just cold determination. The chisel sticks out of his eye like something obscene; his arms flap weakly just beneath the surface – he is losing strength very quickly. He shakes his head frantically, once to the left, once to the right, the chisel comes loose and blood pours out of the hole I have made of his eye, dissipating into clouds in the water. I feel nothing other than determination. It is hard to make somebody die but I am relentless. If I had struck his cheek or missed his head altogether, or not driven

247

the chisel hard enough, I would be dead by now. Air bloats his cheeks, then his mouth opens wide and his final breaths float out as large bubbles. Soon, he is still.

I wait until I am sure there will be no more bubbles. And then I wait some more. His face is around six inches beneath the surface of the water. His hood has fallen back and his beanie hat slipped off, somewhere in the water. His arms are spread and floating loose and lifeless, but I hold him there, my arms iron with pain, one hand on his upper arm, the other cradling his head, holding and observing him, the silky feel of his hair laced through my fingers. How long do I stand there like that? Time has come adrift from meaning. It is not enough to wait until I am sure he is dead. I have to wait until I am sure he is dead and there is time for him to come back and then be dead again. His lungs have emptied of air and his feet are dangling down to the silty surface of the lake, but still I hold him there in the shallow water.

The night is silent and still. He is dead. I am alone again.

In the moonlight I see that the water around him is dirty and disturbed. Even though I am certain he is dead, I don't want to lift his face above the surface but I have to. Blood has pooled in the hole that was his eye socket. His hair is black, he has a boxer's nose and his lips are full. His skin looks very white but maybe that's the moonlight. It is a blank kind of face, like the faces you see on captured soldiers when they are shown on television, an unremarkable face, you could say, perfect for a hired assassin, a face you would have no reason to remember.

I hold two fingers against his neck. He is definitely dead. I let go of his head, allowing the body to turn in the water, but keep hold of a handful of his coat at the shoulder as I haul him towards the shoreline. There will be plenty of large stones to fill his pockets. Once I've done that, I can drag him out with his pockets full. That will be okay while I am still in my depth, but what then? I'm a strong swimmer, but if I try and swim him out to the middle of the lake with his pockets full of stones, the weight will drag us both down. I need a large, spreading branch, from one of the bushes perhaps, to act as a float while I swim him out to the middle of the loch.

Already, I can feel the adrenaline begin to drain – I must not allow that to happen, for then I will be done for, and I need him as far out into the loch and as far down in the water as I can physically manage. I pull him back towards the shore so I can leave him on the shingle while I go hunting for a branch, not too thick but with a lot of spreading twigs, and large enough to form a small raft. I must take care not to swim so far out that I will lose the energy to swim back, or there will be two corpses in the lake before dawn.

I haul him up the shingle by his shoulders. His legs are still in the water but he's far enough up that he won't drift away; the water only reaches his waist. In the gloom, at a glance, it is as if the lake is eating him from the feet upwards. He's face up and I am trying not to look at him now. Instead I rummage in the pockets of his coat, a dark-grey puffa jacket. I am hoping for a phone or a sodden leather wallet that might give me some clues but I find nothing – he must have a bag hidden somewhere out there in the dark. The only thing I find is a knife with a retractable blade, folded and placed in an outside pocket. This was his fatal error. He saw a small, unarmed woman running into the water in a panic and he thought, I don't need the knife for that, I'll hold her head beneath the water. Better to drown me instead of stab or strangle me, in case my body is ever found, and he was confident he could do it without leaving marks. I wonder if he thought all those thoughts as he ran towards me, so certain of how easy I would be to catch, to kill.

I sit beside him for a moment, my knees raised, breathing deeply, but as I begin to shiver I force myself to my feet and think, *Find the branch, quickly, while you still can, while you still have the strength to swim him out to the middle of the loch. Take your shoes and coat off before you go back in – you were only fully submerged for a moment and the money and passport are zipped in a waterproof pocket. Afterwards, retrieve your rucksack from behind the rocks and get some dry clothes on as quickly as you can, or you'll risk exposure.*

The moonlight seems brighter now. Winter moon, I think, even though it's only September: we never associate the moon with summer, after all. The scene is clearly illuminated, should there be anyone around to see, but we are alone here, me and him. As I get to my feet, I look back out across the loch where the moon creates a shimmery, rippled pathway to the dark centre and I see a small shape, floating in the middle of the reflected light. For a moment I think it is the chisel that I stole from the empty rental flat in Glasgow and have just used to kill a man – then I think, that wouldn't float, it must be his beanie, or a twig, or leaf, or something. A cloud slides over the moon and it disappears again.

22

Dawn torments me. It nearly comes, and nearly comes, and I'm lying between two trees on a bed of bracken, more bracken pulled over me, my arms wrapped tight around my torso but shivering, shuddering, so much so that it doesn't feel like the shivering you do when you are cold, which is external, but as if it comes from inside me, radiating out. As soon as the light is certain, I force myself to rise. If I don't move, I'll die.

My rucksack is propped against a tree trunk. I try to lift it onto my shoulders but I can't stop shaking and have to drop it again. On the ground beside me, the wet clothes from the previous night are lying, still sodden, on a patch of stony earth. I should fold them and put them inside a plastic bag and take them with me, but I can't bear to. I know I will never wear them again. I cover them with bracken and leave them there. Then I pick up my rucksack by its straps and drag it over to where a low horizontal branch sticks out, waist height, from one of the firs. I can just about hoist the rucksack onto the branch, then turn, crouch a little, and slip my arms into the shoulder straps. I need to pause for a moment, take a deep breath, before I tip forward and straighten, taking the weight of it onto my shoulders. The trek back into Thurso seems unimaginably hard in that moment. I could walk to Scrabster, to the ferry terminal, in half an hour under normal circumstances, but in my current state I doubt I'll make it. I need something to eat, a hot drink inside me. I'm in delayed shock, and possibly the early stages of exposure. I diagnose myself dispassionately.

I stay the other side of the trees as I trudge slowly away from the loch, but as I come to the end of the woods and head up the rise, back towards Thurso, I stop and look across the water.

The loch seems small and shallow in the daylight – I hope it's deeper than it looks from here. It felt deep last night, when I was treading water in the middle of it in the moonlight. I turned his body so that it slipped soundlessly off the branch, and in an instant it went down, down, down . . . I kicked away immediately, using the branch as a float, flailing my legs to propel me to the shore. Even though there was no doubt he was dead, I could not shake the fear of a hand reaching up through the icy water to grasp my ankle, drag me down. When I finally got back to the shingle beach, I stayed there on my hands and knees for a long time, shaking and shuddering like a dog that has emerged from the water having nearly drowned.

I force myself to scan the loch in the early-morning light, its cool, innocuous glimmer. The water is pale grey. How dreadful it will be if I see the dark shape of a body floating on the surface . . . and what will I do then? But there is nothing. The loch is smooth and unbroken as a mirror. He is at the bottom, where no sun will penetrate. He is amongst the weeds and mud and silt, his lungs full of water and his flesh already mottled. He will decompose more slowly than he would in the open air, but it's a freshwater not a salt lake and a degree of stagnation will provide plenty of bacteria. He'll be bones in three weeks.

I skirt Thurso so that I can walk into the town on the same road that the bus came in on the previous night – I remembered a small row of shops about half a mile before the bus stop; I'm sure there was a café. I will have to wait until it's open. I find a small brick bus shelter not long after I enter the town, covered in graffiti and disused, with a long wooden bench against the wall and a distinct tang of urine in one corner. I daren't lie down in case someone comes by, but I sit on the wooden bench and stretch my legs out in front of me, crossing my arms and leaning back against my rucksack. I close my eyes. I don't exactly doze, but enter some semi-conscious, catatonic state, a mockery of rest.

Eventually, I rouse myself and head towards the shops. The café is at the end of the row but before I get there, I pause and lean against a stone wall, wondering what I look like. Did I kill somebody, the previous night? Did that actually happen? Images flash in my head. I stay where I am for a while and then think, as coldly as I can: you're still in shock. You haven't eaten and your blood sugar must be catastrophically low. You've had no sleep. Don't do anything quickly, you aren't in any fit state.

As I lean against the wall, I hear a noise – a crash and a tinkle, but sonorous, something being smashed. I have a bodily reaction to the sound, more than a flinch, a clenching in of myself. It may not be the sound of someone being attacked, or even a house being burgled or a car being stolen but it is, unmistakeably, the sound of damage being done.

It is coming from an alleyway behind me. I take a few steps down, where, to the right, a gate hangs open, leading through to a tiny backyard with flagstones. There is a wooden crate sitting on a bench. And there is a young man with a beard dressed in jeans and a white T-shirt with a brown apron on top. The young man is picking up items of crockery from the crate and smashing them against the flagstones. I notice that next to the crate on the bench there is a

253

hammer – he could be smashing the items with the hammer and that way he would keep all the bits inside the crate, but maybe he is worried about shards of crockery flying up into his face or maybe he has decided doing it this way is more satisfying. There's a certain aplomb in the way he lifts an item and pauses for a second, gazing down at the rough Victorian flagstones at his feet in a moment of homage towards the damage he is about to do.

He picks up a blue cereal bowl with white spots, holds it – down it goes. It breaks neatly in two. Next, he holds a dinner plate, a garish abstract pattern in red and green and yellow. With this item, he puts a bit of welly behind it – it descends at speed and smashes into multiple shards with a compressed sort of crackle, an immensely satisfying sound, it would seem from the expression on his face. One of the shards bounces towards me. He looks up from his task and sees me stopped in the gateway. Noticing the question in my gaze, he says, 'They don't come back for them. We have to smash the rejects. We give it months, like, but we don't have the space.' Then he shrugs as if I've asked a question. 'I sweep it all up, of course.'

As I turn and walk back down the alleyway to the street, I hear him resume smashing items on the ground. The sound follows me. It is accusatory.

In the street, I see that the shop the yard belongs to is one of those decorate-your-own pottery places – you paint a mug or a plate or a sugar pot and leave it with the shop to be glazed and fired. In the window is a long trestle table hosting a child's birthday party – I wonder why they aren't in school then realise it's a Saturday. Eight or so children sit around the table, each at work on a plain matt-white squirrel. The child nearest to me, a girl of around nine, is taking her task very seriously – her squirrel is brown and she is adding some grey to the tail using a fine brush, her shoulders dropped and tongue protruding in concentration. The boy next to her is painting his squirrel a mad blue-all-over and looking bored. Pretty soon, I think, he'll pick it up and smash it himself.

At the end of the trestle table is a mother, supervising the children, looking anxiously from one to the other – glancing at the clock then back at them, waiting for the moment, I'm guessing, when she will be able to relinquish her duties and return her charges to their parents. She wears a cherry-red cardigan with pearly buttons over neat jeans. There is a kind of perfection in her bored anxiety: she plays the part of arty but slightly harassed mother very well, so well she has forgotten that she was ever anything else. There was a primary school at the end of my road when I lived in London and I used to see mothers like her congregating at pick-up time. They looked like the kind of women who should have been running multinational oil companies, but instead had chosen to put all that energy into organising the candyfloss stall at the summer fete. They frightened the life out of me.

As I stand there, the mother looks up and I see the involuntary shock on her face – it's only momentary, then she composes her expression. The window holds my reflection, translucent, layered over her fleeting but plain distaste. Her expression, and what I can see of myself, combine to tell me what I look like now: a mad person, homeless, thin and dirty, with matted hair and a stark expression that says to her, *No, you're not imagining it, I do hate you for your privileges. I do.*

Dear God, I think, as I turn away from the shop and head to the café. It's there on my face, what I have done. I walk away from her startled stare. Will everyone be able to tell, just by looking at me? It's a disordered thought, I know that, but I feel marked.

Something about the combination of the mum and the children and the young man smashing the artistic efforts of people who couldn't even be bothered to come and pick them up makes me feel angry, then. All at once, I'm glad I'm now beyond the pale of ordinary lives. Is this what normal people do, until they die? Paint fucking squirrels? I realise what is so dreadful about being a person who has done what I have done – it isn't the guilt, it's the contempt.

In the café, I order a full breakfast and drink two mugs of hot tea. Halfway through it, I remember I have a squashed ham and cheese sandwich in my rucksack that I could have eaten as soon as I woke – a sandwich that was bought in a different life, back before I did what I have done. Five minutes after I leave the café, as I stride out towards Scrabster, I turn quickly to a scrubby grass verge and upchuck everything I have just eaten.

I am in a bad way and I need to get to the ferry. As I pass through Thurso, I go to a baker's and buy another tea, and a doughnut with yellow icing, which I consume with small bites as I trudge out of town – sugar, taken in small amounts, is what I need. This time, it stays down.

It's ninety minutes on the ferry from Scrabster to Stromness. I won't be stopping on Orkney unless I have to; I'll get the bus straight over to Kirkwall and hope there is a ferry to Shetland today. I know they go three or four times a week. That second crossing will be seven or eight hours and can be rough, but I'll do anything to put as much distance as possible between myself and Thurso now.

As soon as I board the boat, I go to the stern to watch as we pull away from the British mainland. If it wasn't for the events of the previous night, I might have enjoyed this moment, but I can tell there is a leaden quality to my gaze as I watch the boat slip its moorings and the engines churn the water in the harbour. Who was he, and who sent him? If I was tougher, harder, I think, I would have hunted in the dark for the bag he must have left somewhere that might have had ID or a phone or some kind of clue – unless he had a car, or was staying somewhere in town. Could those two men in the restaurant have been in on it . . . ? I don't think so. If he was part of a team, the others would have turned up like a pack of dogs. I wouldn't have stood a chance.

I think of the young man's pallid face beneath the water – how alone he was in that moment, the desperate thrashing of his head: when it was the other way around, as he tried to drown me, his face was a terrifying blank. He didn't know me, or anything about me. It was nothing personal. He was a hired hand. A properly trained person, like one of our field operatives, would be reporting in every twenty-four hours, but a gangster's hired hand, someone who prefers to work alone – it could be days before he is missed. I am sure he was a solo operator – but somebody still sent him, and sooner or later, that somebody will find out that the job is incomplete. Someone else will be dispatched to complete it.

As we pull away from the mainland, I imagine two men running down the gangway waving their arms frantically above their heads in a big sweeping motion, hands crossing over at the top. We pull out into the bay and there's the hard brown chop of the cliffs, topped with grass, white surf breaking at the bottom. I picture the same two men again, on the cliffs this time, motionless, staring at me as

I stand on the deck of the boat. The mainland shrinks and the men shrink, become like tiny little sticks, disappear.

Stop imagining things, I think; save your ingenuity for when they are really there. You will need every ounce of it then.

There aren't any other men on my trail as yet and as long as I can leave the country before the man is missed and someone else is dispatched, my trail will go cold. I think of all the times on my flight when I wondered if I was being paranoid, and there is no satisfaction, not one cold ounce of it, in the knowledge that I was not.

The ferry is huge and the passengers are sparse. It's freezing in the wind: others come out for a few minutes, then disappear back inside, intimidated by the stiff breeze and the great throb of the engines beneath us. We pass the Old Man of Hoy then head into open water. The wind in my face feels good, as if it is washing me clean. I wonder when I will next be able to have a bath. I need to scrub the loch off my skin. The boat rocks beneath me. If I think about the loch, I'll be sick again.

Out on the water, gulls wheel and shriek. I do not move from the deck – the sea, the wind, the gulls – for the entire journey.

And then, suddenly, I see low-lying land on either side of the boat, green fields, houses – Orkney. We have come into the arms of the island.

23

In Kirkwall, I buy a ticket for the overnight ferry to Lerwick. It's horrible to be forced to wait, even for a few hours, when I want to stay in motion, but the only thing I can do is act like a tourist. I make myself go into the cathedral, hesitating at the door, then forcing myself over the threshold. Inside, I pick up a leaflet from a wooden stand and realise that it's fluttering in my grasp. A picture comes into my head: the mother in the pottery shop, staring at me in shock, the expression on her face when she saw mine. I am different, now. Everything is different now. I see his face again, beneath the water. I think of Flavia, my mother, and wonder if they would have still loved me if they knew what I was capable of. I go back out onto the street, still clutching the leaflet, gulping the air. I pause to catch my breath and an elderly man heading into the cathedral glances my way and I think, this is not good, I am making myself conspicuous.

I've been so strong for the whole of my flight so far, not trying to contact anyone, even Vikram – it's the one way that people always get caught, when they crack and make contact with someone from their old life. As soon as I knew Kieron had the number of my burner phone, I got rid of it. But now I know I have to find a way to speak to Carmella.

I walk around Kirkwall for half an hour or so, looking for likely candidates. Eventually I find them near the harbour, sitting on a bench, two teenagers, a boy and girl. They are dressed in the inadequate way that teenagers often seem to dress on a cold day. The girl has a short skirt and bare legs, flat little pumps on her feet. The boy is in a T-shirt, a thin denim jacket on the bench beside him. He is leaning back on the bench, legs straight out and both arms spread expansively. She is snuggled into one armpit, turned into him, one hand on his upper thigh, staring into his face and smiling. He smiles back, raises one hand to lift the hair on the back of her head, then lets it drop like a curtain. Their mutual obsession, pale and pimply and incontinent, is plain to see.

I approach them with a worried look, stop right in front of them, frowning. I wait until they have both noticed me then say, 'Oh God, look, sorry, there wasn't a phone on that bench when you sat down, was there?'

They shake their heads defensively as if they think I am about to accuse them of taking it.

I pull a face. 'I don't even know if I left it there, might have been in the taxi. Listen, have either of you got a phone?' I have a purse in which I keep my small change. I open it. I am about to take out a fiver, then decide that's a suspiciously large amount to offer. I take out a pound coin. 'Can I borrow it for a sec? Just a sec? I'll stay right here, haha.'

The girl pulls away from the boy as he sits up slowly, languorously. Her gaze slides from his face reluctantly. He takes a phone out of the pocket of the denim jacket lying next to him, keys in a passcode and holds it out, and when I offer the pound coin in return he shakes his head and shrugs. 'Nah, s'okay, you're alright.' His girlfriend smiles at him as if he's just invented penicillin.

I thank him profusely, then turn to face away from them while I dial, entering the code to withhold the number. I cross my fingers that it's Carmella herself who answers rather than her husband Bernard, or one of the kids. I've no idea what their routine is on Saturdays.

The phone rings seven times.

'Hello?' she says.

I stay silent.

'Hello,' she repeats. 'Who is this?'

There is a long pause, a silence in which all the things that aren't being said crackle like static. *Who else can it be, Carmella?* I think desperately. *Don't hang up, don't hang up. Please don't hang up.*

I take a step away from the couple and I say softly and swiftly, 'Carmella, it's me – whatever you've been told isn't true. It's Kieron, he's been dirty for years.'

There's another silence, then she calls to someone in the house, 'Another cold call!'

I keep talking. 'You knew something before that meeting, you knew we were about to be put under investigation. You couldn't tell me, so you told me about Collins instead, you were trying to warn me. If that's true, then just don't reply.'

I hear some background noise – it sounds as though a child has come into the room. Carmella is silent.

'Thank God,' I say. 'I know you don't believe whatever Kieron has said about me.'

She pauses then says, in a derisory tone as if she is talking to someone trying to get her bank details, 'I'm not stupid.'

'Okay, listen . . .' I say. I'm about to tell her she was right to be worried, that someone has tried to kill me, that perhaps Collins was killed by whoever is paying Kieron and the same people are on my trail – and at that point, she hangs up. I want to call right back. I

261

want to ask her a million questions, but it's clear she could listen to me but not talk; even so, just to have her confirm that she doesn't believe Kieron is something.

Still with my back to the couple, I delete the call register – and as I do, it comes to me. That was how Kieron had the number of my burner phone. Whoever broke into my flat discovered the holdall in the hallway cupboard. They turned the phone on, which was so old it wasn't locked, and used it to call their own phone. Then they deleted my call register and turned the phone off again, putting it back in its place. The cigarette stub and the piss in the toilet bowl – they were there to throw me off the scent, to make me think the break-in was a warning, not a search, when in fact it was both. Kieron knew I was making preparations to run, that's why he said something to Richard that triggered an investigation, so that I would be arrested and neutralised like the unfortunate Collins.

I turn back to the couple. 'Not even in, after all that.'

The boy tucks his phone back into his denim jacket and says, 'Bad hair day.' His girlfriend giggles.

'Thanks anyway,' I say, and turn to an orange-fronted café on the other side of the road.

I buy a tea at the counter and take it to the back, the far corner – my days of sitting in windows or near doors are over. I add milk and stir and stir and watch the tepid-looking beige water go round and round in a neat whirlpool. I'm sure that Carmella believed me, that's why she said *I'm not stupid*. The *run* I saw in her eyes . . . she feared for my safety, and she was right.

We had such different ways of being, Carmella and I – me with

my skinny single life and antiseptic flat, her with her husband and three children and expansive garden – and yet, there was something between us, some sense that although our lives were very different from each other's, we still had more in common than we did with those pale public-school boys that we worked with. There was an unspoken grit, a determination, in both of us. We recognised it in each other even if we didn't understand the full complexities of its origins.

One day, I remember, I was coming out of my office when I heard raised voices at the far end. I looked down to the tech room and saw through the glass wall that Carmella was standing over James, who was sitting in his chair, pushed back from the desk and turned to face her. They were having what can only be described as words.

Kit and Samuel had stopped what they were doing and were watching them. James swivelled his chair back towards his terminal while Carmella was still talking to him. Rude, I think.

As she came out of the glass door, I walked towards her and said, 'What was that about?'

Carmella rolled her eyes. 'You, actually.'

I looked at her.

'He's furious I've decided to send you on the malware course. He needs it to complete his indoctrination for his Level Three, so he thinks he has an automatic right to it. Hell hath no fury than an entitled young man.'

I had actually wondered myself why she was sending me, not him. 'Listen, if it's . . .'

She didn't let me finish. 'You're going.'

As I continued down the corridor, I saw James through the glass

wall, raising his hands and gesturing at Samuel and Kit, Kit shaking his head.

I sit in the orange café in Lerwick, stirring my cup of tea, for a long time. Every now and then, the metal spoon scrapes lightly across the inside of the cup with a musical sound. I stir my cuppa, watch the brown liquid go round and round and round. *Ting . . . ting . . .*

On the ferries so far, I have prided myself on my steady stomach – even with a heaving sea, I've usually managed okay. The trick is to go on deck or find a seat next to a window. Then you fix your gaze onto the horizon, that comforting straight line that will remain a straight line however hard the water beneath you heaves and gullies. Neither you nor your gaze moves a centimetre for the whole of the trip.

This is all very well for a daylight journey, but the ferry to Lerwick is an all-nighter, and the boat begins to pitch and roll as soon as we leave port. There is no option but to do what the other passengers are doing, settle down in a reclining seat, close my eyes and hope for the best. I don't imagine I'll be able to sleep – but straightaway I fall into a deep, dead slumber, and pass most of the trip that way, waking at dawn to heaving grey seas and an hour to go.

I stay where I am, turned uncomfortably on my side with my coat wrapped round me. When I open my eyes and rise, it will be to the knowledge that I cannot shake off, however hard I try not to think about what happened in Thurso: somebody tried to kill me, to make me not exist any more. I was supposed to not be here today. Despite what some people think, we don't actually kill people in the Service. Our actions may sometimes result in people's deaths – a

wall, raising his hands and gesturing at Samuel and Kit, Kit shaking his head.

I sit in the orange café in Lerwick, stirring my cup of tea, for a long time. Every now and then, the metal spoon scrapes lightly across the inside of the cup with a musical sound. I stir my cuppa, watch the brown liquid go round and round and round. *Ting . . . ting . . .*

On the ferries so far, I have prided myself on my steady stomach – even with a heaving sea, I've usually managed okay. The trick is to go on deck or find a seat next to a window. Then you fix your gaze onto the horizon, that comforting straight line that will remain a straight line however hard the water beneath you heaves and gullies. Neither you nor your gaze moves a centimetre for the whole of the trip.

This is all very well for a daylight journey, but the ferry to Lerwick is an all-nighter, and the boat begins to pitch and roll as soon as we leave port. There is no option but to do what the other passengers are doing, settle down in a reclining seat, close my eyes and hope for the best. I don't imagine I'll be able to sleep – but straightaway I fall into a deep, dead slumber, and pass most of the trip that way, waking at dawn to heaving grey seas and an hour to go.

I stay where I am, turned uncomfortably on my side with my coat wrapped round me. When I open my eyes and rise, it will be to the knowledge that I cannot shake off, however hard I try not to think about what happened in Thurso: somebody tried to kill me, to make me not exist any more. I was supposed to not be here today. Despite what some people think, we don't actually kill people in the Service. Our actions may sometimes result in people's deaths – a

Cold War is still
nor do we hire o
They would have
and if he was inno
was killed.

I realise somethi
my eyes closed on a
face, what I was drea
saw in the café in Car
happening to me. I wa
wrong about that boy,
unhappy teenager. I thin
journey: the woman with
diagonally opposite me on
two men in the restaurant
head as if they are some str
a football team, and to ma
some I didn't even see. Wei
How organised was the atten
organised, or I'd be dead.

After a while, I open my e
sleeping passengers, the old ma
heaving seas, the two young w
member moving quietly behind
paring it to open for breakfast. Sc

I have to spend a whole week on S
Stuart the yacht guy and I can't risk
I need to stay out of sight as much a

office in Lerwick,
try to book me o
spend so long he
have no choice.

I buy food or
and eating and
during the day,
and making m
to be right by t
wake up if son
at the ceiling.
the small win
narrow gap b

After five day
need fresh ai
so I walk do
covered in r
when thing
There ar
end of the
– almost a
remember
a large m
blue jum
perhaps,
and the
smoke i
beach s

264

265

they locate a cottage for me, out of town. They
n various excursions, which I refuse. It's agony to
re when I'm at the very tip of the country but I

my way to the cottage and I hide there, resting
ecovering from all that has happened. I sleep a lot
bringing the duvet down to the tiny sitting room
yself a bed with sofa cushions on the floor. I want
he doors and windows on the ground floor so I will
eone tries to break in. At night I lie awake, staring
Sometimes I get out from under the duvet and go to
low that looks out over the road, peering through the
etween the window frame and the curtain.

s and nights of this, I'm on the verge of going insane. I
r and I need to bring my body clock round to normal,
wn to the beach one afternoon, a wide sandy stretch
ocks and seaweed. It's breezy, with a light sun: it is a day
s feel possible.
e a few people around, mostly dog walkers. At the far
beach, I see a man collecting seaweed from some rocks
ll seaweed is edible as long as it's still attached to a rock. I
that from survival training. As I get closer, I see that he's
n with a bushy jet-black beard, wearing a ragged brighter. He turns and walks towards a younger man, his son
who is crouched in the sand around halfway between me
waterline, busying himself with a set of rocks from which
drifting – a fire pit. There are several other people on the
retching their legs, so it feels acceptable for me to indulge

my skinny single life and antiseptic flat, her with her husband and three children and expansive garden – and yet, there was something between us, some sense that although our lives were very different from each other's, we still had more in common than we did with those pale public-school boys that we worked with. There was an unspoken grit, a determination, in both of us. We recognised it in each other even if we didn't understand the full complexities of its origins.

One day, I remember, I was coming out of my office when I heard raised voices at the far end. I looked down to the tech room and saw through the glass wall that Carmella was standing over James, who was sitting in his chair, pushed back from the desk and turned to face her. They were having what can only be described as words.

Kit and Samuel had stopped what they were doing and were watching them. James swivelled his chair back towards his terminal while Carmella was still talking to him. Rude, I think.

As she came out of the glass door, I walked towards her and said, 'What was that about?'

Carmella rolled her eyes. 'You, actually.'

I looked at her.

'He's furious I've decided to send you on the malware course. He needs it to complete his indoctrination for his Level Three, so he thinks he has an automatic right to it. Hell hath no fury than an entitled young man.'

I had actually wondered myself why she was sending me, not him. 'Listen, if it's . . .'

She didn't let me finish. 'You're going.'

As I continued down the corridor, I saw James through the glass

my curiosity and sit down on a tuft of long smooth seagrass and watch for a while. The men are cooking fish, slender and speckled, shiny – mackerel, perhaps. A neat row of them lie on a rock.

The older one with the black beard and bright-blue jumper lays the seaweed down on the rock and picks up one of the mackerel, then walks a few paces down to the sea, splits it open and guts it with his bare fingers. He steps towards the shoreline and hurls a smattering of innards out to sea, bringing down a shrieking mass of gulls, then bends and rinses the fish in the sea.

He walks back to the younger man who now has a lemon cupped in one hand and is cutting it into fat slices with a penknife, using the palm of his hand as a chopping board. The fish-gutter holds the mackerel splayed open so fire-pit man can shove the fat slices of lemon into the wet valley of the fish. When all the fish have been gutted in this way, he first layers the seaweed over the smoking rocks, then, with great tenderness, puts the mackerel one by one on top. I am close enough to smell the charring skin, to imagine the ease with which the soft flesh will peel from the fish's spine.

Neither of the men looks my way and I feel at liberty to stare appreciatively at the older man. He can gut fish with his bare hands.

Two things happen then. I think of the young man underwater, staring up at me, one eye open, the other a deep well of blood. In the same moment, I think of the young woman in Kirkwall, on the bench by the harbour, gazing at her beau with all the innocent and unalloyed admiration of youth. The collision between these two images makes me feel dizzy. I am revolted by one and made wretched with envy by the other. Above all, I am overwhelmed with a longing for surrender. I could rise from where I sit, walk over to the man in the bright-blue jumper, and offer myself to him. I would go up to him (in this scenario, the son isn't around) and say, this is the deal, one night together, skin and warmth, then take me to the police, and after that I won't need to make any decisions any more. It's like the moment on Skye when I stayed in my room at the guest house – a plunge into weakness, this time through a prism of desire.

I watch the man in the bright-blue jumper. The need to get away has been so overwhelming that I have not allowed myself to think of my other needs, human needs, but what if the imperative of flight is ever removed, what then?

That night, after leaving the cottage for the first time, after breathing some fresh air and thinking about the man in the blue jumper, I take the duvet in the cottage back upstairs and sleep in the bed. I still feel afraid, and jam the chest of drawers against the back of the bedroom door before I sleep – but I sleep.

In the morning, I wake up and go back to the beach, which is empty now. I walk to one end and back, staring at the wide vista of the sky, the high cloud, breathing the sea air. Today, I will visit the shops, pick up some supplies, and I will go to the harbour and try to find Stuart.

There's no passenger ferry from the UK to Norway. You used to be able to get one from Newcastle to Stavanger, but that route no longer exists. There's still freight, but it's hard to stow away on a freight ship in any case – well, hard for a woman. If I was a man, it might have been possible to pose as crew, as long as I had a contact that could get me in.

It's now the last week of September but with no phone to contact Stuart, my only option is to walk around the harbour every day, checking the boats until I find him. I cannot afford to miss my slot. On the third day of hunting, I start to worry, and so decide to hang around the harbour office and get chatting to the woman behind the counter. I steer the conversation towards holidaymakers who do those crazy crossings, hoping for a holiday that won't feel like a holiday, and how mad they are – to spend all that money just to be tested. Eventually, I work out which area of the moorings I'm likely to find him.

When I do, he is sitting on the edge of the cockpit of a forty-footer, single mast, his head bent over some sewing – it looks like he's stitching up a hole in the armpit of a jacket with some twine. The hatch is back and I can see down below, the nav table and the seating area. My knowledge of yachts is limited, but from the size of it I'm guessing there will be maybe six passengers, maximum eight, due to make the crossing.

I stand on the pontoon looking at Stuart – early thirties, bearded. I'm guessing his parents took him on sailing holidays several times a year when he was young; he has an air of privilege even though he's scruffily dressed in cut-off jeans and a sailing jacket, the jacket unbuttoned to reveal a white vest over a flat, hairy chest. He is engrossed in his task – he doesn't look up.

'Stuart?' I say tentatively.

He looks up and shields his eyes from the light with his hand.

'You're still doing the crossing to Stavanger, aren't you?' I manage to say it with a light laugh. 'Really hope I haven't come all this way for nothing.'

'You must be Sophie,' he says. 'I've been calling you, left a couple of messages, you know.'

'Yeah, sorry, my phone got nicked,' I reply, 'but we're still okay for the trip, aren't we?'

He regards me, up and down, shakes his head. 'Dunno, Sophie, looks like we've got a bit of a problem here.'

Something inside me contracts. If Stuart from North Sea Adventures is not making the crossing to Norway soon, I am finished, done. I am on borrowed time as it is. There is no way I can head back down south, reversing all those miles, all those trains and buses and ferries, to find another way out of the country. I will have to stay in the cottage until they track me down and I still don't even know who they are.

Stuart scratches his stubble. 'Your jacket looks good, glad you bought the heavyweight, storm coming I reckon and you need to be prepared. Those deck shoes won't do though, not on this crossing – you got some sailing boots?'

I feign concern, whereas in fact I am ready to double up, the full hairpin, right there on the harbour, with relief. I bought my sailing jacket the day before, from a chandler on St Olaf Street, and the harbour office sells some clothing and equipment too. 'I can get some proper boots. When do we sail?'

24

The sea is calm as we motor out of the harbour, heading south at first to skirt the end of Bressay, then sail past the cliffs on the Isle of Noss. There are four other paying customers on the yacht, three men and one woman, who have each paid a significant amount of money to cross the North Sea in a small boat, a difficult and potentially dangerous journey that takes twenty-four hours on a good day and forty on a bad. They could have flown it in two. They'll be hoping for some excitement along the way – a good storm, a pod of cresting, monstrous whales, perhaps, although we'll be more likely to see oil rigs than whales, surely. It's hard not to resent my fellow passengers when they're doing this for fun.

We all have different degrees of sailing experience – I've done some basic homework but am probably the rank beginner. As we pass the cliffs, one of my fellows, a spongy-faced man called Jason, comes to stand beside me in the cockpit and tells me he's a fully qualified yachtmaster. He's done the open-water course, and so is Stuart's second in command should things get rough. He starts to explain what the different bits of the boat are called and what they are for, and it's actually quite useful so I'm happy to let him lecture me. Once darkness falls, we will move to a three-hour watch rota, hot bunking down below in the forepeak and the rear berths. Jason informs me, with insincere nonchalance, 'I'll be skipper when Stuart is sleeping. If you're on my watch, I'll put you on the jib, nothing personal but you need a bit more strength and experience to be on main.' He launches into a lengthy anecdote about how heroic he was when he did the Fastnet only fifteen years after that storm when all those people died, how unhappy his wife was about him doing it. Luckily for me, at that point, a huge company of gannets plunges and wheels overhead and their shrieking is so loud I can legitimately flap a hand near my face and shout that I can't hear him.

As we pass into open water, the boat beneath us begins to dive and lift, deeper and stronger each time, finding its stride. The sky above is wide and grey. We are doing the return leg of the Viking route – not excited marauders setting out, but brigands heading home, bloodied but victorious. We are still in the UK maritime zone, so technically I haven't left British legal jurisdiction yet. I think we will cross into Norwegian waters somewhere around the halfway point of the trip. I wonder if I will be awake at that point – I hope so. I'd like to mark the moment.

I am woken at 2 a.m. An alarm is buzzing. I don't know where I am or why I am strapped into a straitjacket until I snap to full consciousness. I'm in a sleeping bag, on a bunk, on a yacht. It's the middle of the night and it's my turn to go up on deck.

As I sit up, I realise the boat is pitching. A red nightlight illuminates the cabin. It's a struggle to push my sleeping bag off me while I'm rolling from side to side. I've been sleeping fully clothed but I still have to pull on my boots and as I bend, the boat gives another lurch and I tip forward. Someone grabs my arms and lifts me – it's Annette, the other woman passenger, waiting to throw herself down on the bunk I am vacating. She holds on to me as the boat lurches again and we sway together, back and forth, until I am able to manoeuvre past her. 'Go up quickly, getting rough out there,' she says.

On deck, it's freezing cold and the wind takes the breath from my throat. The sky is black, the sea is black, the separation between the two invisible. Stuart is at the helm and one of the men is on the mainsheet. He points me to the jib, yelling, 'Put another turn on!' as the boat dives. I do as I'm told, then grab the winch handle, remembering to keep my fingers clear. The noise is deafening; the mainsail flaps as Stuart yells something at my fellow sailor that I don't hear. I can't believe how little I can see. I look behind me and see the tiny glow of the port and starboard lights on the aft, leaping up and down in the dark. Above there is a small light at the top of the mast, swinging wildly, and I think, *We are invisible in this. If a tanker of any sort comes along, we're fucked.* We lurch again and a huge spray of white water shoots up on our port side, hangs in the air for a moment, then crashes down onto us. This bit is exciting, I think, whooping with glee, and I look around to see if the men are having fun too, but Stuart is glaring at me. He pulls the other man towards the wheel, then leans forward and grabs the webbing hanging loose from my self-inflating life jacket, stretches it, and hooks the karabiner onto the safety wire. Then he yells into my face, 'You stay hooked the whole time you're on deck unless you want to die!'

The yacht takes a wild dive. The look on Stuart's face as he returns to the helm makes me feel sick. The boat plunges up and down into the blackness, again and again. At one point, I look behind and see a wall of water behind and above us, like an upright tail attached to the boat. Another wave crashes over and Stuart looks at me and gestures, but I don't know what he wants. I shake my head to indicate I don't understand. He grabs the other man again and hollers to him, 'Keep her steady!' Then he leans over and shouts, 'Can't see the compass!' He unhooks my karabiner from the safety wire, puts his mouth close to my ear and hollers, 'You're in the way, go below!'

I don't want to go below. On deck, I can convince myself that the wild bucking of this small, brittle vessel in the pitch dark, the crashing and the freezing, flying sea spray is exhilarating – the motion of the boat is far more frightening in an enclosed space. Down there it feels as though we are about to sink any minute – but Stuart is the skipper and I obey.

Down below, everything is wet and slippery and the cabin stinks, a plasticky, salty smell overlaid with the acid tang of vomit. Whoever has been sick has gone back to their bunk and I stagger to the one opposite Annette, who is a motionless bundle, grabbing a plastic bowl from the floor as I do. I'm guessing Annette left it there because she thought she was going to be sick but it's empty. One of the others must have thrown up in the forepeak – I wonder if it's Jason. I try to lie down but realise immediately it's going to be impossible – I wonder at Annette's ability to stay where she is. I am being buffeted so badly my only hope of avoiding injury is to sit on the corner by the sink and brace one foot on the floor and the other against the nav table in order to steady myself. It is a position so uncomfortable that any rest will be out of the question, but experimentally, I close my eyes and try not to think of the depths beneath me. *Full fathom five thy father lies.* At its deepest, the North Sea is seven hundred metres – that's two thousand three hundred feet. How many fathoms is that? I don't know, but down down down you would go, to where it was so dark you couldn't see, so dark you would never be found. I think about my body, drifting down into the dense black water, my hair floating and my arms waving above my head like the fronds of some elegant seagrass or kelp. Then it is not my body I imagine drifting down, but a pale-faced young man whose history I will never know, a young man who may never be missed . . . I'm so tired, thinking of these things. I'm tired and the night has hardly begun. I open my eyes and look around the cabin in the red glow of the night-vision light and feel myself being tossed around in this ridiculous coffin, the black sea beneath, and think, *There are hours and hours of this to go, that's if the boat doesn't overturn in this storm, in which case you will be trapped down here and you will drown in a small enclosed space.* My stomach lurches – I gag into the bowl but only spittle comes out. I can't believe I will survive this awful night, nor that I escaped being drowned in a loch just to drown crossing the North Sea in this stupid vessel.

I think about all the different ways there are to die – water for me; for my father, it was nearly fire. The horror of what he went through – isn't that why he wanted to serve his country, in some form or another, to prevent that ever happening again? I think of how that story was baked into my upbringing: the firestorm, the charred corpses that he saw the following morning, aged seventeen. I know that people I went to school with, or university, sometimes wondered why I joined the army – and if they had known about the Service they would have wondered why I wanted to do that too. The best explanation I could have given them is this: good people have to try and stop bad things from happening. An example: somewhere, some time in the sixties, I think, there was a scientist who invented a plastic tough enough to form a casing for high-explosive devices. When the device detonated, this specially invented plastic shattered and embedded itself in the body of a soldier or villager or child much like any other form of shrapnel – but this shrapnel could not be located by X-ray when the wounded soldier or villager or child was taken to hospital. The sole purpose of this invention, funded by taxpayers somewhere, was to ensure further suffering.

When I first heard this story, I remember thinking, *How awful.* But now it comes to me, I don't remember being told where the scientist was located, which government he worked for.

I think about all this as I bump up and down inside a forty-foot yacht in the middle of the North Sea in the dark, the red glimmer of the night-vision light casting a hellish glow, and about how I have always assumed that we are the good people – me, my father, the Service – and that when we did bad things, they didn't count because we did them unwittingly. The suffering we might cause in the course of doing good was terrible and tragic, of course, but it was a price that had to be paid. How glib of me, I realise now, when it wasn't me paying it.

The boat dives again. I vomit more spittle and close my eyes. Isn't it enough that we are fragile, that we are made of soft flesh, and bones we can break by merely slipping on an icy pavement? Apparently not. We have to make the whole world fragile too. We have to be fearful of what can drop from the sky with a scream or a whistle, of the waters rising, of the sky itself rending in two and the air we breathe being sucked into space. We know now, don't we, that there are people who have weapons who think that Armageddon is a good thing, that the polar ice caps will one day become lakes, that somewhere in a laboratory a monkey or a bat is giving an almighty sneeze, that out there in space an asteroid is hurtling towards us surrounded by an aura of blue flame with a tail that can be seen centuries in the future, except that there will be no one left to see it and really, if one more person asks me why I never wanted children the stare I will give them will freeze them to their bones.

He had a fondness for suet puddings, my father, which he cooked in a pressure cooker, a huge rattly thing like a great thick saucepan. I remember him standing by it, twiddling with some small black knob on the top, releasing the steam that came out in a fierce, narrow jet. If he didn't do it, he said, the whole thing could explode – he made it sound more like bomb disposal than pudding.

I was his sidekick, his little apprentice in so many ways, his Bird. He loved nothing better than kidding me. When I was very small, I remember, he would sit in front of me on a chair and lean forward, placing his right elbow on his right knee. 'Bird,' he would say, 'come here.'

I remember standing in front of him.

'Look,' he would say, smiling at me knowingly, and lowering his voice, as if he had a secret that he wanted to confess to only me.

On the other side of the kitchen, my mother, preparing food, would smile and say something like, 'Robert . . .' in a mock-complaining, indulgent sort of voice.

'Look, Bird,' he would say, 'I've got a *mouse* up my sleeve . . .' And he would flex his bicep in his tight white shirt until the bulge of it jumped and twitched.

I pretended to fall for it long after I knew it wasn't true.

Some time around six, Stuart comes down below. I'm still awake and he tells me dawn will break in the next hour and the seas are calmer – maybe I should come up? Soon, we will be able to see the lighthouse at Kivitsøy.

25

Six days after I step off Stuart's yacht in the harbour in Stavanger, I am standing on the edge of a small town that overlooks Sognefjorden, Norway's longest and deepest fjord. Sognefjorden stretches for over a hundred miles through the north region. My name is Sophie Lester. I am forty-nine years old. I've been an English teacher for twenty-five years but a couple of years ago, I took redundancy and, with the help of a small legacy from an aunt, decided to go travelling and gather material for a memoir about an English teacher who gives it all up and goes travelling. I've always wanted to see the fjords.

I am standing halfway up a steep slope that, behind and above me, turns into a mountain. To my right is a slip road that leads to the highway that brought me here; to my left the road curves round the mountain out of sight but within a few minutes becomes the high street of this tiny town: a bakery, a general store, a repair shop, and a white wooden church with a graveyard that has a shelter with shelves where small trowels and forks and gardening gloves sit so that people can tend the graves of their loved ones and nobody ever steals anything because this is Norway, and because when your population is well fed and cared for they tend not to steal from each other so often. Funny that.

Next to me is a Norwegian woman in her sixties who has introduced herself as Ida. She is holding a key. The cabin is fine for the summer, she says as she unlocks the door to show me, but it won't be suitable for the winter months and the temperature is already dropping. She thinks after a few weeks I will need to find somewhere else. Her English is strong and precise, and as she opens the door and pushes it wide to show me around the cabin, I see immediately why it isn't let commercially, why she is prepared to give it to me for a short while at a price that is, for Norway, a bargain.

Inside the cabin, the shutters are all closed, but in the dim light, I can see there are things no Norwegian family would tolerate – a pile of household junk against one wall, a broken armchair upended in one corner, waiting to be fixed, its feet removed and laid neatly next to it, its underbelly torn and springs showing. She explains that her family use the cabin as a holding shed when it isn't let – they had already closed it down for the winter. She goes over to the sagging velvety sofa, pulls off the sheet that is only half covering it and wraps it round one forearm like a bandage, then she bends and unrolls a rug over the floorboards. She walks over to the glass doors and opens them, then flings wide two full-length green-painted shutters. The small sitting room floods with light. She steps out onto the balcony, waving me over.

The balcony is on stilts and looks out directly over the fjord. It's a misty day but even so, the water below us is an unfathomable blue, the mountains on the far side rising as vertical cliffs of strata beribboned with a dozen thin white waterfalls that tumble down the rock.

I stand looking at the view, and exhale so deeply it feels I may never stop – I can feel my shoulders going down, my chest relax. *Here, yes, here.*

Ida looks at me and nods, as if she is thinking, *I knew you would feel that way.*

*

279

At the front, the cabin is quite close to the road, but it's hidden behind a row of trees and we're away from the highway, so there's only the occasional passing car. In the yard, she shows me a tumbledown shed with a woodpile and some mops and buckets and, propped up against one crumbling black wall, a bicycle. It is usable, my landlady tells me, but I'll need to take it to the repair shop to make it work – it's mine if I do, she was going to throw it away. There's a reason I came to this town and a broken bicycle is all the introduction that I need, an unexpected bonus. I thank her profusely.

The small town on the edge of the fjord has a population of one thousand two hundred and forty-six. For the next few weeks, I will make it one thousand two hundred and forty-seven.

Every day I go walking and as I pass through the town on the way to the mountain paths, I get to know its daily life a little. There is a small, low library with an internet desk where, once a day, I check the news from Scotland – no mention of a body being discovered in a loch outside Thurso. It feels odd, searching to see if he has been found, thinking of him at the bottom of the loch, examining myself for signs of guilt about his body down there – but if I feel a flicker of anything, it dissolves when I pause to reflect that the longer he is undiscovered, the more likely it is that my trail has gone cold. Am I safe now I have left the UK? That is the big question. I wish I could call Carmella again, but I can't risk that now – it was one thing when I was in motion, another now I am stationary for a while. I set up an encrypted Gmail account in preparation for my exchanges with Vikram when the time comes.

In the meantime, I am embedding myself in the life of the town. My Norwegian won't stretch to much more than saying hello and thank you in the shops and cafés, but everyone speaks English to me, good English, of course. The bakery does cardamom buns and excellent hot drinks; it's run by a man with three sons who get up early in the morning to help him before school. I learn that the receptionist at the library wants to go and live in Sweden because her boyfriend is there. Nobody questions my presence or is curious about me in any way – I'm guessing I'm not the first person who has come here because it's pretty and out of the way.

The repair shop is the last shop on the high street, a little out of town, just before the turn-off to the mountain path that I use to go on my daily walks. I go past it several times without even glancing in – I want to establish myself as a fixture around town. It's important that I do that, give the locals time to say to each other, *Oh yes, that's the Englishwoman, the teacher who's renting Ida's cabin.* After they have seen me a couple of times, I will be unremarkable. My approach, when it comes, must seem natural, organic.

The mountain path leads steeply up into a pine forest. On wet, misty days, of which there are quite a few, the rain makes a musical patter in the trees. It's a steep uphill climb and sometimes where there is a break in the forest, I can see threads of mist beneath me, hanging over the fjord. I go walking every day to keep in shape. Being stationary for a while is allowing me to look after myself, and every day that passes when no one comes for me, I feel a little less fearful. Yes, I think. *Here.*

I want to get to know these trails well, in case I should ever need them. It's calming, being amongst the trees. Occasionally there is another walker, but often I see no one. I usually make it to the top of the pass and stop to drink some coffee from a flask on a flat stone that forms a lookout point down into the valley on the other side of the ridge.

There's a story about this mountain pass. It sounds like a fable, but the locals swear it's true. It's about a girl called Marta. People always claim Marta was their grandmother or great-grandmother or great-aunt – everybody loves Marta.

Marta was from a farming family in the valley, and one winter, the time came for her to be confirmed into the church. There was no priest in the valley, and so the only way to be confirmed was to cross the mountain pass in the next valley, a walk of several hours. One morning, young Marta set out, her father giving her strict instructions to be back before dark.

After her confirmation, Marta set off for home – but no sooner had she reached the mountain ridge than a thick snowstorm swept in. The weather can change in an instant, in the mountains. Although she had crossed the pass many times, she had never done the journey there and back in one day and had underestimated her exhaustion on the way home. Darkness descended. The snow became a blizzard. Poor Marta realised that she could go no further and would have to lie down. Once she lay down, she knew she would die.

At this point, she commended her spirit to God. Her last act, as she lost consciousness, was to reach out and pick up a long twig that was lying on the ground and hold it upright in her fist, so that when her body was covered by snow, there might still be a marker as to where she lay, and they would be able to dig her up and re-inter her in holy ground.

Meanwhile, Marta's father had been anxiously waiting at home. As darkness fell, and no daughter came home, he set off with a lantern. He climbed his side of the valley, lifting the lantern high all the way and calling out for his daughter. When he reached the mountain pass, he knew for sure that something terrible had happened, for little Marta should at least have reached this spot. He held the lantern up and stood there, calling her name. Just as he was about to give up in despair he saw, in the middle of the path, a long twig sticking up out of the snow. Marta's father fell on his knees, cleared the snow from his daughter's body and carried her all the way back home.

And young Marta, having fallen asleep in a deserted forest, in the dark, in the snow, woke up in her own bed, covered in blankets, with no memory of having been brought home, brought back to life by the firelight, her grateful, praying family gathered around her, the father who saved her life on his knees with gratitude at God's mercy.

The locals believe the moral of this story is simple: faith, courage, endurance, on the part of both father and daughter. They might also mention cleverness. Marta knew she could go no further, but she had the sense, as a canny mountain lass, to grasp that twig. All those qualities are ones I needed to possess for my chosen profession, of course. I can admire every aspect of this story. But something else about it haunts me, as I think about it on my walks – and it is, of course, my own particular interpretation. Why do we run? Is it because we want to be far away, to be hidden – or is it because the most profound of all human desires is to be found?

On my way back through town one day, I stop off at the library to check the news. I am sitting at the small table a few feet away from the reception desk and reading on the large white monitor: the International Monetary Fund thinks the global economy is recovering more quickly than expected from the financial crash. Iran has announced it is ready for a nuclear deal. There have been more earthquakes in Indonesia, underwater this time. The monitor freezes. A couple of zigzag lines appear across the screen, distorting the text.

I rise and approach the desk, where the receptionist is on the phone, but she finishes her call as I approach and before I say anything, she says, 'Ah, has it stopped, again?' She shakes her head.

Back in front of the monitor, she leans forward, wiggles the mouse on the mouse pad a couple of times, shakes her head. 'This happens. It's not the Wi-Fi, it's the machine,' she says. 'It's not that old, I don't know. I will have to reboot, you will lose what you were looking at, is that okay?'

'Yes, sure,' I say.

The receptionist leans behind the monitor to find a button. 'This is not really the thing I am good at,' she says, pulling a face.

'Me neither,' I say chummily, although I'm only saying it to bond. I think how complex that malware course was, the one I went on in London, how by the end I'd got the hang of it pretty well. I think of the pleasing chevron pattern on the tiled floor as I crossed the foyer that day, how long ago that seems, another world, another Heather. I remember Richard calling my name, 'Heather!' And that's when it dawns on me.

It's time to contact Vikram.

The next morning, it is sunny. I go out to the shed in front of the cabin. Propped up against a damp wooden wall, next to a stack of

284

musty-smelling planks, is the landlady's broken bicycle. It is painted pale green, and I see immediately that it has a broken chain. When I wheel it out into the light, I find that the brakes hardly squeeze and the front wheel wobbles when I try and push the bike forward across the yard.

The repair shop is set apart from the other shops in its own little building, somewhat dilapidated by Norwegian standards, with the workshop on the ground floor and a flat above. The workshop has doors that fold right back, like a car garage, so in good weather the whole frontage can be opened and the man who owns it can see the view down the hill to where the white wooden church and small cemetery sit a little apart from the rest of the village, next to the fjord. On a clear day, you can see the waterfalls on the other side of the valley. Most are thin trickles now – it's the end of the summer. I imagine in springtime they will all be in full flood.

It's a sunny day, this day, and warm, but already there's a tightness in the air that hints at the plummet in temperature to come – snow stays on the high peaks all year round here.

It takes me a while to push my wonky bike through town. The repairman is alone in his shop, standing at a rough-hewn wooden work surface that runs alongside one side of the workshop and looking through a technical magazine of some sort while drinking a coffee. The front doors are wide open, folded back.

My shadow falls across him as I enter and he turns, giving me no more than a glance before dropping his stare to the bike, which he regards with something like amusement.

'I'm sorry,' I say, lifting a hand to indicate the counter, the magazine, 'you are taking a break.'

He shakes his head. 'I am finished. Would you like a coffee?'

285

He comes over and takes the bike from me, then in one swift, strong movement, lifts it onto a stand in the middle of the shop. He indicates the high stool he was sitting at when I entered. 'Please.' Then he disappears into an alcove at the back of the workshop.

I sit on the stool and look around. Against the far wall, half a dozen refurbished bikes are on a rack. Next to the bike rack are two vacuum cleaners and a washing machine, and above them a series of shelves with small tools and parts in metal wire cages. Although the interior of the shed is dark and smells pleasingly of some kind of oil, outside the bright light floods the valley and the picture postcard view. Not a bad life, I think, if a solitary one – as long as you like fiddling with things, that is.

He returns with a coffee – it's black but I feel too shy to ask for milk – and places it in front of me. He is a bulky man, fair stubble and scrubby fair hair on a large head, topped with a green beanie that sits on the back of his head. He is wearing overalls.

'Now,' he says, in plain but accentless English, 'let us look at this bicycle.'

He turns his back to me, lifts one finger to the bike on its stand, and spins the front wheel, shaking his head.

I look at his broad back, his solid buttocks in their brown over-alls. It's been a while, after all.

I sip my coffee and watch him as he circles the bike, checking and testing, lifts it down from the stand and pushes it to and fro. He moves it towards the yard in front of the shop to try sitting on it, then wheels it back into the workshop and returns it to the stand. He looks at me then and gives a small smile, one corner of his mouth lifting in a grin that – I think – holds a degree of knowingness, as if he is thinking, have I given you enough time to observe me?

'You are going to have to leave it here, with me.'

'Okay, sure,' I say. 'Thank you.' I extend my hand. 'My name is Sophie.'

'Sophie,' he repeats as he extends his own hand, takes mine in his meaty grasp. 'Welcome, Sophie. My name is Aksel. I will take good care of your bicycle.'

26

The local community round here is close knit and conservative but I'm taking a wild guess that a lot of the local women have a bit of a thing about Aksel. I've been chatting to my landlady Ida and the receptionist in the library and I've gathered snippets of stories. People round here enjoy talking about the community and ask me very few questions about myself, which is just how I like it. When it comes to Aksel, there is something about a bad divorce, a city-born wife who took the kids back to Oslo on the promise they would spend every summer with him but then she fell in love with a Canadian – or maybe it was an Australian – and went back home with him, taking the kids with her. Aksel has been lonely and unhappy ever since, I've been given to understand, and they all hoped he would find romance with a local doctor at some point, but it didn't work out. He's too old for the single girls and most of the older women are too married.

In middle age, Aksel is still a proposition of sorts, but if he grows elderly on his own I imagine that, eventually, people will become suspicious of his solitude. He will become grizzled and fat, rather than just bulky, and spending too much time on his own will solidify into odd tics in behaviour. Rumours about him will begin. He will reach the point where, if he was a character in a TV series and a local teenager went missing, he would be the first to be questioned.

That's what he's facing, is Aksel – or what I have guessed he is facing – he may not be outlining it to himself in quite that amount of detail. Small communities pity single women like me, but at least we're allowed to be odd without being threatening; it's one of our few natural advantages.

I return to the repair shop two days later. Aksel makes me coffee again and we sit on two wooden chairs just outside, facing the narrow road and, beyond it, the fjord. He seems happy to talk about himself – I wonder if he doesn't get much opportunity. He's from a large family in Askvoll, he tells me, and I think, yes, I know. He misses his children. I hint at a divorce of my own, without giving details, a grown-up son. He doesn't hide the fact that he is lonely, talking as he lifts his earthenware coffee cup in his grasp, his fingers too meaty for him to use the small handle.

Aksel's size, his bearishness, adds poignancy to his solitude. I imagine him climbing the outside steps to the flat above his shop. I picture him being quite fastidious about washing his hands when he gets there. He's already done it once in the metal sink in the corner of his workshop, using some industrial cleaner, but he does it again when he gets upstairs with domestic almond-scented soap, using a nail brush. He probably washes his hands so often he has to layer them with thick, creamy moisturiser every night to stop the knuckles from cracking. I imagine him cooking a meal for himself, meat and potatoes, looking forward to the flavourless bulk of it, sitting down in front of a full plate with relish, but then, as he goes to lift the first forkful, pausing, his hand frozen in mid-air, staring straight ahead, the full power of his solitude suddenly apparent in this supper-for-one. All at once, his stomach has filled up with lone-liness and his appetite is gone.

I like Aksel. I wish I could be honest with him about who I am and why I am here. I have the strangest of ideas in my head, that

I could tell my story to him, the real story. For the whole of my journey, in the absence of anyone to talk to, I have been telling my story to myself – which probably isn't healthy. Who else will I get to tell it to, if not to him?

I imagine what it would be like to live with Aksel. I picture me and him together in one of the modern properties I have seen strung out alongside the fjords on my journey through Norway, all blond wood and white surfaces and large windows with views over water. I imagine getting up in the night, as I often do in the cabin, and going to the loo, then slipping back beneath the cloud of the duvet, to have Aksel turn to me and envelop me in the softness of his flesh, those thick arms, making sure I am warm again before we go back to sleep.

Aksel is talking while I fantasise about him, then abruptly he rises and says, 'I must finish work now.' Perhaps my distraction has been noted, although the reason for it misdiagnosed.

I have a small laugh at myself as I walk back through town. All this imagining, just because I am lonely and have the hots for a man with scrubby hair and fair, mottled skin. The fleshiness of him would be a bit much, perhaps – he's a handsome potato of a man, but how much carbohydrate does any woman want?

The question is, how long should I leave it before I find an excuse to use his phone?

I am still pondering this, wondering how to move our friendship on to the next stage, when I am out on my mountain walk one day and something happens that reminds me of the unexpected.

I have not yet reached the ridge, but I have stopped at a small clearing and thought, *How strange*. Looking out across the fjord, the mountains on the other side are drenched in mist. I've been up here on cloudy days but this seems solid and low – perhaps it's oncoming snow.

When the snow comes, it isn't snow. It's hail. It arrives suddenly, dropping from the sky at such speed – a fierce stinging shower of it. It hits my face like needles. I step back from the clearing to the shelter of the trees but the hailstorm is so fierce it rips through the branches of the pine trees and within a minute I am soaked. I am wearing a windcheater but didn't bring a waterproof out that morning, it looked so fine. I have no hat or gloves. I turn back to descend the path, but my face already hurts – I can feel it going red and numb, my cheeks freezing.

The downward path is steep. I have just turned the corner through the woods when I look down and see that, making his way up the path towards me, head down, is Aksel.

I stop and he looks up, sees me, puts his head down again and continues up towards me. He doesn't look up again until he reaches me.

He looks into my face, and I know he reads there that I have been frightened, not because I was stupid enough to have put myself in any real danger, but because I have had a reminder that I am still a stranger here, that however much I thought I knew about mountains, I can still be caught out, as so many have been before me. Poor little Marta was a local and look what nearly happened to her.

Without saying anything, I hold out my hands – they are as white as death, the fingernails grey and purple. The hail is still hailing down.

He stops in front of me and looks at my hands, saying nothing but raising his eyebrows in a gesture that seems to me to be saying,

Are you a complete idiot, to go out walking without a proper coat or hat, without gloves?

'I didn't think I would need my gloves,' I say, and hear a tremble in my voice, the sort of tremble that comes when you are safe again.

He lifts his own hands and rips off his gloves with his teeth, one by one. Then he unzips his jacket a little and stuffs both gloves into the jacket, against his chest. He does up his zip again, then reaches out, takes hold of my hands and encloses them in his.

He keeps them enclosed for a moment or two, then he begins to rub at them, quite hard – his hands are calloused and as the feeling returns to my skin, it hurts a little. He is rough.

Then he encloses my hands again and pulls me towards him, so that he can lift my hands up to his mouth and, still clasping them between his, blow on the ends of my fingers. His breath is hot.

He does this for some time without speaking, then he pauses and says softly, 'You will not go walking again with no gloves.'

I stand before him, shaking my head meekly in agreement. *No, I will not go walking again with no gloves.* Even though my legs are still shuddering from the cold and the effort of the descent, I am feeling this whole episode is already more than worth it to know that Aksel followed me. He must have seen me pass his shop on the way to the mountain path.

After some more blowing on my fingers, he unzips his coat again and withdraws his gloves from his jacket – they are thick, padded workman's gloves, with a silky lining but a torn, rough exterior. I realise that he placed them there to warm them against his chest. He pulls the gloves over my hands – they slip on easily; his hands are so large and mine so small.

292

I make a small mew of protest – his own hands will be cold – but we both know I'm only being polite. He gives his head a small shake, he will brook no argument on this subject, and then, swiftly and softly, he leans forward, lifts one of his calloused hands and places it on the back of my head, on my hair, pulls my head forward slightly and kisses the top of it. He pauses for the briefest of moments, then turns and heads back down the path, and I follow, suddenly every bit as warm as I need to be, a liquid, happy warmth, for something unequivocal has happened between us now and I know that held within that brief moment is the seed of everything else that is going to happen.

We walk back down the path together. By the time we reach the bottom, the hail has stopped as abruptly as it started and the sun has come out again. The tarmac road and bright-green grass outside his workshop are gleaming. When we reach it, he takes my hand without a word, and together we mount the exterior staircase to the flat above his workshop, our feet clanging discordantly on the iron steps. The door leads directly into an open-plan sitting room and kitchenette, much as I imagined it, vanilla walls, a worn leather sofa, a large old-fashioned television, newspapers scattered on a low coffee table and what I take to be repair manuals of some sort stacked in one corner.

Just inside the door, we both perform the same gesture, resting the heel of one foot against the toe of the other, to flip off our boots. He bends and stacks his neatly on the shoe rack behind him and so I do the same. As we straighten, we are facing each other, smiling, and I lift both hands. He looks at me and, one by one, retrieves his gloves, dropping them on top of his shoes. Then, without another word, he takes my hand and leads me to the bedroom.

293

The shutters are closed. The room is warm and dark. We undress each other while we are still standing, him peeling off my damp clothes with a slowness and delicacy that makes me shudder in anticipation. He thumbs one of my nipples with a calloused hand, then lowers me a little clumsily onto the bed and enters me without ceremony. His skin is hot against mine and the old bed creaks. His weight on me feels sweet. Normally, it would not be enough for me, just being entered, but I'm so starved of human touch I feel my abdomen begin to rise. He puts his thumb in my mouth, the other hand holding the back of my head and when I come it is like the falling of water down the side of one of the mountains next to the fjord, direct and involuntary. I even cry a little, which makes him smile. He strokes my hair.

He brings me coffee in bed. He offers to run me a bath, which is about the cutest thing a man has ever said to me – and I would love a bath so it is an effort of will for me to shake my head and say, 'It's okay, let's just talk. Have you ever been to the UK?'

Within five minutes, he is telling me about his cousin who is married to a lawyer near one of the biggest cities in the country and I am saying, 'That's funny, I have a friend who is a lawyer and is married to a Norwegian woman. His name is Vikram.'

'Truly?' Aksel says, his eyes wide.

We both agree – it's the most extraordinary coincidence, we can't believe it. Bulky Aksel glows like a young boy when he is surprised about something, it's very sweet. 'I know our countries are small, but even so!'

I don't want to push my luck, but I can't guarantee there will be another opportunity, so I say eagerly, 'Why don't we call them?

Let's call them now! I haven't spoken to Vikram in ages, I owe him a call.'

Aksel shakes his head, frowns. 'Anne and I were not very close, you know, our fathers did not get on. It's a long story.'

'Oh, go on,' I say. 'I lost Vikram's number when I lost my phone in Bergen. If we call on your phone now I can get him to call me on my new number and I can have a proper catch-up with him another time.'

Aksel shrugs. There is a landline by the bed. 'I would suggest we don't tell them exactly where we are . . .'

'God no,' I say, laughing.

Then, randomly, he adds, 'Are you hungry? I have fruit and cake.'

'Great,' I say, 'let's make the call first.'

Aksel looks a bit bemused as he dials. After a short while, he says, 'Anne . . .' He speaks in Norwegian but I hear him use Vikram's name, and mine, which he pronounces 'Soff-y'. After some chat, he turns to me and says, 'Vikram is not at home, do you want to talk to Anne?'

'No, it's fine,' I say, 'just can she get him to call me, explain I lost my phone. Say, tell him, it's Sophie and my new number is . . .' I rattle off the number of my Norwegian phone and Aksel repeats it into the phone. 'Tell Anne to pass on the message – he could call me tomorrow.'

When he comes off the phone, he shakes his head. 'Well, she thought that was very funny – I haven't spoken to her for nearly two years. Any more coincidences for me?'

'Only that I love cake.'

He rises from the bed.

'Shall I come through?' I ask.

He looks at me softly. 'No,' he says, 'you can stay here.'

It is dark by the time I leave Aksel's flat. He has lent me a thick coat and his spare gloves. He invited me to stay the night, but I wanted to get back to the cabin, to the phone I have left there. I hope when Vikram calls he remembers to do it from a phone box or use a burner phone.

The cabin is cold; the temperature has dropped. I need to light a fire but I go to the phone straightaway, which I keep in the pocket of my waterproof.

There is one voice message.

'Heather. What the fuck. I'll call tomorrow.'

That night, I huddle down in the small bed in the cabin, two old-fashioned eiderdowns over me, and wrap my arms around myself and think about Aksel inside me, his bearish bulk. He has served his purpose now – I have made untraceable contact with Vikram. Still, there would be no harm in continuing to see him while I was here, would there?

I am woken by the phone on the bedside table ringing – my new mobile.

'Vikram,' I say, 'what time is it?'

'I'm on my morning run,' he says, 'it's six o'clock here.'

'Are you in a call box?'

'No, I got a burner phone. If Anne finds it, she's going to think I'm having an affair. I've already had to make up a story about who this Sophie is.' He sounds quite grumpy. 'What the hell is going on?

I didn't even know you'd gone – first I knew of it is when they show up at the office.'

'Ah, sorry. Still, at least your surprise would have been genuine. What did they want to know?'

'Seemed routine enough. They asked me about our contact over the last two years. They didn't know about your visit to the allotment, or at least they didn't give it away if they did.'

'Good,' I say. 'Two things. I've opened the Gmail account, name and password as we agreed. I'm going to log on today and in the draft email folder, there'll be a list of formal instructions for you as my solicitor. Just remember to reply by editing the draft, don't actually send me anything.'

His tone is still testy. 'Yes, I know what foldering is. But as soon as I contact them on your behalf they'll track everything I do – they'll be able to trace your whereabouts sooner or later, you must know that.'

Foldering keeps your communications safe from MTAs, random internet searches, but what you write still appears on the MUA, of course. It's postponement, not protection.

'I know, that's why you're not going to do it just yet. I'll go on the move again once we've opened negotiations.'

'What's the other thing?'

'The other thing?'

'You said two things.'

'I need you to doorstep one of my colleagues.'

'I can't do that.'

'I'll give you her address and tell you the best time to wait outside her house. All you have to do is ask one question.'

'Fuck's sake . . .' he says in a low voice, but it's more to himself than me.

'I really need you to do this, Vikram, and you have to do it before we can open talks with the Service. One question – just say to her, "Whose decision was it to send Heather on the training course in London?"'

Three days later, when the weather is fair, I cycle up to Aksel's shop. I have made a cake, a large cake. I am going to hand it over and thank him for the loan of his coat and his gloves. As I approach the shop, I see that he is standing on the forecourt, wiping his hands on a cloth, facing a man and a woman. Aksel is turned towards the workshop and doesn't see me. The man and woman are facing out but I'm wearing sunglasses and a hat and am on a rickety bike clearly meant just for pottering around town, so even if they glance at me as I pass, they have no reason to think I am anything other than a local.

They, on the other hand, are clearly city dwellers – their coats and boots look new and their hands are jammed into their pockets against the unfamiliar cold. They might be a couple of tourists, just arrived in town, but there is something about the intensity with which they are talking to Aksel, their focus on him.

It is an effort of will not to pick up speed, but I carry on cycling past at a leisurely pace, crossing everything that Aksel does not turn and see me before I'm safely round the bend. Damn, I think, I'm going to have to cycle for ages out of town in order to give them time to move on, just in case. The road starts sloping uphill from here.

On the way back through town, I cycle to the rear of the library and leave the bike behind it, next to the refuse bins. The building is little more than one large L-shaped room and has floor-to-ceiling windows, so it's easy enough for me to do a visual sweep as I walk around to the entrance. It's a quiet day, midweek. Hardly anyone else is around. I've trusted my instinct the whole way and so far it has proved to be right.

Inside the library, I go straight to the monitor and check the Gmail account. Vikram has received my formal instructions – including that he is not to approach the Service and open negotiations (immunity from prosecution and witness protection in return for what I know) until I have decided who, precisely, he should approach. He is confused about the delay – but that is because I have not told him about what happened in Scotland.

At the end of his message, he writes: *I waited outside your friend's house. She was very unimpressed I knew where she lived. She threatened all sorts if I approached her again. I told her I just had one question. When I asked, she looked pretty confused about why I wanted to know, and I think she could tell I had no idea either. Anyway, before she slammed the door in my face she gave me a name. Richard. Does that mean anything?*

I sit back in my chair. Confirmation is gratifying but not always comfortable.

Richard Semple used me as bait. It may even have been the reason I was sent to Birmingham in the first place. Perhaps he thought I was being a bit slow on the uptake, which is why he phoned Carmella and asked her to send me on the malware training course in London instead of James. He would have made up a work excuse – some concern about my technical capabilities that she wasn't to mention to me, perhaps – when in fact it was all so that he could accidentally

299

bump into me in the foyer and give me the piece of information that I needed, about Sidcup Man, that meant I put two and two together about Kieron's activities.

Richard choreographed everything. He knew that Kieron was planting evidence on anyone who suspected him, but he didn't have enough proof, so he put me in harm's way. This time he was going to lie in wait. He knew it was only a matter of time before Kieron tried to discredit me.

Did it ever occur to him that Kieron might tell his gangster friends – or whoever has been paying him to manipulate our internal investigations – that I might be onto him? Did Richard ever consider the danger he could be putting me in then? Perhaps he knew but suppressed any qualms he felt, the risk being acceptable in pursuit of the aim of bringing down an entire network of corruption.

The fucker used me as bait – but he reckoned without me going on the run.

When I get back to the cabin, I am thinking all of this through as I lean the bike against the shed wall, take the cake in its tin out of the basket and go inside. I stand by the coat rack, unwinding my scarf from around my neck.

I am in the kitchen, making a coffee, when my phone buzzes. I pick it up from the counter.

Aksel and I exchanged numbers before I left his place. We have texted a couple of times since then, but neither of us has suggested we might meet again – it is as if we are both waiting for the other to suggest it first – so his text would not seem suspicious to me if I hadn't seen the couple outside his shop.

Hey. I am wondering if you would like to come for dinner tonight. I am not best cook but I have wine.

I look at the text for a long time, as if the letters on the screen might rearrange themselves into answers if only I stare at them for long enough.

I reply: *Sure. I have a cake for you. I'll bring it. What time?*

That sounds good. Come at 7 p.m.

Great, see you then.

There is no need to pack – I have never unpacked. I abandoned my sailing gear in Stavanger and travelled onward with my rucksack. I close the shutters. I put the cake tin on the table and put the key for Ida on top of it. I am out of the cabin and back on the bike within five minutes.

Cycling up to the highway is hard on the old bike and once I get there it's a few more miles to the bus station. The road is quiet and as the occasional car approaches me from behind, I brace and check the terrain either side in case the vehicle behind me pulls ahead then slows to a halt. None of them do. I feel sober as my legs push down on the pedals, rising a little in my saddle to put my weight into it – I'm strong now, after all that mountain walking – but my breath still deepens with the effort. The couple I saw outside Aksel's repair shop might have been the Norwegian authorities at Richard's behest, or new assassins sent by Kieron's paymasters, or entirely innocent tourists, but I can't take the risk.

I imagine how it might have happened. I might have cycled over, the cake in my basket, then mounted the outside staircase to the flat above the cycle shop, lit yellow from within. Aksel would have answered the door and gestured me inside, taking the cake tin from my grasp with an appreciative murmur but without meeting my gaze, then walked over to the countertop and put it down, turning to face me as I straightened from removing my boots. It would be only then, as I was unzipping my coat, that I would have seen the look on his face: half sorrowful, half bemused. At the same time, two other things would happen. I would realise that there was no sign of a meal in preparation, no casserole bubbling on the stove, no vegetables half chopped on a board – and as I noticed this, I would hear a sound, the musical clang of someone mounting the iron staircase I had just ascended, the staircase that is the only way to enter or to leave Aksel's little flat.

Maybe. Or maybe they would be waiting outside to apprehend me as I approached the workshop – or perhaps they would have turned up at the cabin before then. Perhaps they were asking around town while I was wasting time in the library. I had been careful not to tell Aksel where I was staying, but it was a small town; word would have got around. It might have been him who said it, or the receptionist at the library, or the man in the café as he handed over a cardamom bun.

'Oh yes, the Englishwoman, she's staying in Ida's cabin.'

When I reach the bus shelter, I will have to find some undergrowth to abandon the bike, then once I am on the inter-city service, it will be a clear six hours to Bergen.

Norway was a false ending. I had hoped to open negotiations with the Service here and maybe stay for a bit, but I can't do that until I've confirmed my suspicions, and in the meantime, I have to keep running. I mourn a little at the thought that I will never get to tell my story to Aksel. It would be nice to tell it to someone, one day. I think, not without regret, how if I am mistaken about that couple, then he will wonder why I have just left town without coming to see him again. He will wonder what he did wrong.

I did not allow myself to become complacent, though, not even when I was fantasising about staying in that small town by a fjord for a while, being enfolded in Aksel's bearish bulk and feeling safe, not even then.

27

Keflavík Airport is small and clean and shiny. I glance around as I wander, oh so casually, into the Arrivals hall. Two tour guides are awaiting their groups, wearing the different sweatshirts of their companies – turquoise blue and rival orange. There are singles and pairs and trios of relatives. I count five drivers holding boards with the names of the passengers they are waiting for, and these I scan swiftly but closely because if I was going to have someone waiting for me, nothing would be easier than planting a nondescript man holding a clipboard saying *Mr John Edwards*.

As I head towards the car rental desk, I pause – under the guise of bending to rip off the airline tag on the handle of my suitcase – and glance back at the men. They all still have their backs to me. There is no one else in the hall even facing my way. Like Norway, Iceland is outside the remit of the European Arrest Warrant, but while my suspicions about the tourists talking to Aksel remain, I'm going to stay cautious. The Service might have to play it by the book but freelance killers don't bother with warrants.

There is no one waiting to be served at the Europcar desk, nor at either of the car rental desks either side of it. As I approach, the young man looks at me with the polite, blank smile of a boy just doing his job and says immaculately, 'Hello.' His relaxed efficiency is disturbing – I'm still not used to being able to do things easily.

I slide Sophie's IDs across the desk. He takes them with one hand and scans them, using the other hand to push a form across the countertop in my direction.

I stare down at the form, and while I do, I am aware of the boy looking at me, the courteous beam of his attention. I am gripping the borrowed biro between my fingers as if it is a scalpel and I a surgeon about to make the first incision. I glance back up to see that he is watching me with the slightest of smiles, probably thinking I'm one of those weird people who actually reads car hire forms before they sign them – and I wish I could say to him, *I'm sorry, but it's been a while since I've had to do this. I'm not used to it.*

It takes a matter of minutes. He points at a laminated map on an upright clipboard that sits on the countertop to my right, drawing my attention to several roads in the north that have become hazardous due to weather conditions. It is my turn to give a light smile and reassure him that I'm not planning on putting myself in any kind of danger.

I head out to the car park in front of the airport, dragging the wheelie case I bought in Bergen along pavements covered in grey slush. Beneath the slush are occasional patches of snow trodden hard. An icy wind whips my hair across my face, but it isn't worth pausing to put everything down, take my small backpack from my shoulders and find my beanie hat. As I slip and slide along, I realise I am doing a good imitation of an ordinary traveller a little baffled by their journey. Even so, it is only when I pause to look around for the green Europcar sign in Section 1A that the full reality of my new situation dawns on me – and it feels like stepping into the shower to wake yourself when you have a hangover. I have filled in a form. I have handed over the paperwork of my new identity. And most importantly of all – I have car keys in my hand, mobility, the cold metal fact of it between my fingers. It's almost like being a real person again.

My sense of disorientation isn't helped by the fact that the car is an automatic, left-hand drive of course. It isn't that long since I was behind a wheel but it's a while since I've driven one of these. I put the key in the ignition and push some buttons on the steering wheel – one of them will be cruise control, useful on the empty Icelandic roads where everyone drives at a uniform 90 kph. I bought a guide-book in Bergen Airport to carry around ostentatiously. It takes me ages to work out how to pull the seat forward – and when I do I throw myself against the steering wheel.

Eventually, I manage to settle comfortably in the driver's seat and put the car into forward motion, pulling out slowly across the crunchy slush and leaning forward to look for the Exit signs. Oh, I think as I turn the steering wheel, what a simple but profound pleasure – to be driving again, to turn left or right at my own will – and soon I will be able to feel the kilometres slip beneath my wheels. I am going to cover so much ground just by sitting down, without looking left or right all the time and wondering who is watching or following me. I whoop. I actually whoop. *Yes, yes,* I think. *This is much better than Norway. Even fewer people per square kilometre; even more emptiness to lose myself in.*

Small piles of snow sit on the bonnet of my car long after I have left the airport. The voids that are the roads are bliss to gaze upon, stretching far ahead in front of me and behind in the rear-view mirror. Only a handful of cars pass and no one could be following me here without being blindingly obvious. I decide to come off

306

Route 41, which will take me to Reykjavík, and head south, with no aim other than avoiding the capital city.

Above me, the clouds sit low in the sky, soft folds of white here and there shaded the lightest grey or lightest blue and, here and there, a tantalising blend of both. For mile after mile, the road is a straight line of charcoal grey that cuts through black lava fields covered in drifts of whitest snow. I read about lava fields on the plane, but there is no substitute for seeing them – great waves of volcanic lava, like the waves I survived in the North Sea but frozen into stone while they were in motion, crested by icing sugar powder snow. They are so extraordinary that after a while, I park by the side of the road and get out of the car to take a closer look. It's illegal to park by the side of the road in Iceland because the roads are single lane and there are so few passing places – a crash or breakdown could back the traffic up halfway across the country – but I won't be long.

I pull on my beanie hat and thick gloves before I flick the switch on the hazard lights and get out of the car. The wind is so strong I have to push against the car door to open it and the minute I release it, it slams shut behind me. I have a moment of panic that I'm locked out of the car even though that isn't mechanically possible, and I have to open the door and close it again to reassure myself.

I turn to the field, with the sense that I am about to face something, I don't know what. The scrubby grass beneath my feet is frozen. Ahead of me lies an undulation of black frozen rock, pitted and full of holes and crests and valleys of snow – here and there a large puddle of frozen water the colour of charcoal, reflecting the clouds that freight the horizon. It is the bleakest landscape I have ever seen – a place where human habitation, life of any sort, would be impossible. It is like the moon. Iceland feels very, very different when you're not inside a car.

I stay close to my vehicle and stare out across the snow-topped lava and think about impossibility. I think of all the running I have done, what it might be like if I had to cross that field, the effort of scrambling up one frozen wave of rock only to tumble down the other side. Volcanic rock is so rough, so full of holes and ridges, it would tear lumps from you as you attempted it.

I have read about a phenomenon called lava kettles. Many centuries ago, when the lava was molten, bubbles formed in it as it roiled and boiled down the side of the volcanoes and across the fields, great bubbles large enough to hold a cow, a car. When the lava solidified, the convex curve at the top of some of the bubbles formed a thin crust, a crust that looks like solid rock but hides a cavern beneath. You must never go walking alone in a lava field, for if you walk across the top of a lava kettle, you might crash through that eggshell crust, and once in the kettle, you'll find it impossible to get out as the sides will be curved and shiny, and even though you will be able to look up and see the white sky through the hole you have just made in the top of the egg, you will be trapped.

Even if someone is looking for you, scanning the vast black and white landscape with binoculars, cupping their hands round their mouths and calling your name again and again – all they will see is mile after mile of cresting stone waves. Even if they knew you were there somewhere, even if they thought they could hear a thin cry being whipped away by the wind, they would never be able to find you. There's almost certainly an Icelandic folk story, I think, involving a young girl like Norwegian Marta, who gets trapped in a lava kettle but through bravery and ingenuity manages to get herself out. Why do these stories always involve girl children having to be brave?

I picture myself, then, stuck inside the lava kettle, looking up at the patch of white sky above me, visible through the hole my fall has made. Then it is as if I am suspended in the sky above the same hole, looking down at my upturned face with its desperate expression. I rise up in the air slowly, still looking down at myself. Gradually, more and more of the surrounding field is revealed and my face gets smaller and smaller until it is just a pinprick – then I am gone, lost somewhere in the unending swoops and gullies of black rock.

I find myself backing away from the edge of the field until I feel the cold metal of the car door behind me and then I turn and wrench open the door, get in and clunk on the central locking. I throw my hat and gloves onto the passenger seat, buckle the seat belt and restart the car. I pull out with such speed that my tyres squawk on the tarmac and I've gone at least a kilometre before I realise the hazard lights are still on.

I don't fully calm myself until I reach a seaside town called Grindavík, where I park up beside a small fishing port and find a tiny café beside the water's edge that serves lobster soup for 2,300 kronur. I have a debit card now and won't be able to avoid using it for hotels, but every tiny trace still counts in my head, so I use the cash I got at the airport. Old habits die hard.

The lava field has shaken me. I don't feel normal again until I have spooned half the soup inside me. It's hot and gritty and gradually, very gradually, I try to become what I want to be – just a tourist trying the local soup.

*

As I leave the café, I stop to look at a fishing trawler docked by the quay, a neat-looking thing, hull, radar and lifting cranes all painted the same pale grey. A metal gangplank leads up to the bridge, but the side door is open and no one is around. My reflex is to wonder where that trawler is going and whether or not it is large enough for me to find a hiding place inside. I could board without anyone noticing, but the hold would be in constant use, so without the captain's co-operation to pose as a crew member, it wouldn't be an option.

I walk back to the car, shaking my head. Inside, I reach for my small backpack and get out my guidebook. I need to find somewhere to stay for a few days and think.

The hotel is a short drive away from the main highway, away from a town or village to maximise the chances of the Northern Lights – although it has to be said it's not hard to be away from a town or village in Iceland. The building is long and low, ranch style, with the rooms on the ground floor, everything made of wood, and a stuffed polar bear on his hind legs in a tense stand-off position in the foyer, which strikes me as a little funny when there are no polar bears in Iceland – lava kettles, glaciers, volcanoes, yes – it has plenty of natural hazards, but it's a little short on predators.

I stay there for three days with my phone turned off, feeling lonely and wondering whether the couple talking to Aksel really were people I needed to flee from or whether I've become too in love with motion. It's happy hour in the bar between 3 p.m. and 6 p.m. They make a house cocktail that tastes of vodka and forest. Each night I have a couple of those before a dinner involving whatever combination of fish and fat and carbohydrate I fancy and that, along with a glass or two of Sauvignon, helps me sleep. Restaurant eating still feels novel. I wake each morning bleary and weighted from consumption. I haven't had the opportunity to weigh myself in a long time but I'm guessing I lost a stone during my flight – I'll put it back on pretty quickly at this rate.

Everyone else staying here is in couples and families, although a wedding party arrives at the weekend and I make a point of stopping and chatting to a couple of guests in the breakfast room so other people in the room will think I'm part of that group. Everything is wood – wood-lined reception area, wood-lined corridors. My room is at the far end of one of the corridors and, like a wooden sauna, secret and secluded. I spend a lot of time in it.

A river flows past behind the hotel, less than one hundred metres from my room. I have a back door and a small terrace sheltered from the fearsome Icelandic winds by rough planks. From the terrace, I can descend a couple of steps to a patch of scrubland covered in a light frosting of crunchy snow and walk down and watch the river slip by, thin films of ice on its surface floating past like discarded sheets of plastic. Few other guests venture out the back and I have the illusion of complete seclusion, although on the horizon, if I squint, I can see tourist buses thundering along Route 1, the main road that circles the island and takes British and Dutch and Japanese and Indian and American people to see the largest glacier in Europe, and Diamond Beach, where lumps of ice as big as garden sheds sit on a shoreline of black volcanic sand.

People come to Iceland. It's only two and a half hours to fly from London to Reykjavík. They come in their planeloads to see the wilderness and why not? Not long ago, the wilderness was prohibitively expensive, but the financial crash has brought it within reach of the middle classes, if not the masses. It would be easy enough for anyone in the UK to get here.

I descend the steps of my wooden terrace and crunch across the snow in my boots and stand by the river, watching it slip by. There are no bodies in the river, floating alongside the sheets of ice. There are no faces staring up at me from the water. It's just a river, a cold, semi-frozen river. I wonder how long you'd last if you fell in.

I am still frightened, and there is only one thing that can happen that will make me less frightened. Since I went on the run, the only power I have had is to stay one step ahead of the people who have been looking for me, but it's a negative power, the power of flight. That has to change if I ever want to stop running. I stare at the river. The only thing I can do is make the people who have real power think that it is in their interests to help me, and for that, I have to have something that they want.

While I am staying at the ranch hotel, I do some local exploration, and one day I stop at a village called Vík, just over an hour's drive away, close to the black beaches: a white church with a red roof, little houses and a large-windowed café at the petrol station as you pull into town.

I pull up to the petrol station and as I fill up the car, I realise how much I am still enjoying the novelty of being able to do ordinary things. I park up after and go and buy a coffee and a spinach roll from the café. Every small, ordinary act is one step away from what I have been and towards what I hope to be – someone who no longer looks over their shoulder.

After my snack, I decide to stretch my legs and head down towards the beach. The grey clouds are heavy and low above me, but here and there they break and there is a glimpse of icy blue. The wind is freezing cold and fearsome. Signs warn tourists to be careful – there are something called sneaker waves, apparently, that suddenly crash onto the shoreline much higher up the beach than visitors are expecting. Every now and then, a sneaker wave takes a man or a woman or child, snatching them back into the icy ocean. We are talking about waves that can chuck ice floes around as if they were confetti. If one of those takes you, you are lost.

I stand on the boardwalk. A few feet away are two tourists, a mother in her forties with a teenage daughter. The mother is trying to enthuse the teenager with the majesty of nature. 'Just look,' she is saying, 'look at those waves, look at how huge they are. Isn't it incredible, the Vikings came here on wooden boats when the island was completely uninhabited and they landed here? Look how barren it all is, but they built a whole society – they must have been so brave.'

The teenager shrugs. 'Mum, the Vikings, you know, I think that was just their jam.'

In front of me, white-crested waves the size of double-deckers lift and crash onto the black lava sand. The wind snatches the breath from my throat. I have come here, to this place where human beings are puny, and it comes to me that I can't spend the rest of my life dodging sneaker waves.

Back inside my car, I turn on my phone, open up the Gmail account and leave a message for Vikram in the drafts folder. *Okay, it's time. Contact Richard Semple. Tell him I know he used me as bait to gather evidence against Kieron Blythe, and by doing so, placed me in an unacceptable level of danger. Terms as follows: no question of me*

313

co-operating with the Service until Kieron Blythe has been arrested and
my safety guaranteed. Even then I will need full witness protection in
a country of my choice. I am not to be approached by any authorities,
British or otherwise, while we sort out the details. If I am, I'll disappear
and the lying bastard will never find out what I know — I guess you'll
put that last bit more tactfully.

I'm bluffing, of course. Richard will not want to arrest Kieron
until he has hard evidence not just against him, but against whoever
he has been working for. My message implies that once I know I
am safe, I can provide it. I can't, of course. I know less than Richard
knows about Kieron's activities, but until he finds that out, he
has every incentive to make sure that Kieron Blythe is taken into
custody. I google short-term rentals in Vík – pricey, but still a lot
cheaper than living in hotels. It looks like there is a cabin on the
edge of town that's available for six months. I won't need it for that
long, I think.

I don't know it yet, but there is another force building that
will mean I stay in Iceland for rather longer than I had planned.
Sometimes, something bigger than you makes the decision for you
after all.

28

Vikram does put it more tactfully, of course – so tactfully that my opening terms run to eight pages. In response, I receive an interim order from Her Majesty's Government: the Service denies categorically that I was manipulated in any way in their investigations into corruption within the Department of Standards. It will, however, agree not to pursue me, nor apply for extradition, while they investigate my conduct, and in return, I agree not to contact Kieron Blythe, Carmella Adebayo or any of my former colleagues in Birmingham or London – nor will I talk to the press: in person, by phone, online or via a proxy of any sort. In short, I have successfully gone to ground and they will leave me alone for the time being as long as I stay there.

'So they haven't arrested Kieron Blythe?' I type in a message to Vikram one day. 'Do they think I was complicit with him?' We still use foldering to contact each other, although in the New Year, we will abandon it.

He responds with two words. 'I guess.'

I have not told Vikram about what happened that night outside Thurso. As things stand, if the Service plays dirty, I could find myself charged with bribery and corruption, fraud, breaching the Official Secrets Act – and murder.

I ask Vikram to keep pressing for Kieron Blythe's arrest as a condition of my full co-operation. The Service is not the only thing I have to worry about, after all – don't they understand that?

*

Christmas approaches. I do not attempt to integrate myself into the life of the village in any way. This is easy enough with the daylight hours so short – and even when it's daylight, sometimes a jet-black cloud drifts across the icy blue sky, as if the weather is saying, *Don't forget, you're not normal.* The air smells funny round here. My suitcase stays by the door of my little white chalet on the edge of Vík, just as my rucksack did in Norway, just as Flavia's cases stayed packed when she stayed in the cottage in Plockton. I lay it flat on the floor and lift the lid up to use it as a chest of drawers, folding clean clothes back into it the minute they are dry after washing. I'm ready to slam down the lid, zip it up and go at a moment's notice.

There are many dark hours. I think about Flavia, and I think about my mother. I think about the few friends I had in London, the feeling of camaraderie I had with my colleagues in Liaison 2.6 before it all went bung. How thin is a life, I think – and how few people are aware of that fact. A death, a debt, a move across the country – even just a job loss, and before we know it the fabric of what we believe to be a complex and rooted existence begins to come apart like damp tissue. *Face it, you had no life to run out on in the first place.*

In the cottage in Plockton, Flavia painted my nails. 'C'mon,' she said, laughing at me, 'we're not in the army any more, we can be *women!*'

I lowered my gaze pointedly to her pregnant belly, pulling a face.

'I know, I know!' she said. 'I've gone from nought to sixty on that front but hey, maybe you should try it some time.'

'No thanks,' I said.

316

She grabbed my left hand and pulled it towards her. 'Crystal rose or pale dawn?'

'Pale dawn,' I said. 'No one has ever accused me of being a rose.'

In January, the darkness and the waiting start to get to me. At this time of the year, the sun rises mid-morning and sets again mid-afternoon. There are only so many walks you can do in the half light and freezing cold, only so many books you can read or so much television you can watch in the evenings. Icelandic nights are long, my skin is drying out and I've developed a nasty cough.

One slow stretch of an afternoon, I google Adelina Bianchi. She is a research fellow at Bristol University, in the Department of Anthropology. I find a picture of her with a group of other humanities research fellows, taken on the steps of some department building. She is wearing a long wool coat and a heavy knitted snood, her dark hair in a loose ponytail from which tendrils are escaping. The group are all friends, it would seem, clutching at each other, all in the age range from mid-twenties to early thirties. She is on the right of the picture, holding on to the arm of another young woman and bent over slightly as she laughs. She is the very image of a happy, confident young woman, liked and loved, her whole life ahead of her.

I stare and stare at the picture, as if I will be able to read in it the history of her life since I last saw her at the age of eight – the much-loved child of a single parent, the tragic loss, the going on bravely to make a success of her life. I choose to see all that in her happy expression. *A fine young woman* is the phrase that comes to mind, the kind of woman any mother would be proud of. I think about the fact that Flavia is not here to see how fine her daughter

317

is. I think about my own mother, and wonder if she felt that way about me when I was Adelina's age. Unusually for me, I cry, for the first time since Plockton.

Afterwards, I feel tired. I make myself a coffee, wrap a blanket round my shoulders and go out onto my balcony to watch the light fade from the sky. It has a strange lilac quality. It is below freezing outside and even though my cup of coffee is cradled in my grasp, the liquid in it is cold in an instant. As I raise the cup to my lips, my teeth clank glancingly against the porcelain.

One night, I am awoken by a rumble. I start awake, senses straining as they always do when something unexpected wakes me. The night is silent. It feels as though whatever happened was both loud and distant. It had the quality of a dream, but I know it was real. I throw the duvet off because I am sweating, but I cool rapidly. I pull the duvet over myself and go back to sleep.

I never dream about him. You would think I would. You would think I would dream about the soles of my feet slipping on the mud as I struggled through the water; about the way his arms flew wide as he fell backwards; about being in the middle of the loch in the pitch-black night and rolling him off the spreading branch, the water closing over him like oil.

If they don't arrest Kieron Blythe soon, I'm going to go on the move again. I can't stand the waiting.

A week later, I receive a parcel from Vikram. I pick it up from my postal box at the petrol station and walk home with it tucked under my arm. Inside my little plain kitchen, I open the padded envelope and slide out the folders onto the table, reaching up to twist the anglepoise lamp so it illuminates them, the light is so bad today. Inside the first folder is a file with my name and code number on the front. It's the Service's file on my case that Vikram has demanded as part of our negotiations.

I leave it on the table while I go to the fridge and get out the remainder of some pasta that I made myself the night before. I heat the pasta in the microwave and then sit at the table eating it straight from the Tupperware with a mechanical hand, looking at the file in the same way that I might look at a birthday present I have resisted opening because I want to enjoy the delayed gratification, or an unexploded bomb – somewhere between the two, perhaps.

Inside, it is so heavily redacted as to be infuriating – page after page covered with thick black stripes. But reading through the observations, I understand that for an extended period, the DOS did indeed suspect me of corruption – not instead of Kieron, as he was hoping, but as his accomplice. Their information on him was already damning, but they were sure he had help from inside the Service, possibly from more than one source. They knew about my financial difficulties, they knew about Cheltenham – and when I went on the run they did indeed issue a warrant for me and, to my dark but distinct gratification, sent police officers to Carlisle railway station. They were monitoring Kieron's phone and when he rang my burner they triangulated the number to get my location. The police officers arrived on the platform just after the train had pulled out – by which time I was striding off down English Street. I'd turned my phone off by then, so they assumed I was still on board. The train was halted at a junction just outside Glasgow to allow other officers to board, but I was in a car with a man in a pale-blue short-sleeved shirt, shortly to be restraining myself from breaking his finger in a lay-by. It is gratifying to know that I was not wrong about everything.

Once I was in Scotland, the trail went cold for them. Not for the young man with the pale skin and dark hair, though.

The authorities didn't pick me up again until Lerwick. In my haste to get rid of the burner phone, there was one thing I had forgotten – I had called Stuart on it before I got rid of it. They tracked the yacht across the North Sea using a radar system called See Me that small boats use in order to avoid being run over by tankers in busy shipping lanes. They lost me for a while after Stavanger, but there is a partially redacted reference to assistance from the Norwegian secret services – the couple who spoke to Aksel, I presume.

There's one thing I don't understand. If they knew about Stuart the yacht guy, then why didn't they send someone to arrest me on the quay at Lerwick Harbour, before I got onto the yacht and left their jurisdiction?

After I have read the redacted papers, I call Vikram. We talk about the papers for a bit, but he sounds distracted. When I dry to a halt he pauses, and in that pause, I realise he has some news.

'So,' he says, his voice holding a trace of boyish glee, 'fancy a very late Christmas present?'

'Yes . . .'

'Kieron Blythe was detained two days ago at the office in Birmingham – they've just let me know. I was wondering why they suddenly agreed to release the papers to us. They weren't going to do it until they had enough to arrest him.'

It doesn't give me as much pleasure as I would have thought. It is long overdue, and I'm not even sure what it means for my situation any more. 'Where exactly, which room?' I ask. 'How much detail do you have?'

Vikram gives a small laugh. 'Why does it matter which room? He was probably taken down the service stairwell in handcuffs and put in a van with someone's hand on the back of his head to bend him a bit. I thought you'd be pleased.'

'I am . . . I am . . .' I say, unable to explain that the image I am fantasising about is different: Kieron in Alaska by the floor-to-ceiling window, looking out across Birmingham and raising a coffee cup to his lips, turning back to the room as they come through the door.

Vikram has no further information about Kieron's arrest. We talk some more about the papers. I ask him why he thinks I wasn't arrested in Lerwick, and he can't explain it either. There is far more bureaucracy in these things than the public understands, less efficiency, more paperwork, requests that have to be put in to various police forces and between agencies, more cock-up than conspiracy in every aspect of apprehending someone. Even so.

Something occurs to me. My voice becomes a little lower, slower. 'There's something else I need you to help me with.'

Vikram picks up on the change of tone. Over the last few weeks, he has acquired a slightly anxious response to my requests. He tries to sound jokey without success. 'Does this involve me doorstepping one of your former colleagues again? Because if so, the answer is no. Under the terms of your interim agreement you would be breaking the law and I would be colluding with your law-breaking.'

'No, no,' I say. 'This is just about helping me with some detective work online, completely legal.'

The Family Records Centre in London closed in 2008. You have to put in online requests now in order to find anyone's birth,

321

marriage or death certificates. Kieron Blythe would have been born in 1963 or 1964. I explain to Vikram that we need his birth certificate to begin with so that we can trace his parents and get their certificates, which will give us Kieron's grandparents. 'I want to trace any siblings his parents might have had, and their descendants, which will mean choosing a childbearing window and doing a name search over quite a span, depending on how many there are. It means working backwards in time then forward again, if you get my drift.'

'What are we looking for?'

'I need to know if Kieron Blythe has ever had a cousin called Ruth.'

After I finish talking to Vikram, I go out for a short walk. The village is getting busier these days, with tourists and volcanologists come to assess the nearby rumblings. I take my favourite route, down to the black sand shoreline, where I look at the white and grey heave of the sea – there have been some bad storms recently. I stare at the rock pillars, the huge dark-grey vertical formations of basalt, dusted with snow. Local folklore has it that they are three trolls caught out too late and frozen by the early-morning sunlight. I think of them more as knowing old ladies, silent in their wisdom. I like to go and commune with them, watching the huge rolling breakers of icy sea crash onto the black lava sand, and think about how puny I am, how little I matter in the grand scheme of things. It's a comforting thought.

I miss my mother. I understand that in her own quiet way, there was a small centre to her, moral goodness, you might call it, and that moral goodness came from her capacity to love. She was happy because she loved. Kieron Blythe is in custody. It may be that the gangsters lost my trail when I left the UK – but even if they didn't, now Kieron has been arrested, their primary focus will be him, not me. My negotiations with the Service are ongoing. I should be feeling pleased. I should be feeling safer, finally.

As I trudge back up the path, I think, *Come on. It's time to stop now.* And if I'm going to stop, here or anywhere else, there is something else I need to do.

29

It takes a fortnight. I draft the email, then I redraft and redraft. Then I leave it a few days and redraft again. Then I delete it and start it all over again from scratch. Even with all that rewriting, it's hardly my finest hour – but I don't want it to seem too polished. I want it to seem sincere, because it is sincere.

I send it one evening when the cabin is draped with the pitch dark and it's a freezing night outside. I warm up some soup first, tear some bread from a loaf, light a fire – all displacement activities – then I sit beside the fire eating the soup slowly. Eventually, I rise and put my soup bowl and plate in the sink, get my laptop and bring it back to the fire. I have tracked down her university email. That was the easy bit.

Dear Adelina,
This email will come out of the blue, so I hope you will bear with me, and allow me to introduce myself. I knew you quite well when you were small – until you were almost nine, in fact, so you may have some memories of me. My name is Heather Berriman. My nickname since childhood has been Bird, but your mother always called me Heather and you called me Heather too, although you had a strong lisp as a toddler and it came out more like 'Fevver'.

Your mother and I first met when we trained together in the Women's Royal Army Corps in the 1970s. I don't know how much she told you about that time, but we remained close friends after she left, when she became pregnant with you. At that time, it was obligatory to leave the WRAC if you fell pregnant and in fact even if you got married.

First, I must begin with an apology. I have no idea what your mother might have said about me so perhaps you know some of this already, but she and I were exceptionally close, to the extent that, although I never lived close by enough to be a daily feature in your life, I considered myself much in the role of an aunt. We holidayed together a few times, when you were probably too small to remember, and you were in many ways the closest thing I ever had to a family of my own – and then I took on a new job that prevented me from seeing you and your mother as much as I would have liked.

Just before your ninth birthday, your mother and I had a falling out, a rather bad one, although to be honest the details seem so vague to me now that I can't help thinking that if we had talked it through it could have been resolved. But we were both stubborn – we had that in common – and the weeks went by while we each waited for the other to apologise, and the weeks turned into months and the months years, and then, ludicrous as it seems, two people who had been so close were no longer even in contact, just like that. I hope you don't think it presumptuous of me to admit that it was the hardest 'break-up' of my life. I think, in the back of my mind, I always thought that one of us would get in touch – there always seemed to be plenty of time for that. Until, of course, there was no more time.

It came as a great shock to me to learn of your mother's accident. And here I must offer my deepest condolences to you. I can only begin to imagine what it must have been like to lose your mother in such circumstances. Whatever shock and sadness I felt pales into insignificance in the knowledge of what it must have been like for you.

This is the thing I want to explain most clearly, even though it is something I am sincerely ashamed of: I only learned of your mother's passing years after it had happened. It shocks me, even now, that I could have allowed this gap in our lives to occur. By the time I found out you were motherless, you were a young adult, but even so, I will never forgive myself that for the years between you losing your mother so suddenly and my finding out, I was not available to you. I will, to the end of my days, regard it as the greatest of failures on my part that I was not part of your life. There have been others, I might say.

So now you understand the somewhat formal tone of this email: it is because it comes as a most profound apology, as someone who cared for you a great deal when you were little, someone who was very close to your mother. For me to not be there to support you, even in a small way, when your mother died was a dereliction of duty, and one that was ultimately my loss every bit as much as yours.

I have always believed in duty, in the concept of duty as an abiding principle by which it was possible to live a life, regardless of religious belief or patriotism. I used to believe that, at the most basic level, we were here on this earth in order to serve, in order to stop bad things happening to people who had done nothing wrong. That is why, a few years after leaving the army, I returned to another form of public service, a civil service role that involved a certain amount of travel.

But there is something that your mother accused me of that I must now concede she had right, that sometimes we use duty as an evasion – we tell ourselves we are serving a higher cause when in fact we are using it as an excuse for not looking after those closest to us. I was not a very good aunty, Adelina, although I cared for you a good deal. I dropped in and out of your life when it suited me, and your mother was right to admonish me for it. And then, when I eventually learned of her death, I told myself you were grown up, the restrictions of my job meant I couldn't play a full part in your life in any case – but the truth was, I used those undoubted truths as an excuse for not making the effort I should have done towards you, and because I felt guilty about the falling out with your mother.

I am sorry from the bottom of my heart.

My dearest wish is that whatever you are doing now, you are thriving – who knows, you may even have a family of your own. If you find this email in any way intrusive, then please forgive me for that too, and ignore it, but should you ever wish to be in touch, either to talk about your mother or to reconnect in any way, nothing would please me more than to hear from you.

With love from an old aunty from the past,

Heather

x

Once I arrive at this final version, I hit send, and then brace myself for a long wait or – more likely – no reply. I reread it multiple times even after I send it and try to imagine what it would be like to receive it from Adelina's point of view. Some woman from your dead mother's army days, who you scarcely remember, gets in touch out of the blue wanting – what? Absolution? To talk about how tough your mother's death was on her, how hard it was that she didn't find out for years?

I try to remember what I was like at Adelina's age and when I do, my best guess is that she will read the email, hit the delete button and get on with her life.

I am low for a while after I send the email – I don't know why. It has prompted me to dwell too much, I suppose, on the multiple ways in which I have let people down. I think about my father and my mother, how I always assumed there would be plenty of time in some vague future when it would be the right moment to take an interest in them. I think about my distant brothers, and the niece and nephews I know nothing about. I think about that trip to Margate, and how much Mum would have liked to come along, and how I didn't invite her because I wanted to walk on the beach on my own and think about my life. I assumed there would be other chances. There weren't. I leave Vikram to finish the research into Kieron's family tree. In my black mood, it hardly seems to matter.

Nobody has come to find me, here in Vík. The Service is leaving me alone while we negotiate, and the gangsters seem to have given up as well. Has my trail gone cold or has their focus shifted to Kieron? Silencing him will be their priority now. Maybe nobody cares about me either way, not any more.

A week later, Vikram rings. His voice is perky. There will always be a part of Vikram who is the pleased, clever schoolboy he undoubtedly once was. 'Just checking, but Kieron Blythe *is* completely white, isn't he?'

'As white as driven snow.'

'Okay. I thought so. My lot use the word cousin more loosely but I know with white people it tends to be literal, so it did take a while, as you said, because I looked into second cousins and cousins by marriage as well, but I'm pretty sure now. Kieron Blythe has a maiden aunt on his father's side and two uncles on his mother's side, both married, three kids each so six cousins in total, but none of them are or have ever been called Ruth. None of them are even married to a Ruth. I checked his wife's relatives too. As far as I can tell, there's never been a Ruth.'

I pause on the other end of the line, and something surges through me: I think of it later as cold, hard anger, but it isn't as certain as that. It's a bolt of something clicking into place – my capacity for determination reawakening itself.

'Contact Richard Semple. Tell him he has to come to Reykjavík. I want to talk to him in person.'

There is the little pause that I have come to know well, the space in a conversation where I can tell that, internally, Vikram is giving a little sigh. 'Why would Richard Semple come to Reykjavík?'

'He might not,' I say, 'but give it a go.'

If I am right, Richard will come. I know he will come.

Three weeks after my email to her, Adelina replies.

Dear 'Fevver',

Yes, of course I remember you! You brought me that HUGE Lego set, remember? I think it was my sixth birthday. You were very generous on my birthdays. Mum would buy me stuff, of course, but you would arrive with the most ginormous parcels!

It's great of you to get in touch after all these years and sorry it's taken me so long to reply. I wanted to wait until I could do it properly. I don't think you need to apologise at all. I'm really sorry you and Mum fell out, but I don't remember being told about it or you disappearing. I think it must have been just before she met my stepdad. They got married when I was ten so that must be it.

Yes, it was really awful when Mum died, just such a random, stupid accident. I had my stepdad and my little brother Gabriel by then and when we lost Mum it was so awful for him, I kind of threw myself into being a surrogate mum for him in some ways, and of course it was awful for me too, but nothing was more important than looking after him so I just had to get on with it. He was a typical teenager and went through some bad stuff, but he's coming through it really well. I'm so proud of him. My stepdad's family helped as well. His parents are my granny and granddad like they've been there from the start. Granddad is the best cook in the world.

Funny, though, you getting in touch now, because I've been thinking about my mum a lot recently. One of my friends had a baby boy and I went to visit when he was four days old. Seeing her mum with the baby and realising I'll never have that upset me quite a bit.

I pause at this point and try to imagine the reality of Adelina's grief – all the events she must know are lying in wait for her in her future, happy events that her mother will be absent from. For all her cheery, practical tone, I can feel the sadness beneath her words.

I would actually really like to be in touch more and talk about Mum. She was a brilliant mum, but because she died young, I never got the chance to ask her more about her early life – she told me about her father dying once, when she was explaining that she had grown up without one as well. My stepdad used to get so upset when I brought her up and anyway he'd only known her for three years when she died so he couldn't really help. So yes, let's keep in touch – maybe we can meet for lunch or something?

Ah, I think. Lunch, well that would be lovely, but . . . sooner or later, I will have to explain to Adelina that that might be a little tricky.

It's really great to hear from you though and you mustn't worry at all about not being in touch for so long. These things happen, I guess. Let me know where you're living now. I'm in Bristol – maybe I can come and visit? Not just after more presents, I promise!
Let's make sure we stay in touch,
Love
Adelina
Xoxox

I read the email again and again – it's fanciful I know, but I can't help hearing Flavia in Adelina's turn of phrase. She wants to stay in touch with me. It comes naturally to her, I can already tell – her warmth, her chattiness.

I write a brief reply of pleased acknowledgement, saying I'll be in touch soon about the possibility of meeting up – I need to stall on that for the time being.

The next day, in a new mood of happiness and exploration, I drive out towards Evindarhólar. There is an open-air swimming pool up there I want to try – I have taken to swimming every day, as well as walking. I am on Route 1, wondering whether to stop on the way and do the walk to see the Sólheimasandur Plane Wreck on the beach, when I see, up ahead, a row of cars parked by the side of the road, people standing by them raising binoculars and pointing.

The smell I have been smelling for several weeks in Vík is overwhelming as soon as I get out of my car. It fills my lungs. Beyond and above where the people are parked, pointing, I see it, the darkness of the sky, as if there is a film over it, a fine gossamer waterfall of grey. If I didn't know better, I would think it was rain, whereas of course it's the opposite of rain.

From far off in the distance comes an almighty, elemental groan, a deep, rock-filled undulation of sound. I have never heard anything like it before.

On my return to Vík, I pull in at the petrol station and the woman who runs it comes out and says I should know that they have opened the church in case the civil defence authority need to bring people in from the surrounding farms. There are going to be drills. She wants to make sure I know that the church is the place to run to if an eruption causes a glacial flood because it is on higher ground. I have to plan ahead, she says, in case they get an ash fall. The pollution will be dangerous and I might have to stay inside, maybe for a few days, so I must make sure I am stocked up with food. I ask her what it is like, an ash fall. She shakes her head and says it comes down so thickly, it's like a blizzard. It falls in such volume you think the whole town will be buried – but then there's a strong wind and it vanishes. The local farmers will be worried about their livestock.

*

I make sure I have supplies in and become glued to the news. My balcony looks away from town, across a stretch of open tundra. In daylight hours, I go out there each day as darkness gathers, to look at the sky. In Iceland, there is always a good reason to stare at the sky, but now, we have another one. During eruptions, dust particles shoot into the air then get suspended in the atmosphere. At dusk, they scatter the light. It's called a volcanic lavender, caused by minute particles of glass in the ash – but it's every colour: purple, orange, blue. It's because the volcano is erupting under glacial ice, apparently, something about the meltwater making the lava cool very fast and become very brittle, that's how you end up with glass. Glass in the sky. Volcanic lavenders. Lava kettles. Why would I ever want to go back to reality?

Then I hear the rumour, one day in the petrol station shop, that if the volcano blows big, the ash cloud could close Icelandic airspace. I message Vikram and tell him to put pressure on Richard. I tell him to imply that if he doesn't come soon, I'll disappear again.

It's time to write to Adelina and own up that I'm actually out of the country and not quite sure when I'll be back – we'll have to stick to email correspondence for the time being. It's the start of regular messages between us. She tells me more about her life – there's a boyfriend called Pieter; she met him in Amsterdam. She thinks it might be serious but as they both have jobs in different countries they are doing the long-distance thing. She loves Amsterdam, though. I'm sorry that in return I can't tell her what it's like living in a remote village on the south coast of Iceland. It would be lovely to have someone to describe it to. I would like to tell her how white snow and black sand make the whole world seem monochrome, so that when you see the red roof of the church, it startles you. I would like to say *There are so many places in the world, it is so various. Whatever else you do with your life, don't miss the world.*

When I think back to that correspondence, it seems drenched with hope – the hope that there was something more for me than what I had become.

30

I set off at 4 a.m. There's been a cold snap the last few days and when the wind blows it's still below freezing. It takes me a while to defrost the windscreen in the dark, scraping away with the cold air harsh in my throat. A few flakes of snow drift in the dark-blue air but don't settle. Even though I scattered grit around my parking space the evening before, the wheels slip and spin on some thin ice before they find purchase and allow me to pull slowly and carefully out onto the road.

No one else is around at this hour. As I reach the highway, it feels as though I am driving through a lunar landscape at night, the sole explorer passing through dim and distant mountainsides and wide plains on the dark side of the moon. Then I see a tantalising green glow in the distant sky, the hint of some Northern Lights that never properly materialise, even though I lean forward clutching the steering wheel and peer out of the windscreen and will them to appear.

Clouds cover the night sky as I near my destination and there is still no hint of dawn as I reach the airport. I drive around for a while in the dark, looking for the right building. The police office is round the back at the end of a series of hangars and is roughly the same size as a police station in a small town in the UK. I park up next to the main entrance and go inside, where two officers in black uniforms with yellow badges on their sleeves are standing by the door, drinking coffee. A bulky young lady sits behind a sliding window in a hole in the wall. I tell her why I am here and she writes down my name on a clipboard, then rises and opens a door to one side of the window, beckoning me through. She leads me down a short but confusing maze of corridors with so many turns that my internal compass tells me we must be back where we began. At the final turn is a prefabricated door – we seem to be in some kind of temporary annex. An aeroplane takes off overhead and the whole corridor rattles.

The policewoman opens the door and gestures me into a small meeting room – a plain room with light-grey walls and a functional table around which are ranged four chairs. It reminds me a bit of Alaska. Standing by the window, looking out over a runway and holding a styrofoam cup, is Richard.

He turns to me and smiles – and I feel something unexpected, a kind of warmth towards him. It's so long since I've seen anyone from my old life in person. His hair seems a little thinner and he looks tired. The styrofoam cup in his hand feels like an obscure insult to his personal taste – he's strictly a china-cup-and-saucer man. He's wearing a pea coat over a soft-white shirt and dark-grey slacks, rather than his usual suit, but I notice his fingernails are as manicured as ever, his shoes polished.

'Heather,' he says simply, and there seems to be genuine warmth in his voice. 'Do you . . . ?' He raises the cup in his hand.

I shake my head.

He looks at the cup, then places it on the table, turns it once thoughtfully, sits.

I sit down opposite and look at him expectantly.

'I'm sorry the way things have turned out, Heather,' he says.

'You used me as bait.'

He concedes the point with a series of small, slow nods. Then he says, 'We had no idea how far it would go, of course. We thought that once you realised Blythe was corrupt, you would investigate him and that your proximity would mean . . .'

'Yes, well, I didn't get very far with that, few problems of my own. You overestimated me.'

'. . . and once that happened, he would start planting evidence on you, the way he did with my Level Four deputy.'

'Collins.'

'Yes, Collins. Blythe's case against him was incredible, I must say. If we hadn't suspected Blythe already, Collins would be in a lot of trouble.'

I make an incredulous huffing sound. 'You mean in a lot of trouble rather than dead, bumped off by a bunch of Kazakh gangsters or whoever else . . .'

Richard interrupts me with a hearty smile. 'Oh Heather, Heather, what a monster you must think I am! Collins isn't *dead*. That's just a rumour we set going so that Blythe wouldn't realise we were onto him. We arrested poor Collins at dawn, that much is true, frightened the life out of the silly bugger, but once he was in custody and we could contain the rumours we sent him off to New Zealand. His whole family joined him two weeks later. They're going to be there for six months while he works online and goes mountain climbing every weekend. He's having the time of his life.'

'You used me as bait,' I repeat. 'And you let others in the Service think I might be Kieron's accomplice in order to justify it, even though you knew I wasn't.'

'Well, to be accurate, I didn't know that for certain.'

I sit back in my chair. 'You knew I wasn't corrupt. You've known me for years – my father. You were reckless with me, Richard, all

336

because you wanted him to fuck up when he tried to discredit me. I suppose it was you who told him about my debt and my friend Flavia? You handed him the tools to manipulate me.'

He shakes his head. 'Absolutely not. We didn't give him any help – that would have been hugely unethical. Whatever he found out about you, he did it on his own.' He pauses, then says, 'He must have accessed your full Service records somehow. Perhaps he had help within the London office. Yes, maybe you're right about that, I can look into it.'

At that, he looks down at his lap, at his hands. He twists his wedding ring round and round his finger. He blows air out of his mouth. He has to put on a show of contrition even if he doesn't feel it. 'We had absolutely no idea what Blythe would do. In fact, it wasn't even him that was responsible, you know?'

He's lost me.

'We found the body, my dear, or rather the Scottish police did. We managed to keep it out of the press, just, but your DNA was all over it. If you return to the UK any time soon, you'll be liable for arrest. It's out of my hands.'

'It was self-defence – he nearly killed me.'

Richard looks at me evenly. 'That will be for a court to decide, of course.' Then he continues smoothly on. 'Blythe was exceptionally clever, and we're pretty sure he wasn't working alone. It wasn't your friend Carmella, by the way. The only thing she did wrong was to believe what he told her about you. Mind you, it didn't help she caught you going through his office out of hours.'

He pauses. Something childish in me wants to say *so you're saying it's my fault, the mess I was in?* There is a small element of truth in that that I don't want to admit.

337

'The Birmingham unit has been disbanded,' he says then. 'Pressure from above. Shame, because it was actually doing some good work apart from the cases that Blythe was fixing. Now we've got to work out which – it's an unholy mess, I can tell you. We need a complete account of your time there, every detail of every case as well as everything you know about Blythe. Not now, of course, it will take days. I'll send a team.'

Can Richard really be such a dedicated bureaucrat that all that matters to him is the investigation? What happened to me in Thurso, what might have happened, doesn't that matter? They found some remains in the loch and they knew I was responsible – and Richard has not, at any point, imagined the reality of that incident. No one has ever pushed his head beneath the water.

I, on the other hand, cannot let it go so easily. 'What do you mean Kieron Blythe wasn't responsible?'

Richard raises his hands, fingers spread wide, in a gesture of speculation. 'We don't think it was Blythe's idea, but we know he was reporting back to his paymasters about the possibility of you being onto him, having evidence against him. When you went on the run, he would have been panic-stricken. It was probably them that set a man on you, to hunt you down. Blythe would have been terrified for his own life, of course. I don't know.'

'But you have him in custody. What has he said?'

Richard presses his lips together in an expression of regret. 'Sadly not. We released him on bail, under observation of course, and it seems he has slipped from our grasp.'

There is absolutely no way that the DOS would have released Kieron, or lost track of him, unless it was deliberate.

'He's on the run?'

Richard smiles. 'I am guessing that the irony of that does not escape either of us, but I don't know, m'dear – he doesn't have your talents. Possibly. We've let it be known through one of our other channels that he was co-operating with us.'

'Was he?'

'No, of course not – he's far too scared of the lot he was working for. Rightly so, one might say.'

'So you've done to him what you pretended to do to Collins.'

Richard doesn't reply.

'You've executed him.'

He gets a little angry then, as if I have just cast a slur on his character. 'That is pure speculation, as you well know.' He sits back in his chair, makes a small explosive sound with his mouth, then says scornfully, 'I don't know, Heather. At least the traitors of your father's generation betrayed their countries out of principle. Now it's all about money. People sell their souls for a swimming pool. Kieron Blythe was on the take, pure and simple. He was a puppet being controlled by criminals who sold secrets on to the highest bidder – don't ask me to get all anxious about it coming back to bite him on the arse.'

I rise from the chair and go to the window. We have only been talking for a few minutes, but it feels much longer. I gaze out across the runway, where an aeroplane is taxiing for take-off, and wonder where the dawn is, why it is taking so long. I should feel no compunction for Kieron's fate either – even less than Richard – but now the people who were after me are probably after him I feel no pleasure, not even of a grim sort. I feel confused.

Richard says, 'Funny, you know, but as you came in, I saw your father in you, something in the eyes. Never noticed it before.'

I do not turn from the window.

'How old was he when he joined the Service?' Richard says.

'I don't know,' I say, my back still turned, 'but it was before the end of the war. The raid was what did it. The Moonlight Sonata.'

'Yes, I know,' Richard says.

I turn back to him.

He is looking at the table. 'I wonder if you know that story?'

'Of course I do,' I say. 'He was in the shelter with his mother but his father and brother were in the centre of town. He went looking for them as soon as the all-clear sounded, but he never found them.'

Richard is silent for a while. 'Men of that generation,' he says quietly, 'there were things they didn't tell their wives, their daughters – details I mean.' He picks up the empty styrofoam cup and puts it down again. He looks at me. 'He did find them. The firestorm was still going in some places. Looking for them must have been very dangerous. He found their blackened corpses at the back of his father's workshop, where they had tried to shelter. He never told his mother, or your mother for that matter. He carried it all his life, and he never said what he had seen. He told me all at once when we were on a mission, drinking whisky from our flasks, one night, while we waited in a car.'

I do not respond.

'He was quite senior by the time I joined, and you know most officers of his rank wouldn't have given a stripling like me the time of day. But your father took me under his wing.'

I return to the table and we sit in silence for a while then. 'I understand why you ran,' Richard says. 'I wasn't expecting it, but knowing your father, his ingenuity, maybe I should have done.'

I don't want to talk about my father any more, or myself. It offends me that Richard is telling me things about my own father, as if he thinks he'll get round me that way. I suppose I should ask him for more details about the deal, but Vikram will be the one who has to negotiate all that. Exile. It's such a simple word. There's a cleanness to it, like an icicle.

He senses that I might be about to bring our discussion to a close. 'You haven't got to it yet,' he says, 'why you wanted me to come in person.'

I look him straight in the face as I lie to him and I make it good, which isn't difficult. My anger is quite genuine. 'Whatever the official line is back home, I want you to apologise face to face for using me as bait. You could have explained to me and asked for my help rather than using me like that. It was a disgusting thing to do.'

He looks back at me. His gaze is cool and pale – he doesn't want to overdo the sincerity. 'I'm sorry.'

Richard and I talk a little more and as I stand to go, he rises from his chair, comes over to me, bends his head and kisses my hair.

I wait to see if he will make another reference to my father. But after a moment or two, he murmurs, 'The world is changing, Heather.'

No, it isn't, I think, *not really.* Isn't that the problem, that it never does?

At the door of the small room, I turn before I reach for the handle and say, 'What was his name?'

Richard looks at me.

'The man I killed, what was his name?'

That tight smile again. 'You don't need to know that. We're onto them, that's all you need to know. You're safe here for the time being and the less you know, the better.'

I pause. 'Okay, just tell me one thing then.'

Unexpectedly, Richard sneezes. It is such a human thing to do, we both smile, despite our mutual scorn. I wait until the moment has passed, until he has pulled a handkerchief from his pocket, blown his nose and the smiles have faded from both our faces.

'How old was he?'

Richard gives me a full look, a sad look, then says softly, 'Twenty-three.'

The woman officer is sitting on a plastic chair outside the room. She rises as I come out and walks back down the corridor without speaking. I follow her.

By the entrance, the officers who were drinking coffee are still there, talking to each other, nodding. As I exit the building, I see the merest hint of dawn at the far edge of the sky, a line of light lying low along the horizon. I wonder how long Richard will have to wait for the first flight back to London.

I drive out of the airport slowly. They've cleared the slip roads. Slush is still heaped either side in the dark but it's dirty and collapsing, becoming pockmarked with air – one sunny day and it will melt. Spring is not far away unless the volcano goes up big time and brings a different kind of winter. They are saying that if the small eruptions are building to one massive one, the plume of ash could go as high as thirty thousand feet and close most of the airspace in Western Europe. A few months ago, I would have found it hard to believe, because the world seemed solid and knowable, but here and now, it feels that anything could happen, even something that could ground aeroplanes, prevent flight. When the unexpected happens, then afterwards, you always know it *can* happen. There is no unknowing that fact.

As I leave the airport behind, I know that soon the road will bifurcate – and then I will have a choice. If I head north-east, I will continue on Route 41 to Reykjavík. If I take the right fork I will find myself at a roundabout, where another right turn will take me onto Route 43 towards Grindavík, after which I can follow the same route I took the day I arrived, along the south coast. It will take around three hours to get home. I think of the little village by the black sand beach. Would it be so hard to build a life there, after all? Maybe I could get a job in the café or the petrol station. The winters would be hard. I think of Norway, then, of Aksel, who was so bulky and so real he would banish shadows simply by existing. I remember my fantasy of sharing a bed with him, of slipping down into the cave he would make of himself and the linen, the way he would draw me in close, spooning me. It would be like being held beneath a swan.

I think of all the places I have been, all the places that I am – icy, frosted, cold. I want to stop running. I want to build a life full of the things that are too mundane to make a story – and Adelina is part of that, even though I know I can't expect her to regard me as a part of her life. That kind of trust needs to be earned, after all, and it remains to be seen whether Adelina can thaw the winter inside this old bird. But I want to be the kind of person who has a visitor, someone whose arrival is anticipated – someone, perhaps, whose company is joyous but who is a little irritating when they don't put their dirty mug in the sink.

I imagine Adelina arriving at Reykjavík airport, me waiting in the Arrivals hall and reaching out a hand to take her luggage as she approaches, how I will keep the conversation light as we walk back to my car because she might feel a little awkward. I imagine her sitting next to me in the passenger seat right now, as I ask her about her life. It will probably be only later, when I am sure she is comfortable in my company, that I will tell her some of my story, an edited version, of course, about how I have ended up here.

Perhaps one day, I will talk to her about her mother, Flavia, and how we met in the British Army, of all places, that home for lost souls who can run a bit. And how we loved and supported each other and how the great sadness of my life was that she and I fell out and that I just assumed we would make it up eventually, but eventually never came. If I feel able to speak freely to her, I might say there's no point in regrets, dear Adelina, but I do regret, most sincerely, that I missed out on watching you grow for the rest of your childhood. I regret I wasn't there to say to your mother: I'm sorry, you were right, I was always running from attachment because I viewed it as a burden rather than a privilege. I love the silver bracelet. I love you. Please be careful when you go out to the shops and if you walk past a toddler in a stroller who has dropped a toy, ignore it, don't be so soft.

I can't be a mother to Adelina – it's too late and I don't have the right – but I could be something. I could be a presence.

The road ahead is empty. Behind me is a distant car, its headlights bright white. Still slowly, the sky is growing paler, the navy hue at the horizon blurring with the coming dawn. Not long now.

*

I think of the sincerity on Richard's face, how he raised the subject of my father because he thought he could bond with me over our shared memories. He may as well have been standing above me holding a needle, looking down at me, wondering about the best place to insert it, the one that would encounter least resistance – how to avoid bone and muscle, and find flesh.

Fuck that.

Kieron Blythe doesn't have a cousin called Ruth and even if he did, the idea that he bumped into Michael at a party is preposterous. If I hadn't been so shocked at learning that Flavia had died, I would have seen through that invention at the time. Kieron Blythe had done his homework. He had seen my files, the full files, that only the London heads of departments have access to – or maybe somebody who knew about me said to him: *Here is everything you need to know about her, all her weak points. Do with them what you will.*

How was the young man able to track me from some point during my flight across Scotland to the loch outside Thurso? If the Service knew about Stuart's yacht, why weren't they waiting to arrest me as soon as I appeared on the harbour at Lerwick? It was because someone was hoping all along I would be found by a killer before I was detained by the authorities.

The truth is in the picture. I think of Kieron standing and gazing out of the floor-to-ceiling window in Alaska, raising his coffee cup to his lips. Instead of staying at the table, looking at us all to gauge our reactions, he rose and took a leisurely pace or two away, coffee cup in hand. I see the coffee cup again, being raised to his lips by his automatic arm. I see the way his fingers tightened on Carmella's shoulder a moment or two later. Why wasn't he more worried? There could only be one reason. He did not fear a powerful investigation because he had powerful protection. He only became fearful when I went on the run.

Your father was wary of him.

If you are lucky enough to have loving parents, they continue to protect you long after they are dead.

The road continues. The car in my rear-view mirror keeps its distance. Icelandic drivers are polite like that. I estimate I have around ten minutes before I have to decide which route to take.

There's no ferry to Greenland, that's the catch. Shame. It's a huge country, but if you traversed the southern peninsula to Nuuk, you'd miss out the bulgy bit at the top, and from there you're almost in Newfoundland, just a hop across the Davis Strait. Crossing Canada would be a breeze. They're a friendly lot there, the coffee is good and they still do the train journey through the Rockies in the tourist season. From there, you could head to Alaska. The Bering Strait, mind you – sounds cold and scary and it probably is, but it must be crossable somehow. There's a Trans-Siberian express across all those steppes now, and granted Russia is huge, it'd take you a while – but one day, you'd be back at the gates of Europe, with its art galleries and cafés and centuries-old arguments about the nation state. From there, you could miss out the grey little island you've always called home and head back up to Scandinavia and spend the rest of your life going round and round and round . . . It's just about time, money and endurance – and ingenuity of course. The distances, the impossibilities, only exist in our heads.

Route 1 is a circular road that goes round the whole of Iceland, 821 miles. Perhaps if they close the airspace, I could drive round and round it, again and again, stopping here and there to sleep in different places one night at a time. It would give me the illusion of perpetual flight even though I never left the country. If I got tired of driving, I could make the circle even tighter – spinning on the spot, perhaps that is the ultimate escape.

I think I have successfully convinced Richard I am going to co-operate: demanding that apology will have helped. It will buy me some time. He doesn't know that I put my suitcase in the boot of the car before I left Vík four hours ago, just in case.

If I am right, then there will be a price on my head for a long time to come, which means I must never contact Adelina again. For a moment, at this thought, a kind of darkness descends upon me, as I drive towards my decision. I think of my image of myself on the first day I got to Iceland, trapped inside a lava kettle.

I square my shoulders as I approach the fork in the road and slow the car. Behind me, in the west, there is light now, pale but decisive and growing every minute. Either side of the road, snow covers the landscape in a thin, crisp crust and the expanding dawn throws a golden glaze across the fields, making them twinkle like fields of tiny diamonds. Who knows what colours the sky will show me as the day begins?

Acknowledgements

Although this book is based in the world of British intelligence, I have created my own version of it – in particular the departments that I refer to as Liaison 2.6 and the DOS. When it came to researching what was possible or plausible, I owe a great debt to two employees of an organisation I have promised not to name – they know who they are. I was also lucky enough to be granted an interview with Lord Evans of Weardale, former Director General of MI5. It's not often I get to offload my ignorance on such a big cheese – he was very good about it. In terms of research into the army and the WRAC, I am much indebted to Colonel (Retired) Frances E. Castle MBE and Lieutenant Colonel (Retired) Sue Westlake MBE, and to Paul Weatherald. Chief Superintendent Tara McGovern of the Metropolitan Police Service and the author Mark Thompson gave invaluable assistance regarding other matters. I hope all the above will forgive the bits in this book where I misrepresented their worlds, played fast and loose with the truth, or just plain made it up.

I am grateful for permission to use epigraphs from Tom Burgis and the estates of John Le Carré and Geoffrey Household; I recommend each of the works quoted. On research trips to Norway and Scotland, I listened to the podcast *Death in Ice Valley*, from the BBC World Service and NRK, presented by Marit Higraff and Neil McCarthy. The identity and fate of the Isdal Woman still haunt me and I commend their investigation of that enduring mystery to you, although the wisdom of listening to it while hiking alone in remote areas is perhaps debatable. Pétur Már Ólafsson and Michael Ridpath both helped with Icelandic details.

Thank you to Heather Kneale for her donation to Young Lives vs Cancer in return for her name in a novel. I struggle with names and am always grateful when people offer theirs up, even better if it's for a good cause. A significant chunk of this book was written at Château de Lavigny in Switzerland; thank you to the Fondation Heinrich Maria and Jane Ledig-Rowohlt.

My friends Jacqui Lofthouse, Raj Kohli and Russell Celyn Jones all read the manuscript for me and offered comments at a stage when this book was all over the place – I couldn't be more grateful for their input. There was still a huge amount for my peerless Faber editor, Louisa Joyner, to do. This book would be nowhere near the finished article without her help. Thanks to Lesley Jones for combing out the commas and much else besides.

As ever, my career would not exist without all of those above and my other key allies: Antony Harwood of Antony Harwood Ltd, Rebecca Watson of Valerie Hoskins Associates and a host of brilliant and unfailingly supportive staff at Faber & Faber UK Ltd, too numerous to name. When it comes to the multiple people who make it all happen I am still, on this my tenth novel, unable to believe my luck.